More Than Once

by Dominique Wolf

More Than Once
Copyright 2021 Dominique Wolf
All rights reserved.

ISBN: 979-8-541434-79-8

Published by Dominique Wolf
Interior book design by Bob Houston eBook Formatting
Editing by TC Media
Cover design by Dominique Wolf (Picture supplied through Canva Pro
    License - by rabbit75_cav)

TO MIGUEL

Thank you for making me feel like I am living a real-life romance story.

CHAPTER 1:

"**O**h, Isabella, come on!" Reyna, my roommate and long-time friend, yelled over the sound of the water from my shower.

I rolled my eyes knowing very well that she couldn't see me.

"Reyna," I sighed. "You know, I don't do the whole 'going out' thing because it makes me so uncomfortable."

"That's because you don't even try to have a good time."

"I do!" I retorted.

Reyna snorted, "As if! You need to come out with Kat and I and actually *try* to enjoy yourself."

I sighed. Reyna was always so damn persistent and I had a feeling I wasn't going to win this fight.

Reyna and Katrina Cazarez were sisters who were eighteen months apart, but looked almost identical. They were both gifted with long, thick black hair that had the most perfect curls. The kind that started right from their roots. Their olive skin was a blessing from their father's Spanish ancestry, and their light blue eyes were from their half-French, half-Spanish mother.

Reyna and I had been friends since the first day of high school, when she walked in and offered me gum, despite the fact that we weren't allowed to have gum during class. Her shirt's top button was undone, and her tie was pulled to the side. She couldn't care less about the rules, which terrified my control-freak tendencies, but I was fascinated by her spontaneous nature.

Her family lived in Madrid, and they had decided that sending their daughters to a posh international school in the UK would be the best option. So she was enrolled in the boarding school side of Queen's College - Somerset, one of the country's most prestigious private schools. She moved back to Spain after graduation and yet, we still managed to stay just as close.

Reyna and I were polar opposites in every conceivable way - from our personalities to our looks. My longer wavy brown hair and hazel eyes were never features I considered to be striking like hers. Reyna thrived on being the center of attention, and thanks to my introverted tendencies, I couldn't think of anything worse. We may have been opposites, but we always managed to bring out the best in each other. She was the dreamer and I was the realist. She had always been the closest person to me - not even my older sister Camila and I were half as close.

"Izzy, I know how difficult this has all been for you," Reyna began, a sliver of her Spanish accent visible. "But you deserve at least one night to go out and have fun."

The ache in my heart still lingered. She was referring to the latest life-altering event that I didn't see coming. My now ex-boyfriend, Nate Cameron, with whom I had spent the previous six years of my life with, dumped me. We were dubbed "high-school sweethearts" by everyone, and we had our entire lives planned out.

The perfect job, the perfect apartment, the perfect life.

Until he left me and that all went for a ball of shit.

It was one of our regularly scheduled date nights... Everything in our lives had always been meticulously planned to the last detail, but something about this night felt different.

Everyone around us had been talking about marriage for a while now and we knew they were expecting an engagement. A part of me was terrified of making such a long-term commitment, but my mother always reminded me that it was the next logical step.

Nate, a prominent architect based in London, was planning to head to Madrid to work with an old family friend who was heading up a project there. I was happy Nate was getting all these amazing opportunities but initially, the idea of leaving London riddled me with anxiety. I had a clear plan for my life, which didn't include leaving, but I had to stick by my boyfriend. We had talked about settling down there if everything went as planned. I was actually looking forward to the change, which was completely out of character for me. Change terrified me. I had to coordinate everything, but we talked about going to Madrid together, and that became part of our new plan. My mother wasn't thrilled that I was leaving London, but she was determined to make it work. She claimed that quitting my job was not an option, so after much convincing, my boss agreed that I could work remotely for the time being.

I was getting ready to meet him at our favourite Italian restaurant when Nate stumbled into our apartment.

"Are you drunk?" I asked, shocked and confused by this out-of-character behaviour. This was not Nate's style. We were simple people who enjoyed the "finer things in life", and he never drank or even went out. I never wanted to use the word "boring" at the time, but if I'm being honest, that's exactly what our lives were. Boring! There was no room in the plan for any distractions, which I had learned to accept. He walked over to the kitchen counter, leaning against it to keep himself upright. He undid his tie and threw it across the kitchen. He began unbuttoning the top of his shirt, avoiding direct eye contact.

"Isabella," he slurred, "I can't do this anymore."

I held my breath.

"What?" I asked, even though I had heard exactly what he said.

"This," he indicated to mean him and I. "I can't do this relationship anymore. I'm sorry but this is getting way too serious for me. Everyone wants us to get engaged and get married. I can't handle this pressure. I don't want it. I haven't even lived yet and I'm not ready for that kind of commitment."

I waited for the tears to come, but they didn't. Instead, I went numb.

"You're breaking up with me?" I tried to remain calm, but I couldn't deny the confusion bubbling over inside of me.

He nodded, "I'm sorry, but you deserve someone who can give you what you want right now and that's isn't me."

"We don't have to get engaged right now, Nate,"

"I know but it's what your family wants, and I don't even know if I want to get married at all."

Given how openly we discussed the next step in our relationship, his sudden admission of his true feelings caught me off guard. He finally met my gaze. His light blue eyes were filled with pain, and I could tell he was ashamed of what he was doing. I wish I could say I could have predicted it, but it appears we were not on the same page, and I had no idea. This came as a complete surprise to me. I watched him bury his head in his hands. I tried to feel something, but there was nothing left. No sadness. No anger. I felt nothing as the numbness spread across my body.

"Please, Nate, just let me deal with telling my family," I murmured, my voice devoid of any emotion.

"Of course, Izzy. I'm sorry, I never wanted to hur-"

I lifted a finger to cut him off. He never wanted to hurt me and yet, here we were. I turned around and returned to our room, locking the door behind me. I was in shock. The very last

thing I expected Nate to do was dump me. We had it all figured
out; every step of our lives had been laid out and ready to go.
But that was the problem.

I thought my heart broke that night until I admitted to myself that once
the initial shock wore off, it was actually relief that washed over me. I
had always been too afraid to admit it, but I wasn't in love with Nate
anymore. I loved him, but I wasn't in love with him.

I was just bored.

The blindside, on the other hand, did not make the months
following our breakup any easier. My entire life had a plan, and then it
was suddenly thrown out the window, leaving me unsure of what to do
next.

So long story short, I moved to Barcelona with Reyna, who had
already been living here for a few years. While their family still lived
in Madrid, Reyna and Katrina had moved to Barcelona when they
decided to attend university here. They had been sharing an apartment
and opened their home up to me when I needed it. We lived just outside
the city center, but everything we needed was just a train ride away.

Barcelona was rich in fascinating history and culture, right down
to the architecture of the old buildings that were still standing after all
these years. The apartment building's exterior was archaic, but the
interior was as modern and spacious as it could be.

When I moved to Barcelona, I didn't even tell my parents the full
story. There was no way I could explain to them that I had been dumped
by my picture-perfect boyfriend just days before we were supposed to
move to a new country together, especially since everyone was
expecting an engagement. Everyone already assumed we were going to
get married. I went to Spain in the end; I just left out the part about not
going with Nate.

I've been told my entire life that I need to have everything together.
I had grown up terrified of disappointing my parents if I didn't follow

the plan laid out for me. My mother was a control freak by nature, and it didn't change when she had children; she was adamant about directing the course of our lives, as it was her way of ensuring that we were, in her words, "going to be a success." In my 'perfect' household, there was no room for failure.

Nate dumped me and then in the very same week, the publishing company I worked for declined to promote me. After all my hard work and my mother stepping in, convincing them I could do my job from Spain. I wasn't a fan of nepotism but my mother got me the job in the first place. She didn't care about involving herself in my life, she would do whatever was necessary to ensure her children would not be failures.

How do you do that? Well, according to her, you get involved in every aspect of your children's lives and smother them with the plan you believed was best for them.

Everything in my life seemed to be falling apart and I was suffocating. Reyna welcomed me with open arms four months ago, and I haven't looked back.

Reyna brought me back to reality. "You have to admit that you could use a night out."

I turned off the water and grabbed my towel, wrapping it around my body. Reyna had just finished applying the last of her makeup in front of the large mirror we shared. I was always envious of her beauty and the way she carried herself. I'd always wished for that level of confidence.

"You're right," I admitted with a sigh. "I'm just the worst at it."

"It's because you overthink it," Katrina shouted from outside the bathroom.

She strolled in with a pair of black heels in her hand. Her beautiful dark hair hung perfectly straight over her shoulders and she was dressed in a tight red dress. She was all set to go.

"Why are you dressed already?" I asked, knowing it was still too early to head out.

"I'm meeting Sergio," she explained, smiling as she leaned over to put on her shoes.

Katrina had been seeing Sergio for a couple of months now, and although she would never admit it, I could tell she was really starting to fall for him.

"Can we stop changing the subject here?" Reyna turned and grabbed me by the shoulders. "Izzy, you are coming out with us, okay? I'm not taking no for an answer!"

"When do you ever?" I rolled my eyes.

"Never," she said with a smug smile.

She was right about needing to go out. I could sense it deep within me, this hidden desire to break through and do something I'd never done before. The desire to be spontaneous and live a little for the first time in my life.

"Where are we going?" I sighed, slowly building up the courage to join her.

"Mala Mía," she said with a smirk.

Mala Mía was the hottest club in town situated in the city center of Plaza Catalunya. It was still a fairly new addition in the area when compared to the other standing businesses surrounding it. Every weekend, the place was packed with locals and tourists who came to enjoy the city's best reggaeton club. The vibrant atmosphere of the area consumed Mala Mía and made it one of the most popular clubs in town.

Reyna was a VIP there, and although she always invited me to join her, I was too caught up in my own fears to take her up on her offer.

Tonight, she wasn't giving me a choice.

"Fine," I caved. "What should I wear?"

CHAPTER 2:

Maybe this wasn't such a bad idea.

We were standing in the entrance line to the club, which was already packed with people. I was feeling surprisingly good about myself, and a glimmer of excitement was bubbling inside of me. I curled my hair, and thankfully it cooperated tonight. Katrina loaned me an off-the-shoulder long sleeve black dress with an uncomfortably high but beautiful pair of black heels.

Would I normally put on an outfit like this? Certainly not. Was I in love with how it looked on me tonight? Surprisingly, yes.

I'd never felt this confident before, so it was both terrifying and exciting for me. It could be related to the shots Reyna forced us to take before leaving the apartment. Right now, I needed all the liquid confidence I could get. We made it to the front, paid the cover charge, and received our stamp.

We were all set to go.

When I walked into Mala Mía, I was immediately consumed by it. We took the stairs down to the dance floor, which was already flooded with people. The club was fantastic. The high ceilings made you feel as if you were in a place like no other. The interior was extremely modern, which, like most places in Barcelona, was in stark contrast to the architecture on the outside. The walls were gold-plated, and the flashing lights bouncing off them caused you to lose your senses. The most expensive alcohol was placed in a pyramid formation in the middle of the dance floor. Long leather couches and booths lined the sides of the dance floor, filled with people having a good time. I followed Reyna's gaze as she pointed up to the VIP section. The DJ booth was elevated and extended above parts of the dance floor in the same section. As the DJ played a hot reggaeton beat, I watched as the crowd threw their hands in the air. Strangely, even I couldn't stop moving to the music. You immediately were entranced by the atmosphere.

"Let's get a drink." Reyna shouted over the music.

I nodded and followed her. She looked like a goddess in her tight gold dress. If this club was a kingdom, she would be the queen. She walked effortlessly in her heels, turning heads as we made our way to the bar.

The music blaring from the speakers had an effect on me, and I couldn't help but continue to move to it as we walked. We came to a halt at the bar's counter, and I was relieved when she ordered another round of shots. Her go-to drink was always tequila, and while I despised the taste, I needed all the confidence I could get right now. She handed two of them to me.

"Two?" I shouted.

"Go big or go home baby!"

I laughed and knew I was in for a treat tonight. I took the shots, one right after the other. It burned going down, but I could already feel it making its way through my body. I needed a night to just let go of everything I was holding on to. I decided to allow myself to have fun for a change.

"Come on, let's dance!" Reyna exclaimed and pulled me to the dance floor.

We pushed our way through the crowd until we were in the middle of the dance floor, right under a huge gold chandelier that dangled and shimmered above us. It was extravagant for a club but it added a touch of sophistication to it.

I put my hands in the air as we moved from side to side, allowing the music to take over.

I danced and danced. Not once stopping to care if anyone was watching me. Not once stopping to think too much about what I was doing.

I was living my best life.

After dancing for what seemed like an eternity, Reyna grabbed me and led me through the club and up the stairs to the VIP section she had pointed out when we first arrived. Katrina and Sergio were at the private bar in the back of it when we noticed them. We made our way over to join them.

"Isabella!" Sergio shouted over the music. "I didn't expect to see you here!"

"Well, I never expected to be here either and yet, here I am," I said excitedly as he pulled me in for a quick hug.

Sergio was at the apartment so often, we already considered them a couple. Their choice not to put a label on it didn't make it any less of a relationship. When I first arrived in Barcelona, the lack of relationship was a culture shock to me - everyone avoided it. It was unusual to someone like me, who had always been around long-term commitments. I liked Sergio a lot - he was a genuinely nice guy and I couldn't deny he had a certain attractiveness to him that was underrated. He stood out with his dirty blonde hair and beautiful green eyes, always hidden behind a pair of glasses. He was tall, a full head taller than the rest of us. And he was attractive in the sense that he was a smart looking guy, bordering on the cliché of the nerdy typecast. Sergio ordered another round of tequila shots for us, and we threw them down.

"Where's the rest of your clan?" Reyna asked Sergio.

"They actually just arrived," Sergio nodded to a group of men walking towards us. "Perfect timing."

Our group got bigger now with the addition of Sergio's friends. Two of them introduced themselves to be Jose and Alonzo but I couldn't keep my eyes off the third one who just walked in.

Oh my...

He took my breath away. I allowed myself a moment to take him in. With his dark olive skin and dark brown hair, he was undeniably Spanish. His hair almost appeared black, but when the lights flashed, I noticed it was a rich chestnut color. He had a full dark brown beard to match and it was so perfectly kept that I wanted to reach out and touch it. His deep dark brown eyes surprised me, and I had to physically restrain myself from reacting to these new impulses.

Everything about him was the polar opposite of what I had ever thought of as "my type." I usually prefer lighter hair and eyes, but I was drawn to his dark features. In his leather jacket and all-black ensemble, he exuded sex appeal. If this were a teen movie, he'd be the bad boy character everyone warned you to avoid.

"*Hola,* I'm Giovanni," he smiled and extended his hand to me.

I reached out and took it in mine. That touch alone was enough to confirm this strange sensation I suddenly felt over me. He leaned in and kissed both of my cheeks, as was the customary greeting here. I was completely taken back by him. Who was this dark handsome man and why did he have such an impact on me?

Was it the alcohol?

Probably.

"Nice to meet you," I stammered. "I'm Isabella"

The music was becoming louder, and I could tell he wasn't hearing what I was saying. He leaned in closer, prompting me to say it again.

"Isabella," I murmured in his ear.

He pulled back to look at me but was still close enough that I could hear him.

"Beautiful." he said.

The dormant arousal deep in the pit of my stomach came to life and I couldn't fight the urge to bite my lip. I was thankful for Reyna shoving a drink in my face to distract me from this new physical reaction I had no control over. He went over to stand with Sergio and I couldn't help but steal a glance in his direction while they were attempting to have a conversation over the blaring music in the club. His leather jacket hugged his arms in the perfect way, exposing his muscles. The jacket fits him like a glove and I wanted nothing more than to rip it off him.

What was happening to me?

I gulped down more of my drink in an attempt to drown out these thoughts. Was it the fact that I hadn't been with anyone in months? Or was he just *that* attractive?

I watched as a beautiful blonde walked over to him, her long hair flicking side to side as she strutted toward him. She threw her arms around him and he wrapped his around her waist. There was definite chemistry between them - you could see it with their body language. She kept close to him as they spoke and his arms remained around her. Just observing their close proximity caused an unexpected stir inside and I realized I wanted that to be me. I was so taken aback by this sudden wave of jealousy I was feeling for this attractive stranger. *What the fuck Isabella?*

I shook my head and turned my attention back to the music. I was here to have fun - not to get jealous over some stranger I just met. He was just so hot and I had never experienced this kind of physical attraction before - it was unusual for me. I handed my empty glass back to Reyna, suddenly, desperately needing her to top me off.

"Look at you!" she shouted, laughing as she reached for the vodka bottle. "Who would've thought you'd be out drinking with us?"

"Not a big drinker huh?" Giovanni suddenly joined the conversation.

I took my glass from Reyna and turned away from him, glancing down at the dance floor. He stepped closer and casually stood next to me with his hands in his pockets.

"Not usually." I admitted, sipping my drink.

"So, where do you usually spend your Saturday nights then, Isabella?" my name rolled off his tongue.

Fuck. I wanted him to keep saying my name.

"I'm more of a book or Netflix kind of person."

"Netflix and chill?" he winked at me and I couldn't help but laugh knowing the urban culture meaning of that phrase.

Oh, what I'd give to Netflix and chill with him right now.

"So what do you do?" I asked him, changing the subject before my mind wandered off again.

"Just run a few businesses here and there," he replied.

"How vague," I scoffed. "I'm not asking you to spill trade secrets here."

"You never know," he challenged. "These businesses could be top secret."

"Guess I'll never know."

"Well, I'll give you a hint about one of them," he murmured in my ear.

I pulled back to look at him, waiting for him to give me the hint.

"You're currently standing in one of them," he said, smiling at me.

"You own this club?" I blurted out.

He shrugged, "Family business."

There was no doubt that they were doing very well for themselves here. Every weekend this place was packed and judging by the amount of alcohol our group alone had bought, I could only imagine how much their bars made per night. Not to mention the cover charge..

"Well, good for you guys." I sipped on my drink as Reyna stumbled into the conversation.

"I see you've met Giovanni." she smiled smugly.

"*Hola, Reyna.*" he greeted.

"How do you two know each other?" I asked.

"She used to sleep with my brother." Giovanni said bluntly.

Reyna laughed, "I did but that was years ago."

Giovanni laughed and what a beautiful sound it was. He was so close to me now that his arm brushed up against mine. The most simple physical touch and yet it went beyond just that - it crawled across my body, lighting it up with desire.

"Nice to see you out and about and not stuck in that office of yours," Reyna continued to say to Giovanni. "I was starting to think you were becoming an old man."

He scoffed, "Someone has to keep this place running."

She rolled her eyes.

"How come you've never brought Isabella out here before?"

He turned and smiled at me. There was a flicker of interest in his eyes and I was surprised to see he was reciprocating the very obvious chemistry between us.

"Oh trust me, I've tried," Reyna rolled her eyes. "After months of convincing her to come out, she finally gave in."

"Lucky me." Giovanni smirked revealing a deep dimple in his left cheek that I never noticed till now.

I blushed, surprised by his blatant flirting. I had never experienced this kind of attention and I couldn't deny the excitement I felt. I was careful not to give anything away on the surface but deep down I was enjoying how he was making me feel.

"This really isn't her scene," Reyna started again, her intoxicated state allowing her to run her mouth. "She's usually hiding out in our soon-to-be coffee shop."

"You guys own a coffee store?" Giovanni asked me.

"We're trying to," I mumbled awkwardly. "There's so much we still have to fix up."

"That's great though," he said, smiling. "I'd love to come by."

"You really should! It's going to be great," Reyna interrupted. "Coffee would be so great right now!"

She was definitely starting to feel the alcohol.

Ignoring her, Giovanni turned to me. "Well, I hope you'll be coming around here more often," he continued, stepping closer to me.

He was so close now that I could smell the cologne he was wearing and it was intoxicating. I breathed him in and allowed my mind to wander to where it truly wanted to be.

"That really depends." The alcohol was turning my flirt on.

"Oh?" he smirked.

"Yeah, it has to be worth my while."

The tension between us was palpable. Pure, raw, sexual tension surrounded us and for the first time in my life, I was completely overcome by it. Desire was a strong sensation and there was no fighting it now. We clearly weren't the only ones who noticed it - even Reyna picked up on what was happening between us.

"What the fuck you guys?" she started and reached for my hand. "Come, Isabella, you need to dance girl."

She started to lead me away from him. He laughed but never took his eyes off me and I couldn't help but steal a glance or two back at him. I was drawn to him in a way I had never been drawn to anyone before. Sure, I had been attracted to people in the past but this was different. This was the kind of desire that came from a deep pit in my stomach. It was the kind of desire that I had never experienced but always craved. I craved the attention. I craved having someone look at me in the way he was looking at me right now. The alcohol was definitely assisting the situation by giving me the confidence I usually kept hidden. My intoxicated state just allowed me to be free - it allowed me to give in to what I truly wanted and what I had always fought so hard to keep hidden. Right now, I wanted Giovanni. I tried to keep my cool as we made our way back to the center of the dance floor and let the music consume me once more.

CHAPTER 3:

"This was such a great idea." I shouted to Reyna.

We were still on the dance floor and both Katrina and Sergio had joined us. I couldn't help but constantly notice Giovanni's movements. He was in a booth in the corner talking to one of the other guys I met. His name was Jose? Or was it Alonzo? Right now I couldn't remember which one was which. My focus was just on him. The beautiful blonde from earlier was sitting across from him but he wasn't paying attention to her and a small part of me was glad about that. I didn't want him to pay attention to anyone else - I wanted him to pay attention to me.

"Of course, it was a great idea," she replied. "You should listen to me more often."

Katrina snorted, "No one should ever take advice from you, *hermana*."

"What are you talking about?"

"Reyna, you and I are both sitting with ridiculous tattoos because of your so-called 'good life' advice," Katrina said as she sipped on her drink.

We all burst out laughing. One drunken night and another 'Reyna knows best' life session led to her and Kat finding a 24-hour tattoo parlour and getting what they thought would be each other's names on their ankles. They realized the next day they were too drunk to have even remembered their names and instead of getting each other's names, they got their own.

"Oh God, that was a bad idea," Reyna admitted and turned back to me. "But this wasn't bad advice was it?"

"Not at all." I smiled.

"You know what else you should do though?" Reyna shouted with excitement.

We all waited for her to finish her thought.

"You should have a one night stand!"

I choked on my drink. "Reyna I-," I started but she interrupted me.

"Hear me out, Izzy," she said. "Let's all be frank here - Nate was boring as hell."

I started to object, but quickly shut my mouth knowing she was right.

"See!" she laughed. "You can't even deny it."

Sergio ordered a round of shots earlier and one of the bartenders brought them to the dance floor. Katrina handed us each one while Reyna carried on her explanation.

"So, back to my point," she continued. "Nate was boring and you don't need boring. You need excitement. And what is more exciting than a one-night stand?"

I remained silent, unable to think of an answer.

"Nothing!" she shouted. "Nothing is more exciting than a one-night stand!"

Was she being serious? I had never in my life had a one-night stand. I had never even considered it. My only sexual encounters were all with Nate and I couldn't deny that those were pretty vanilla. But sleeping with someone I just met? *Could I even do that?* A surprising glimmer of excitement awoke from within at the mere thought of it. The thought of being with someone like that again. My mind immediately went to Giovanni. I tried to stop myself, but I decided to stop fighting it. So what if I was sexually attracted to him? So what if I just wanted to take him home and have my way with him? Was that so bad?

"I couldn't do that." I meekly protested.

"Why not?" Katrina joined the conversation. "It could be fun."

"It *would* be fun," Reyna emphasized. "In fact, I dare you to do it."

I couldn't help but laugh.

"You dare me?" I repeated.

"I dare you!"

Reyna enjoyed her games, and she enjoyed them even more after a few drinks. I pondered this for a moment, fully aware that my confidence was derived from the numerous shots I had taken throughout the evening. A part of me was terrified of doing something so unusual, but another part of me was ecstatic at the prospect.

Fuck it - why not?

"I'll do it!"

Reyna and Katrina shrieked in excitement. I could even tell that Sergio was enjoying observing this little game of ours.

"Okay, some ground rules," Reyna started to explain. "You have got to be the first to wake up and you leave right away, okay?"

"Yeah, don't stay for breakfast," Katrina interjected.

"Otherwise you'll end up like us," Sergio joked and pulled Katrina closer to him.

They were so into each other.

"Don't give out too much information about yourself," Reyna continued. "Not that you should be doing much talking anyways."

I blushed.

"Always use protection," she continued. "You're still on the pill right?"

I nodded.

"Smart girl," she said smiling. "And just have fun okay? You'll probably never see him again so who cares what happens?"

Was I seriously considering this? The hookup culture was very much alive among society here. You couldn't escape it. Everywhere you went people were more interested in experimenting and enjoying themselves with whoever they pleased rather than getting into a relationship. It was intriguing to someone like me who had never been a part of something like that.

"Okay, I get it. Now let's not overthink. Let's just see what happens."

They both shrieked in excitement, and I couldn't help but laugh at their reactions to all of this. Reyna laughed and pulled me in for a hug before we went back to throwing ourselves into the night.

CHAPTER 4:

I was having the time of my life.

I never expected to be enjoying this as much as I was but it's so different when you decide not to worry about what other people think. We were still on the dance floor, laughing and moving to the music. It had been a while since my last drink so I decided I needed another one. For someone who hardly drank alcohol, I seemed to be handling it better than I expected. I did notice that the alcohol was definitely doing most of the talking for me tonight though.

Reyna had found a partner in some attractive man on the dance floor. We locked eyes and I made a gesture towards the bar. She winked and I knew she was not joining me - she was too interested in her new dance partner. She could put any man under her spell. I often felt bad for some of these men because she tossed them to the side as quickly as she found them.

I walked through the crowd still moving to the music. The bar was full of people but I managed to squeeze my way through a gap I found and leaned against it. I could feel my feet were aching but I ignored it, once I started dancing again, it wouldn't matter anyway. I waved down one of the bartenders.

"Can I please get two gold tequilas?" I shouted.

He nodded and was off.

"Are you expecting company?" A voice said from next to me. I turned to see who it was and Giovanni took his place next to me, casually leaning against the bar.

Isabella, get your shit together.

"No," I replied.

The bartender placed the two shots in front of me. I reached into my bag to grab my purse

"No, no I got this." He placed his hand against mine that was holding my purse and turned to the bartender to tell him to add it to his tab. The perks of running the club I suppose.

"I can pay for my own drink," I remarked

"I'm sure you can."

I raised my eyebrow at him. There was a clear power struggle here and I was adamant to own it. He may have paid for the shots but I reached over to grab them both before he thought of taking one for himself. I downed the first one and then the next one. No matter how much it burned me to do that, I would stand my ground. I was annoyingly stubborn like that.

"Thank you for the shots." I placed the empty shot glasses back on the bar.

I turned to leave but he grabbed my arm. I looked back at him and there was something about the way he was looking at me that made me weak. He made me forget that we were in a club full of people - he was all I saw.

"You dance, Isabella?"

I nodded.

He grabbed my hand and led me through the crowd to the dance floor. I was not drunk but I was intoxicated enough that my bold ambition was sitting front row. We stopped and he pulled me closer to him. The beat blaring through the speakers seeped into my body and I knew the same was happening to him. I wrapped my hands around his neck and allowed my body to move against his.

It was like someone ignited a fire inside of me. I had never in my life experienced such an instant attraction to someone. Reyna's words of having a one-night stand rang in my ears. I had never been the type of girl to even consider that but I had also never felt desire like this. The way he held me close and moved his body against mine was enough for me to hand myself over to him.

He looked down at me and his desire mirrored my own. The tension was suffocating and I had to have him. I knew what I wanted and I was tired of being the girl that never did what she wanted. Today I was going to be different.

I pulled into him.

His kiss was soft and careful at first until I couldn't help but pull him closer to me - letting him know exactly how I was feeling. He kissed me back, this time with more aggression. He ran his hands down the side of my body, awakening every part of me.

I pulled away. The desire in his eyes was undeniable and I knew he wanted me as much as I wanted him.

"Do you wanna get out of here?" I asked him, surprising myself with this question.

He smirked. "Oh yes."

"Give me one second," I said. "Don't move."

I pushed my way back to Reyna who was now standing at the bar with her dance partner from earlier.

"So, I'm leaving now," I announced, trying my best to sound casual.

Her eyes flickered over to Giovanni and smiled. "You could not have found anyone better."

"How well do you know him?" I was curious to know more about this sexy mystery man I was about to leave with.

"Izzy, he owns this club," she said excitedly. "So I know him pretty well, and trust me, he's the easiest target for a one night stand."

Easiest target? This was news to me but I was too high on the desire to care.

"Seriously, he'll be amazing for you!" she exclaimed.

"Have you slept with him?" I asked, a little unsure if I'd want to share that kind of thing with her.

She burst out laughing.

"Hell no!" she shouted, "I slept with his older brother, Alvaro. But believe me when I say that Giovanni is all about the hook-ups and he's fucking hot."

She wasn't wrong.

"Don't overthink this, Izzy," she encouraged, "You really need this."

My doubt dissolved, "You're right. I do need this."

"Now, go and get him," she smirked, "And remind him that I know where he lives, just in case."

I laughed and pulled her in for a quick hug. Her encouragement helped that little voice in the back of my mind telling me that this was a bad idea to dissolve into nothing more than a faint murmur. My desire was sitting front and center and I needed to get to Giovanni now. I pushed my way through the crowd and made my way back to him.

He leaned into my ear, "You ready to go?"

I tugged at my bottom lip. His breath on my ear was already sending my body into a frenzy.

"Hell yes." I breathed.

He grabbed my hand and led me through the crowd. We slipped to the back and I was surprised to find an elevator next to a very stylish office with his name on it.

"Are we going to your place?" I asked

"Yeah, it's above the club."

Convenient.

The elevator doors opened and we stepped inside. The doors closed and the tension surrounded us. He was still holding my hand and the fire between us was suffocating me. I couldn't hold it back any longer, so I turned and threw myself at him. He wrapped his arms around me and his lips came down on mine. Our kiss was urgent, both of us high on arousal. His lips moved from my mouth down my neck.

"Giovanni," I breathed his name, not being able to hold back.

Each kiss burned against my skin and I felt the tension build between my legs. It had been so long since I'd been touched and yet my body had never felt such an awakening.

The elevator came to a stop and the doors opened. We broke the kiss, both of us breathing heavily. He grabbed my hand and led me through his apartment. I didn't have time to admire it before we made it upstairs to his bedroom. He opened the door to a huge modern looking bedroom with high ceilings and a double-bed in the middle. A painting hung above his bed but I wasn't interested in the decor in his room. I was interested in him. He turned to face me.

"You sure you want to do this, Isabella?" he asked seductively.

"Oh, yes." I managed to breathe.

He smiled and pulled me into his arms, his lips crashing down on mine again. My hands found their way into his hair and I pulled him closer to me. I had to have him. My hands ran down his chest to the buttons on his shirt, I fumbled at them for a while before ripping the shirt open to reveal the tattoos covering his body.

"*Fuck*," I breathed.

"You like what you see?" he smirked before kissing me again.

There was no time to analyse each one but all I knew was that they were hot as hell. We stumbled towards the bed and I kicked my shoes off, never breaking the kiss and he fell back onto the bed. I climbed over him, straddling him as I found his lips again. His hands ran down my back where he found my zipper and pulled it down. I was so thankful for my decision to wear matching underwear tonight. I ran my fingers down his perfect body feeling every sculpted muscle.

I broke the kiss and got off the bed.

"What are you…" he started before he realised that I was getting rid of my dress.

"*Joder,*" he moaned and pulled me down to him, this time flipping me over so that I was against the bed.

He started kissing me down my neck and along my collarbone. I felt like I was going to explode from the pleasure rippling through me - the feeling of his lips against my skin was enough to make my body fall apart.

His hand ran down my chest and he cupped my breast. He ran his thumb over the material, teasing me and my breath quickened.

"Do you like this?"

"Mmm-hmm."

His hand snaked around my back, reaching for my bra clasp. I arched my back to allow him enough space to unclip it. I pulled it off my arms and flung it across the room. The arousal in his eyes was driving me crazy. I felt wanted and desired and I was thriving off that feeling. He brought his hand back down to my breast and started to rub gently. My body reacted and I could feel the tension between my legs intensify with each touch. He ran his other hand down my body until he reached my underwear. In one swift movement, he removed them. I kicked them onto the floor and there I was, lying on the bed of a man I didn't know, all exposed and waiting for more. My body was dying for more. This kind of passion and electricity was new to me - I didn't know how to handle it.

He brought his lips back down to mine while I felt his fingers run over me.

"You're so ready for me." he murmured. His words were so explicit and usually, I would have been uncomfortable by this kind of talk but hearing those words from his lips was only making me want him more.

And slowly I felt him slide a finger inside of me.

I gasped.

"Ohhh," I purred as he started to move.

"Isabella," he breathed my name.

I couldn't form any words. I couldn't even breathe, I was so caught up in the pleasure. He went faster and faster and I could feel my body reacting, the tension waiting to reach its release.

"Yes," I murmured, "Don't stop."

"Let go," he whispered in my ear and my body obliged. I couldn't control it any longer - he was just too much!

He brought his lips back down on mine and I knew I had to have him. All of him. Now! My hands reached for the button on his pants before he eventually got up and took them off. He brought himself back against me and I could feel him. He was hard against my body and that excited me even more. It excited me to know I had this effect on him. I pulled at his underwear, needing him to know what I was asking for. He pulled them down and exposed himself to me.

Oh fuck. I had to feel him inside me.

"I need you," I breathed. "Now."

He reached over to his bedside table and grabbed a condom. He tore it open and rolled it down over himself. The anticipation was killing me. He leaned over me and spread my legs. I was still wet so I knew it wouldn't be difficult to welcome him. With one swift push he was inside of me and I cried out in pleasure.

"Are you okay?" he breathed.

"Hell yes."

There was a little pain but it was nothing compared to the pleasure. He started to move his body and I followed his rhythm. I had never felt pleasure like this before. He continued to kiss along my neck and run his hands down my arms. He brought them up over my head and pinned them down. I started to move faster, I felt consumed by him, and yet I still needed more. I needed more of him. Uncontrollable gasps escaped my lips.

"Oh, Giovanni," I panted.

"Yes baby," he breathed. "Say my name."

His encouragement sent me over the edge. We started to move faster with each other, him getting deeper with every thrust. I could feel myself tighten around him. My body was about to explode.

"Yes, yes, yes!"

I could hear a few breaths escape from his lips.

"Giovanni," I moaned.

He pushed deeper inside of me and my body came undone. Moments later he joined me in his own climax. His body collapsed on top of mine. We both lay there, both trying to catch our breath, soaking in the aftermath of the pleasure.

"Certainly didn't think I would've done this tonight," I murmured, smiling to myself.

"Are you happy you came?" he smirked, knowing very well that it had a double meaning.

I laughed.

"Oh yes."

We laid next to each other, still. Basking in the memory of what had just happened. It wasn't long before we both drifted off into a deep peaceful sleep.

CHAPTER 5:

I woke to the bright morning sun shining in my eyes. I slowly opened them, confused by where the light was coming from. My curtains were usually so dark, they never allowed any sunlight to peep through. Did I forget to close them last night?

Wait a minute…

I opened my eyes completely.

I wasn't at home.

I sat up immediately and took in my surroundings, the memories of the night before suddenly flooding back to me. I turned to the side to find the bed empty.

Giovanni?

Where did he go? I rubbed my eyes and tried to gain my composure. The first rule of Reyna's one-night stand rules was to leave before the person woke up and here I was almost sleeping the day away.

What time was it? I was far too comfortable in his bed, I really had to force myself out of it. I was still naked so I gathered the sheet on the bed, wrapping myself in it as I started searching for my clothes. This room really was a mess - our clothes were everywhere. My mind wandered back to last night and my body immediately reacted. That was amazing. The small feeling deep within the pit of my stomach reminded me that the desire was still there and the lingering pain between my legs confirmed his presence. I found my underwear and slid them back on. My bra was next. Looking around the room, I couldn't quite place where my dress was.

"Come on," I murmured to myself.

I finally spotted it across the room. I lunged for it and put it on as quickly as I could. I had to try to sneak out of here without bumping into Giovanni again. Not that I wouldn't want to see him again, I just knew I was already breaking the rules that were given to me. I eventually had my shoes, my cell phone, and my purse in my hand - I was ready to go. I tried to check the time on my phone but it was dead.

Of course, it was dead!

I slipped out through the door and found the staircase that led to the rest of his apartment. I tiptoed down the stairs, careful not to make any noise. I could hear movement from the kitchen and figured Giovanni was probably in there. The problem with his apartment, it was an open floor plan and you had to pass the kitchen to get to the elevator.

"Shit!" I muttered to myself.

I peered around the corner and saw that he was in the kitchen with his back towards me. If I sprinted past the kitchen quietly enough, I could definitely make it across to the elevator without him seeing me. Was that a good idea though? Running away like a scared little girl? I seriously needed Reyna and her brilliant plans right now to get me out of this one. I peeped my head out again but this time he had turned around and noticed me.

Crap!

"Well, good morning." Giovanni smiled at me.

I shifted uncomfortably and stepped out from behind the wall.

"Uh, hello."

"Coffee?" he asked casually.

I nodded and walked towards the kitchen counter. I sat down on one of the barstools and placed the stuff I was holding down next to me. He caught me and there was no way I could just leave right now. One cup of coffee wouldn't do any harm, right?

He placed a cup in front of me.

"Sugar?" he asked.

I shook my head. "Just milk, thanks."

He opened the fridge door, grabbing the milk for me. He placed it in front of me and smiled. I allowed myself to take him in. *How was he so sexy after just waking up?* His hair was disheveled but it suited him and he was only wearing a pair of briefs with black shorts. His body was so lean and it took every ounce of self-control I had not to reach out across this counter. I noticed his tattoos properly this time. He had a full sleeve running down his left arm and a couple starting on his right shoulder. He had a large wolf on his back by his left shoulder - it was detailed and beautiful. I had never been one to find tattoos attractive, especially so many but they suited him. I forced myself to look away from his body and averted my eyes to take in the rest of his apartment for the first time. It was very modern with a black and white colour scheme throughout. Across from the kitchen was a lounge area with a huge flat-screen TV against the wall. An acoustic guitar stood in the corner next to the TV and I wondered if he could play or if it was just for decoration. I was impressed by how neat it was. Nothing was out of place. The curtains were still drawn closed but there was enough light from the sun to remind me that I should get my day started. I turned back around and sipped on my coffee. I really needed this - I had a lingering headache but I was surprised I didn't have a hangover given how much I had to drink. *Maybe it would hit me later?*

"So last night was pretty amazing." he remarked, watching me over his cup as he took a sip.

"Yeah, it was," I admitted. "Never done that before."

"Never had sex?" he mocked.

I rolled my eyes and smiled. "Never had a one night stand."

"A one-night stand huh?" he smirked, "And what makes you think this would be a one-time thing?"

I looked over at him. He was amused by this but I could sense the tension between us still lingering. My body was captivated by him and the memories of last night resurfaced making it more difficult to want to leave right now

"This is definitely a one-time thing," I reminded him, knowing very well that I was actually trying to convince myself here and not him. "Not going to happen again."

He nodded, "Okay, if you say so."

My eyes flickered over to him. *Why did he have to be so damn tempting?* He looked at me and I could feel the tension rising between us. He gently placed his cup down and walked around the counter to where I was sitting and stood next to me.

"I should go." I murmured, nervously placing my cup back down.

"Okay."

I looked over at him. He was so close now and by the way he was looking at me, I could tell exactly what he wanted. I slipped off the barstool and he stepped right in front of me now.

"You sure you need to go?" he murmured.

Absolutely not.

"Yes I do." I said weakly.

He stepped closer to me, "Okay then."

He reached out and tucked a stray hair behind my ear. His touch set my body alight and my brain was no longer in control. My rejuvenated desire came knocking and I couldn't ignore it. Without thinking, I reached out and kissed him.

His lips were soft and I could feel him smiling as he kissed me back. I arched my body closer to his and his arms encircled me. He lifted me up onto the counter, never breaking the kiss. My hands found his hair and I couldn't help but tug on it. Just kissing him was enough to send me over the edge. You'd think the desire I felt last night would have been satisfied after being with him but no, it seemed to have a mind of its own. This was all fascinating to me. To crave someone like this was unprecedented territory. His lips left mine and instantly found my neck. He kissed down my neck and across my shoulder. He knew I loved what he was doing to me. My neck was a sensitive spot for me and he picked up on that last night quickly. He leaned against me and I felt his body come alive. I wrapped my legs around his waist, encouraging him to get closer to me. His hands ran down my body and over my thighs. He started to push the material of my dress up, exposing me in the necessary way.

Was I seriously going to do this again?

Hell yes.

I ran my hands down his body to his briefs and yanked them down to his thighs. I could feel he was ready for me.

He moved his hand up the inside of my thigh again and reached for my underwear. He used both hands to slide them down my legs. My body happily obliged. It was thrilling to give in to my deepest desires, there was a freedom to it that I never expected and it exhilarated me. He kicked his briefs from around his ankles next and the tension between my thighs increased just at the sight of him. The memory of what it felt like to have him inside of me lingered and that only increased the throbbing between my legs. I needed him to take me again. He positioned me just right on the kitchen counter and buried himself deep inside of me in one sweeping motion.

"Yesss," I breathed out, throwing my head back.

There he was again. Inside of me. Just what I wanted.

I wrapped my legs around his waist again and he supported my body with his arms. We started to move, this time with more urgency than before. We were both consumed by the ecstasy - here and now, we were the closest we could ever be and it enthralled me. It was just us and our bodies. No strings attached and not a single care in the world. All that mattered was relieving us of this overwhelming tension.

"Giovanni," I moaned.

"Say my name, baby," he encouraged.

I obliged. Here on his kitchen counter, I moaned his name like no one could hear me. I had never felt such a rush before - he was like a new drug to me that I couldn't get enough of. He pushed deeper and faster inside of me and I felt like I was on the edge.

"Don't stop," I moaned.

He didn't stop. He kept going until we both came undone, moaning each other's names in this haven of pleasure. I held onto him, both of us trying to catch our breaths. He brought his lips down to mine. It was a sweet kiss this time and it made me smile.

"Now you can go," he smirked.

I giggled and gathered myself, again. Dressing quickly, I was ready to finally leave.

What a way to start the day.

***

It took all the self-control I had left, but I managed to pull myself away from Giovanni and walk out his door. I finally made it back to my apartment.

Standing outside the building almost frozen, I was on cloud nine.

I couldn't stop smiling. I successfully managed to have one night to myself and I let loose in every way possible. I couldn't stop thinking about him. Every kiss, every touch, every moment with him was unlike anything I could've ever imagined. A part of me was hoping I would see him again but another part of me knew that wouldn't be the smartest decision. The goal was to have a one-night stand and that's what I did - no strings attached, no feelings, nothing.

I grabbed my keys out of my purse and unlocked the door. As I stepped inside, I was greeted by Reyna who stood there with her arms crossed.

"And where have you been, young lady?" she mocked.

We both burst out laughing. I couldn't take her seriously. Especially in her oversized gown and fluffy slippers.

"You're getting in really late for someone who was just supposed to have a one-night stand." she mused

The heat spread across my cheeks, "Yeah I know. I broke your rules."

"Ugh, who cares about the rules," she shrugged and pulled me in for a hug, "Did you have fun?"

I blushed again and this time she noticed.

"Of course you did!" she squealed, "Look at how you're blushing!"

"Giovanni is amazing. I mean, seriously… wow."

I dropped down onto the couch and she came over to join me.

"I told you that you'd have fun with him!" she slapped my arm playfully.

"I know and you were so right," I replied. "I just never expected to have *that* much fun though."

"You've been missing out with all your overthinking," she mused, "Sometimes you just have to live a little."

I smiled at her. She was the closest person to me and I was lucky to have her. She felt more like a sister to me than my actual sister did. She pushed me to take chances and do things I wouldn't ordinarily do because she knew it was best for me. My sister and I hardly even had a relationship.

"You were right," I replied. "This is the first time in a long time that I actually feel at peace."

"See that's also a side effect of an orgasm." Reyna said as she raised her eyebrows and gave me a sexy wink.

I burst out laughing. "Well, you're not wrong."

She tapped my thigh and stood up. "Look at you, all you needed to do was to sleep with someone once and you'd feel better."

"Twice actually," I confessed.

Her jaw dropped. "You little slut!"

I slapped her leg and we started laughing again. Uncontrollable, silly laughter and for the first time in a long while, I felt genuinely happy. There was no pressure, no judgment and no plan. The control freak side of me was in a state but I was learning to ignore her. She was no fun.

"Okay, I am making popcorn." Reyna announced as she strolled over to our kitchen.

"That sounds great," I said as I stood up. "You pick a movie, I am going to have a quick shower."

***

The rest of the weekend was spent lounging around and recovering from my first night out in years. My feet were killing me from pairing all the dancing we did with the uncomfortable heels I had chosen to wear. As much as Reyna's persistent ways could be considered annoying to most people, I found it quite endearing that she always had my back. She could always tell exactly what I needed.

It was just after nine on a Sunday evening and I was already in bed. I was working the afternoon shift at the restaurant tomorrow and I wanted to make sure I was well-rested and ready to face the week. When I first got to Barcelona, I didn't do anything. Which was great for a little while, but got boring. I eventually had to talk myself into getting a temporary job. Luckily, there was a small family restaurant called *La Senda* just down the road. They were hiring and with their flexible work hours, above minimum wage pay, and the fact it was also an English speaking restaurant, how could I not try it out? My savings weren't going to be able to carry me forever. I didn't mind working there but it was definitely a temporary solution. I had no choice though - I needed something to do and needed to have some extra income while Reyna and I fixed up our soon-to-be coffee shop.

About three weeks into my stay with Reyna, we were walking along the promenade as I was taking in my new surroundings. I loved everything about Barcelona. There was something so calming about it that really helped me attempt to work through everything that I was going through at the time. We made it to the corner and found a quaint little store that was up for sale. I went inside and immediately fell in love with it. Despite the fact it was falling apart, both Reyna and I could sense the potential in it. While we both had different reasons for wanting the place, it was an investment we were both heavily interested in and when the opportunity presented itself, we couldn't turn it away. She was interested in investing in a small business on the side and she knew how much I needed this. I needed something to put my energy into while I figured my life out. We got chatting to the owners and we learned that they were selling the shop and relocating. They were desperate to find a buyer and for the first time in weeks, I felt a glimmer of excitement. *What if I could make it my own?* My own little book store with a coffee shop? I had always wanted to own my own business and there was nothing better than my two favorite things - books and caffeine. Reyna loved coffee and she loved me. She was more than happy for us to explore this investment together.

It was at that very moment I was thankful for my money-savvy ways. I had been saving since I could remember. My parents had always given us an allowance from the day I turned thirteen and I was smart enough to save most of it over the years. I had managed to save enough to go half-way in for a deposit for the shop and we worked out an arrangement for the balance that suited the owners as well as Reyna and me. They were so desperate to get rid of the place that they were happy with what we had to offer them.

A few weeks later they were out of there and it was time to start working on it. There wasn't much we wanted to change in terms of layout but we did have a lot to fix up. It wasn't in the best condition so the price they sold it to us made a lot of sense. The paint was chipping and there was a terrible water leak that stained the carpets near the back. Fixing the plumbing issues was a top priority to avoid another leak in the shop. We decided we wanted to start from scratch so we removed all the furniture they had into Reyna's storage unit. Thankfully through Reyna's family's contacts, we found people willing to assist at a reasonable price. We got people in for the improvements and repairs we weren't able to complete ourselves. Once the leak was sorted out, we got the carpets removed and replaced with tiles. Everything after that was up to us to sort out. I didn't mind having to work on the shop, it was great having a distraction. I didn't want to think about my failed relationship or failed job. I didn't want to think about the fact that my parents still thought I was in Madrid with Nate. He had spoken so openly to them about marriage and how much he loved me and wanted to be with me. How could I possibly blindside them too? Deep down I sensed my father would be more understanding but my mother was not the kind of woman you could open up to, so I hid the truth from them. As far as I knew, Nate was still working on the project in Madrid. I tried to stay up to date with him but it wasn't easy since someone like Nate avoided social media like the plague. After a while, I stopped checking in and after the fallout I ended up having with my mother, I avoided my family as much as possible. I was sure they all most definitely had some suspicions. I knew avoiding them made the situation worse, but out of sight, out of mind. It was what I usually did - when things got difficult, I had this terrible tendency to always run away.

Growing up, I was always made to feel like I had to control my emotions since my family hardly shared theirs. I couldn't remember the last time my parents were even affectionate in front of me. It made me feel like an outsider and more often than not, I struggled to relate to them. I was the one who found it difficult to contain my emotions. Love, pain, anger, sadness, lust - I feel it all and it often has the ability to consume me.

Like it did this weekend.

I smiled to myself thinking back to my time with Giovanni. I hadn't been able to get him off my mind since I left his apartment - every passionate kiss, every touch, every moment was ingrained in my brain and I had a strong suspicion that it wasn't going anywhere anytime soon. I reached for my phone on my bedside table and did what any sane woman would do. I social media stalked him. I didn't have much to go on except his name and the fact he owned Mala Mía. I typed it into my search bar and his name popped up on my screen immediately.

Giovanni Velázquez

It had a nice ring to it. There were plenty of articles about him - about his family and the club, all of which were in Spanish. I scanned through those quite quickly but the further I scrolled down, the more articles started to pop up about his Casanova ways. There were tons of pictures of him with different women. Tons of speculation as to who he was dating and there was no secret that he seemed to get around. A flicker of jealousy overcame me and I had to mentally scold myself. There was no reason for that. I found his Instagram page and was surprised at the fifty-eight thousand followers he had - he clearly had a public persona I wasn't aware of. Scrolling down his page was making it so much harder to put him out of my mind but I couldn't look away. I was so attracted to him - it was borderline ridiculous. He woke something up inside of me and my body burned for him. My toes curled at the thought of him touching me again. His kisses along my neck and collar bone. The way his hand felt against my back. His fingers making their way between my thighs.

Thoughts of him consumed me and I was starting to wonder how I was ever going to get rid of them.

CHAPTER 6:

I t's Thursday night and I just strolled back into the apartment after finishing my last shift for the week. Tonight was madness at the restaurant. I was serving a family with three young lively children which resulted in having a chocolate milkshake knocked over as I was serving the food. Luckily, my arm was able to catch most of it before it spilled onto the floor. Unlucky for me however, but it was unintentional. I spent the rest of the night sticky and uncomfortable.

But finally, I was home.

It was just after ten-thirty as I stepped through the door to a chorus of voices from the living room.

"I'm home," I announced.

I hung up my keys on the key rack and made my way to the living room. Reyna, Katrina and Sergio were lounging around laughing at some series they were watching.

"Welcome home," Reyna said, suddenly noticing the chocolate stains on my arm and shirt. "What the hell happened to you?"

I sighed, "Some child thought it would be fun to knock their milkshake over."

"Ah, so it was one of those nights huh?" Katrina laughed.

She was leaning against Sergio's chest and he was smiling down at her. The simple intimacy of the way they were around each other made my heart ache. I've always been a relationship person so I couldn't help but feel a little jealous seeing them like that.

"You're going to need a new shirt," Sergio joined the conversation, stating the obvious. "That one is stained."

"Yeah I figured," I said, rolling my eyes. "I should've charged them extra for clothing damages."

"Whose clothes are damaged?" I heard a voice say from behind me. I turned around and caught my breath.

Giovanni.

Here he was standing in the hallway, in my apartment, looking sexy as hell and he didn't even have to try. He was wearing a casual pair of jeans and a black jersey. His hair was messy today, strands falling forward and I had to physically stop myself from reaching out and moving them back.

What was he doing here? Or better yet, why did Reyna not warn me he would be here? I suddenly became aware of my appearance and how I probably looked like an absolute mess to him right now.

"Mine," I said, indicating the big brown stain on my once white shirt. "This was a clear fatality of the night."

He laughed. "Oh shit."

His laugh was the most wonderful sound. I just wanted to keep hearing it.

"I didn't know you were going to be here," I said as casually as I could manage.

"Just stopped by on my way out," he replied. "Nice to see you though."

I smiled, "Nice to see you too, Giovanni."

I was using every ounce of self-control I had to keep the conversation as casual as I could manage and not freak out about the fact that my body was calling out for him. *What the hell was up with that?* When I was around him, I seemed to lose all control. My body surrendered itself to him and he didn't even have to ask for it.

"I'm going to go shower," I announced. "I've been sticky all night."

Reyna, Kat, and Sergio were so engrossed in the series they were currently binge-watching that they didn't say a word.

"What are they watching?" I turned to Giovanni.

"No idea," he said. "But it's clearly more entertaining than what you're saying."

I chuckled. "Clearly."

I stood there awkwardly, not sure if I should leave him standing in the corridor of the apartment. He was looking at me as if he was waiting for me to invite him to come with me. He tried to hide it but the interest in his eyes was still there. The last thing I wanted to do was to drag myself away from him, no matter how uncomfortable I was right now.

"Are you going to just stand in the hallway all night?" I teased.

"Well I was thinking about it but then you mentioned you were going to shower and that sounds way more fun," he said in a low, almost whispering voice.

Did he just say that? *Holy shit.* He had no filter.

"And what makes you think I would want you to join me?"

He smirked. "Intuition."

I hated that he knew the effect he had on me. No matter how much I tried to hide it, I couldn't control the physical reaction he caused me. The tension between us was palpable. I couldn't control my thoughts from wandering off to a lascivious place.

"Don't worry though, I know last time was just a one-time thing," he quipped. "Well, a two-time thing."

The heat spread across my cheeks turning them pink.

"I should probably get going anyway," he announced. "Too many people around."

He winked at me before reaching for his wallet and keys on the table. *How could he be so brazen?* He was so confident and didn't seem to care what anyone thought. His departure announcement did bring on a wave of disappointment. He had been on my mind all week - even with my conscious efforts to push thoughts of him away. My body would not let me forget him.

"It was really nice to see you again, Isabella," he murmured, smirking at me. "Enjoy your shower."

He said his goodbyes to the others with a general wave and headed towards the door. I figured I should let him out since neither Reyna nor Katrina made any movement to suggest they would be the ones doing it. *What in the world were they watching?* I strolled to the front door and pulled it open. He stepped out and turned back to face me.

"So will I be seeing you at Mala Mía again this weekend?" he asked.

"I told you, it has to be worth my while."

He bit his lip in a quick motion before smiling down at me. "I think you know now that I can make it worth your while."

His confidence was a major turn-on.

"You know where to find me." he smirked and turned to leave.

"Goodbye, Giovanni." I said, smiling at him as he strolled to the elevator that just arrived.

"Oh, Isabella," he called out, turning to face me again. "Shower sex is fun too - if you ever want to try it sometime."

He winked at me and stepped inside, disappearing from my view.

I let out the breath I didn't know I was holding. *Fuck.* Now I really need a cold shower.

CHAPTER 7:

I knew he was here somewhere. Giovanni had awoken something in me that I just couldn't shake. An itch I couldn't seem to scratch. The fact that I joined Reyna at Mala Mía again just at the slight chance of seeing him again proved that something had changed. I didn't think it was a bad thing but I wasn't used to this. I wasn't used to a man having such physical control over me. Every time I thought of him, my body burned. His kisses along my neck or his hands running up my thighs. I swore to myself that it would be a one-time thing but I hadn't been able to stop thinking about him, especially not since he dropped by the apartment.

Reyna and I were on the dance floor but my head wasn't in it. I wasn't nearly drunk enough to not care and I couldn't help but constantly scan the room for him. My eyes flickered over to the bar.

Found him.

And he wasn't alone.

A pang of disappointment hit and I had to remind myself that there is no place for jealousy in this arrangement. I wanted to sleep with him and if I got to do that then what was the problem here?

Why did I want him so much?

He stood by the bar with the same beautiful blonde I had seen here with him previously. She was leaning against it, smiling at him. They were standing close to each other and I could tell by her body language there was definitely interest from her side. He, on the other hand, was difficult to read. He had his back towards me and I just wanted him to turn around. I wanted to see if he was interested in her too. If so, that would be it. I would accept that it was a once-off thing and move on with my life. I didn't own him - he wasn't my boyfriend so I had no reason to feel possessive over him.

Get your shit together Isabella!

I managed to drag my eyes away from him and focused on having a good time on the dance floor. I allowed the music to take me away, even if it was only for a quick moment.

Not a lot of time had passed before I found myself scanning the bar for Giovanni again.

He was gone but the blonde remained.

That's a good sign.

I scanned the rest of the club but I couldn't find him. I wondered if he headed to his office in the back.

I turned to Reyna. "I'll be right back."

She nodded but carried on dancing. If there was one thing Reyna enjoyed more than forcing me out of the house, it was dancing. I pushed my way through the crowd and followed the corridor to the back. The music was still loud but it wasn't blaring in my ears anymore. I made it to his office door. I took a moment to think about what I was doing. I wanted him and I was going after what I wanted. I could just spend my time thinking about it or I could be the type of woman that took control of a situation.

I tapped on the door lightly and pushed it open.

"*Sí?*" he said before looking up and noticing it was me. "Oh, Isabella! Hi!"

I stepped inside and closed the door, locking it behind me.

"I thought I'd find you here." I looked around, taking in his office.

It was modern, spacious, and when you closed the door, no one could see inside it. He stood by his large wooden desk flicking through a pile of papers. His businessman demeanor was an attractive look on him. He was in charge and I loved that he brought that same energy to the bedroom. He had a simple black button-up top on with his sleeves rolled up, exposing his many tattoos that lined his arms. I strolled past the black chairs right in front of his desk.

"I didn't even know you'd be here." He placed the papers he had in his hand down on his desk. "Thought this wasn't really your scene?"

I was in front of his desk now and I was thankful for the flicker of liquid courage my body managed to retain. I wasn't sure I would've had the confidence to do this without it. I wasn't nearly as confident as I wished I could be so I needed a helping hand to truly give in to my true desires.

"Yeah it isn't," I murmured. "But I couldn't stop thinking about you."

"Oh?" he quipped, the interest in his voice was undeniable.

I stepped closer to him. He was leaning against the side of his desk and I positioned myself in between his legs. Instinctively, his hands went to my waist, pulling me closer to him. His cologne surrounded us, allowing me to breathe in that familiar smell of his.

"Have you been thinking about me?" I asked.

"Haven't been able to stop."

My eyes jumped up to meet his. Desire was flaring in his eyes. We were so close now. All I've wanted since I last saw him was to feel his hands on my body again. He ran a single finger up and down my bare thigh as his eyes traveled down to my mouth. I brought my hands to his chest and leaned into him. It was a soft kiss at first and with that, the memory of the first time we kissed resurfaced. I wanted more from him. His tongue flickered over mine, deepening the kiss. My hands slowly made their way into his hair, tugging at him, needing him closer to me. I focused on nothing else but his hands on my body. This was what I'd been wanting. I wanted him. This physical connection consumed me and there was no stopping us now. His hand found my waist and he turned me around so my back was against his desk. He lifted me up onto it, pushing the files and papers that were on his desk, to the floor.

I smiled against his lips and ran my hands down his shirt, reaching for the buttons. I started to unbutton his shirt as his lips left mine, leaving kisses along my neck instead.

I couldn't help but moan. My legs tightened around his waist, pulling him closer to me. He was all I was focused on right now. I didn't care that we were in a club full of people, all I cared about was the burning desire for him. He ignited my body with every touch against my skin.

"Giovanni," I moaned.

He needed to know the effect he had on me. Every kiss, every touch burned against me and the tension between my legs increased at an expeditious pace.

He ran his hands up my legs, pushing the material of my dress up along with it. Thank goodness I decided to wear a dress again. *Easy access.*

"Tell me what you want, Isabella..." he whispered in my ear, sending an overwhelming feeling up and down my body. His breath on my ear was such a trigger for me and I couldn't control how it made me feel.

I had never been one to express what I wanted but he made me feel comfortable enough to do so.

"I want you, Giovanni," I looked up at him. "Right here, right now."

He tugged at his lips before smiling as he brought his lips down to mine with a new rejuvenated sense of urgency. My hands reached for his pants and I fumbled for his button. I got it open and rocked my hips against him, needing to feel him against me. He slid my underwear down my legs and dropped them to the floor. He pushed his pants down, finally revealing himself to me. Just seeing how I made him feel intensified my own arousal.

"Now, Giovanni," I moaned.

He chuckled. "Patience baby."

That was one thing I definitely didn't have right now. The thrill of being in a public place brought on a wave of excitement that I had never experienced before. It was exhilarating. He grabbed a condom from his top drawer, ripped it open and rolled it over himself. I was so ready for him. I couldn't help it - my body was under his spell. I wrapped my arms around his neck as he lifted me up, bringing me down on him. He slipped inside and filled me up, giving me exactly what I had been wanting.

"Yessss," I gasped and started to move my body with his.

I threw my head back and allowed myself to take him in. He was strong enough to hold me up while he entered me again and again. The moans were uncontrollable and I was thankful for the loud music from the club masking my vocal pleasure. His hand slipped underneath my dress and over my breast. He rubbed me softly at first but when I nipped at his bottom lip, he could tell the intensity I needed. I knew I was close already. I could feel it. This was what I had been craving. I craved him. The harder and deeper he went, the more my body was slipping further and further from control. He couldn't hide his own pleasure, it was written all over his face. Loose strands of hair fell in front of his eyes as we moved as one. Just seeing his pleasure made me tighten around him - it was fucking hot. I ran my hands up and down his body, needing to feel every inch of him. Every curve of his muscles, every carefully drawn marking against his skin, every part of him that I could touch.

He leaned forward towards my ear and nibbled the top. I tightened my grip on his hair and pulled myself closer to him, pushing him deeper.

Uncontrollable gasps escaped my lips. "Don't stop. I'm so close."

And he didn't stop. He kept giving my body what it wanted, increasing the urgency with each movement.

"Let go, Isabella," he murmured in my ear.

My body obliged. He was my master and I surrendered myself to him. He pushed deep inside of me one last time before joining me in my climax. He was panting and leaned his forehead against mine. My breathing matched his and the aftermath of the pleasure spread across my body.

"I've never been so glad to have someone enter my office before." he murmured, smiling down at me.

I laughed. "I certainly hope this doesn't happen too often."

"I never kiss and tell," he joked.

I smiled but the memory of what Reyna said about him being the perfect one-night stand resurfaced. He clearly did this a lot. I started to wonder how many others he had been with. I couldn't be angry at that - I didn't even know him that well and I still didn't have any right to feel the jealousy that was lingering in the back of my mind. Just knowing how he made me feel, I couldn't help but feel possessive. I was drawn to him and I wasn't used to being so out of control. I pushed my overthinking out of my mind. I really needed to stop that. I was here now, with him, and I finally got what I had been wanting - to have him again. But I knew myself and I knew that I probably shouldn't seek him out like this again. I already couldn't control the way he made me feel physically and I needed to find a way to make sure that these feelings didn't spill over to my emotional side.

I wasn't ready for any of that.

We were both fully clothed again and ready to face the crowds in the club. The last thing I wanted to do was head back to the dance floor. I wanted to take his hand and have him take me back to his apartment and do this all again but I knew that would be a bad idea. I had my three doses of him and it was probably a good time to start my Giovanni detox.

I strolled to the door of his office and he followed closely behind me. The post-orgasm calmness finally settled throughout my body. I reached for the handle but he was quicker than me, putting his hand on the door keeping it closed. I turned to face him and he leaned closer to me. I could feel his breath on my face and the close proximity was driving me crazy.

"I'm really glad you came in here tonight, Isabella," he murmured.

"I can't seem to stay away from you it seems," I confessed.

"You don't have to."

Oh yes, I did. The effect he had on me was terrifying. I was a control freak and the fact I couldn't seem to control myself around him was not something I wanted to get used to. I had already lost control of so many things in my life. I couldn't afford to lose control of myself.

"I think I have to," I murmured. "I'm not looking for anything right now."

"And who said I was?" He asked, raising an eyebrow.

Good point.

"You're over-thinking all of this," he continued. "We're just having some fun here. No strings attached."

As appealing as that sounded to my body, my mind didn't quite agree. Would I be able to keep my physical and emotional feelings separate? It was never something I had to do in the past. I had always felt an emotional connection that led to a physical one. Not the other way round. But then again I had never felt this kind of physical connection to anyone before. He excited me and brought out a side of me that I didn't even know existed. I would have never dubbed myself as the kind of woman to sleep with someone I wasn't dating, especially repeatedly. It was new and terrifying and I wasn't exactly sure how to feel about all of this.

"No strings attached." I repeated.

"You do you and I'll do me and if we happen to do each other then great." he replied.

I burst out laughing.

"You're something else, Giovanni." I reached out and kissed his cheek before turning and making my way back to the dance floor.

CHAPTER 8:

"So we ended up having sex on my bosses desk." Reyna chuckled.

My jaw dropped as I turned to face her. "You didn't!"

It had been a while since Reyna and I had a chance to head over to the coffee shop so we decided to make some time today to do just that. We finally settled on a colour to paint the walls. We went back and forth for a while - her wanting a dark maroon and me wanting a light lilac colour. We met in the middle and went the complete opposite of both and settled on a baby blue - for one side of the shop at least. After getting all we needed from the closest hardware store, we were in our old clothes painting on a Saturday morning.

"Of course I did, Izzy," she smirked. "There was no one there and I've always wanted to do it on a desk at work."

I burst out laughing. Reyna went on telling me all about the hot new campaign manager her company hired for the latest project they were working on.

"And I was surprised Diego was into it because he's the polar opposite of the type of guys I'm usually into."

She had been seeing him since the start of the project and she was more than happy to share their latest sexual encounter. Her mention of having sex on the desk at work made my mind wander back to the last time I saw Giovanni. I had never thought of having sex in a place where the chances of getting caught were very high, but that was before I met him. I didn't care that we were in a club full of people that night - I had to have him. He brought out this new side to me and it was exhilarating. My mind wandered back to that night - his strong arms around my waist, bringing me down onto him while his lips found my neck and I - ...

"Hello? Izzy?" Reyna clicked her fingers, bringing me out of my unexpected sexual daydream. The heat spread across my cheeks. I couldn't help it, the thoughts of him inside of me lived rent-free in my mind lately.

"What in the world were you thinking about?"

"Nothing." I brushed the conversation off. "Back to Diego - so when are you seeing him again?"

"Well, that's actually what I wanted to speak to you about. He's going for some drinks later with friends of his at one of those *Vai Moana* beach parties, and he asked me to meet him there."

I brought my roller down to the paint in the tray next to me. "Meeting his friends already. That's a big step in the right direction."

"Yes but I need you to come with me." She eyed me, awaiting my reaction.

I knew she needed me right now. She wouldn't admit it but I could tell she liked him more than she ever expected to. The way she spoke about him was different and I wanted this to work out for her. For them.

I brought the roller back to the wall and continued painting. "Of course I'll come."

She squealed, "Ah Izzy, thank you so much. I know how much you hate going out so thi-"

"I don't hate it so much anymore," I interrupted.

"Even better then," she smirked. "And you can meet some of Diego's friends. Maybe there's a cute one you could take for a spin?"

I rolled my eyes and smiled. "I think I'm fine for now."

I knew she meant well by this but there was no way I could even think about being with anyone else when I couldn't get Giovanni out of my head. How could I when every thought of him invaded my mind?

My body was going through an awakening and I didn't know how to make it stop. I hadn't seen Giovanni in days and I wasn't entirely sure of where we stood. Would this be a recurring thing between him and I, or was that it now? The feeling of disappointment lingered at just the thought of it being over. A part of me didn't want that to be it. After I left the club that last night I had seen him and thought about what was said, I realized that I was probably not the best candidate for an arrangement of "no strings attached". How could I be? I had never been very good at separating my emotions from anything and I certainly wasn't going to be able to stop myself from developing something for him if I continued. I decided from that moment on that I wouldn't seek him out. I would stay away.

My body didn't seem to agree with this decision - in fact, she was pretty pissed off about it.

I had to keep reminding myself to take each interaction with him for what it was. I wanted him and I got to have him - there was nothing more than the pure, raw, physical attraction between us. I needed to put him out of my mind.

"There are other guys out there besides Giovanni. I'm sure you could easily land up under one of them."

"Reyna!" I exclaimed.

"What?" she chuckled. "Stop acting like a prude. I know you had sex in his office the last time so you're not as innocent as you try to be."

I couldn't help but laugh. I was still getting used to the nonchalant attitude people had here towards sex.

"I knew I shouldn't have told you that."

"Oh please! Your messy hair and flushed cheeks gave you away. I know a post-orgasm look when I see one."

I nudged her playfully. "God you are so brazen."

"And that's why you love me," she said as she smiled.

***

Vai Moana was packed. It wasn't a very big bar to begin with but that didn't matter as people spread out onto the beach. We were supposed to be headed into autumn but the beating sun shining down on us wasn't ready to let the heat go just yet. I followed Reyna onto the deck where she threw her arms around a tall, slender man who I assumed to be Diego. Reyna did warn me he was the complete opposite of the type of man she usually went for so I wasn't too surprised. While she usually went for the dark, handsome, and dangerous type, I was always the one who drifted more towards the shy ones who were attractive in the "your-mind-is-attractive" kind of way. It would appear that we had now swapped tastes in men.

She pulled away from him and stepped to the side. "Diego, meet Isabella. *Mi amiga de la escuela.*"

"*Hola, Isabella, soy Diego.*" He reached out and pulled me in for a hug.

"*Hola, Diego,* nice to meet you."

Reyna turned to me. "Don't mind his English. He can speak it but he prefers to speak Spanish."

"*Lo siento.* I speak English - but it's not great," he said sheepishly, his Spanish accent coming through.

I shrugged. "No problem. I'm really the one who should be learning Spanish anyway."

Reyna leaned into him and her eyes were full of affection as she looked up at him. She was so smitten already. I had never seen her like this before.

"*Mi amigo, Matías,*" Diego started to speak in Spanish but switched over for my inclusion. "*Lo siento*, my friend Matías just went to get us drinks. What can I get you guys?"

Reyna reached for the cocktail menu off the high table we were standing around. She leaned closer to me so we could both look.

"Should we get a jug of Sangria for now?" She asked me. "We can share."

"Sounds good to me."

"Let me get that for you," Diego said as he smiled. "I'll be back."

He leaned over and left a kiss on Reyna's cheek before heading to the already packed bar to get us some drinks.

"You weren't kidding when you said he was the opposite of your type," I teased.

She snorted. "I told you! But I can't help it - there's something about him that really makes me want to jump him all the time."

I chuckled. "It's like you're in heat."

"Right?" she giggled. "All jokes aside though. I don't know why I like him so much, but I do. So it would mean a lot to me for you to get to know him."

I squeezed her hand. "Of course Reyna. I'll do anything for you."

Minutes later Diego returned with a jug of Sangria and two glasses in hand. Following closely behind him must have been his friend, Matías. His thick curly hair made him cuter than I expected. He wiggled himself between Reyna and me and placed down a tray of shots he was holding. He turned to me with a bright smile on his face.

"*Soy, Matías*," he opened his arms and pulled me in for a quick hug.

"Nice to meet you, Matías, I'm Isabella."

"Is that an English accent I hear?"

"I guess so," I chuckled. "I'm originally from London."

Diego grabbed a shot glass in each hand and handed it over to us, "We're not going to have a good time if we just stand around here."

That sounded just like something Reyna would say and I was starting to see the similarities between the two of them. They both shared the same zest for life and just like Reyna, Diego was ready to have a good time. I psyched myself up to get onto their level. Hell, I was at a beach party in Barcelona for crying out loud. I've been going out so regularly lately, why stop now? We lifted our shot glasses together, cheersing to our new meeting and coming together. I brought the shot to my lips and tilted my head back, allowing it to slide down my throat.

Oh God. Tequila.

It burned going down like it always did but there was no going back now. It made its way through me and all the tension I was holding onto started to slowly fade away like it always did. Alcohol - the true illusionist.

Another two shots later and we were standing outside by one of the beer pong tables the bar had set up. Reyna and Diego were playing against another couple we had just met and I sat on the sidelines with Matías cheering them on. The music was blaring through the bar. I leaned my head back and closed my eyes, soaking in the moment.

"Yes, baby!" Reyna exclaimed and I turned to watch as she high-fived Diego for getting the ball into her opponent's plastic cup again. Three in a row - even I was impressed by his skill. I sipped on the cocktail next to me. Reyna and I made our way through that Sangria quite quickly and I had moved onto another suggestion from Diego. I didn't know what it was but it was strong. My stomach rumbled and I realized I needed food. I was drinking quite a bit and if I didn't get food into my system now, I was going to be a wreck.

"Can I order food from here?" I asked Matías.

He shook his head, "When they have these parties they close their kitchen. They're all about the bar being open."

There were quite a few other places along the beach so I was going to have to go and find something.

"You can try a place down there," he pointed in the direction he was referring to. "They should have something."

I reached for my purse and stood up.

"Do you want me to come with you?" he offered.

I shook my head, "No - you stay here and watch their victory."

He chuckled.

"I won't be too long. Let Reyna know where I've gone please."

As soon as I turned to walk down the wooden walkway, the alcohol hit me. I had been sitting for a couple of hours now as we continued to enjoy our drinks so this was the first time I allowed it to make its way through me. A lingering dizziness hovered over me and I had to remind myself to focus extra hard now. And to not fall over.

I reached the restaurant that Matías pointed out and strolled through it to the counter. It was packed with people and they had long white couches on the beach itself filled with different groups of people. I picked up the menu and scanned through it. I quickly realized I forgot to ask if anyone else wanted anything so I was going to have to order double - just in case. I settled on a tapas platter that would be enough for all of us to share. I signaled for the waiter and quickly placed my order.

"You can take a seat and wait there." he pointed to an area of empty bar stools right by the beach.

"Gracias," I said.

I started to walk towards the barstools but someone caught my eye. I turned to a group of people scattered across one of the white couches. In the middle, I watched a couple wrapped up in an intimate moment with a fresh-faced brunette woman leaning into his ear as he ran his hands up and down her bare thigh. I caught my breath at the sight of him.

Giovanni

Of course, he'd be here with someone else. She was nibbling on his ear and that made him slowly lean his head back, soaking in what she was doing. I couldn't look away and the stab of jealousy started creeping over me. It made my skin crawl to see her doing that to him. I wanted to be her right now.

Isabella, get yourself together.

The combination of alcohol and jealousy was lethal and I had to get out of there. Just as I started to look away, he brought his head forward again and we locked eyes. Eye contact - one of the purest forms of intimacy. The ability to hold power over one another from across the room by the simple flick of the eye. I quickly turned away, pretending that I didn't see him. I didn't want to see him right now. I couldn't get him out of my mind lately but judging by the tongue shoved in his ear at the moment, he wasn't thinking of me at all. He was with someone else now and a sick feeling settled in my stomach. The reminder that I was just another one on his list wasn't something I wanted to be reminded of. I pulled out my cell phone to text Reyna. I started typing but I felt a light tap on my shoulder that made me stop without pressing send. I turned and there he stood. He was wearing a bright emerald shirt that looked great against his dark olive skin. The shirt exposed his tattoos and I was fascinated by them. They were so fucking attractive.

"I didn't know you would be here." he smiled.

"I could say the same thing about you."

I was too intoxicated for a conversation with him but I was adamant to keep myself together. I sat up straight and instructed myself to focus.

"Well the odds of me being here are way more likely than you," he teased. "Who are you here with?"

"Reyna. We're here with her new boyfriend, thing, I don't know what they are." I started to ramble.

"Boyfriend, thing?" he bemused. "Interesting title."

I smiled awkwardly. I scolded myself for drinking too much - I couldn't even string together a coherent sentence in front of him.

"Well I'm glad I bumped into you," he said.

"You are?"

He stepped closer to me, brushing up against me. *Why did he have to touch me?* Just the simple skin-to-skin contact reminded me of what it was like to really have him against me.

And inside of me.

Isabella, no.

That was the last thing I wanted to think about but now it was too late. A slight throbbing between my legs made an appearance and I really had to get away from him. He had such an effect on me and that became worse in my inebriated state.

"Of course," he breathed. "Do you want to get a drink?"

Wait, what? *Was he being serious?* How could he be asking me to go and get a drink when not even two minutes before he had some other woman's tongue in his ear?

"A drink? With you?"

"Yes with me."

I leaned past him to where he was sitting before and the brunette was now staring me down - she clearly wasn't impressed that he ditched her. I leaned out of her view and looked up at him. His eyes were brimming with interest and a few strands of hair had fallen forward over his eyes.

"No thanks."

He was taken aback, "No?"

"I don't think your date is very happy with you right now."

"She's not my date."

"I think her tongue would disagree." I quipped.

He shrugged, "That was nothing."

The waiter brought my order and handed me the packet. I slipped off the barstool and thanked him. A wave of dizziness washed over me and I had to focus on keeping myself steady. Giovanni's presence was enough to suck away all the air around me. I felt like I couldn't breathe around him - it was terrifying.

"Seriously, Isabella, that was nothing." he reached out and grabbed my hand.

I held my breath. His touch burned against me and it was no longer the heat from the sun that I was feeling. *Why did I want him so much?* He was not a one-woman kind of man and seeing him with someone else reminded me of that. There was an internal battle between my brain and my body. I was dying to have him again but the logical part of me was waving the red flag at an incessant pace.

"You don't owe me an explanation, Giovanni. There's nothing going on between us."

As I said it I knew I was trying to convince myself of that because I didn't believe it one bit. There was something between us - our chemistry was undeniable.

He stepped closer to me and we were inches apart, "You don't mean that."

I didn't.

"Yes I do," I lied meekly. "I told you it was just a one-time thing."

"It happened more than once, Isabella." he breathed.

My name rolled off his tongue and his breath on my skin intoxicated my senses. At that moment I could have just thrown myself at him. It was what I wanted to do. I wanted to feel his strong arms around me and his hands all over my body. I wanted his lips on my neck. I wanted to rub my hands down his body and take him in my hand and...

I mentally blocked the rest of those thoughts but the tension between my legs was rising and I needed to get out of there. I had to keep reminding myself that he was here with someone else and I needed to save face. Seeing him with someone else made me so jealous and I was angry at myself for the investment I had in him. Sleeping with him three times was a momentary lapse of judgment and I needed to continue my Giovanni detox.

"One drink, Isabella." he persisted.

One drink wouldn't hurt, right?

He was with someone else Isabella!

"No thanks," I pulled my hand away from his. "I'm here with someone else anyway so I should really get back."

I didn't know why I said that but I did. Drunk me wanted to prove to him that I didn't care if he was with someone else - I could do the same.

"You're here with Reyna."

"And Reyna's boyfriend-thing who happened to have a very cute friend." I couldn't control what was coming out of my mouth. It had a mind of its own right now.

"A very cute friend?" He lifted an eyebrow and I could see the amusement in his eyes. This wasn't funny. I was trying to get a reaction out of him but I certainly didn't think it would be one of amusement. I wanted him to take me seriously. I didn't need him - I could easily find someone else.

Drunk me was in charge right now, sitting front row to the Giovanni and Isabella show. Sober me was hanging her head in shame knowing there was nothing she could do except watch on the sideline.

"That's what I said."

"You're cocky when you've been drinking." He was challenging me and it was such a turn-on.

"I'm lots of things," I slurred. "You just won't get to find out."

"But what if I want to?" he murmured. "What if I want to get to know more about you, Isabella?"

His low voice was thick with desire. He was doing all he could to get to me and he already had. From the moment he touched me, I was ready for him but I didn't want him to know that. I needed to regain some control of the situation. He was saying all the right things right now but how could I trust him? I was made well-aware of his reputation and seeing him with someone else again drove me into a fit of envy that I didn't want.

"Sorry, that right is reserved for my date."

I was seriously going on about this date thing. I didn't know a thing about Matías - he wasn't even as interesting as I thought he would be but thankfully Giovanni didn't know that.

"I'd love to meet him." he quipped.

"What?" I asked, even though I heard him clearly.

"Your date," he said. "I'd love to meet him."

"Oh no," I protested. "He wouldn't wa-"

"There's no harm in meeting him right?" he continued. "Since you said there's nothing going on between us, what would be the problem?"

He was enjoying this. I could see it in his eyes. He wanted to catch me in my lie but I wouldn't allow that. I was way too stubborn and even though Matías was not my date, he would be now.

"No problem," I smiled. "I'd love for you to meet him."

"Great then," he smirked. "Lead the way."

"Fine…"

I turned and we started to make our way back to *Vai Moana.* I scolded myself on the way there - *what the fuck was I thinking?* Why did I lie about Matías being my date? I had no idea how I was going to get out of this one so I was really hoping that he would be on board with me springing this one on him. I didn't know a single thing about him but I just needed to convince Giovanni that he was in fact my date. Giovanni remained close to me as we made our way through the crowds of people. I saw Reyna and Diego at the tall table we had before they went off to play beer pong again. I quickened my pace and reached Reyna before Giovanni did.

"There you a-" she started to say but I interrupted.

"Reyna, play along with whatever happens now." I said in a hushed voice and placed the food on the table.

"What?" She was confused until she saw Giovanni step out from behind me.

"Giovanni! Hi," she was shocked at his presence but she did her best to try to hide it. "Didn't expect to see you here."

"I could say the same about Isabella." he smirked.

"Oh, she's full of surprises," she smiled and turned to her date. "This is Diego." He politely introduced himself and I was looking around for Matías who was nowhere in sight. I started to panic a bit. *Why did I have to be so stupid and say he was my date?* That was a terrible idea.

"I bumped into Isabella a couple places over and she told me all about her date." He announced casually.

"Her da-..." Diego looked confused but Reyna quickly jumped in to save my story.

"Yes, her date!" she exclaimed. "Matías is great."

Diego couldn't hide the confusion in his eyes but she nudged him, "Remember we set Isabella and Matías up today."

Diego was definitely not on board and I could feel the heat spread across my cheeks.

"He's got to be around here somewhere." I said as casually as I could manage.

"Oh, I'm sure he is." Giovanni sneered.

"He is."

Giovanni had a look of amusement on his face and I really didn't want him to catch me in this lie.

"So what does this Matías do?" he asked.

He was relentless.

"Marketing," I said at the exact same time that Diego announced he was, in fact, an accountant.

"A marketing accountant." I said quickly.

What the fuck was a marketing accountant Isabella?

"A marketing accountant?" Giovanni repeated. "Can't say I've ever heard of that."

"Oh, it's all the rave. Super interesting to hear about." I rambled on. I could have crawled into a hole at that very moment. Diego leaned over to Reyna and whispered something in her ear. I had no idea what he said but she turned abruptly to the door. I followed her gaze and Matías was walking towards us.

Hand in hand with a pretty, young blonde.

Oh fuck!

They reached us and Reyna stepped forward to greet him again, "Ah Juan, you're back!"

She was trying to save the situation here but Matías had no idea what was going on and said, "Reyna - you can't be that drunk to forget my name."

He noticed Giovanni and politely extended his hand, *"Hola, Soy Matías."*

My cover was blown. Giovanni looked over at me and I could tell he was trying to hold back his laughter.

"Ah, the marketing accountant," he remarked.

Matias looked confused but Giovanni continued, "Nice to meet you, Matías," he introduced himself and turned to the pretty blond on his arm. "Sorry, and you are?"

She smiled politely, "I'm Selena, Matías's girlfriend."

"Matías's girlfriend?" he repeated. "Well, it's lovely to meet you, Selena."

Selena introduced herself to everyone else and Giovanni stepped closer to me.

"So did you know your date had a girlfriend?" he murmured in my ear.

There was really no way to get out of this one. I had to accept defeat. The heat continued to spread across my cheeks, "News to me."

He chuckled, "Well now I guess you can have a drink with me."

I had lost this. Badly.

"Fine, one drink."

He winked at me and opened his mouth to say something but I held my finger up, stopping him.

"But there's one condition." I announced.

"And what's that?"

"You don't mention anything that just happened ever again."

He chuckled, "I can't promise that. You put on quite a show just now."

I was humiliated and angry at myself. *Why did I have to be so stupid?* I didn't have to say anything about a date but of course, the sight of Giovanni with someone else made me do it. He had so much power over me and I hated it. I wanted to be the one in control.

I crossed my arms, "One drink and no mention of this or I'm staying right here."

"Fine," he smiled. "Shall we?"

CHAPTER 9:

"You seriously said he was a marketing accountant." Giovanni laughed.

I hung my head in my hands, "I told you I didn't want to talk about that."

Giovanni reached over and removed my hands from my face, still keeping them in his. We were sitting on a bench on the beach away from the music from all the parties going on. The sun was beginning to set and I loved the way it reflected against the water.

"Why'd you lie about having a date?"

I really didn't want to get into that with him. I'd have to admit my unexpected jealousy of seeing him with someone else and I didn't want him to have any more power over me than he already did. I should have left the situation alone when I had a chance. I remained silent and looked up at him, an amused look spread across his face.

"Do you want to know what I think?" he asked casually.

"Not in the slightest."

He ignored my sarcastic comment and continued, "I think you like me."

I scoffed, "Oh please."

"Don't deny it," he teased and leaned closer to me. "You can admit you have a thing for me, Isabella."

"I don't have a thing for you, Giovanni."

That was a big fat lie but I didn't want him to know that. I needed to convince him that I didn't care what, or who, he did.

"Keep telling yourself that." he mused and lifted his drink to his lips. He was enjoying this so much. I could see the amusement on his face and as much as it frustrated me that he had all this control, I couldn't help the burning attraction I still had towards him. We ate our way through a couple of the tapas I bought and I was thankful for the food in my system. It was balancing itself out against the alcohol now.

"Why do you care if I have a thing for you?" I asked. "Which for the record, I don't. By the looks of things, you've been pretty occupied. Doesn't seem like you're in short supply when it comes to women."

"And how would you know that?"

Besides the tongue in his ear earlier, the articles, and everyone's mention of it, it really rounded his "player" image out.

"You know what, I actually don't want to talk about this anymore," I snapped. "Why did you want to have a drink with me, Giovanni?"

He was playing games here. All of that to have one drink with me and now he wouldn't stop with the questions. It was starting to frustrate me. I hated being out of control and whenever I was around him, that was exactly what happened. I needed to stop this before it went any further.

"Is it so hard for you to believe that I want to get to know you better?"

I flicked my eyes to his and the interest in them was as clear as day. He was looking at me the same way he looked at me that first night at Mala Mía. My nerves started to flicker inside - he was making me so nervous. There was a part of me that was ready to throw myself at him and another part wanted to sit here and get to know him. He intrigued me. His ability to command my body and now my mind was unexpected but it happened and now I couldn't get rid of the lingering feeling he had left me with.

"For the record, yes it is," I said quickly but carried on with my thought. "But fine. Since you say you want to know me, ask me something. Nothing deep and personal, we are keeping this as platonic as possible."

"Platonic?" he laughed.

I nodded and he leaned over to me to whisper in my ear, "There's nothing platonic about wanting you in my bed again screaming my name."

Fuck. The throbbing between my legs returned and I wanted him again.

Bad idea, Isabella.

"That's not going to happen again." I said, while also trying to convince myself of that statement.

"We'll see." he smirked.

"You really think you can always get what you want hey?"

He shrugged, "If I want something, I go for it."

That could apply to anything in life but right now in this context, he wanted me and he didn't care about hiding it. He was confident and had no filter when it came to the things he said. He could casually throw around something like that without realizing what that meant for me. Giovanni had piqued my interest and I was obviously drawn to him. I wanted him so badly. While I wanted him to take me back to his apartment so I could moan his name to the night, there was something more than that. There was also a part of me that was interested in him - he was intriguing and spontaneous and it excited me in ways I had never experienced before.

No strings attached

That's what he said to me and given the countless mentions of his one-night stand tendencies, it was bad news to have any sort of feelings involved here.

"You're quite arrogant." I commented.

"Confident," he corrected. "There's nothing wrong with confidence."

"There is when you become arrogant about it."

He smirked, "So is it arrogant to say that I know you want to kiss me right now?"

He was insufferable. He didn't hide his arrogance and as much as it was annoying me, it was turning me on at the same time. I didn't know how it was possible but it was happening. I wanted him to touch me. I wanted him to take me. I wanted him to kiss me.

But of course I didn't want him to know that. That was the stubbornness inside of me. There was a lingering amount of alcohol in my system and I reminded myself that two could play this game.

"I don't want to kiss you," I said as casually as I could manage. "But this is now the second or third time you've mentioned something like that so by the sounds of it Giovanni, it would appear that you're the one who wants to kiss me."

I shifted closer to him on the bench, wanting to remove as much distance between us as possible. If he wanted to play this game then I'd be happy to join in. This wasn't a one-sided situation. I leaned closer to him, my lips hovering close to his. He couldn't keep his eyes off them and if I wasn't so stubborn I would have brought my lips up to his.

But I didn't.

Instead, I brought my drink up to my lips and took a slow sip. Never losing eye contact, he watched me repeat that action.

"You're playing games now, Isabella." he breathed.

"I'm sure you're used to being the one doing that." I murmured.

He rested his hand on my bare thigh, waiting for a reaction from me but I remained unchanged. He wasn't going to have me that easily. I reached out and slowly ran my nails through his hair, stopping at the back to tug on it a little bit.

"You're not as innocent as you look are you?"

"Not in the slightest..." I took the last sip of my drink.

He cocked an eyebrow.

"I bet you're thinking about me running my hands up and down your body."

I didn't know where it was coming from but I suddenly wanted to get a reaction out of him. He couldn't be the only one that had power in this situation and I had to know he wanted me as much as I wanted him.

"And what it would be like to hear me moan your name again."

"I love hearing you moan my name, Isabella," he breathed. "You know what I can do to your body."

I was so turned on. We were sitting in a place filled with people all around us but once again, he was all I saw. I just wanted him. He leaned closer to my ear and graced it with the tip of his tongue. I couldn't control the moan that escaped my lips.

"See, I already know you love it when I do that to you because I pay attention," he murmured. "I pay attention to your body and what it wants."

He leaned closer to my ear again but this time I was reminded of the image of the fresh-faced brunette from earlier doing the exact same thing to him. I suddenly pulled away from him. An hour ago he was here with someone else and that just confirmed I needed to continue to stay away from him. He was bad news.

"I promised you one drink." I stood up.

"Where are you going?" he asked, surprised by my sudden change in demeanour.

"Home." I announced.

If I headed home now, I would leave him wanting more and selfishly, that's what I wanted. I wanted him to think of me when I wasn't around. I wanted him to want me. I wanted him to be the one to lose control.

"You're leaving?"

"You asked me to get one drink with you and now I have, so I'm going to head home."

His eyes shone with amusement and sexual frustration. I could tell a part of him was enjoying me taking control of the situation - he wasn't used to it.

"You're trouble aren't you, Isabella?" he mused.

I leaned down and kissed his cheek. I wanted to do so much more but I couldn't ignore the constant red flags. If I didn't leave now, I was without a doubt going to end up in his bed again.

"I'll see you around, Giovanni."

"I hope so."

CHAPTER 10:

It's been just over two weeks since I had last seen Giovanni. I was proud of myself for walking away from him that day at the beach but I couldn't get him out of my mind. We never made any further plans or exchanged numbers and I couldn't stop the constant disappointment I felt. No matter what though, I was adamant to stay away from him.

Every inch of my body screamed out for him but my mind was the one in control for now. I needed to take those interactions for what they were - a time where I needed to let loose. That was over now and I was focused on moving past this "Giovanni phase" of mine. He wasn't looking for anything and after seeing him with someone else, I had to remind myself that I wasn't the only one and I wouldn't be okay with that long-term. It was only meant to be one casual night with him but now that we had been together more than once, I didn't know how I was going to stop wanting him. He thrilled me in a way I had never experienced before.

I hadn't been with anyone since Nate. I had managed to successfully build walls around my heart to avoid anything like that from happening again. As relieved as I was when Nate ended it, I was still hurt by the situation. He was in my life for so long and the fact he managed to turn it upside down in one swift moment was where the real pain came in. The loss of control was something I hated. I was disappointed and angry at myself and I hadn't quite worked through all of that yet and the last thing I needed was to add any complications that would arise from being around Giovanni.

I was clearing up the last of the dishes in the sink when Reyna wandered in.

"So you know I'm treating this weekend as my birthday weekend right?" she asked, strolling over to the counter and bringing herself up onto it.

"You know that you've been reminding me of this for the last two weeks, right?" I teased.

Reyna's birthday wasn't until a couple of weeks from now but she was heading up to Madrid to visit her family for it. She was turning twenty-four and still got as excited each time her birthday rolled around. Birthdays were never a big deal in my household growing up but to the Cazares family, it was always meant to be a celebration.

"I'm just making sure," she smiled at me. "I invited Diego to join us tomorrow night."

Reyna's relationship with Diego had escalated significantly over the last couple of weeks. Typically, Reyna jumped from man to man constantly avoiding her fear of commitment but since Diego came around, that was starting to change. She talked about him all the time and the fact she was letting him in on a personal celebration like her birthday just proved that there was more than just a hook-up going on there. She was very good at keeping her interactions as casual as could be which included avoiding anything that could prompt her to develop feelings for the guy. Having him join her friends and family for something like her birthday was a big step for her. Case in point, Diego was different.

"Have you decided where you want to go?" I asked, hoping that she would opt for a change of scenery and allow me to continue to avoid Mala Mía.

"Giovanni has secured a booth in that fancy private area of theirs and opened up a bar tab for us," she exclaimed.

Damn

"Of course he has," I mumbled. "I suppose it's convenient when you own the place."

"I'm sensing some hostility here," she mused. "Do you not want to go there?"

"No of course I do," I answered quickly. "I want you to have the best birthday."

"But you don't want to see Giovanni?"

I sighed and grabbed the cloth that was hanging up and started to dry my hands.

"It's not that either," I confessed. "Of course I want to see him but I don't trust myself around him."

"Who don't you trust yourself around?" Sergio asked as he casually strolled into the kitchen.

Sergio was at the apartment so often now since he and Katrina had finally decided to take their relationship to the next level. They were going on dates now and Katrina was currently getting ready for their dinner date they had planned for tonight.

"Giovanni," Reyna answered and turned back to me. "Giovanni has never been the relationship type. He gets around Izzy."

"Take it from me, Isabella," Sergio started to explain, "Giovanni is a good friend of mine and I've known him for years. If you're looking for something more, he is not the guy for you."

I already knew that but hearing it again brought on another wave of unexpected disappointment. I didn't want to hear that. I wanted to believe that there was something different between us but that would be naive to think.

I sighed, "I know. I'm not even looking for anything though. I just can't seem to shake him and I know if I don't stay away from him that I am going to end up falling for him and I'm not ready for that."

"Then staying away from him is probably the best move." Sergio shrugged.

"Sergio's right. Giovanni is just one of those guys you take for a casual spin around the block. Nothing more." Reyna said as she reached for a box of cookies we had on the counter and started eating as we spoke. "But you need to not let the fear of getting hurt again, stop you from living your life either."

She was right but I was apprehensive. There was still so much I hadn't dealt with after Nate left. I hadn't dealt with my parents or the friends we used to have. I hadn't dealt with the fact I left what I thought was my dream job. I hadn't dealt with the fact that I was twenty-four years old and my life was the complete opposite of what I had always imagined it would be. I wanted to be married, living in a nice house, working my dream job… but instead I had none of that. For years it was ingrained in me that my life would only be successful if I had all of that and now look at where I was. I wasn't used to not having control over my life. It was unprecedented territory. The last thing I needed was to fall for a textbook "bad boy" that was going to end up breaking my heart.

"You deserve to be happy, Izzy," Reyna said, bringing me out of my own thoughts. "You need to allow yourself to find your happiness again. Whatever that may be."

"What do you think I should do?"

"If you want to go out, then you go out. If you want to stay in then stay in. If you want to kiss every random guy you meet then go for it. Or if you want to just kiss Giovanni then why not?"

"As long as you are fine with it being something casual." Sergio repeated.

I rolled my eyes, "Trust me, Sergio, I get it. Giovanni is a no-go for anything more than a hook-up."

"I'm just watching out for you, Izzy. Giovanni is my friend but so are you."

I smiled at him, "Thank you for that."

"I think you need to just do what you want without the fear you currently have. Heartbreak is going to happen. You just have to decide what's worth getting your heartbroken over." Reyna advised.

She was right. Pain was inevitable but I had only just managed to get most of mine under control. I pushed it to the back of my mind and sealed it in a tightly shut box.

"Look at you with your wise TedTalk again." I mused.

Sergio chuckled.

"Just think about it," she said, placing her hand on my arm and squeezing it. "You deserve to be happy."

I smiled at her.

"You're right," I sighed. "You always are."

CHAPTER 11:

Saturday night rolled around and we were all in the VIP section of Mala Mía for Reyna's birthday celebrations. It was a full house tonight with Reyna inviting her friends from work to join our usual group. Diego also brought a few of his friends around but thankfully Matías wasn't one of them. The last time I saw him was humiliating enough. We had been here for a few hours now and Reyna was having the best time with Diego. She was glowing. Just watching them interact with each other brought on a wave of jealousy I couldn't control. There was a connection there and they were both happy to explore it. I hadn't figured out exactly what I wanted at this point in my life but I would never turn down the opportunity to have what they were starting to have. I mentally scolded myself and pushed all unnecessary thoughts out of my head. I was here for Reyna and that was all that mattered. We had all made our way through several bottles of alcohol but I needed another drink. I reached over the table and grabbed the bottle of tequila from the ice bucket we had. I scanned the area for shot glasses but was unsuccessful.

"Fuck it," I mumbled to myself.

I stood up and walked over to Reyna and Diego. They were leaning against the railing looking down at the dance floor. I tapped her on the shoulder and she turned around.

"There you are!" she exclaimed. "Please can we go dance?"

"We can," I said as I presented the bottle up in front of her. "But first, you and I are taking a shot of this."

"Where are the shot glasses?" Diego asked.

Reyna laughed, "As if we need one."

She reached for the bottle from me and removed the lid. One quick motion and she took a big swig. She pushed the bottle back to me, laughing at how she successfully managed to down that without gagging. I took it back from her and repeated the action, trying my hardest to keep my face composed. I was clearly unsuccessful since both she and Diego burst out laughing.

"You did not enjoy that." Diego mused.

"And what about you?" I shoved the bottle in his face. "You can't let us drink alone."

He smirked and took a sip. The alcohol was still burning my chest and I could feel it slowly traveling to every inch of my body. I could physically feel the tension I was holding started to melt away. I was reaching for the bottle again when I suddenly noticed Giovanni casually stroll into our section. I held my breath. That man literally takes my breath away. I had forgotten how damn attractive he was. He was wearing that leather jacket I loved so much and I rolled my eyes at his typical chosen bad boy attire. I decided to take Sergio's advice and remove myself from the situation. He was so sexy though and it took everything I had to avoid him. I wanted Giovanni badly but I also knew myself. I grabbed the bottle from Diego and turned to go put it back in the ice bucket, happy that it was in the opposite direction to where Giovanni was headed. I snuck one more sip, knowing I was going to need it. I placed it down and felt a tap on my shoulder. I turned and was surprised to see Alessandro, one of Diego's friends that I met earlier. There was no denying that he was attractive as well but in a very different way to Giovanni. His long dark hair was pulled into a bun and even in the dark lighting of the club, I could notice his pretty grey-blue eyes.

"Are you not going to share?" he mused, eyeing the bottle I just put down.

"Help yourself," I gestured to the bucket. "It's a free for all around here."

"I can tell." he reached past me to grab the bottle. His movement was deliberate in ensuring he was in close proximity to me. He removed the lid and downed some, never taking his eyes off me.

"Good?" I smirked.

"We can all agree that it tastes pretty shit," he quipped. "But we don't drink it for the taste."

"Ain't that the truth." I laughed.

"You've got a great laugh."

I blushed, "Are you flirting with me, Alessandro?"

My inebriated state came out to play now and there was no way I could control what was coming out of my mouth.

He cocked an eyebrow at me and smiled, "Would that be a bad thing?"

"Not at all."

There was tension between us but not even close to what I experienced with Giovanni. I shouldn't be comparing but I couldn't help it. The thought of him made me quickly scan the area. He must have left because I couldn't see him anywhere. Maybe that was a good thing. Here was a cute guy flirting with me and I was looking for someone else. I needed to stop and focus on Alessandro. Even if it was just for tonight.

"Can I buy you a drink?" he shouted over the blaring music. "I think we could both do with something better than tequila."

I nodded and grabbed his hand, "That would be great."

I led him through the crowd and down the stairs. We had to slip through the main dance floor to get to the bar. As we made our way through the crowds of people, Giovanni caught my eye. He was on the other side of the bar now standing with Alonzo and Sergio. I tried to avert my eyes but he was staring at me. The way he was looking at me brought my body to life. There was something more to it. The desire was there in his eyes but so was the jealousy. *Was it jealousy?* Was he jealous of Alessandro right now? We made it to the bar and I could still feel his eyes on me but I forced myself to ignore it.

If he wanted me, he would come and get me.

"What can I get you?" Alessandro asked, leaning in closer to me so I could hear him.

"Surprise me."

His hand slid down to the small of my back and he rested it there. It made my body tingle but only because thoughts of Giovanni running his hands down my body decided to pop up. *What the fuck was happening to me?* Every thought was of him and our time together. He had me addicted and I didn't know how much longer I was going to last without another dose. I shook the thought away as Alessandro passed me my drink.

"Thank you." I brought the drink to my lips. I had no idea what I was drinking but it was great.

"This is pretty good." I said. Which was going to be a problem honestly, because it was way too easy to drink.

Alessandro leaned against the bar, "So, have you always lived in Barcelona?"

I shook my head, "No, I'm originally from London."

"Ah, I thought I sensed a bit of an accent," he commented.

"I moved here about five or six months ago." I couldn't even remember anymore. These past few months have felt like a blur and it gave me a warped perception of time.

"Change of scenery?" he asked.

"I guess you could say that."

I couldn't help but flick my eyes over to where Giovanni stood. Some girl I had never met had joined him and they were in close proximity to one another. Too close for my liking. I had to physically hold myself back from allowing my jealousy to consume me, yet again.

Was he trying to make me jealous now? He couldn't do that. I had already experienced an annoying amount of jealousy the last time I saw him. Witnessing the way he was with that brunette at the beach was one of the many red flags that wouldn't stop waving excessively in my head and yet here I was unable to get him out of my mind. Just knowing he was in the same vicinity as I brought my desire to life. Why did he have this effect on me?

"So you moved out here to Barcelona months ago," Alessandro recaps. "Why'd you leave?"

Sober me knew I didn't want to have this conversation right now but unfortunately, she wasn't here at the moment.

"I got dumped." I announced, laughing at the ridiculousness of that statement. It was the facts. Nate dumped me but I was more upset at the fact he turned my life upside down rather than him actually leaving me. I wasn't even in love with him anymore, so shouldn't I have been happy that we broke up? Did I want to end up marrying someone I wasn't in love with? Did I want to end up with someone that I had no passion with? No - I wanted it all. I wanted the hearts and flowers and sex and passion. I wanted to have my life under control again. I wanted to live the life I had always dreamed.

But what was that now? What did I want? I pushed all those thoughts out of my mind. Now was not the time to let all that consume me.

"I'm sorry to hear that." Alessandro said sincerely.

There was a kindness to him that I found endearing. I smiled at him, "That's okay. It happens to all of us."

"I'll drink to that," Alessandro smirked, sipping his drink. "My ex-girlfriend left me for someone else."

"What a bitch."

Alessandro laughed and shrugged it off, "What can you do hey? Like you said, it happens to all of us."

"Well, it doesn't need to," I said, smiling at him. "So how do you know Diego?" I wanted to avoid any further talk about either of our exes. I didn't know him and the last thing I wanted to do was explain anything more about Nate and I certainly didn't expect him to do the same with his cheating ex. He jumped right into explaining how they had known each other since middle school and they'd been inseparable ever since.

"You wouldn't know it, but Diego became a naughty shit all throughout high school," he chuckled. "And I always went along with his crazy plans."

"Sounds just like Reyna."

"Yeah it would seem that those two really have something," he commented. "I think Reyna is great for him."

"I'm glad you feel that way. She's the best and I just want her to be happy."

"I've never seen Diego like this with anyone." he mentioned.

"That's the same with Reyna. She always had a tendency to run away from any real commitment."

"It's starting to sound scary at how many similarities those two have in common." he joked. I laughed and placed my empty glass on the bar.

"I'm guessing you enjoyed that." Alessandro laughed, eyeing my empty glass.

I shrugged, "That was actually really, really good. Unlike that tequila we had."

He chuckled, "You want me to order another one?" He was sweet. He was really trying with me but in the back of my mind, I was just too distracted to give him the attention he deserved. Over and above everything going on in my mind, I was insanely jealous of the blonde with Giovanni right now. I couldn't even bring myself to look over at him again. I was already on the edge and something as simple as seeing that could easily push me over.

"I'll get us another round," I said to him. "Can you go get Reyna and Diego? We should get a drink together."

He nodded and turned to head back upstairs to the VIP section. I leaned against the bar, trying really hard to stop the room from spinning right now. I was more intoxicated than I realized. I didn't seem to care though as I ordered another round of drinks from the handsome bartender behind the bar. I ran my fingers through my hair and leaned my head against my hand.

"Who's the guy?" I heard him say from behind me. "Another date of yours?"

I turned to the side and Giovanni took his place next to me. I rolled my eyes at his reference to the previous interaction we had around Matías being my date. I had done plenty of overthinking since the last time I saw him at the beach and I was not in the mood to get into anything with him right now. But that didn't stop my body from awakening at his mere presence and I scolded myself for my lack of self-control. I had managed to pull myself away from him a few weeks ago but my body felt so deprived, I wasn't sure how much longer I was going to be able to keep this up.

"Not that it's any of your business but he's not my date." I slurred. I had to force myself to look away from him. I couldn't help that he was so damn attractive but my drunken self couldn't handle looking at him for too long without my mind wandering off again.

"And so what if he was my date?" I shouted over the music, the words flowing out of me, "There's nothing going on between you and I anymore."

"Isn't there?"

"Is there?" I turned back to him. "As I recall you said you weren't looking for anything." I blamed the alcohol again for my inability to keep my mouth shut right now. He moved closer to me and leaned on the bar. He was calm and collected and I was using every ounce of my self-control to keep it together.

"You said it first." he reminded me.

Touché.

I could see the amusement in his eyes again. He was enjoying this back and forth banter. I wanted to see if I could make him jealous. I already knew that my jealousy was there and I couldn't control it but what about him? Was he jealous I was with someone else? Did it bother him if I was? What if I left with Alessandro? Would he come after me?

"Well I've decided that I need to stay away from you so might as well have something casual with him." I shrugged.

The bartender placed our next round of drinks in front of me. I couldn't carry all four so I decided to get a head start and reached for mine. I brought it to my lips and sipped on it. My body warmed as the alcohol burned through it, creating the illusion of a sense of calm in this rowdy environment.

Giovanni laughed and leaned closer to my ear, "He can't drive your body crazy like I can."

Oh my. I squeezed my thighs together to try to contain the excitement that just came to life. Fuck. He was so sexy. His words, his looks, his body - he was just too much for me and after making a comment like that, I had no idea how I was going to keep my distance. I downed more of my drink.

"There's that arrogance again." I commented.

"Confidence." He corrected me, just like he did last time.

He was so close to me now. I turned my body to face his and looked up at him. He was ready for me just like I was ready for him. I wanted nothing more than to reach out and kiss him. I needed to feel his lips on mine again. I needed his hands on my body - the sexual tension consumed me.

"This is a bad idea, I need to stay away from you." I breathed.

"Why would you want to stay away from me?"

"I can't control myself around you, Giovanni." I let out a breath and reminded myself not to give into him.

"Don't…," he lifted his hand to my chin and ran a finger across my cheek.

That single word was hypnotic. Every inch of my body called for him. He was so close that I could smell his cologne. I groaned - it was intoxicating. I regretted the amount of alcohol I had up till now because I was slipping further from my sane thoughts and closer to my deepest desires.

"I know you love it when I touch you." he ran his other hand up my thigh, lifting my dress just enough to get his message across.

I bit my lip trying to control my arousal. Here we were again in a crowd full of people but all I saw was him and what I wanted him to do to me right here, right now. I was staring into his eyes and was just about to hand myself over to him when Alessandro returned with Reyna and Diego.

"I've been looking for you." Reyna said.

Giovanni and I broke out of the trace we were in. He stepped away from me and we turned to the group. I didn't want any of them to be here right now. I just wanted him.

"Here I am." I smiled, reminding myself I was here for her.

Alessandro came to stand on the other side of me. He noticed Giovanni and extended his hand, "*Hola,* I'm Alessandro. Nice to meet you."

Giovanni nodded and returned the handshake, "Likewise."

Liar.

I flicked my eyes over to him and I knew he was still reeling from the unfulfilled tension just like I was. I turned to grab the drinks I ordered and handed them out.

"Okay this is my last one," Reyna took the glass from me. "I actually came to let you know that Diego and I are going to get out of here. He says he has a surprise for me."

I raised an eyebrow at her and she winked.

"I just wanted to find out how you're going to get home," she continued. "Cause I'm probably going to stay with him and Kat just left with Sergio."

"She's actually going to stay with me." Giovanni announced, interrupting our conversation.

I flicked my eyes over to him, surprised by his interjection. How could I possibly convince myself not to leave with him when every inch of my body was ready for him to take me right now?

"Oh?" Alessandro didn't hide his surprise, "I didn't realize you had a boyfriend."

"He's not my-" I started to say but Giovanni interjected again, "She's a forgetful one when she drinks." He placed his arm around my waist.

This was awkward. Reyna jerked her head back, eyeing me at this new piece of information that just came to light. Of course, she knew we weren't dating but she wasn't dumb, this was a classic clash of the egos. She leaned into Diego and whispered something that made him smile. I wanted to tell Giovanni off but his hand on my body was making it difficult to do so.

"Bad thing to be forgetting." Alessandro murmured softly, probably hoping I wouldn't hear although I did. I felt bad for him.

"Anyway!" Reyna shouted, saving me from his incredibly awkward situation I was in, "I'm leaving now. You be safe. I'll text you in the morning,"

We exchanged goodbyes with everyone and then they were off. Alessandro left with them without so much of a goodbye. I couldn't blame him. He was trying really hard and I was blatantly flirting with him too. I turned to face Giovanni. I contemplated confronting him about why he didn't correct Alessandro, but I was too tempted by the possibility of being alone with him right now that I let it slip from my mind.

"So," he started. "Your place or mine?"

CHAPTER 12:

There was no debate when it came to whose place we were heading to. I loved my apartment but I wouldn't be able to control myself until we got there. It was quite convenient to have his apartment just a few floors up. We made it to his apartment and I strolled into the lounge area. His curtains were still open and the full moon shone down on us. I smiled at the peaceful sight. The rollercoaster of feelings that occurred in my own mind had subsided at the sight of the calming nature of the night sky. I could sit and stare at it for hours.

"Can I get you something to drink?"

I turned to him as he headed to the counter in his kitchen. He slipped his jacket off and placed it down. He was wearing a well-fitted black t-shirt that exposed the markings on his skin. I wanted to spend some time analyzing each one but now was not the time.

"I've had so much to drink already so why stop now?" I dropped onto the couch.

"That's the spirit." he mused.

Giovanni attended to the drinks and I made myself at home on his big black leather couch that was surprisingly more comfortable than I thought it would be. He had a big flat-screen TV on the wall in front of it and I noticed the surround sound setup. My eyes wandered over to the guitar standing in the corner.

"Do you play?" I asked.

He strolled in and handed me my drink.

"Yeah, a little bit." he replied, taking his place next to me.

"Play me something."

He shook his head and sipped his drink, "Not right now."

I pouted, "Why not?"

"Don't pout," he laughed. "I'll play for you later, but I have other things on my mind right now." I tugged at my bottom lip knowing we were both thinking the same thing. There was one thing that neither of us would be able to hide and that was our desire for one another. It was magnetic. It was an all-consuming passion that, at times, took my breath away. Okay, pretty much all the time.

I had never considered passion to be a major factor in a relationship but now that I had gotten a taste of it, I didn't know how I could have another relationship without it. The overpowering feeling of needing someone so badly that you just had to have them no matter what was new to me. It was hypnotic and at times a little frightening. I continued sipping on my drink to ensure that I didn't attack him. I wanted to see who would make the first move here. As if right on schedule, Giovanni reached out and placed his hand on my thigh. It was a simple gesture but it was all I needed. He continued to sip his drink, pretending that he didn't know what a simple touch like that could do to me. He had the power over me and he knew it. He knew any touch would drive my body crazy and he thrived off that. As much as I wanted to throw myself at him, I also wanted him to work for it more.

"How's your drink?" he asked.

"I really don't think you care about my drink right now." I took a big sip and placed it down on the table in front of us. I turned to face him, forcing him to move his hand off my leg.

"Why didn't you correct Alessandro when he referred to you as my boyfriend?"

"Why didn't you correct him?" He challenged me in return.

I rolled my eyes, "No, no, no. Don't answer my question with a question."

He smirked and downed the rest of his drink, "Does it matter?"

"Of course it matters," I replied. "I didn't want to lie to him."

"So you want him to know that you're single?"

"What would be the harm in that? It's the truth." He flicked his eyes to meet mine and I could see the jealousy in them. I didn't expect to see it but it was as clear as day.

"You don't want him, Isabella."

I raised an eyebrow, "And who says I don't?" He rolled his eyes at me.

"I'm serious. He was a really attractive guy - I'd be happy to go a few rounds with him."

He let out an exasperated sigh, "Are you trying to drive me crazy?"

Yes, yes I am!

The alcohol was still very much in the driver's seat and I couldn't really control the words coming out of my mouth. I wanted to know that he cared. I couldn't be the only one feeling what I was feeling. Call it what you want but there was something going on between us that I had never felt before.

"Why would I be driving you crazy?" I probed. "Alessandro and I were clearly flirting so I don't blame him for being confused when you said that."

Giovanni ran his hand up my thigh. We locked eyes as he reached for me, lifting me on top of him. My legs straddled his waist.

"Don't tell me that you were flirting with him," he murmured. "You were just trying to make me jealous."

"Is it working?" Sober me would never push and pry like this but she was nowhere in sight. I needed to know that I could drive him as crazy as he was driving me. I needed to know that I had the same effect on him. It was daunting to feel this kind of loss of control around someone. He didn't even have to try and he already had me. He never demanded control but he had it. My body was ready to surrender itself to him with a single touch.

He pulled me closer to him. He ran his hands up and down my body, knowing exactly what that did to me. I rocked my body against his, feeling him come alive beneath me.

"You only want me, Isabella." he breathed. "Don't fool yourself into thinking that anyone else could make you feel this way."

He pulled me closer to him. He was so close now, I could feel his breath on me. I wanted to kiss him. I was dying to kiss him. His words were both a huge turn-on and completely terrifying. I was trapped. He had me and I wasn't going anywhere. No matter how hard I tried, I knew that I would never be able to shake him. I ran my fingers through his hair and tugged at it, just a little. He ran his hands up my thighs, pushing my dress up with it. I needed to release the tension building between my thighs.

"Can anyone else do this to you?" he asked, running his hand up and down the inside of my thighs, brushing over me, again.

I groaned.

"Can anyone else make you feel this way?" he murmured, sliding his finger underneath my underwear. "You're so ready for me baby."

I bit my lip.

"Why do you have to make me jealous?" he whispered in my ear, leaving kisses along my jawline.

"I don't know." I admitted.

"You drive me crazy when you do that, Isabella."

He slipped one finger inside of me and I moaned. This was what I had been craving. This was what I wanted and what I needed. I needed to feel him again. I needed him to drive my body crazy. I was so eager for him. I rocked against him, moving with the rhythm he had going on.

"Say my name." He whispered in my ear.

I obliged. I couldn't even help it. He was pushing me to my limit already. I needed to feel him, all of him. I brought my lips down to his. It was passionate and with more urgency than I intended. He kissed me back. He removed his fingers from me, making me groan since the pressure was still there.

"Why did you stop?"

"Does it drive you crazy?" he answered between our kisses.

"Does what drive me crazy?"

"When I do that to you, but then I stop?" He brought his fingers back inside me. I threw my head back and moaned. It was uncontrollable. He was driving my body crazy. I rocked against him and ran my fingers through his hair, tugging on it more.

"Don't stop, Giovanni." I breathed.

But he did. He removed his fingers again.

"Fuuuuuck," I shouted. "What are you doing to me?"

"This is how you make me feel. You drive me crazy," he said. "So I needed to return the favour."

This was fucking messy but something about it was a major turn-on. I got to him. I was driving him crazy with jealousy which gave me the power I didn't think I had. I didn't think he wanted me as much as I wanted him. Turned out we were both feeling this magnetic pull towards each other.

"I only want you." I groaned in his ear.

He brought his lips down on me, leaving kisses along my neck. In one swift movement, he lifted me up and turned me around, laying me down against the couch. He ran his hands down my body and made it down between my thighs. He pushed my dress up, exposing my underwear and quickly removed them. He spread my legs and boy, was I was ready for him. He slowly teased me by running a finger over me. My body had been ready for him for weeks so his simple touch was enough to make me come undone. He started kissing me along my thigh. He left kisses up from my knee and made it so close to my center but then moved away. He was driving my body insane right now and I was losing control.

"Giovanni, please... " I pleaded.

"Please what?" he murmured. "What do you want Isabella? Tell me."

He knew exactly what I wanted but he was playing this little game to get back at me for making him jealous. As much as it was driving me crazy, my arousal was through the roof.

"I want you, Giovanni." I breathed out heavily.

He was kissing my thigh again. Letting his tongue trace down my leg. The image of him between my legs was so damn sexy. He flicked his eyes up to mine. Never breaking eye contact, he stood up and removed his shirt. I reached out to touch his body, feeling every muscle. His pants were next along with his underwear till he stood ready for me. I pulled my dress over my head and tossed it across the room, my bra joining it. I lay my arms above my head on the couch as he spread my legs even more. He reached for a condom from his jeans pocket, rolled it over himself and positioned himself in front of me.

"You're mine, Isabella." He breathed and with one swift motion he entered me. It was euphoric. The tension that I had been building up for the past two weeks was finally getting what it wanted. Hearing those words from his mouth was the cherry on top. He claimed me. I was his and he was mine. It didn't matter what happened outside of this very moment. This was everything to me. We both moved with urgency, soaking in every moment. It had been too long since we'd last been together and that was evident in the urgency of our movements. I dug my nails into his arms. This was exactly what I wanted. This was what I needed.

"Say you're mine." Giovanni breathed.

"I'm yours, Giovanni." And that was the honest truth. I was his. He had consumed my body and invaded my thoughts. I tried to get rid of him. I tried to push him out of my mind but I was done with that. I couldn't. I was so overcome by passion and pleasure that I wanted to be in control of it. I pushed him off me and instructed him to sit. I pushed him against the back of his couch so he was in a seated position. My legs were on either side of his body and I placed my hands on his shoulders for balance. I brought myself over him, then up and down on him again. I bit my lip to quiet my cry of pleasure.

"Fuck, Isabella." He exhaled.

Knowing what I was doing to him only made me want to do more. I continued the motion and found my rhythm. Small breaths escaped his lips and I couldn't help but moan his name. The tension was becoming unbearable. I picked up speed and pushed down on him. The pressure between my legs was overwhelming and I knew I was close. I moved my body, pushing for the release to come. He was close too. I could feel it. I kept going. Pushing against him as hard and as fast as I could. His hand found its way into my hair and he pulled on it. It was so sexy. I threw my head back and cried out in pleasure as we both reached our climax. I wrapped my arms around him and tried to control my breathing. He was doing the same. We didn't move. We sat there for a long moment while he was still inside of me, but neither of us wanted to ruin this moment. We soaked it in as much as we could. I pulled away from him enough to look down at him. He smiled at me. The smile reached his eyes and for the first time, I noticed a softer look to them. Usually, they are filled with desire and quite often, amusement but now there was something different. I couldn't quite put my finger on it but it made me feel warm inside.

Oh no. *What was that?* Was I feeling something more towards him? I ignored that thought and pushed it right to the back of my mind with all the other things I had yet to address. I focused on right now. I focused on him.

"You drive me crazy." He repeated and started kissing my neck gently.

"Yeah well, you do the same to me."

He smiled and kissed my lips. It made me smile. I pushed myself off of him, immediately regretting the emptiness my body felt. I leaned against the armrest of the couch, looking up at him. He was a beautiful man. My eyes wandered across his body and down his arm with all his tattoos.

"How many tattoos do you have?" I asked.

"Way too many to count."

"I never liked tattoos." I admitted.

"Oh yeah?" He lifted an eyebrow.

"Yeah, but I love them now."

He smirked, "So you should get one then."

"Oh no," I said quickly. "I love them on you. They suit you."

"Well thank you." He got off the couch and reached for his underwear and jeans. He slipped them both back on and strolled into the kitchen, disposing of the condom in the trash can. I just laid there and watched him. I watched how he moved and soaked in his body. He must have a really great gym routine because his body was in great shape. He returned with two glasses of water. The alcohol still lingered in my body but the pleasure I felt took over it all. He handed me a glass and I drank it in one go, not realizing how thirsty I was until that moment. I was still lying naked on his couch but I had no intention of getting up. I was comfortable. The most comfortable I had ever been around a man. He made me feel like a woman. I didn't feel the need to shy away from him or get dressed. I could lie here on the couch with him and be perfectly comfortable. He strolled over to the window and opened it a bit for some fresh air. There was a door leading to a small balcony. It must be peaceful to have this view every day. I loved everything about this city but especially the buildings. They were so old and yet so well kept. There was so much history to it that needed to be preserved.

He turned back to me and leaned against the wall, "What are you thinking about?"

So many thoughts were running through my mind and I didn't know where to start. I opted for a simple answer for now.

"How long have you played for?" I eyed the guitar.

"On and off for about twenty years or so. First started when I was eight." He replied.

"That's a really long time. You must be pretty good at it then."

"I'm not bad," he admitted. "I do it more as a hobby than anything else. It calms me."

"I'd love to hear you play." He smiled at me and this time he reached for the guitar. I grabbed the soft blanket at the end of his couch and covered myself with it while I made myself more comfortable. He brought it with him and sat on the couch opposite where I was. The moonlight was shining down on him and he was picture perfect right now.

"Now, I'm a little rusty," he said. "So you have to go easy on me."

"I'll try my hardest not to judge you." I joked.

He smiled, took a deep breath in and started to play. I was surprised by how skillful he was with the guitar - he downplayed how well he could play. It was beautiful. He was playing a Spanish guitar melody that was so peaceful. The fingers on his left hand slid up and down the neck of the guitar with ease while the other fingers picked at the strings on the bridge, moving from string to string with a sense of purpose. I couldn't keep my eyes off him as I watched him in his element. He nipped at his bottom lip and his tongue slid swiftly over it as he deepened his concentration. He leaned forward as he played and stray strands of his hair fell forward. The curves of his muscles pulled with each stroke of the guitar strings. I was completely taken by him. I closed my eyes and moved with the music. I was in the perfect place. I was high on the passion from what we just did and now to hear him play something like this, I was feeling more vulnerable. I was trying to avoid it but there it was. A brief flash of feelings inside of me. A fondness I had towards Giovanni. It terrified me - I didn't want to admit it to myself but there were feelings now. Something more than just a physical attraction. I slowly opened my eyes and watched as he came to the end of his song. His eyes were closed as he finished the last few soft notes. I was in awe of him. He looked up at me.

"So?" he hesitated, awaiting my reaction.

I shook my head and smiled. I got up from the couch I was on, bringing the blanket with me, and walked over to him. He placed the guitar next to him and welcomed me onto his lap. I wrapped my arms around his neck.

"That was absolutely beautiful." I ran my fingers through his hair and then softly ran the back of my hand across his cheek. It was more intimate than I intended it to be and I could see in his eyes that he didn't expect that. I jerked my hand away quickly, hoping that he wouldn't dwell on it but instead he grabbed my hand again and placed it back where it was.

"Don't," he murmured. "I like that."

I smiled at him. My heart grew three sizes with that simple interaction.

"You play so beautifully," I continued, "Where did you learn to play?"

"Back in the day my dad used to teach me," he explained. "Music had always been in my family so he decided I should learn too."

"Are you and your dad close?"

I wanted to know more about him. Up until now we hardly had any conversations where we got to know each other better and that was what I wanted. I wanted more of him, anyway I could get it.

He shrugged, "No, we stopped being close a long time ago."

I could see a brief flash of anger in his eyes. This piqued my curiosity but I also didn't want to pry so I shared a bit about my dad and me.

"My dad and I aren't close anymore either," I admitted. "I'm actually not close with anyone in my family."

"Why not?"

"We don't have anything in common. I can't relate to them - my mom and sister the most. I know that might be a strange thing to say about one's family but I have always felt like I was adopted."

He chuckled, "I know exactly what you mean. My family used to be close and then the older I got, the more I noticed the bullshit."

"Are you close with your brother?"

I remembered him mentioning that Reyna used to sleep with his brother so I already knew he wasn't an only child.

"So-so. We're business partners and both started Mala Mía so we are close in some ways."

"I never see him at the club."

"You probably won't. He's got a wife now who's pregnant so he's not interested in the clubbing scene. I hold down the fort on site."

Mala Mía was the fastest-growing club in the city. Their success escalated each weekend with each event landing them on every "clubs to visit in Barcelona" list out there. It was a very successful club so they were definitely doing something right.

"And you?" he asked, "Any siblings?"

"An older sister. Her name is Camila and she lives back in London with my parents." I slowly ran my fingers across his chest.

"And you're not close?"

I shook my head, "Not at all. She's the golden child. Followed every rule set out by our parents so someone had to be the disappointment of the family."

"Hey," He ran his thumb across my cheek, "You're not a disappointment."

"You don't know enough about me to say that Giovanni." I averted my eyes away from him.

He slowly turned my face to look at him, "There's no way someone like you could be a disappointment. Beautiful. Smart. Confident."

I blushed.

"If it makes you feel any better, I know I'm not my parent's favourite child either," he murmured. "Maybe we should start a club."

I laughed and leaned against his chest. The alcohol was starting to leave my system and I couldn't help but yawn now.

"Someone's tired." he quipped.

"It's been a long day."

He ran his finger across my collarbone and up my neck. We had been with each other enough times now for him to know that I loved it when he did that. We were starting to become more to each other. We could try and deny it but there was something more starting to develop here and I don't think either of us expected it. *Giovanni is not the relationship type.* That phrase kept replaying in my head over and over again but here we were. Surely this is more than just a casual relationship? I'm not saying he has to be my boyfriend. Hell, I don't even think I am ready for that right now but there is no way that this is a touch-and-go situation. He feels something for me too. *He has to. Right?*

"Play for me again?" I murmured. I slipped off him to give him enough space to reach for the guitar again. He started to play again and I smiled, drifting off into a deep peaceful sleep.

CHAPTER 13:

I spent the next few days over-thinking. I'd gotten pretty good at it - in fact, I couldn't control it anymore. I kept replaying the time I spent with Giovanni over and over again. There was something more to it, more than just a physical attraction. It had to be. There was no way we could have that much passion and chemistry and it not develop into something more. Or was this a thing that I just didn't know about? I had never been the kind of woman to have once-off physical interactions with men, but here I was stuck in that exact situation. I'm not the same woman I used to be and I wasn't sure yet if that was a good thing or not. All I knew was that the way Giovanni was making me feel was new and exciting but also absolutely terrifying.

I didn't want to be feeling anything for anyone. When we were together, I was consumed by him and then when I left, I started to doubt what was happening. When it's just him and I, I knew he was feeling it too but then we didn't see each other, and I didn't hear from him for days or weeks, it turned my overthinking into overdrive. Reyna kept reminding me that she has never known him to have a girlfriend. He had never committed to one woman and I hated hearing that. A huge part of me got disappointed every time she mentioned it but then I think back to how we are together and I go crazy thinking this is possibly one-sided? *Surely not.* I couldn't be the only one stuck dealing with these unwanted feelings. The way he looked at me and touched me… you couldn't tell me he did that to others?

But then when I didn't hear from him, I started to feel like a statistic. I was also way too stubborn to be the one to reach out first. It was a terrible defense mechanism that I just couldn't break through. If this was how it was going to be then I should be able to flirt with whoever I want without him interrupting.

But I didn't want to be flirting with anyone else. I only wanted him.

This back and forth continued in my mind as Reyna and I walked into one of the bars on our road. It was a Sunday evening and *Paradiso* was the only place open that had energy to it. It was filled with people but nothing compared to Mala Mía. We were relaxing at home before Diego called and convinced us to join him for drinks. I wasn't working tomorrow and I didn't feel like continuing to wallow in my thoughts so I agreed to join. There was a crisp cold wind lingering in the air - Autumn was here but each day it was starting to feel more like winter already.

I scanned the area. I had never been here before but I was already enjoying the atmosphere. It had a dance-floor right in front of the bar and the rest of the place was scattered with high tables and bar stools. It wasn't meant to be a club but had the same vibe as one. We probably would've gone to Mala Mía but it was only open from Thursday to Saturday and I was actually glad for the change of scenery. It was already making me feel more at ease as it helped distract me from the on-going thoughts in my head. The DJ was playing my favourite kind of music - *reggaeton*. The type of music you couldn't help but move to. This was the Barcelona that I fell in love with.

We strolled through the crowd and found Diego at one of the high tables. His face lit up as soon as he saw Reyna. It made me smile. He was falling for her and as much as she ran away from her feelings, she was doing the same thing. I found Diego to be quite cute with his dirty blonde hair and light brown eyes that were a great combination. He was more on the skinnier side but he wasn't obsessed with his image like a lot of the other guys she has been with. He was kind-hearted and I was rooting for the two of them.

"Hey, Izzy." Diego pulled me in for a quick hug.

"Thank you for letting me tag along," I said, hopping onto the barstool. "Please don't tell me I'm going to be a third wheel though."

He laughed, "Sergio and Katrina are coming too."

"So I'm a fifth wheel?"

"Sergio mentioned he invited a few of his boys."

"Maybe you'll get to see Giovanni?" Reyna quipped.

A part of me was hoping for that but the other part was honestly dreading it.

"What's going on between you two?" Diego asked casually.

"I don't know," I admitted. "Nothing really."

I wish I knew but I just didn't have the answers. I didn't know how to explain the situation to people.

"Well, Alessandro might be pleased to hear that." Diego joked.

"I felt so bad for him last week. I don't know why Giovanni said he was my boyfriend."

"He clearly wants people to think you're taken."

"Well I'm not, so I should be able to do what I want." I mumbled.

I didn't know why this conversation was annoying me so much. Who was Giovanni to dictate who I could have a relationship with? I could've definitely tried with Alessandro - he was attractive and interested in me. But no, Giovanni had to interrupt and take control of the situation.

"I thought you wanted Giovanni?" Reyna asked.

"The only thing I want right now is a drink." I deflected and gestured for the nearest waiter. Diego and Reyna didn't push the conversation any further and I was thankful for that. I didn't know how to answer their questions and that was where most of my frustration stemmed from. I knew I wanted him - hell, all day every day, but I didn't know if I wanted *wanted* him. Or maybe I was trying to convince myself I didn't.

A pretty waitress came by and we ordered a round of cocktails to start off. A year ago, if someone had told me that I would be spending most of my weekends out in Barcelona drinking, I never would have believed it. *Who would have thought?*

***

A few hours had passed and Katrina, Sergio, Alonzo and Jose joined us. We were on our third round of drinks and Reyna and I were definitely already intoxicated. This was evident by our uncontrollable laughter. We didn't even know why we were laughing, but we were. Diego came back to the table with a bottle of tequila in his hands.

Reyna and I groaned in perfect unity which only made us laugh even more. Alcohol really created the illusion that everything was fine. When you're intoxicated, you don't have to care about things that you otherwise would. After a round of shots, the music was blaring *Con Calma by Daddy Yankee* louder than ever.

"My song!" Reyna shrieked and reached for my arm, pulling me to the dance floor.

I reached for Katrina and made her join us too. The three of us were in the middle of the dance floor singing the words at the top of our lungs. Granted I only knew the one line but I didn't care, I was enjoying this way too much. I put my hands in the air and swung my hips from side to side. I accidentally swung my arms too much to the side and ended up knocking someone in the head. He reached for his head as I turned to face him.

"Oh shit! I am so sorry!" I shouted and reached for his head, rubbing it better.

I was pretty sure he didn't need that but I felt so bad.

"It's okay," he chuckled. "You've got to be careful with those killer dance moves you've got there."

I giggled. He was super cute. Dark brown hair and light brown eyes but his soft features made him so sweet looking. Don't get me wrong, he didn't look like a child with his beard that was starting to grow out but there was nothing "bad boy" about him. I was starting to realize that most men in Barcelona were a sight to behold in their own way.

"Please forgive me. Sometimes the music just takes over." I shouted.

He nodded and smiled, "I'm Lorenzo."

"Isabella," I said, extending my hand.

"Oh no, I'm a hugger." He opened his arms. I was thrown off but in a good way. He pulled me in and I couldn't help but breathe him in. *Fuck, he smelled so good.* I was aware of my tolerance level and I had already passed the filter checkpoint.

"You smell so good." I blurted out.

"Thank you, Isabella," he laughed. "Can I buy you a drink?"

I nodded. I caught Reyna's attention and gestured to Lorenzo and the bar. She smirked at me and continued dancing. We made it to the bar and I found one of the few barstools still open. I slid myself onto one, giving my feet a break from all the dancing.

"Are you here alone?" I asked, leaning my elbow on the bar. Lorenzo ordered us two drinks and turned back to me.

"I'm not," he explained. "I'm actually here for my sister's birthday." He pointed out a petite brunette in the crowd and she was just as attractive as he was.

"How old is she turning?"

"Twenty-three,"

"Are you older or younger?"

"Older. I'm twenty-six. What about you?"

"Twenty-four."

The bartender handed us our drinks. I sipped on it and it was strong, I couldn't help but make a funny face which immediately made Lorenzo burst out laughing.

"What is this?" I asked, trying to regain composure of my face.

"Long Island Iced Tea." he sipped on his with such ease.

"Obviously your drink of choice since you're sipping on it with no problem."

He chuckled, "Yeah I've clearly had more practice than you."

The more I looked at him, the more attractive he became. That was another one of the many perks to living in Spain - all the men were attractive. I didn't know if it was something in the water but they all had it.

"So, is this the part where we exchange awkward small talk?" I mused.

"God I hope not, I hate that."

"Me too!" I exclaimed. "We can just jump right into the deep stuff then."

"Let's not get too deep," he chuckled. "I'm only on my first drink."

"I am way ahead of you then," I said laughing. "Drink number four right here. Excluding a shot of tequila."

"Well, you seem to be handling your alcohol really well. Most people would be falling over."

"I have a surprisingly high tolerance for someone who never used to drink."

"Never used to drink huh?" he repeated. "So what changed?"

"I didn't feel like being stuck up anymore." I admitted. A part of me always knew I had that tendency. It wasn't intentional but everything in my life before moving to Barcelona molded me that way. I was such a bore and way more judgemental than I wanted to be. Now... I didn't care.

"I like your honesty." he smiled.

Someone pushed in next to Lorenzo to get the bartender's attention which forced him to scoot closer to me. Close enough that I could smell that cologne of his. A great smelling cologne on an attractive man was my weakness. Just another one, of the many reasons, I found myself attracted to Giovanni.

Why did he always have to invade my thoughts?

"Here's some more honesty for you," my mouth was running away with itself and I couldn't stop it. "You're very attractive."

He gave me a crooked smile and his eyes lit up. He placed his hand on my thigh and I didn't remove it. I actually kind of liked it.

"Well, Isabella," Lorenzo murmured. "You're quite beautiful yourself."

I couldn't help but blush. I was terrible at accepting compliments but it made me smile.

"Look at that," I announced. "We went straight to being attracted to each other. No small talk needed."

Lorenzo smiled and moved closer to me, his arm brushing up against mine, "So what should we do about that?"

There was definitely something here and it intrigued me. I was sipping on my drink when a figure caught the corner of my eye. I turned to the door and there he was.

Giovanni.

And he wasn't alone.

Strolling in on his arm was the same tall, blonde beauty I had seen a couple of times before at Mala Mía. There was definitely something between the two of them - I had seen it previously in the way they would interact with each other. I had never met her but I noticed her. Even from this distance, you could tell she was beautiful.

And she was here with him.

They moved like a couple and a huge rush of disappointment washed over me. I didn't hear from him for weeks and now this? I was actually pretty pissed off about it. My eyes immediately searched for Reyna who was already looking at me with concerned eyes.

I turned back to Lorenzo, "Could you please give me one second?" I asked, trying my best to keep it all together. "Don't go anywhere."

"Sure." Lorenzo said.

He was clearly confused but he said nothing further. He took a seat on the barstool I got off of and I pushed my way through the crowd to Reyna. Katrina was still with her and Diego joined them too.

"Who is that?" I asked her.

She nodded, "Casey Fonseca. She's a model that he's hooked up with in the past."

A model? Of course he was sleeping with models. My eyes flicked back to Giovanni and Casey who had now joined our table.

"Not a fuck," I blurted out. "Is he seriously joining us?"

"Sergio invited him." Diego said, sheepishly.

I rolled my eyes. *Of course, he did.* Giovanni brought someone else to a place where he knew I'd be? After sleeping with me? Multiple times? And making it out like he was my boyfriend the last time we were together? He acted possessive but then pulled this on me?

Now I was really angry.

"Forget about him, Isabella," Katrina said softly, placing a reassuring hand on my arm. "He's bad news."

"I just feel so stupid." I admitted.

"What do you have to feel stupid about?" Reyna tried to comfort me. "Just think of him as multiple one-night stands. You got what you wanted out of him, not the other way round."

She was right. I was attracted to him and wanted to sleep with him, which I got to do, so I technically got what I wanted. What I didn't want was this rush of feelings that consumed me on top of the magnetic sexual attraction I had to him.

Fuck, I knew he was trouble.

"You know what, let's forget this," I announced. "I'm going back to Lorenzo and I'm not going to let this affect me."

They all cheered me on with an underlying tone of concern that I ignored. I didn't care about Giovanni. He could be with whoever the fuck he wanted. If he wanted to be like that then so could I. I knew the amount of alcohol in my system was probably making me completely unreasonable but there was no way to stop it. As I turned to go back to Lorenzo, I caught Giovanni's eye. He looked straight at me but I looked away immediately, not interested in giving him any attention.

I apologized to Lorenzo for taking too long and made some space for myself against the bar. We were closer now. We had to be considering the place had filled up even more. I turned to the bartender and ordered two tequilas.

"Sorry, I didn't even ask if you drank tequila." I said to Lorenzo.

"Well, I do so that works out."

I smiled. He was so nice. Here was a nice, attractive guy - just like Alessandro. We were both attracted to each other and I was not going to let Giovanni ruin that for me this time around. The bartender placed the shot glasses down in front of us. We both took them and placed the empty glasses back down on the table. It burned through me but this time, I was enjoying it. I turned to Lorenzo and out of nowhere, I threw myself at him. My lips crashed down on his. He tasted of tequila and faint cigarettes. I was scared that he would push me away but he didn't. Instead, his arms encircled my waist and he pulled me closer to him. I flicked my tongue over his and my hands found his hair. I couldn't help it - everything I was feeling just reached its climax and I didn't want to face any of it. I just wanted to make out with this attractive man at the bar. My body wasn't nearly as awake as it was to Giovanni's body, but I didn't want to think of him right now. I wanted to focus on Lorenzo. I felt his hand slide down the small of my back and rest over my ass. A feeling that should have set me alight but instead, suddenly made me aware of what I was doing. I pulled away, trying to catch my breath.

"I'm sorry, I don't know why I did that." I said, embarrassed by my actions.

"I'm not complaining," he reached out and grabbed my hand. "No need to apologize."

I looked at him and he was being sincere. In fact, he was smiling and my embarrassment subsided temporarily. This time he pulled into me and I didn't stop him. His tongue flicked over mine and my hand made its way through his hair again. *Fuck - he was a great kisser.* I pulled away to catch my breath and he smiled down at me.

"Do you want to dance?" he asked.

"I'd love to."

With my hand in his, he led me to the dance floor. As soon as I turned from the bar to the rest of the area, my eyes found his again. Giovanni was glaring at me from across the room and I knew he had just witnessed what happened between Lorenzo and me. This time I didn't look away. I stared right back at him, showing that he didn't dictate my actions. He didn't have control over me.

Even if I was lying to myself, I would put up the front. He didn't get to parade around here with some other woman and expect me to wait on the sidelines. Not going to happen. I was so angry with him. I knew we had no obligations to each other and that this was supposed to be a casual arrangement but it felt like more than that. It felt like more than just a hookup and the fact that I was clearly wrong about all of this was what hurt the most. I was embarrassed and disappointed in myself for handing myself over to him so easily. Not that I felt I had any choice in the matter - even now, standing in this public place with all these people, his mere presence had awoken my body. I was betrayed by it and I had to work incredibly hard to ignore my screaming desire.

Lorenzo guided me to the middle of the dance floor and placed my hands around his neck. His hands slowly slid down my back and ended up on either side of my waist. We let the music guide us and our bodies found the perfect rhythm to the music. He knew exactly what he was doing with his body and it increased his sex-appeal. I pushed myself closer to him, trying to ignite something inside of me. It was there but only a faint flicker. There was no way my body could hand itself over to anyone else knowing very well that Giovanni was in the room. I allowed my eyes to flick over to our table. He was still there but this time he wasn't looking at me. He was whispering something in Casey's ear.

Fuck. I was jealous.

Something I never wanted to feel and yet I was. It made me feel sick to my stomach. Giovanni showed me a world of pleasure and passion but also his softer side. His more vulnerable side when he played for me. His soft kisses and intimate gestures. The small little moments like that were what made it impossible for me to believe that this was one-sided. I was starting to feel suffocated by all of this bubbling over in my mind.

I broke away from Lorenzo's rhythm, "I'm sorry, I just need some air."

Without even a second glance, I turned towards the exit. I pushed myself through the crowds of people and finally made it outside. I took in a deep breath as the fresh air filled my lungs. The sun had set but the lights on the street kept the area perfectly illuminated. I ran my fingers through my hair and leaned against the wall. *What was I doing?* I was incredibly frustrated at myself for what I was feeling. I gave myself strict instructions to keep my walls up and yet a few of those damn annoying feelings had found their way through. This was ridiculous. I was being ridiculous now. So I slept with some guy a few times? Big deal.

Get over it, Isabella.

But I couldn't. I was too intoxicated to control my true feelings. What I needed was to get out of here. I could just walk right now and head back home but I didn't want Reyna to worry and I left my bag at the table. The table where Giovanni and Casey were. The table I didn't feel like having to go to.

"Are you alright?"

I turned and there Lorenzo stood. He was concerned for me. It made me smile, but I knew I was being unfair to him. He was a sweet stranger and I didn't want to involve him in my problems.

"Yes. I'm sorry. I'm just suddenly not feeling well." I lied.

"Do you want me to take you home?" he offered.

Ah, my heart.

"You're so sweet for offering Lorenzo but it's okay."

"Let me take you home, Isabella," he insisted. "I promise I just want to make sure that you get there safely."

I reached out to him and rubbed my thumb over his cheek, "You are so wonderful but I promise I'll be okay. I'm not that far from here and I'm going to see if my roommate is ready to leave too."

As much as I wanted to take Lorenzo up on his offer, I really needed to be alone right now.

"Okay. Can I call you though?"

I nodded and gestured for him to give me his phone. He did and I quickly put my number in.

"You'll be hearing from me." he announced proudly and leaned down, leaving a kiss on my cheek.

We went our separate ways as we stepped inside. I needed to find Reyna and get out of here. I scanned the area and noticed that Giovanni and Casey were no longer by the table. I made my way there and reached for my bag.

"Are you leaving?" Jose asked, which startled me and made me jump.

I nodded, "Have you seen Reyna?"

He pointed to the bar where Reyna and Katrina were. I pushed through the crowd to get to them.

"I was wondering where you went. You had me worried," Reyna noticed my bag. "Are you leaving?"

"Yeah. I have too much alcohol in my system to make any good decisions so I need to head home."

"Okay let me grab my-...." Reyna started but I interrupted her.

"No, you're staying," I commanded. "I'm just going home, Rey. It's literally up the road and I need some time to think."

"Are you sure?" Katrina asked.

I nodded, "Yes. You guys enjoy, okay? I promise I'm fine."

After exchanging goodbyes, I turned to leave. I didn't even bother saying goodbye to the guys, I knew Reyna would do it for me. I just wanted to get home right now. As I made it to the door, someone grabbed my arm. I turned around and it was Giovanni.

"Where are you going?" he asked.

I stopped and jerked my head back, "Seriously?"

"What?"

I did not have the energy to get into anything with him right now. I needed to get out of here.

"I'm going home." I jerked my arm out of his grip and pushed through the door.

He followed me onto the street. I was consumed by so many emotions right now and I was afraid I wouldn't be able to hold it together.

"Hold on, Isabella." He reached for my arm again, forcing me to stop.

I pulled my arm away from him again.

"What do you want?" I snapped.

"I think we need to talk."

I rolled my eyes and laughed. *Was he being serious?* I looked at him and it hurt more that he was looking as good as ever. He was always looking good and I hated that.

"Look, Giovanni," I started. "You and I have nothing to talk about. There's clearly nothing going on between us and I have no energy left in me to continue to be just one of the girls you sleep with. That's not happening again. It was fun while it lasted but now please just leave me the hell alone."

And with that, I was gone.

And he didn't follow.

CHAPTER 14:

A journey that normally would have taken me roughly ten minutes ended up being extended to a thirty-minute walk around the block. I just kept walking, trying to figure out all that was going on in my head. Most of the alcohol had left my system and now I was just cold and hungry. I dragged myself upstairs and unlocked the door to an empty apartment. The silence was deafening. I had nothing else to focus on but my thoughts and I couldn't even get those under control.

Here's what I knew - I was hurt by Giovanni. He hurt me by bringing Casey. And I was aware he, *technically,* had no obligation to me but I was hurt because obviously I cared about him. I knew from the beginning what I was getting myself into but I didn't think that I was going to have such an instant connection with him. And such a passionate one. I had never felt passion till I met him and besides the fact he could drive my body crazy, there was something about what was inside of him that made me want to know more about him. He had a soft side too and with his witty humour and sexy confidence, how could I not be intrigued? He didn't have to play for me that night. He didn't have to share what he did about his family. He didn't have to listen to me talk about mine. But he did.

I refused to believe that he did that with all the girls he slept with. Why the hell did he tell Alessandro he was my boyfriend? He couldn't do that and then do what he did tonight. He didn't get to dictate who I could be with while he continued to act like it was a free for all for him.

It made it so difficult for me to believe he didn't feel anything more for me. There were real emotions involved now and I worked so hard to avoid this from happening. Now look where it's gotten me. When Nate left, I was forced to face the fact that I didn't know who I was and I didn't know what I wanted. My life's plan was ripped from under me and all that was left were pieces of who I used to be. Who was Isabella Avery? There was no flicker of life in me for months. Maybe even years.

Until I met Giovanni.

He awoke something inside of me and allowed me to explore parts of myself that were previously undiscovered. It made me happy. I was happy to feel this light inside of me and he was the one who flipped the switch. Turns out I am actually a lot more sexual than realized. He excited me and somehow made me comfortable enough that I wasn't afraid to embrace who I really was around him. He made me feel alive. But that's done now. The walk around the block reminded me that no matter what, I could never just continue to be a number on someone's body count.

My stomach growled but I was too drained to eat anything. I dragged myself to the couch and flopped down. I pulled my phone from my bag and searched Casey's name. There she popped up with her beautiful, care-free smile. I didn't know why I was doing this to myself - it certainly wasn't healthy. I scrolled down and found a number of articles in reference to her on-again-off-again relationship with, as they called him, "Barcelona's sexy businessman", Giovanni Velázquez. I groaned and threw my phone on the couch. *Why the fuck did I just do that to myself?* That was dumb and I made me feel so much worse than before.

I just needed to figure my life out.

I had to.

***

I woke to a loud insistent banging. I sat right up getting the fright of my life. It took me a while to realize that I must have fallen asleep on the couch and that someone was at my door. I reached for my phone and saw it was two-thirty in the morning.

"What the hell?" I mumbled, confused by the unnecessary amount of noise coming from outside.

I stumbled to the door and jerked it open. Giovanni stood there with his arm leaning on the side of the door frame.

"Giovanni, do you know what time it is? What the hell are you doing here?" I grumbled, still groggy by being woken up so suddenly.

He stumbled past me into my apartment and I could smell the alcohol on him.

"Are you drunk?" I asked, closing the door behind me.

He ignored my question. "I told you we needed to talk."

I watched him stumble all the way to the lounge as he pulled off his jacket and threw it on the couch. I went to the kitchen and grabbed him a glass of water. As angry as I was at him, he was drunk and I was not about to have him throw up in my apartment. He needed to get himself under control.

"Sit," I instructed.

He obeyed and dropped onto my couch. He ran his hands through his hair and looked up at me. I handed him the glass of water.

"Drink it all."

He didn't argue with me and instead finished the whole glass. I took it from him and placed it on the coffee table in front of the couch. I sat on the table and looked at him, waiting for an explanation.

"Is there a reason you are in my apartment drunk at two-thirty in the morning?" I huffed.

"Why did you leave earlier?" There was a glimmer of sadness and confusion in his eyes.

I sighed. "You're joking right?"

"No Isabella, I'm not." He mimicked my tone.

I was tired, hungry and seemed to be a tad hungover already so I had no patience at this point to deal with his questions.

"Do you need me to spell it out for you?" I asked, the sarcasm dripping from my voice. "Did you forget who you brought with you tonight?"

He still looked confused and I wanted to shake him.

"Giovanni, you cannot tell me that you don't understand why I was hurt tonight."

"Casey?" he asked. "Are you referring to Casey?"

"Of course I am."

"She wasn't my date or anything like that, Isabella."

"Sure looked like she was from where I was standing," I mumbled. "Please don't lie to me. Just be honest, get some more water and see yourself out."

I had no energy to deal with this. He drained me. I stood up ready to leave but as I turned he reached for my hand. That touch sent shivers through my body. I couldn't control my physical reaction to him. It was still unbelievable to me.

"She wasn't my date." he repeated

"Do you realize how often you say that?"

"She's just a friend."

"A friend you've slept with. A friend that the press refers to you as her on-again-off-again boyfriend."

"You searched her?" he was confused. "Why would you do that?"

"Why wouldn't I do that?" I huffed. "There's so much about you and your *many* relationships that I wasn't aware of."

He said nothing.

"I really don't care anymore," I sighed. "You went out of your way to make it known to Alessandro last week that you're my boyfriend, which might I remind you, you are not and then you bring another woman to a place that you knew I'd be? How many times must I see you with someone else, Giovanni? One minute you're interested in me then you're not. I mean, what the fuck? Please explain all of this to me because I really can't seem to figure you out."

He remained silent which only angered me more.

"If you're not going to answer my questions then you need to leave right now, Giovanni," I snapped. "I'm not going to continue to be just another number on your list."

"That's not what you are."

"Oh really?" I huffed. "Cause it sure feels like that."

"I don't know why I brought Casey," he admitted. "I don't even give a shit about her."

"Well, that's nice," I remarked, not even bothering to control my sarcasm at this point. "You play a dirty game, Giovanni."

"Something's going on Isabella and I don't know how to handle it."

"What are you talking about?"

"You," he huffed. "I can't get you out of my head."

I held my breath.

"You literally consume my every fucking thought lately and that's never happened to me before."

He let go of my hand and stood up, pacing back and forth. "I don't know how to handle all of this so it's just easier for me to try and push you away."

My anger subsided and was replaced with a wave of relief. I knew I wasn't going crazy. It was impossible for him to not be feeling what I was feeling. It was way too real.

"I knew bringing Casey would get this reaction but it's what I do. I fuck things up." He ran his fingers through his hair.

I stood up to go to him but he paced right past me.

"And then I saw you kiss Lorenzo and that made this all very clear to me."

"Wait, how do you know Lorenzo?" I asked, surprised that he knew his name.

"He and I had got into a fight a while back, I actually broke his nose." He shrugged casually.

"Giovanni! What did you fight about?"

He averted his gaze and I figured it out. "Did you sleep with his sister?" Lorenzo's sister was quite a catch and clearly, Giovanni had a thing for really beautiful women given how Casey looked too. He didn't need to say anything, I could see the answer in his eyes.

"Of course," I mumbled and sat back down on the couch. "How many others have you slept with?"

"Isabella, I don't want to talk about the others," he said softly. He walked back to the couch and sat down next to me. He reached out for my hand and I didn't push it away.

"When I saw you kiss Lorenzo." His hand tightened. "It made it very clear to me that I don't want to see you with other guys. It drives me fucking crazy. I've never felt like this before." He was saying everything I needed to hear. There was no way what was happening between us was one-sided. The feelings were very much there and I didn't think either of us expected that. I certainly wasn't looking for it. After everything that had happened in my life, the last thing I needed was to involve someone else in it. But Giovanni came out of nowhere and I was feeling things I'd never felt before.

"Don't you think it drives me crazy to see you with someone else?" I explained, "Why do you think I was so hurt tonight? I can't help myself, Giovanni. There's something about you that I just can't shake."

I didn't want to admit any of this out loud but here he was saying all the right things and I needed him to know I was feeling the same.

"I'm not good at this shit, Isabella."

I squeezed his hand. "Trust me, neither am I. There is still so much we don't know about each other."

"Maybe we should start there." I smiled. I couldn't help it. Everything I was feeling for him started bubbling over - there was no way to control it now. He was saying what I needed to hear and that opened the floodgates to everything I was trying to fight. A part of me was terrified of this. I knew if Giovanni was to break my heart that it would be unlike any heartbreak I had experienced before - that's how real our connection was already. I didn't know how it was possible to have this kind of connection with someone I only met a few months ago but here we were. I reached out for him and caressed my thumb across his cheek. It was a soft gesture but I knew he needed it right now. He leaned into my touch and closed his eyes. He was so beautiful. Everything about him was just beautiful to me. All the hurt and confusion I was feeling earlier slipped away. All that mattered to me right now was that he was right here. I leaned forward and kissed him. A soft kiss but it was exactly what we needed. I pulled away from him and we looked at each other.

"Are you trying to take advantage of me in my drunken state?" He murmured, smiling.

I laughed. "I was actually going to suggest we go to bed." I stood up and extended my hand to him. "Come with me," I instructed.

He slid his hand in mine and stood up. I led him to my bedroom and walked him over to the bed. He was sleepy now and I could tell we weren't going to discuss anything further tonight. He kicked his shoes off and laid down against the pillow.

"Do not throw up in my bed. I won't be cleaning that up." His eyes were already closed but he cracked a small smile.

"Come lie with me," he mumbled and reached out for me.

"Let me go get changed." I turned but he pulled me back again.

"Don't be too long."

I kissed his cheek. "I'll be right back."

I could already hear his soft breathing and snores from just outside the room. I stopped at the door of the bathroom and looked back at him. He was so peaceful. Looking at him made me smile and I could feel the warmth inside my heart. I was already in too deep. There was no way I could stop myself from falling now.

It was far too late for that.

CHAPTER 15:

I was hot.

I could feel myself sweating under the weight laid on top of me. I was so disoriented, it took me a while to finally get my eyes completely open. Giovanni's arm was draped across me and his head was on my pillow right next to my head. The memories of our conversation from very early this morning came back to me and I couldn't help but smile. I looked over at him and watched as he slept. His soft breaths were all I needed to hear right now. Strands of hair had fallen over his face so I slowly tucked it behind his ear. He didn't move, he was too deeply asleep and I figured it could be a while until he would be up. Judging by the alcohol I could smell on him last night, I was expecting a real hangover when he woke up. I reached for my phone on the bedside table and checked the time. It was just after seven in the morning and I had only bagged a few hours of sleep. I could feel I was exhausted but my mind was racing and I couldn't even attempt to go back to sleep. I decided I would head out for a morning run to try and release all this pent-up tension I had. If I had it my way, I would be doing another physical activity first thing in the morning but I knew that Giovanni needed the rest. I managed to slip out from under him without him waking up and went to get changed. I used to run every morning - it was always a great way for me to clear my mind and it had been a while since I had a chance to do that. I quickly got changed, reached for my running shoes, earphones and cell phone - I was ready to go. I couldn't run in silence. I always made sure I had my music with me. I gave Giovanni a kiss on the cheek and left a message on a little piece of paper by the bedside table letting him know where I was going. I didn't think he was going to wake up before I got back but just in case he did, he'd know where I went.

I made it downstairs and was greeted by the bright sun shining down on me. Autumn was upon us and I loved everything about it. The leaves were turning into so many shades of reds and oranges and although the sun was shining, there was a cold wind in the air. My long sleeve shirt was all I had to protect me from the fresh breeze but once I started running, the cold air wasn't a problem anymore. I placed my earphones in and headed down the street in a light jog. Running always had calming effects on me. The burn in my chest that spread after running for a good amount of time made me feel like I could conquer anything.

As I ran I tried to go over everything in my mind again. I never expected Giovanni to end up at my apartment, especially not after what happened last night. I hated seeing him with Casey. At that moment I accepted that I was done with him and his games but when he told me everything I needed to hear, I had to admit to myself that I was already in too deep. I knew exactly the type of person he was when I first met him and yet, I still pursued him. I wasn't sure what I thought would happen but I certainly never expected to develop actual feelings for him. I was convinced that I could have a one-night stand. I was actually adamant about it but I never thought he was going to introduce me to a world of passion and pleasure the way he did. He had ways with my body and I could never back out now. I was hooked on him and addicted to how he made me feel. Both physically and emotionally. After our conversation, we both knew that there was more between us than just a physical connection. It excited me. He excited me.

After a couple of laps around my area, I made it back to my apartment building. Kat and Reyna were spending the day with their significant others so we had the apartment all to ourselves. I made it back upstairs and went straight for a bottle of water. I finished it all in one go - my breathing was still heavy from the intensity of the run. The apartment was still quiet so I figured Giovanni was still asleep. I placed my earphones and cellphone down on the kitchen counter and went to check on him.

He was still sleeping peacefully.

The sight of him in my bed made me smile. It was nice to have him here - it was nice to have him around again. I made sure I was quiet with my movements as I went to fetch my towel and hairbrush. I pulled my hair out of its ponytail and let it fall over my shoulder. It needed a good wash. I tiptoed to the bathroom and slipped inside, closing the door behind me. I placed the towel on the counter and brushed through my hair. I was feeling calm. Giovanni was here because he wanted something more and we were both on the same page now with that. We were both reluctant to jump into a relationship but we didn't need that right now. All I needed was the confirmation that I wasn't going crazy and that he was feeling this too.

And now I have it.

I smiled to myself and stepped into the shower. The hot water burned against my skin, a feeling of relaxation spreading over me. I felt like I was finally at a point where I was starting to get a handle on everything again. I knew at some point I was going to have to deal with my family and stop avoiding them the way I had been but that was not today's problem. I was focused on my life here in Barcelona. I didn't want to leave here. When I first joined Reyna here, she didn't even ask how long I was staying for. She let me move in and made it clear that this was my home now. I was incredibly lucky to have her - I honestly didn't know what I would have done if she wasn't in my life. She was always my knight in shining armour. There was nothing for me in London. This really was my home now.

I washed the last of the conditioner out of my hair and turned the water off. I reached for the towel as I stepped out of the shower. I wrapped it around my body and brushed the knots out of my hair once again. I strolled back into my room, headed straight for my underwear draw, slipped on a pair of underwear and clipped my bra in place, dropping the towel to the floor.

"Now that's a sight I could get used to," Giovanni said from behind me.

I jumped. "Oh! I thought you were still asleep!"

"Nope," he mused. "And I'm really glad I'm not."

I blushed and turned to face him. He had his arms behind his head and was smiling up at me. He looked at ease and seeing him like that warmed my heart. I strolled over to the bed and sat down next to him.

"How are you feeling today?"

"Like I was hit by a ton of bricks," he answered casually. "How did I end up here?"

I froze. "Do you not remember banging on my door at two in the morning?"

He shook his head.

Oh no. Did he not remember what we spoke about?

"Uh well, you showed up here this morning because you said we had a lot to talk about," I explained slowly. "Which we did."

"Oh?" he asked, "So what did we talk about?"

This was not happening!

Did he seriously not remember this morning? Did he not remember saying everything I needed to hear? Was he going to deny it all now? Oh no, the overthinking was back. He could clearly see the panic and confusion on my face because he suddenly burst out laughing.

"Oh, Isabella." He pulled me closer to him. "I'm just messing with you. Of course, I remember what we spoke about."

Oh, thank goodness!

I punched his arm lightly. "Don't do that to me!"

He chuckled. "But it's just way too much fun."

He pulled himself closer and kissed me. He touched me and my body was suddenly open for business. I pulled myself onto his lap, intensifying the kiss. His hands ran up and down my back and I was thankful I didn't get around to putting clothes on. Now there wasn't much for him to remove. My tongue found his and the intensity of his kiss was driving my body crazy. I was ready for him and he didn't even have to do much. I was always ready for him. I ran my hand down his body and found the bottom of his shirt. I started pushing it up and he pulled it up and over his head.

He broke the kiss. "Don't you have roommates?"

"They're not going to be home anytime soon."

His lips collided with mine again. I ran my fingers over his bare body, feeling every inch of him. His lips moved to my neck and I threw my head back, enjoying every kiss. It sent shock waves through my body. I couldn't control how his lips on my body made me feel. He consumed me. He lifted me up and laid me against the bed. He ran his hands down my body and reached my legs. He slowly spread them, watching my reaction the whole time. I held my breath. He was so close to me. He slowly slid my underwear down and started leaving kisses by my knee, slowly making his way closer to me. My breathing picked up, the tension was becoming too much and just the sight of him in between my legs was overwhelming me. He inched closer to me and I closed my eyes, anticipating the release. I felt his tongue flick over me and my body jerked.

My eyes flew open. "Giovanni, wait."

He stopped and looked up at me. "What's wrong?" I was embarrassed. I had never had anyone do that to me before and as intrigued as I was in that moment, I was also apprehensive.

"I've never had anyone," I mumbled shyly. "Do that to me."

He smirked and his eyes lit up. "Oh, baby." He positioned himself back down between my legs, still looking at me. I bit my lip, not knowing what I was in for.

"Just lie back, Isabella," he murmured. "I got you."

I instructed myself to calm down and lay back against the pillow. I watched him as he brought his tongue down on me again.

Oh my. He found his rhythm against me and I threw my head back, biting down hard on my lip. It was amazing. He was amazing. Whatever he was doing, my body was agreeing with and I couldn't even try to control it. He was driving my pleasure levels through the roof. My hand involuntarily found his hair and I pulled on it. Soft moans escaping my lips. I was so close now. I pushed my hips up against him. He slid a finger inside while flicking his tongue over me and I came undone. I couldn't hold back anymore.

"Giovanni," I moaned. Closing my eyes and basking in the pleasure that consumed my entire body. He kissed the inside of each thigh one last time before moving himself from between my legs. My eyes were still closed but I could sense him next to me. I tried to get a handle on my breathing. I opened one eye to peep up at him and he was smiling down at me. I loved his smile.

"So?" he smirked.

I covered my face with my hands. "I don't even have the words."

He chuckled.. "That's what I like to hear." He jumped off the bed.

"Where are you going?" I asked.

"To make breakfast," he replied. "I've just had dessert so..."

I threw a pillow at him, laughing. "Don't say stuff like that." He dodged it and I could hear him laughing all the way to the kitchen. I smiled to myself. I was feeling pure bliss right now. There was something different about him today. He had a different energy about him. He was so care-free. There was nothing holding us back now and we were free to discover where this was going to lead us. I didn't know much about Giovanni's cooking skills so I jumped out of bed, got dressed and went to find him.

CHAPTER 16:

"**S**o what are your plans for today?" I asked him.

It turned out his cooking skills were non-existent so we figured out a great system of him passing me ingredients while I made us some breakfast. I was standing in front of the stove frying the last of the eggs while Giovanni took a seat on the barstool by the kitchen counter.

"I've got a few meetings with some potential partners today," he explained. "We're actually looking to expand Mala Mía to other places in Spain."

"That's great news!" I exclaimed. "Where are you guys looking at now?"

I boiled the kettle and then placed the eggs I was frying on his plate. It completed the already laid-out bacon, toast and mushrooms in front of him. He had quite the hangover so we were trying to rectify that with a greasy yet hardy breakfast.

"This looks amazing," he commented. "Very English of you. I'm just used to coffee and a sandwich for breakfast."

I chuckled. "I think this would help with your hangover much better than that." He smiled before continuing our previous conversation. "We're looking at a few places. Sevilla, Madrid but our focus, for now, is Valencia."

"I've never been to any of those places. I've heard Sevilla is beautiful though."

"They all are," he said, as he took another bite of his food. "You know, I never learned how you came to Barcelona. I've known Reyna for a few years now so I know you haven't been living here for very long."

Just as I was about to answer, my phone started to ring. *Saved by the bell.* I was busy pouring the hot water into our mugs so I asked Giovanni to answer.

"Isabella's phone," he answered formally.

I placed his mug in front of him and gestured for him to pass me the phone but he didn't.

"This is Giovanni. What can I do for you, Lorenzo?"

Oh no. I reached for the phone now but Giovanni jumped off the stool. He was clearly finding this entire situation amusing.

"I'll have to let Isabella know you called."

"Giovanni!" I hissed.

"Goodbye, Lorenzo," he said as he hung up, strolling back to the counter and sat on the barstool again, casually continuing his meal. "So that was Lorenzo."

"Yes, I got that," I mumbled sarcastically. "Why didn't you let me speak to him?"

"And what could you possibly have to talk to him about?"

"Well, I wanted to see why he called."

"He called because he wants you."

"He doesn't want me."

Giovanni snorted. "Don't be naive, Isabella. I know Lorenzo and he always goes after what he wants which, after that kiss last night, is you."

I blushed. I was embarrassed by that and it was even worse that Giovanni watched it happen. I knew I wanted him to see but that was not the smartest decision I had made.

"Are you mad about the kiss?"

He shook his head and took a bite of his bacon. "I was but that's not going to happen again." I raised an eyebrow and sipped on my coffee, waiting for him to explain.

"You're mine now," he announced proudly. "This is delicious by the way."

I was thankful for the subject change. The last thing I wanted to do was continue to talk about Lorenzo. I did feel bad. I led him on the same way I did with Alessandro but I couldn't help the way I felt about Giovanni. In the end, he was all I wanted and to hear him call me his was music to my ears.

"You never answered my question about how you ended up in Barcelona?"

I sighed. There was really no point in prolonging the inevitable. I took a seat on the barstool across from him.

"Well, I moved here from London just over half a year ago," I explained. "Long story short, I got dumped."

"What was his name?"

"Nate Cameron," I said. "We were together for about six years and then..."

"Six years?" Giovanni interrupted me. "Holy shit."

"Yeah, we had been together since I was in high school."

"That's a long time to invest in one person. What happened?"

"There had been so much talk about marriage and everyone around us was expecting it so just when I thought he was going to propose, he dumped me instead. It turned out he wasn't ready for the commitment."

"I really want to say sorry but I know that if that never happened, I never would have met you and I couldn't think of anything worse." Giovanni reached for my hand.

I smiled up at him. He was right. I never would have ended up in Barcelona had Nate not decided to end things. I never would have started a life here and I never would have met Giovanni. He brought light to my life again and I couldn't imagine living in darkness again.

"Did you want to marry him?"

I shook my head. "I don't really think I was ready for that either."

"Were you sad when he ended it?" He asked, softly.

"I wasn't sad over losing him but rather sad over the fact that I actually had no idea who I was without him," I admitted. "My life had been so perfectly planned by everyone around me and he was a huge part of that. When he left, I didn't know what to do. I didn't even tell my family the whole story - we were planning to come to Spain for his work anyway but that was in Madrid. They were shocked that there wasn't an engagement so imagine if I had to tell them that there wasn't a relationship at all."

I couldn't explain what happened with Nate. At the time, I wasn't ready to accept it myself.

I continued to explain this to Giovanni. "My mother and I had a bit of a fallout after she found out I quit my job. I avoided their calls but when I arrived in Barcelona, I had to rip the band-aid off. I told them that Reyna had some family emergency so that's why I was in Barcelona and that I was going to meet Nate in Madrid after."

"Where do they think you are now?" he asked.

"In Madrid with Nate. At least that's what I'm assuming. I haven't really spoken to them enough over these past few months to know for sure,"

"You're going to have to tell them the truth eventually."

I sighed. "Don't you think I know that? You don't know them, Giovanni. Especially my mother - she's a control freak. There is no room for failure in my family and who would be more of a failure than a daughter who runs off to Barcelona of all places after being dumped and quitting her job. A job that they got for me, might I add. My mother was not happy with me 'ruining my life' as she explained. She really didn't want any part in my new life since it wasn't what she had planned. I knew Nate wouldn't say anything to them about what happened between us. He knew what they were like. I'm not an idiot, I know they probably suspect something but out of sight, out of mind and honestly, I don't want to be reminded that I'm a disappointment to them."

"You're not a disappointment, Isabella."

"I used to feel like I was. The first few months were tough but now that I've started to build my own life here, I'm happier than I have ever been."

"You're pretty fucking brave." Giovanni leaned over and kissed my forehead. "Don't let anyone tell you otherwise."

He's right. Not many people could pack up their life and move to another country just like that. It was a spur of the moment decision and I remember the day as if it was yesterday.

"Isabella," he slurred. "I can't do this anymore."

I held my breath.

"What?" I asked, even though I had heard exactly what he said.

"This." He indicated to him and I. "I can't do this relationship anymore. I'm sorry but this is getting way too serious for me. Everyone wants us to get engaged and get married and I can't handle this pressure, I don't want it. I haven't even lived yet and I'm not ready for that kind of commitment."

I waited for the tears but they never came. Instead, I went numb.

"You're breaking up with me?" I tried to remain calm but I couldn't deny the confusion bubbling over inside.

He nodded, "I'm sorry but you deserve someone who can give you what you want right now and that's not me."

"We don't have to get engaged right now, Nate."

"I know but it's what your family wants and I don't even know if I want to get married at all."

Given how openly we discussed the next step in our relationship, his sudden admission of his true feelings caught me off guard. He finally met my gaze. His light blue eyes were filled with pain, and I could tell he was ashamed of what he was doing. I wish I could say I could have predicted it, but it appears we were not on the same page, and I had no idea. This came as a complete surprise to me. I watched him bury his head in his hands. I tried to feel something, but there was nothing left. No sadness. No anger. I felt nothing as the numbness spread across my body.

"Please, Nate, just let me deal with telling my family," I murmured, my voice devoid of any emotion.

"Of course, Izzy. I'm sorry, I never wanted to hur-"

I lifted a finger to cut him off. He never wanted to hurt me and yet, here we were. I turned around and returned to our room, locking the door behind me. I was in shock. The very last thing I expected Nate to do was dump me. We had it all figured out; every step of our lives had been laid out and ready to go.

But that was the problem.

He didn't want that next step and I couldn't even blame him. I wasn't even sure I wanted it but all I knew was that I had to stick to the plan. My mother made it very clear to me how my life was going to be. I never bothered to question it because my parents always explained that the only way to lead a successful life was to plan for it. I had to get straight A's and study English at University. I had to complete my internship at Oak Tree Publishing and become Junior Editor. The end goal was to become Senior Editor of my parent's newspaper alongside Camila. While ensuring I had my work life under control I had to have the perfect relationship for our society. They had immersed themselves in the upper-class society of London since before I was born. Reputation was everything and every step of our lives had to be as perfect as could be. We had to keep up with the standard. I needed to marry a nice boy from a well-off family. Nate fit the profile perfectly with his family being just as involved in the upper-class society as mine was. We both knew the next step was to get engaged. My family expected me to be married and in the next phase of my work life by next year.

Now that was not going to happen.

I dragged myself to the bed we shared and dropped onto it. I caught a glimpse of myself in the mirror by my dressing table and stared at my reflection. I didn't know this woman looking back at me. She was lost and unfulfilled. She was more concerned about the reaction of her family to this break-up than how she actually felt about it.

I began to panic. What was I going to do? Where was I going to go? I couldn't tell them. I didn't know what I was going to say to them but I knew I needed to leave. The air around me became thin and I started to feel suffocated. I couldn't control my breathing and I welcomed the tears streaming down my face. My emotions hit me like a ton of bricks. I needed to get out of here. I grabbed my suitcase and began filling it with as much as possible. Clothes, shoes, toiletries, books, and anything of mine that would fit. I changed out of my date night clothes which were now tainted with this memory. I tossed the clothes on the bed and changed into something more comfortable - a pair of tights and a shirt would cover it. I reached for my big jacket knowing how unpredictable London's weather could be. I was ready to leave. I turned back to the room one more time - it was strange to look at now. A room that I put so much energy into and one that was supposed to be my safe haven was now unfamiliar to me - I didn't belong here.

I opened the door and checked to see where Nate was but he was nowhere to be found. He must have left while I was packing up and that act alone made me so angry at him. How dare he dump me and then leave like it was nothing? No goodbye? Not even a last glance? Did our time together mean nothing to him? I grabbed my handbag and shoved my cell phone and purse into it. I needed to find a place to stay for tonight and then after work tomorrow, I would figure out what I was going to do.

Where was I going to go? I couldn't go home without exposing what happened tonight. I couldn't go to a friend's place. I didn't have a friend that Nate and I didn't share. There was no Reyna in London. I was alone.

A few hours later I was in a cheap hotel room, staring up at the ceiling trying to compartmentalize what to deal with first. The thoughts were running through my mind and I couldn't grasp my emotions - I was angry, sad and confused all at the same time. I didn't know what to do or how to react - I just wanted to sleep.

And so I did.

The next morning I shut away all my emotions in a tightly closed box in my mind and focused on the day ahead. Today they were announcing the new Junior Editor position that I had been working towards for the last year and a half. I really put all my energy into it and although my personal life plan was uncertain, I was adamant to stick to my work plan. After weeks of discussion, all the elements were in place for me to continue working for them, even from Madrid. I couldn't exactly follow Nate to Madrid now could I? What was I going to do?

I shook those thoughts away as I entered the doors at Oak Tree Publishing and went straight to the boardroom. Everyone had already gathered and we were just waiting on the head of the company, Nigel Oak, to join us. He was a much older man and had been in the business for a long time. My parents were good friends with him and essentially, that's how they convinced him to give me a shot. I felt I needed to go above and beyond to prove myself since I got a foot in the door thanks to them. I didn't agree with nepotism but my mother didn't care. My focus was learning as much from him as possible and putting my best foot forward to ensure I landed this new position. I worked harder than ever these past few months. Nigel walked in and greeted the team. He placed his briefcase down on the table and took a seat at the head.

"Thank you all for making time this morning," he started. "It's always a great day when you get to welcome a new team member into a new position. Everyone here works incredibly hard and as a boss, I always want to see people excel."

The door to the boardroom opened and Cindy sauntered in. Cindy was another intern that I worked closely with over the last six months. She was still fairly new to the industry. Her long blonde hair and big blue eyes attracted men to her like a moth to a flame. Her work ethic on the other hand lacked the necessary drive that one needs in her job position. She was happy to be the pretty face and allow those around her to pick up her slack.

"Ah Cindy!" Nigel exclaimed. "You're just in time - ladies and gentlemen, meet your new Junior Editor, Miss Cindy Smalls."

My stomach dropped.

No. Fucking. Way.

"You have got to be kidding me," I sputtered.

Now I snapped. Everyone stopped clapping and turned to face me. Cindy glared at me from across the table. She knew how much I wanted this position. She knew how hard I worked for it.

"Is there a problem, Miss Avery?" Nigel asked.

This was the last thread of my life I was holding onto and it just snapped. Everything I was feeling reached the surface and I exploded.

"Is there a problem?" I repeated, laughing. "That's a joke right?"

The entire boardroom went silent.

"Can you explain to me how Cindy could possibly be the best person for this position?"

"Miss Avery," Nigel started but I interrupted.

"Anyone at this table is more qualified for this position than her. Everything she has managed to achieve at this company has been because of us around her having to pick up her slack."

I knew I was being a childish bitch now but I couldn't stop. We all knew Cindy was sleeping with Nigel on the side but I really thought I had proven myself with the countless hours and dedication I had given to the company.

"Jealousy makes you nasty," Cindy said, crossing her arms.

I laughed. "Congratulations on hiring an actual 12-year-old in this position. I know it says Junior but surely this is taking it a bit far?"

I would never act like this. I was being completely immature but I was done with this all. I felt nothing and I just had to get out of there.

"Miss Avery, I hardly think this is the way to express how you're feeling," Nigel reprimanded.

I grabbed my bag and stood up. "Nigel, consider this my resignation."

And I turned on my heels and left. I was done with this job. I was done with London. I was done with it all and I needed to get out of here. NOW!

Without even thinking about it, I dialed Reyna.

"Hello?" she said.

"Rey, listen, it's me. I know this is out of the blue but I am

buying a ticket to Barcelona right now. Please can I come to you?" I was holding back my tears.

"What time must I pick you up?" That was all she said and the rest was history.

"Isabella?" Giovanni's faint voice brought me out of my memory. I shook those thoughts away and looked up at him. He was standing close to me now looking concerned. "Are you alright?"

"Yes, sorry. Just talking about this brings up a lot," I confessed.

"I understand. We don't have to talk about this anymore. When is Reyna going to be back?" he asked.

I collected the dishes on the counter and placed them in the sink. "Probably a bit later. She's leaving on Thursday to spend her birthday with her family."

Giovanni glanced down at his watch. "Listen, I have to head out to that meeting, but can I call you later?"

I turned the tap off and placed the last of the dishes on the drying rack. I reached for the cloth, wiped my hands down and turned to him.

"I don't even think you have my number," I teased.

"I've actually had it since the first night I met you," he said in a matter-of-fact tone.

"And yet, you never used it."

"We've already established that I've been an idiot up until now," he mused and walked over to me, pulling me into his arms.

I was so calm when he was around. He made me feel safe and wanted. I wanted to hold onto these feelings for as long as I possibly could. I wanted to hold onto him.

"You should go or you're going to be late." I reached up and kissed him. "Call me later since you say you have my number."

"Keep your phone close." He smiled, quickly gathered his things and was out the door in a flash.

The moment he left, I felt the loneliness creeping in again. I missed him. It took me by surprise at how much I already missed him but I did. I sighed and forced myself to head to my bedroom, cell phone in hand. I lay against the pillow he slept in and smiled. It still smelled like him and I wandered off to sleep with the image of him lying next to me.

CHAPTER 17:

I made it to the coffee shop as the skies opened up to the world. The rain was coming down harder now and I was thankful for the coffee I bought on the way here. Even though our little shop was supposed to sell coffee, there was still so much that had to be done - including needing the equipment necessary to brew a steaming hot cup. Today was painting day and I had been looking forward to it. Reyna was stuck with a deadline for work so it was just me today. I enjoyed the painting process - it was a surprisingly calming activity and with my favourite weather outside, I was looking forward to it.

The only thing that would make this better was seeing Giovanni.

He kept his word and phoned me yesterday afternoon after his meetings but I had passed out, exhausted from my recent lack of sleep. When I woke up, it was late at night and he left me a message saying he called Reyna and she told him I was sleeping so he would call me tomorrow. His message made me smile.

When I woke up this morning, I was actually thankful for all the hours of sleep I managed to get in. I had this new refound energy that I couldn't wait to put to work. I turned the lights on and pulled the plastic covers we had over the floor again. We had been painting wall by wall and so everything was already in place to carry on. The last time I was here was the day of the beach party at *Vai Moana*. I placed my bag and umbrella on the counter and went to the back to get the paint. Moments later, I had filled my paint tray with the baby blue we had been using for the walls and placed it on the ground. The previous colour was a faded brown that lacked the comforting feeling we wanted this place to bring. I wanted this place to be a safe haven people could head to when they needed time to themselves with a book and a good cup of coffee. I also wanted it to be a place where people could spend time with a loved one. I wanted it to be warm and welcoming. Barcelona was warm and welcoming to me and I wanted to build on that atmosphere with a place that was entirely mine. I wanted to leave a mark here and remind myself that just because this wasn't part of my original life plan doesn't mean that my life would be any less successful. Working on creating our shop really gave me a sense of purpose that I so desperately needed. I had changed into an old shirt that I had left in the back, so I was ready. I reached for the roller and dipped it in the paint. I brought the roller against the wall and I was off.

After an hour or so, I finished the paint in the tray and headed to the back to refill it. I placed the tray on the ground and reached for the big tin of paint and started pouring. I heard the bell from the front door jingle as it does when someone opens it.

"Hello?" I shouted and placed the tin back on the ground.

Who could possibly be here? There was a clear sign on the door that said we were not open and given by the chaos going on in front, surely no one would think otherwise. I peeped my head around the corner and I was surprised to see Giovanni standing there with two coffees in hand.

"There you are!" He exclaimed and strolled over to the counter, placing everything he was holding down.

My eyes lit up. "How did you know where I was?"

"Reyna," he reached for a cup of coffee and held it out to me. "This one is yours. Milk. No sugar."

He remembered. I smiled and took it from him. "Thank you so much."

"I know this is going to be a coffee shop but I didn't know yet if you had anything up and running to make your own and it's cold today so I figured I'd just bring us some."

I sipped on it and the warmth spread through me. The cold draft he brought with him from opening the door still lingered but I was thankful for the coffee that was now warming me up again. He ran his fingers through his wet hair and pulled off the navy jacket that he was wearing that was soaked from the rain. He wore a tight white long sleeve shirt underneath paired with a pair of dark jeans. The shirt sat so well on him. I didn't know if he wore these kinds of shirts on purpose to show off his build but I was happy with the view. His clothes were way too nice to be hanging around wet paint though.

"You guessed correctly. There's still so much to be done including moving all the equipment back in. So what are you doing here?" I asked, casually.

I was so happy to see him but I had to remind myself to remain calm and collected about this situation. We were being casual and taking it slow so I didn't want to come across as too eager.

"Do you not want me here, Isabella?" He pretended to be offended.

I giggled. "Of course I do but you certainly don't look like you came to help me paint."

"That's exactly why I am here actually. I thought you could use the company and I could show off my underrated painting skills."

"Your painting skills?" I laughed and rolled my eyes. "I am happy that you are here though. I'm sorry I missed your call yesterday."

He stepped closer to me and tucked a stray strand of hair behind my ear, "Don't sweat it. You needed the rest."

He leaned down and kissed me. *So this was how we were going to greet each other from now on?* I could definitely get on board with that. He smiled at me and reached for his coffee. I watched him scan the place.

"It's coming together nicely," he gestured to the already painted walls. "I like that colour."

"Me too. It took a while for Reyna and I to agree on a colour but this one works. There is still so much to be done but it's starting to slowly come together."

The last thing I expected today was for Giovanni to pop in. Just having him here brightened my day.

"What?" he smirked, catching me staring at him.

"Nothing. Just glad you're here."

"Well, you said we needed to get to know each other better so that's what we're going to do," he announced. "We're going to paint and we're going to talk."

"You cannot paint in a white shirt and those jeans," I commented. "You didn't come prepared for this."

He snickered. "It's just clothing Isabella."

He scanned the area with a confused look on his face.

"Are you looking for something?"

"Where's your paint?"

I chuckled and pointed to the back. "I was refilling the tray when you came in."

He nodded and escaped to the back. I was smiling from ear to ear. He had such a care-free spirit to him again and I was engrossed in his energy. Don't get me wrong, I loved sexy, bad-boy Giovanni but I was definitely captured by this other side to him. A few minutes later he came back into the room, tray of paint in hand. He placed it down and I leaned against the counter, enjoying the show. He reached for the roller and brought it to the wall, starting to roll on the paint.

"Please tell me you don't do this in silence," he mused.

"I usually have earphones in but I suppose that would be rude now wouldn't it?" I joked, finishing the last of my coffee.

I tossed the empty cup into the trash can and went to join him. I pulled my phone from my back pocket to find a playlist.

"What kind of music do you want to listen to?"

"Surprise me," he replied. "And no pressure but it better be good cause I don't know if I could be with someone with poor taste in music."

Be with someone? How was this the same man who Reyna said wasn't looking for a relationship? He was so open and casual about where our relationship was headed that it made me feel all giddy inside. I felt like a child.

"Well, I don't know if I could be with someone with such poor painting skills," I mocked pointing at an area on the wall that he missed.

He turned to me. "Does it look like I'm finished yet?"

I giggled.

"Where's your paintbrush, *mi hermosa*?" he mused and gestured to the other roller on the floor. "You're not going to stand and watch me the whole time."

"Oh, but it's such a nice view," I flirted, biting down on my lip to hide my smile.

He chuckled and turned back, concentrating on his painting skills. I decided on a reggaeton music playlist and placed my phone on the chair behind me. I picked up the other roller and dipped it in the paint. The beautiful guitar of *Bota Fuego by Mau y Ricky* filled the room immediately making me sway to the music.

"You're lucky I already approve of your music choices," he mused. "So you like reggaeton music I take it?"

"I love it. I may not understand what they're singing about but I am obsessed with it,"

He laughed, "I take it you don't speak any Spanish then?"

I shook my head. *"Un poco."*

He smirked.

"I've started to pick up on it since moving here. I definitely want to learn properly though."

"I'll teach you," he said as he peeped at me from the corner of his eye. "Repeat after me - *puta madre.*"

I burst out laughing, knowing exactly what that meant. "I'm aware of the bad words, Giovanni."

"Then what more do you need to know?" he chuckled."You're

obviously not Spanish then?"

I shook my head, "Mom's Portuguese. Dad's British."

"And you don't speak Portuguese?"

"Nope," I brought my roller down to get more paint. "I grew up in a very English household away from my mom's side of the family. She had an older sister but we never saw her or my grandparents - they've always had an estranged relationship."

He nodded along as I spoke.

"I hardly remember my grandparents. When my sister and I asked why we didn't see them, my father explained that my aunt fell pregnant way too young and my grandmother ended up kicking her out,"

"Oh shit."

"Things pretty much went downhill from there. There's a lot more to that story but I think a lot of what happened made my mother the way she is now. She's always been closed off. I don't even recall my parents being very sentimental or loving in any way. Don't know how else to explain it but my family has always been very cold. I started to really notice it when I became friends with Reyna - her family has always been so loving and open. I wanted that."

"You are the furthest thing from cold."

"Hence the reason I felt like a complete outsider growing up."

"I'm sorry about that."

I shrugged, "Don't be."

He turned and dipped the roller back in the tray. He lifted it and brought it back down on the wall, finishing off the spot he missed. We were side by side now in perfect rhythm with our painting.

"And you?" I asked, changing the subject, "Are both your parents Spanish?" He nodded, "Yeah, they were both born and raised in Madrid. I lived there until I was about eight before we moved to Barcelona for my dad's work."

"What does your dad do?"

I remembered Reyna mentioned something once about his dad

being in construction but the details escaped me.

"He owns a construction business. *Velázquez Constructora.* 'Velázquez' as in our surname. He started that business back in the day and built it up nicely for himself."

"So, how did you come to own a club?"

I wanted to know him better. He didn't seem to be heading out anytime soon and this was the perfect opportunity for us to share the basic information about ourselves that we completely skipped past. Our relationship started off pretty unconventional so now we were working our way back.

"That's a fun story," he said as he smirked. "My dad got tired of my brother and I always going out, going drinking and he'd just finished the construction of the building where Mala Mía is now. He gave it to us and told us to make something of ourselves 'cause he was tired of us living off his money so we started our own club."

"So the going out and drinking didn't stop then? You just did it in your own place." I chuckled.

"Precisely," he mused. "I'll admit that Alvaro and I were a lost cause for a while and thinking back, we were pretty spoiled but Mala Mía helped us get our shit together and we're not like that anymore. In the beginning, it seemed like our dad gave us the place but when he asked for the first month of rent, we had to grow up quickly and make it work. It's not as easy as it looks to run a club."

"Of course. Any business has its challenges so I can imagine that this was no different. What does your father think of it?"

"He wasn't happy at all when we told him what we were doing with the place but we did it anyway. He's not the type to give praise or acknowledgment so when he doesn't make any comments, then we're at least in the clear."

There was a different energy to him when he spoke about his dad. I could sense the underlying hostility in his voice and remembered what he said about them not being close so I knew there was something more to the situation. I wanted to know more but I didn't want to overstep. If he wanted to tell me, he would.

"You mentioned you had a sister right?" He changed the subject back to my family.

"Yeah, an older sister. Camila."

Camila and I were six years apart and the complete opposite of each other in every way except our looks. We managed to have enough similarities for people to often ask us if we were twins. The main difference now between us was her recent decision to cut her hair to shoulder length while I continued to grow mine out. The age difference between us had always felt quite significant and there were very few times in my life that I felt like we actually got along. I often felt like my arrival into the world probably surprised my parents because I never understood why there were so many years between Camila and me.

"And where does Camila live?"

"In London. She got married a few years back and works for the newspaper that my parents own."

Camila and Smith had only been married for a few years but had been together since she was in University. It was convenient for her when she met Smith since he was the perfect candidate for the role of her boyfriend. They were both studying English literature and Smith's family ran another one of the successful publishing houses in London. "Olympic Publishers" had been around for years and was started by Smith's great-grandfather. It was eerie how many similarities his family had to ours but apparently, that made their relationship work. My parents were over the moon by her choice and her nuptials only put more pressure on me to follow in her footsteps. I often reminded my parents of how long it took Camila to actually get married but they didn't care about that. If I could get that out of the way early enough then I could have more time to focus on my work - that was what they believed anyway.

"They own a newspaper?" he repeated. "Which one?"

"The London Herald."

He stopped painting and looked at me, clearly recognizing the name. "Isn't that quite a big one in London?"

I nodded slowly. My parent's newspaper was one of the biggest in London and there was no doubt that they were running a successful business. Their taste for success was what drove them to ensure that Camila and I did the same. They wanted us to all eventually work for the paper and make it a true family business. Back then I welcomed the idea but now I was reluctant to ever head back to London. My mother was already overbearing as a parent, I couldn't imagine what she'd be like as a boss.

"That's pretty impressive," he commented and continued. "Did you use to work for them when you were in London?"

"No. The plan was to end up working there but I used to work at a publishing house called Oak Tree Publishing before coming here."

"Sounds boring."

I sighed, "It was not boring. I actually really enjoyed my job."

"So why'd you leave it?" He eyed me. "Was it 'cause of Nathan?"

"Nate," I corrected him. "And I guess he did play a role in me leaving but someone else got a promotion over me the very next day after I got dumped and so I was pretty much done with everything in London."

He reached the end of his side of the wall and placed the roller down. I completed my side and turned to place the roller down but didn't notice that I ended up flicking paint straight onto his white shirt in the process.

"Now you've done it." Giovanni yelled playfully.

I turned back to him and there were blue paint drops all over his shirt.

"Oh no!" I exclaimed, reaching for him, "I am so so sorry."

He looked down at his shirt and laughed. That shirt was definitely ruined now.

"See this is exactly why you should be wearing old clothes," I walked over to him and examined my paint stains. "I really am sorry though."

"It's okay, it's just a shirt."

"Yeah but it was a really nice one."

I needed to at least try and get the stains out. I felt too bad about ruining it.

"Let me see if I can wash it out." I gestured to his shirt. "Come on, take it off."

"You just want to see me without my shirt," he teased, cocking an eyebrow.

I rolled my eyes playfully. "Don't flatter yourself."

He smirked and pulled the shirt over his head handing it to me. He was right. Shirtless Giovanni was one of my favourite sights and I couldn't even hide it. I was standing close to him and I couldn't help but reach out for him. I ran my fingers over the tattoo on his chest. It was a side view of a roaring lion. It was so beautiful and detailed - whoever his tattoo artist was, they did an amazing job on this. I flicked my eyes up to his and he was already looking down at me. I looked back down, taking in the artwork on his body. I ran my fingers across his chest to his shoulder. He had a huge owl over the whole top of his arm. I was mesmerized by all of it. It was so precise and the detail was unbelievable. He had tattoos all the way down his arm until his hand. I ran my fingers down his arms, soaking in the details. He didn't stop me. He just watched me intently as I soaked him in. Being this close, touching him was creating a series of lascivious thoughts that I couldn't control. I didn't notice the cold air anymore because the heat between us was enough to keep us warm.

"Do you like what you see?" he murmured.

"Mm-hmm," I said as I bit my lip. "Do you like it when I touch you like this?"

"I love it." He breathed.

We made eye contact and the tension between us started to push its way to the surface. I ran my fingers down his chest and over his abs. They were so defined and I just wanted to kiss every inch of him. My breathing picked up and I had to remind myself that we weren't at home and I couldn't just give into my deepest desires.

"As much as I would love to take you right here, we should probably wait till we're in a more private place," he murmured.

He was right. The large windows peering out onto the street didn't allow for enough privacy for us to do something like that. As much as my desire was fighting through, I managed to get a hold of it and calmed myself down.

"You're right." I sighed.

He pulled me closer to him and his thumb caressed my cheek. There was a deep desire in his eyes and I knew it was taking every inch of self-control for him to stop this from happening right now.

"Let's finish this last wall so we can get out of here," he said and leaned down to kiss me.

I pulled away reluctantly from him and agreed. I took his shirt to the back and tried to wash the stains out but I was unsuccessful. It needed a proper soak at this point.

We went back to our routine of refilling the paint and finishing the last wall we had left to complete. I spent most of the time stealing looks at him and his half-naked body. He could've kept his shirt on because as much as I tried to wash the paint off, it was a lost cause but I wasn't about to complain about the view. I was thankful for the heaters keeping him warm. It was surreal to see him here doing something as mundane as helping me paint my walls.

It was drilled into my head that Giovanni was not the relationship type and never would be and yet, here we were. While there were no official labels for what was happening between us, there was no stopping us from acting like a couple. A part of me was excited at the prospect of a new relationship but the other part of me was terrified.

The way he made me feel actually terrified me - he had so much control over me, even though it was completely unintentional on his part. He didn't fight to have control of me, I just couldn't control how intense my feelings were for him. Physical and otherwise. I had yet to address my feelings head-on and I was just focused on taking what was happening between us step by step.

All I knew was that I wanted to be around him and I would take every opportunity I could to get to know him more. I wanted to know his likes, dislikes, pet peeves, favourite food, favourite movie - I wanted to know it all. The music coming from my phone suddenly stopped.

"And now?" Giovanni asked.

I strolled over to my phone. "Battery. When I fell asleep yesterday I forgot to charge it."

"Grab mine." He gestured to his big jacket on the counter while he carried on with the last wall.

I strolled over and slipped it out of his jacket pocket. I swiped my finger across it and it required a password. I turned to him and asked, "Password?"

"0-5-0-5."

I typed it in and the screen welcomed me. "Is there any significance to those numbers?"

"My birthday."

I made a mental note of that.

"So we're that close now huh? Look at you giving me your password," I joked.

"I have nothing to hide."

I smiled to myself and found his music app. I played the last song on his playlist and the slow reggaeton beat blared through his speaker. Giovanni started to sway to the music and it reminded me of that first night when we danced at Mala Mía. I already knew he could dance and it was hot.

"Now, this is a good song," he said as he placed his roller down on the floor, turned to me and extended his hand.

"Come dance."

"Oh no," I answered quickly. "I don't know how to dance."

He scoffed. "Oh please, I remember how you danced the first night we met."

I blushed. The alcohol in my system really assisted me that night and gave me the confidence to move my body in a way I'd never done before. Now that I was stone-cold sober, I was too shy to try that again.

"The alcohol gave me those moves."

He stepped closer to me and grabbed my hand, pulling me to an open spot away from the paint.

"Just follow my lead," he murmured.

He pulled me close to him and I felt his body against mine. His hand slid down my back and rested on my waist while his other hand held mine. He started to move to the music - swaying side to side. My body followed his and I was surprised at how perfectly we fit together. I followed his rhythm and he knew exactly how to move to the music. He moved his fingers across the small of my back and I was overly aware of his touch. It burned through my shirt and I couldn't help but bite my lip. *Was he doing this on purpose?* How could I possibly control myself when he was making my body feel this way? I slowly lifted my head to meet his eyes and we were inches from each other. I slid my hand around his neck, running my fingers through his hair. He closed his eyes and I knew he was enjoying my touch. I slowly scratched the back of his neck with my nails and he pulled me closer to him. I could feel him come alive beneath me. Our eyes met and we were both thinking the same thing.

"Forget the rest of the wall," I murmured.

He brought his lips down to meet mine. They were soft and the coffee on his breath still lingered. I flicked my tongue across his. I needed him. I had done so well up until now controlling myself but it was too late. He nipped at my lower lip and my hands found his hair again. He ran his hands down my body and lifted me up, my legs instinctively wrapping around his waist. Suddenly the problem of being in a public place didn't matter to me - I needed him. He placed me down on my counter, never breaking the kiss. My legs tightened around him, pulling him closer to me. I nipped at his bottom lip softly and he groaned.

"You're killing me." He breathed.

I ran my fingers down his body. He was so hot and his body was enough to drive me crazy. His lips moved to my ear sending goosebumps all over my body. He nibbled at my ear and I couldn't control the moans that escaped my lips. That was such a sensitive spot for me and he knew it. He knew exactly what to do to drive me crazy. Just as I reached for the button on his jeans a massive boom of thunder rippled through the sky, giving us both such a fright that we immediately stopped what we were doing. We both looked at each other and burst out laughing.

"Holy shit." I breathed.

"Talk about a mood kill." Giovanni laughed.

Maybe it was a good thing that the thunder interrupted us because I was just about ready to have sex with him on this counter.

"Maybe we should get out of here?" I suggested.

"That's a great idea." He leaned down and kissed me, my arousal still lingering.

Giovanni took the tray of paint to the back and made sure that the tins were all closed properly. The last thing I needed was for anything to spill over. I cleared the rest of the area and folded up the plastic into the same corner I had it in. The wall wasn't finished but there was no way we were going to get that done today. We had been here for a few hours but all I cared about now was Giovanni. He pulled his ruined white shirt back on and slid his big jacket over it, hiding the stains. I quickly went to the back and changed back into my oversized grey jersey I originally had on. My scarf and jacket were hanging by the front door. I grabbed my bag and strolled over to put my jacket on.

"How did you get here?" I turned to Giovanni who was ready to go now.

He held up a pair of car keys. "And you? Did you walk?"

I nodded. "It wasn't too bad. I missed the rain."

"Well, aren't you lucky that I'm here to make sure you don't get wet," he mused. "Wet because of the rain I mean. I still have other plans for you."

I gasped. "You can't say things like that."

"Oh, please," he said as he leaned into my ear. "You love it."

Yes, I did.

He was so brazen about these things and I was surprised at how much I loved it. By the time we closed up and stepped outside, the rain had been reduced to a light drizzle but the thunder still roared across the sky. The clouds were still dark and there was definitely another storm on its way. I opened my umbrella for us to share.

"Where did you park?"

"Just down the road." He grabbed the umbrella from me and gestured for me to scoot closer to him. I slipped my hand around his arm as we turned and strolled down the street. I was thankful for my decision to wear boots today because they were protecting me from the river of water on the streets. Giovanni pointed out his car in the distance but as we were slowly approaching it, a well-dressed older man stepped out of one of the shops and stopped us in our tracks. He was much older but quite attractive for his age. He had dark brown hair with flickers of grey spread throughout. His face held his age through his wrinkles and I guessed he must have been in his late 50's. He was immaculately dressed in a well-fitted navy suit and I was impressed by his style. I noticed his deep brown eyes had a familiarity to them.

"*Papá,*" Giovanni said from beside me. "*¿Qué haces aquí?*"

Papá? That's why he seemed so familiar. He reminded me of

Giovanni. I suddenly noticed the similarities between the two of them along with the sudden change in Giovanni's demeanor. His father scanned his eyes over me and then back to Giovanni.

"I was just making a purchase. Needed a new suit for a benefit I'm attending," he replied, his tone more formal than you'd expect between a father and a son.

He flicked his eyes back over to me, "*¿Quien es está?* The new flavour of the day?"

I was thrown off by his comment. I wasn't sure how to respond to that so I just stood there. I looked to Giovanni for help but he was glaring at his father.

"This is Isabella," he seethed. "And please do not refer to her like that."

His tone suddenly became just as formal as his fathers but he couldn't hide his frustration.

"I just can't keep up with this one," his father said as he shrugged and extended his hand to mine. "*Hola,* Isabella. I'm Cecilio."

I took his hand and shook it. "*Hola,* Nice to meet you *señor*."

I was uncomfortable. The animosity between these two men surrounded us and I wasn't sure I wanted to be in the middle of it. His father clearly had no tact given by his tasteless comment towards me. I knew that Giovanni had a reputation but his father seemed to want to remind him of that.

"I should be going." Cecilio reached for his car keys and pulled it out of his pocket. "*llama a tu madre*, Giovanni. She's been trying to get a hold of you."

And with that, he was off. I turned to Giovanni and a flicker of anger spread across his face. I squeezed his arm in an attempt to remind him that I was here for him.

"Let's go," I said calmly. He was angry now and as much as I wanted to know the real reason behind his broken relationship with his father, now was not the time.

Giovanni turned to me and the look on his face softened. "I'm sorry about him."

I reached up and caressed his cheek, needing to reassure him, "It's okay. We don't have to talk about that. Let's just get out of here before it starts raining again."

He leaned down and kissed my forehead before leading me to his car. He stopped in front of a stunning black Audi R8.

"No way," I gasped. "There is no way this is your car."

He chuckled and unlocked the car to prove to me that it was his. I was shocked. This was a sexy car but also crazy expensive. I clearly underestimated how well-off he was. He left me with the umbrella and went over to the driver's side.

"Get in," he gestured.

I closed my umbrella and reached for the door handle. I slipped inside and closed it behind me. His car smelled just like his cologne mixed with the leather from the seats. The interior was lined with red and I had to admit that this car suited him perfectly.

"This is a great car," I commented. "How long have you had it?"

He started the car and the engine roared to life. I pulled my seatbelt across me and secured it. He pulled out of his parking and we were off.

"Almost a year. This is my most prized possession."

"I can see why."

He turned the radio on and it automatically connected to his cell phone. The same song we were listening to back at the shop came on and I smiled at the new memory I now had. Having him close to me while we moved to the music together will forever be ingrained in my mind. His energy was contagious. He was so carefree and spontaneous. I was so drawn to him - everything I was learning about him was pulling me in emotionally, deeper and deeper. The whole ride back to his apartment I stole looks at him from the corner of my eye. *How was he so attractive?* He still looked tense though, the animosity from our earlier interaction with his father still lingered. He was so deep in thought. He was seriously bothered by his father and I could see he was holding onto that tension. Even in his tense state, I couldn't get enough of looking at him. His facial hair was my favourite - it made him look so sexy and I wondered how I ever found anyone clean-shaven attractive before. We sat in comfortable silence, our fingers interlocked all the way back and I welcomed it.

CHAPTER 18:

It took about fifteen minutes to get back to Giovanni's place. He parked in the basement parking lot and we took the elevator up to his apartment. The doors opened and I was welcomed back to his home. It was warm inside and the cold breeze from outside quickly disappeared. The curtains in his living room were open and I watched the storm release itself to the world. I found it oddly calming to watch. The raindrops beat down against the buildings, washing away the unnecessary residue of the day. The lightning scattered across the sky, waiting for the opportune moment to light it up from behind the dark clouds. Giovanni strolled into the kitchen and brought the kettle to boil. I placed my handbag down on his kitchen counter and slipped my big jacket off. He disappeared upstairs and returned shortly after that with a new shirt on.

"I'm sorry again about your shirt." I lifted myself onto the barstool by his kitchen counter. He grabbed two cups from the cupboard above his stove and placed them next to the kettle. "Please don't worry about that. It's just a shirt."

I could tell he was still holding onto the tension that came from the interaction with his father. That was definitely not the way I wanted to meet a member of his family but I didn't expect the relationship between the two of them to be so strained. He placed a cup of coffee in front of me and leaned against the counter, looking over at me. He looked like he wanted to say something but he remained silent.

"Giovanni, I want you to know that you can talk to me about

anything." I reached out and grabbed his hand.

He kept his eyes firmly on his cup of coffee and squeezed my hand. I figured that sharing his feelings wasn't something that came easy to him so I was willing to wait until he was ready.

"I care about you," I murmured softly. He sighed and his eyes met mine.

"My dad had no right to say that to you," he glowered. "He can be a real asshole."

"It's ok-," I started to say but he interrupted me.

"It's not okay, Isabella," he continued. "You are not the flavour of the day. You are not like any of the others and I don't want you thinking that you are."

I caressed his hand with my thumb. "I don't think that." And that was the truth. I may have felt that before but I trust what we spoke about and I knew that what was happening between us had more to it. I didn't know why I trusted him so much so quickly but I did. His effort in the last 24 hours alone just proved that he felt for me what I was feeling for him. I sipped my coffee and I waited to see if he would say anything more about the situation. The last thing I wanted to do was push him into talking about things if he didn't want to.

"Are you hungry?" he asked.

I was disappointed at his choice to change the subject but I didn't want to push him.

"Starving." I smiled.

***

Hours later we were still sitting by the kitchen counter, this time with empty plates in front of us. Since we had already established that he seriously lacked skills when it came to making food, I ended up making us a delicious Spaghetti Bolognese. I made sure I taught him step by step how to make the meal - he was going to have to learn to cook at some point in his life. I didn't understand how he lived alone without the ability to cook but he assured me that pre-cooked meals were a very big part of keeping him well-fed and he took full advantage of that convenient way of living.

"That was really delicious," he commented. "Where did you learn to cook?"

"My dad actually taught me. He used to love to cook and I spent most of the time in the kitchen with him when I was younger."

"You mentioned that you weren't close with anyone in your family. Has it always been like that?" he asked.

"With my mom and sister, yes. It was a strange dynamic - my mother has always been strict and very formal and my sister seemed to have absorbed her traits. My dad and I had a close relationship when I was growing up but the more successful the newspaper got, the less time he and I had together."

My dad was always a kind man. That was one thing about him that never changed but we drifted apart when he and my mother started to spend more time focusing on the success of their newspaper rather than their family. He was also the quieter parent, always going along with what my mother decided. She was so focused on their business that she never had time to be a mother. She and I never saw eye to eye with each other so I made sure to always keep our communication as brief as possible. It wasn't ideal but over the years I had come to accept that she was the way she was and I couldn't change that. I tried to bond with her but it was impossible.

"They still think you're in Madrid, right?"

"To be honest, I don't know what they know and I don't care anymore. After everything that happened - getting dumped, losing my job, moving here - I didn't exactly want to keep in touch with them."

"You know they're going to find out one day, right?" He glanced over at me. "How do they not know already? Surely they can tell through speaking to yo-..."

I interrupted him. "I hardly speak to them. I had a bad fallout with my mother after the whole 'quitting my job' thing so she keeps me at arm's length. She wants me to suffer by not having their help. She thinks she's punishing me by forcing me to do things by myself but it was what I wanted the whole time anyways."

I was thankful for our decision to replace our coffee with wine as I brought my wine glass to my lips. I thought back to that last conversation with my mother...

The next few hours were a blur. I still hadn't quite absorbed what happened between Nate and I but that wasn't the most recent issue I had to deal with. I was ashamed of how I acted in the boardroom today but I couldn't help it. I couldn't control all the emotions that flooded through me. It was the last straw. I quickly went back to the hotel to grab my stuff and check out. I managed to book the last flight to Barcelona and now I was sitting at the airport waiting for Reyna to fetch me. The last 24 hours had changed every part of my life and I didn't know how to even begin dealing with it. My phone started to vibrate again and I glanced down to see my mother's name on the screen. I sighed. I couldn't avoid her anymore. She had been trying to call me since I got on the plane and I knew she was going to give me an earful now.

I took a deep breath in and answered, "Hello?"

"Isabella Avery, where the hell have you been?" My mother shouted from the other end. "You have so much explaining to do young lady. We got an upsetting phone call from Nigel earlier today. He said you quit and stormed out of the office and..."

Stormed out? That was a bit dramatic.

"I didn't sto-," I started to say but she cut me off.

"You better get yourself home right now. You have created such a big problem and we need to fi-,"

This time I cut her off. "I can't come home."

"What do you mean you can't come home? Where the hell are you?"

"I'm in Barcelona."

She shrieked. "Barcelona?!?"

I heard murmurs from the other end, probably from my sister who was listening to everything we were saying. I was so numb at this point, I couldn't really comprehend anything that was being said and I really didn't care.

"Isabella, what the hell have you done to your life? You're in Barcelona? Why are you in Barcelona? You and Nate were supposed to leave at the end of the week and weren't you going to Madrid?"

"Mom, please stop," I snapped. "Look, Reyna had a family emergency and she asked me to come here."

I was lying but I needed some kind of story to get her off my back for now.

"I don't care who has an emergency," she shouted. "You quit your job! Why the hell would you do that? Do you have any idea how hard we worked to get you that job in the first place?"

"I didn't ask you to do that."

"You didn't ask? How ungrateful," she snapped. "We've always done everything we could to give you the best life and this is how you repay us? By humiliating us?"

I hung my head in my hands. She was driving me fucking crazy right now and I was on the brink of a collapse.

"Where is Nate? How could he let you run off like this?"

My heart tightened. I couldn't tell them what happened with Nate, especially not right now. I felt sick enough already.

"I'm going to meet him in Madrid. I told you, Reyna had a family emergency and you kn-..."

She cut me off again, "I don't care about Reyna's family

emergency. I care about my daughter not throwing away everything in her life. We've worked so hard-..."

"*I never wanted this!*" I shouted. "*You always forced all this fucking shit on me and I didn't want it!*"

"*Don't you dare speak to me like that!*" She spat. "*Who the hell do you think you are?*"

"*I'm sick and tired of you dictating my life. It's enough now.*"

"*You ungrateful little brat! If this is what you want then fine, good luck trying to make something of your life without us. You've already disappointed us enough.*"

And with that, I disconnected the line. I had nothing left to say to her.

That phone call destroyed whatever was left of my relationship with my mother. The lingering anger I had towards her was still there but I worked really hard to shove it into a box in my mind that I didn't have to deal with.

"I pretty much told her to stay out of my life so she has. This is the least involved she's ever been and I'm sure it's driving her mad," I said as I shrugged and sipped my wine again. "I cut off everything from my previous life - my social media, no communication with past friends, nothing. The less interaction I had with people from my parent's society, the better."

"And how do you know Nate wouldn't say anything to them?"

"He wouldn't," I answered quickly. "He knew how overbearing they've been and he wouldn't want to deal with them anyway. My mother also hated his mother for some reason so it's not like our families were close. The chances of them crossing paths were low, it was only when Nate and I needed to get them together and that wasn't going to happen anymore."

A part of me resented them for embedding this idea of a perfect life in my head. The idea that if I didn't follow what they wanted, I wouldn't be happy or successful was just their own propaganda. Here I was living my own life without restrictions and I have never been happier. It wasn't the life I thought I would have but at least it was mine.

"You're going to have to tell them," Giovanni repeated as he sipped on his wine.

"I know but that's not today's problem." I reached for the plates and started to clear up the dishes.

"What if I wanted to meet them?" Giovanni asked.

"Trust me, you don't."

He didn't push the subject any further and instead, he hopped off the barstool to help me clear everything and load it into the dishwasher. It was strange to be this comfortable with him and yet, I was. We moved as if it was our everyday routine, as if we had been doing this for years.

"How long have you lived in this apartment?" I asked, as I walked over to his couch and made myself comfortable.

"About two and a half years now."

"It's a really great apartment."

"Yeah, it was convenient when we opened up the club to turn this into an apartment. Alvaro was already looking at houses with his wife so this worked out perfectly for me."

He came to join me on the couch with a small tub of ice-cream and two spoons in hand. I smiled and took a spoon from him.

"I hope you like chocolate ice-cream," he murmured and scooted closer to me.

"Who doesn't like chocolate ice-cream?" I chuckled and draped my legs across his. It was still storming outside and I was comfortably cuddling up to a beautiful man in his beautiful apartment. I couldn't believe the genuine calmness I felt around him. It took a while after the run in with his dad, but eventually Giovanni let go of the tension he was holding onto. I never brought it up again and care-free Giovanni was back. He popped the lid off of the ice-cream and I took a spoonful.

"Thank you for helping me paint today," I said in between our spoonfuls of ice-cream.

"You're welcome." He smiled. "It's coming together really nicely."

"Yeah it is," I agreed.

"So, why a coffee shop?" he asked.

"Well, my idea was to have it be both a coffee shop and a bookstore in one. Reyna's always wanted to invest in a small business so she trusted my judgment with the place. I think she felt bad and wanted me to have something to invest my energy in. I've always loved books and I wanted to create a place where people could come and enjoy a good book and hopefully, a really good cup of coffee too."

"I'm not much of a reader so I hope that's not a deal-breaker."

"You should've told me that before. Now I need to reconsider some things..." I nudged him playfully.

He smirked. "Have you guys decided on a name yet?"

"Haven't decided yet but I'm really leaning towards calling it *'Aroma'*."

"*Aroma*," he repeated. "That's a great name." He took another spoonful of ice-cream and passed the tub over to me. I took it from him and continued eating.

"You're the first person I've shared that name with."

"Well, I'm honored to be part of your inner circle," he quipped. I smiled and as I brought another spoonful of ice-cream to my mouth, it dripped right off the spoon and onto my chest.

"Shit!" I exclaimed, wanting to keep it from messing up my shirt. "Please, could you get me something to clean this up with."

"I can help." He took the ice-cream tub and spoon from my hand and placed it down on the table. I wasn't sure what he was doing at first but he pulled me closer to him and leaned closer to my chest. I watched him as he kissed me right where the ice-cream dropped. I let out a soft gasp - not expecting him to be cleaning it up with his tongue. I was aroused by his touch. He licked the ice-cream up and flicked his eyes to mine.

"Is that better?"

I bit my lip. "Much better."

He still had his spoon in his hand and he reached over for the tub again. He took a small spoonful of ice-cream and brought it down against my chest.

"My bad," he mused. It was cold against my skin and I couldn't help the goosebumps that spread across me. I wasn't sure if that was just from the cold or from what he was doing to me. Never taking his eyes off me, he brought his tongue back down on me and licked it up. My body awoke at his touch and I didn't want him to stop.

"Take your shirt off," he demanded.

I happily obliged, pulling the shirt over my head and tossing it across the room. My bra joined it on the floor. The tub of ice-cream and spoon was still in his hand, I knew this was becoming a fun little game. I lay back against the couch and he positioned himself next to me. He filled the spoon and brought it down across my body creating a line of ice-cream from my chest all the way to my belly button. He placed the tub and spoon on his table and brought himself over me, his hands on either side of me. The way he was looking at me was driving me crazy. The desire burned in his eyes and I knew it mirrored my own. The ice-cream was cold against my skin but I was so hot for him that I didn't even care. He brought his lips down on my body, licking me slowly along the path he created on my body. I couldn't control the small moans - they escaped my lips and I tugged a fist full of his hair. This was so hot and the tension inside of me was starting to escalate.

"Giovanni," I breathed.

"Do you like what I'm doing to you, Isabella?"

"Yes." I absolutely loved it but I couldn't form enough words to explain that to him. My body was too caught up in his kisses. He licked up every bit of ice-cream but that didn't stop him. He moved across my body, kissing and sucking softly. I pushed my thighs together in an attempt to control the tension building. I was unsuccessful - my body was ready for him now.

"I want you," I moaned.

The desire in his eyes flared and he brought his hands to the button on my jeans. He kissed me right above my jeans as he opened them and slid my zip down. He pulled my jeans off and my underwear next. I reached for his shirt, tugging at it - I need it off. I needed to feel his body. He reached for it and pulled it over his head. My hands immediately found his body, running them all over him. I just couldn't get enough of him. The curves of his muscles and the ink on his skin - it was so sexy. He brought his lips down to mine and I welcomed him with my tongue. The taste of chocolate ice-cream still lingered and just the memory of him licking it off of me made me pull him closer. I needed to feel him. Every inch of him. He slid his hand down my body and he reached between my legs. Without hesitation, he slipped one finger into me and I gasped against his lips. A second finger followed. He didn't hold back and found the perfect rhythm that had me throwing my head back against the couch. His lips moved to my neck and I had to bite down on my lip to keep the moans from escaping.

"Don't keep quiet, Isabella, I want to hear you."

The moans left my lips and I didn't hold back. I couldn't even control it anymore, everything he was doing was pushing me closer and closer to the edge. My hand found its way through his hair, tugging at it uncontrollably. He was amazing in every way and I couldn't control the overwhelming desire I felt whenever he was around.

"Giovanni, I need you," I breathed urgently.

He pulled himself away from me and my body felt the emptiness. He removed his pants and underwear and reached for a condom from his wallet. I was so ready to have him again. The view I had right now of him and his body against the crazy storm outside was picture perfect. He was everything I needed right now, in this moment, and I was more than ready. I spread my legs for him, inviting him in. He brought his body back down on mine and positioned himself between me. With one swift motion he was inside me and I gasped in pleasure. It was euphoric. His hands dug into the couch on either side of me as I wrapped my legs around his body. I pushed myself closer to him, needing to feel him deeper inside of me. He thrust deeper into me and a few soft gasps escaped his lips. Just the sight of him above me, basking in the pleasure we were both feeling, was pushing me over. He was beautiful. I never really thought that would be an accurate way to describe a man but that's what he was. He was unreal to me. He quickened his pace and I pushed my body against his, moving to his rhythm. He grabbed my arms and placed them over my head, holding them in place. He kept me from touching him which only drove my body more crazy.

"Isabella..." he breathed.

The sound of my name on his lips was beguiling. I tightened around him. It was the most intoxicating sound and I wanted my name to be the only name to leave his lips out of pure pleasure. We savoured each moment as we moved in perfect rhythm together. Deeper and faster he went and I was on the brink of my climax.

"Yes, Giovanni," I moaned. "Don't stop."

He didn't. He continued to push himself deeper inside of me as I tightened around him. I soaked him up - his ability to push me to my climax was unlike anything I had experienced and yet, he managed to do that to me every time. He knew exactly what to do to me - he had mastered my body and it only wanted him. He let go of my arms and I held onto his back, my nails dug deeper into his skin as I welcomed my climax, moaning his name for the world to hear. He joined me shortly after that and dropped against me, both of us breathing heavily and without control. I ran my fingers through his hair and he looked up at me with those big brown eyes that I just couldn't get enough of.

"You're something else, Giovanni," I murmured.

I've said that before but I meant it. I've never known someone like him. If someone had told me months ago that I'd be here with Giovanni, I would never have believed it. I never expected to find him and now that I have, I knew I wasn't going to be able to let him go. I was hooked on him and there was nothing I could do about it. He moved up and laid against the couch while my head found its way to his chest, my legs draped across his body. He slowly ran his fingers through my hair, his breathing starting to slow.

"Will you stay with me tonight?" he asked softly.

I turned to look up at him and ran my finger along his jaw. "Of course."

His arms tightened around me and for the first time in months I felt like I belonged. Right here in Giovanni's arms was where I was meant to be. I was falling.

CHAPTER 19:

Wednesday evening after work I strolled into my apartment and was welcomed by the smell of something delicious brewing in the air.

"Oh my word, that smells amazing!" I shouted and slipped my jacket off, hanging it on our coat rack by the door.

I walked to the kitchen and Reyna stood behind the stove, stirring a hot pot of simmering soup. I breathed it in - the delightful aroma of spices filling the air.

"I'm making my famous tomato soup," she announced proudly. She turned and reached for one of the spices next to the pot and tossed some in. She had an apron on and her thick hair was pulled into an untidy bun.

"You look like the perfect housewife right now."

She chuckled. "Don't get used to this."

I smiled and brought myself onto the barstool in front of her. She already had a bottle of white wine and two glasses laid out on the counter so I reached for the bottle and filled our glasses.

"How have you been?" she asked. "I feel like I haven't seen you."

She was right. We kept missing each other these last few days. I spent the rest of Monday and Tuesday with Giovanni and by the time I got back this morning to get ready for work, she had already left. Between her seeing Diego and me having shifts at the restaurant, we didn't see each other as often.

"I've been good," I admitted. "What about you? Are you excited to be going home tomorrow?"

She nodded and reached for her glass. "Oh yes. I can't wait! I love living in Barcelona but you know how much I miss my parents."

For as long as I have known Reyna, her family has always been close. Her parents were the most loving people you could ever meet. They were always so warm and welcoming and they made you feel like you were part of their family. I went to Madrid with Reyna during my first few weeks here and the energy of the Cazarez family helped a lot with this crazy life transition I was going through. They loved their hometown too much to move to Barcelona where Reyna and Katrina lived, but birthdays and special holidays were always very important to them.

"They're going to be so happy to see you. Have you told them about Diego?"

"Not yet. I wasn't sure if I wanted to at first but now I know I have to."

Her eyes lit up as she spoke about him and she couldn't contain the smile that spread across her face. I had never seen Reyna like this with a man. She was always so calm and collected about these sorts of things but Diego had her hooked.

"Look at you," I teased. "Diego is a great guy. I really think your parents will like him."

"Oh, I know they'll love him! I'll probably take him to meet them next time around."

"So things are getting pretty serious then?" I sipped on my wine.

She blushed, "Yeah they are. I didn't think this would happen but he's just amazing and for the first time in my life I can actually see a future with someone."

I was so happy for her. Reyna was the best person I'd ever known and I'd always wanted her to find someone that would make her happy. It was what she deserved. She had always been hard-headed and independent but now she finally found someone that was not intimidated by that. Too many guys ran away from what made her, her. She didn't mean to be overpowering, she was just very clear about what she wanted. I never understood the intimidation in the first place and thankfully, Diego wasn't threatened by it either.

I reached for her hand and squeezed it. "You deserve this. You deserve to be happy."

"Thanks, Izzy. I'm so glad that you're here." She smiled. I was happy to be living here and it was all thanks to her. She allowed me the escape I was so desperately seeking and the pieces of my life had started to fall back into place.

"Me too, Rey."

She stirred the pot again and filled the spoon with just enough to taste. She brought it to her lips, "That is good if I do say so myself."

I reached for her spoon and repeated her action. I brought the soup to my lips. The tangy tomato and basil was the perfect combination and my stomach rumbled at the taste.

"This is amazing." I stole another quick spoon before she tapped my hand away.

"Save some for dinner," she mused.

She moved the pot off the stove and allowed it to simmer. She pulled herself a barstool and pushed herself onto it, now seated in front of me. We continued to sip on our wine.

"So, are you not going to update me on you and Giovanni? Last I knew you were angry at him for bringing Casey but then he called me trying to get a hold of you so I figured there must have been some sort of progress."

"He actually came banging on our door at two in the morning after the whole Casey thing."

"Two in the morning?" She repeated, shocked. "I'm guessing he was drunk."

"Of course. He said we needed to talk so we did. At first, I didn't even want him here - I actually told him to leave but he told me that

Casey wasn't his date."

Reyna snorted. "That's not what it looked like."

"That's exactly what I said but then he said that he couldn't stop thinking about me but he doesn't know how to handle this 'cause it's all so new to him," I explained.

"I've known Giovanni for a few years now and I have never known him to be in a relationship. He has major commitment issues."

"Why does he have commitment issues?" I asked, curious to know more. "Where does it come from?"

Reyna placed her glass back down and leaned on the counter, "So we're not close so I'm sure there is more to this story but all I know is a couple of years back a story broke in the press about his father having an affair."

I choked on my wine. "What?!"

"Yeah it was a really big scandal," she recalled. "His dad's company was in talks to work on the *La Sagrada Familia* which, you know, is the most popular tourist site here so anything that happened with it, everyone had to know about it. And then the story broke with pictures and everything and apparently that was how his wife found out."

I was shocked. I already got the feeling that Cecilio Velázquez was a difficult man and I already had a small taste of his general disrespect but I did not expect to hear that he was unfaithful to his wife. I felt so bad for Giovanni's mother - to find out something like that in the press must have been awful.

"No wonder he has such a problem with his dad." It gave me a better insight into the very clear animosity between Giovanni and Cecilio. That could be the kind of action that would cause a child to harbor the kind of anger that Giovanni had. Especially if he was closer to his mother.

"Yeah, I heard he even physically retaliated towards his dad," she explained. "I don't know the exact details but that could probably be a reason why he avoids relationships."

I couldn't blame him. A situation like that could leave some underlying issues. I would have liked to find out from him but I was glad that I was aware now - it made me understand him a bit better.

She shrugged. "I'm sure there is more to it though but you must know that I have never known him to make the kind of effort he's made for you."

I smiled. I was surprised by his appearance at the coffee shop and the way he made an effort with me. I could notice it too.

"Look at that smile!" Reyna teased. "You are so smitten with him." I could feel the heat spread across my cheeks. It was impossible to deny that I had feelings for Giovanni. They were as clear as day.

"I can't help it," I admitted. "He's amazing."

"Well, I am rooting for the two of you. I just hope he keeps his shit together because you don't deserve any more hurt in your life."

She downed the rest of her wine and got off the chair. She got two bowls out for us and placed them on the counter. She grabbed a brown paper packet from the bread bin and pulled a loaf out.

"This is going to be great with the soup," she said and started cutting it into slices before going back to our previous conversation. "So, where do the two of you stand now?"

"I don't know to be honest. We're just getting to know each other better but I'd be lying to you if I said I wasn't already feeling something more for him. I didn't want to, I really didn't, but I can't seem to stop it."

"I think it's great that you guys are getting to know each other but I hope he's not still seeing someone else."

"He's not," I answered quickly.

"I'm on your side, Izzy, I want you two to work out because honestly, he could use someone like you in his life and I can already see the way he excites yours. I'm just being a friend and wanting you to be careful."

I understood where she was coming from and as much as the thought of him seeing someone else disappointed me, I really believed that was not the case. I knew now that he felt the same as me but I really didn't want to be blindsided again. I could allow my lingering fear to creep in and take over but I could also choose to trust him and just focus on where things could go.

"I understand. For now, I'm okay with us getting to know each other. I don't want to put pressure on us with labels and all that. I just want him."

"Then you have him," she mused and placed a hot steaming bowl of soup in front of me. "Enjoy!"

I breathed it in. "This is great, thank you."

She placed her own bowl in front of her and sat down on the barstool again. I dipped a piece of bread in my soup and brought it to my mouth. It was amazing. The perfect meal for this colder day that we were experiencing. Autumn went from breezy to freezing very quickly and we were going to have to break out our full winter clothing pretty soon, but for now, we had our soup to keep us warm.

"When are you coming back again?" I asked her.

"Next week, Friday. I actually forgot to let you know that I extended my trip a bit longer. Are you going to be okay here by yourself?"

I reached for the wine and filled our glasses up again, "I'm a big girl, I'll be fine. Plus I already have plans with Giovanni so I am sure I'll be with him for most of the week anyway."

She nodded. "Okay, that's good. You seem really happy, Izzy and I am so glad about that."

Here we sat on this cold autumn day eating a bowl of delicious soup and talking about our romantic lives. My life was nowhere close to what I expected it to be and I was actually so glad about that. I wanted a simple life. I wanted a happy one.

"I am happy."

And I truly meant that.

CHAPTER 20:

"I'll see you next week," I said to my manager as I clocked out of my shift. I had been working the morning shift today, it was late afternoon now and I was thankful I still had the rest of my Saturday evening to myself. It was starting to get colder and I was noticing a change in people's habits. Less people were making their way to the restaurant and I spent a lot of my time at the back clearing out some old cutlery.

I pulled my coat closer to me and swung my bag over my shoulder as I pushed through the front doors. I was welcomed by the lingering heat from the sun peeking from behind the clouds. I dropped my head back, allowing myself to soak it in for a moment. It was nice to take in the little heat that we had left before becoming consumed by winter entirely. I brought my head forward again, my gaze locking with his.

"Giovanni?" I blurted.

There he was, casually leaning against his car with his hands in his pockets. My breath caught in my throat at the sight of him. He was dressed in all black except for the emerald green jersey he was sporting underneath his leather jacket. I loved him in emerald - that colour complemented his olive skin tone so well. I could stare at him for hours. He smiled a big smile and I couldn't help but mirror his happiness.

"What are you doing here?" I skipped up to him and wrapped my arms around his neck as he instinctively wrapped his around my waist.

"Hello baby," he chuckled. "I came to steal you away."

I was so happy to see him. We had been texting back and forth but

I wasn't expecting to see him today at all. Reyna and Katrina left on Thursday and I'd been swamped with shifts at the restaurant. He had been stuck in meetings all week with his team for the expansion of Mala Mía. I was convinced I was going to have a day of binge-watching something mind-numbing on Netflix but now here he was.

"Steal me away?" I cocked an eyebrow and leaned into him. "I thought you were stuck in meetings all weekend?"

"Change of plans. You and I are going out."

Going out? A glimmer of excitement simmered from within. His spontaneous nature excited me - there was always something unexpected to look forward to with him.

"And where are we going?"

"It's a surprise."

I pouted. "You may not know it yet, but I hate surprises."

"You'll love this one."

He leaned down and his lips met mine. He smelled of body wash and his strong cologne, all mixed with his natural scent to form the smell I loved so much. I cupped his face with my hand and pulled away to meet his eyes.

"You ready?" he asked, a boyish grin spread across his face.

"I don't know," I chuckled. "Do I look okay? You're giving me no indication of where we're going."

"You look perfect," he said as he leaned down and kissed my hair. "It's nothing fancy."

I was intrigued. He excited me. We broke away from our embrace and he took my bag from me. "Let's get going."

I walked around the car to the passenger seat as he placed my bag in the back. We slipped inside and he pulled his seatbelt across him.

"Have I ever told you I love that colour on you?" I said, allowing myself to take him in again.

"You haven't but it just might be my favourite colour now." He winked. I smiled and fastened my seatbelt as the engine roared to life.

His phone connected automatically and a relaxed reggaeton beat seeped through the speakers. He turned down the street and made his way through the city. I soaked it all in as we turned every corner. There was just something about this place that I couldn't get enough of. He reached his hand over and rested it on my thigh. I laced my fingers with his.

"How did your meetings go?" I asked.

"Pretty good actually. We're waiting for this one building in Valencia to become available. We've been hearing some back and forth from the contractors there but nothing is set in stone yet."

I nodded and slowly rubbed my thumb over his hand, "How soon do you want to open in Valencia?"

"As soon as possible would be ideal. Our investors are itching to start the expansion but there are still so many elements to consider." He relaxed in his seat as we headed down a long road through the city, "And how was your day?"

"It was actually really quiet. Not a lot of people seem to want to leave their houses in the winter."

"Can you blame them? This is still bearable but let me warn you that a Barcelona winter can be unforgiving on some days."

"Good thing I happen to love winter then."

He turned to me, surprised. "Who in their right mind loves winter?"

I laughed. "What do you mean? It's the best."

"Being cold is the best?" he chuckled. "Absolutely not. Summer is the way to go."

I snorted. "So you enjoy being sweaty and uncomfortable? And it being so hot that you can't sleep because you're practically stuck to your bed?"

"I don't think I want to sleep next to you in summer," he teased. "How much do you sweat?"

"A normal amount," I chuckled. "I just hate the feeling of being sweaty. It makes me all sticky."

"That's the best!" he exclaimed. I turned to him and cocked an eyebrow playfully, "Absolutely not! And summer clothes suck. Winter fashion is on another level."

"Okay, I can't disagree. Winter clothing is elite but c'mon, you can't hate a perfect summer day at the beach catching a tan."

I scoffed. "There's the problem of being sweaty again."

"That's what the ocean is for. You know if you go in, it cools you down." he joked, peeping at me from the corner of his eye.

"Is that what the big body of water is for? I had no idea." I mirrored his playful sarcasm.

"Surprising isn't it?" he smirked.

He had such a care-free energy to him again and it made me relax instantly. I always felt so calm around him. He was smiling, his dimple on full display and my heart swelled at the sight of him. I loved seeing him like this. We sat comfortably together, our fingers intertwined the whole way. He indicated and turned down a quiet street.

"We're almost there."

He found a parking spot available and maneuvered his way into it.

"I am so glad I don't drive in this city," I commented.

"How come?"

"I am terrible at parallel parking."

"Okay, Olivia Rodrigo,"

I couldn't help but laugh at the unexpected pop culture reference, "Is this the part where you tell me you actually listen to her album when you're alone?"

He chuckled. "Yup. I wallow in sadness when you're not around,"

I giggled as he turned the engine off. I glanced outside and the streets weren't giving me much of an indication as to where we were.

"So what are we doing?" I asked.

"They've got a show in a couple hours at the *Magic Fountain of Montjuïc* and I happen to know the best spot to watch it from."

The Magic Fountain of Montjuïc was a fountain located below the *Palau Nacional* in the *Montjuïc* neighborhood. It was a major tourist destination as it displayed a beautiful water acrobatics show with lights and music. I had passed it once or twice in previous months but had never actually sat to enjoy a show.

"Is this a date?" I mused.

"Of course it is," he scoffed. "I thought that much was clear."

I chuckled. "I'm just making sure. This is my first time meeting romantic Giovanni."

"Well, let's see how he does 'cause I don't think he's ever come out to play." He joked. I laughed as we stepped outside the car. Giovanni locked it behind us and reached for my hand, intertwining his fingers in mine again. It was such a natural thing to do now. We moved together as if we had been doing it for years. A level of comfortability surrounded us and I relaxed. He was making an effort to be romantic and I couldn't help but smile. I felt like an idiot with a huge smile plastered across my face but I couldn't control it. I was genuinely happy. He led me through the streets and as we turned, there ahead of us was the fountain with *The Palau Nacional* behind it. The iconic four pillars stood behind the fountain that remained off for now. The show was a night-time only event and the sun still had a couple of hours left until it's full departure.

"So, where's the best spot?" I asked.

"Patience, *mi hermosa*," he squeezed my hand and smiled. "We're using this time to get to know each more since, as you pointed out the other day, there's still so much we need to learn about each other."

"You're right. We have to see how compatible we really are." I joked.

He smirked, "Favourite sport?"

"Football."

"No way!" he chuckled. "Are you just saying that because I like football?"

I laughed "How would I have possibly known you liked football? I grew up in the UK, Giovanni, football is like a religion there."

"You're right. Now the important question is what team do you support?" He eyed me playfully.

"Tottenham Hotspur," I answered proudly.

"What? Tottenham? Why?" he laughed.

I tapped his arm playfully. "Don't laugh. They're a great team. I grew up watching them cause my dad was a huge Spurs fan. He never missed a match."

"Okay I'll admit, your answer could have been worse. You could have said Liverpool and then that would have been a deal-breaker."

I laughed. "Don't tell me you're a United fan."

"Of course I am but if we're talking football, I'm more into *La Liga*."

"Let me guess, you're a huge Barcelona fan?" I smirked.

He stopped in his tracks, "Absolutely not!" I burst out laughing at how insulted he looked.

"I'm from Madrid so don't ever classify me as a *Barça* fan." He pretended to be insulted again but I could see the amusement in his eyes and it made me laugh again.

"Real Madrid it is then." I giggled. "Probably a bad time to tell you I'm the biggest Messi fan." He turned to me with a shocked look on his face and I couldn't control my laughter. He was way too easy to make fun of.

"Oh Gio, you're too easy to fool." I nudged.

"You were about to ruin the perfect image I have of you in my head."

"You don't think I'm perfect," I retorted.

"I think you're pretty close," he leaned down and kissed my forehead. "How do you feel about getting ice-cream?"

At first my mind wandered back to the last time Giovanni and I had ice-cream. I wouldn't mind doing that again. He must have picked up on the change in my expression as he chuckled and cocked an eyebrow playfully, "I know exactly where your mind just went,"

I tugged at my lip. "I didn't say anything,"

"You didn't have to. I can see it in your eyes. I know you enjoyed that,"

Hell yes

"Don't worry, we can do that again. Just not now while we're out," He winked at me.

I liked the sound of that but for now, I pushed the lascivious thoughts out of my mind. "You really want to get ice-cream in this cold though?"

He scoffed, "It's really not that cold."

He was right. The sun was assisting with keeping the lingering cold air from taking over. If Giovanni was going to be spontaneous and make an effort then I was going to go along with whatever he had planned.

"You're right. Let's get ice-cream."

We strolled over to a casual vendor along the walkway. Giovanni paid for two chocolate ice-creams and handed one to me. I removed the packaging and started enjoying it. We continued to stroll down the path leading up to the fountains.

"Harry Potter? Do we love or hate?" I asked playfully.

"Oh, we love!"

I laughed. "Yes, we do love!"

"Are you going to ask me if I'm on Team Jacob or Team Edward next?" He squinted his eyes at me.

"Well, of course I am. I need to know your taste in men."

He chuckled. "Now's probably a good time to tell you that I think those movies were really bad."

I gasped. "How dare you say that? And right when I was going to ask you to have a Twilight marathon."

"I'll still do that, but only for you." He winked.

"You probably secretly love those movies but you had to act cool back in the day."

"You caught me."

I was enjoying our date so much. Every moment with him was so easy and care-free. He was so attractive but also incredibly funny. He made me laugh so much and I loved it. I loved being around him. I was completely enthralled by him.

"How come romantic Giovanni has never made an appearance before?"

"There was never anyone I wanted to make more of an effort for." He said with a matter-of-fact tone. The butterflies inside me fluttered and I couldn't hold back my smile.

"You know everyone warned me about you," I admitted.

"Who's everyone?" He lifted an eyebrow.

"Well, Reyna did but also Sergio. He gave me quite the briefing on how I should stay away from you cause you aren't a relationship person."

He chuckled. "That's cause Sergio knows me well enough."

I was dying to know more about the reasons for his commitment issues. I was already falling for him. How could I not? Especially when he made such an effort with things like this. I was getting to know all the sides to him and I was intrigued by everything about him.

"So, you're telling me that you've never ever been in a relationship? Like at all?" We climbed a few steps and Giovanni led me down a path moving further from the fountain itself.

"So we're going to have that conversation now?"

I shrugged. "I'm just trying to get to know you better. You know all about my previous relationships. All one of them."

"Your almost engagement."

"That's the one."

There were empty concrete benches along the side against a short wall. He stopped by the wall and he pulled himself onto it with his feet resting on the bench in front of him. It overlooked the road below and in the distance was the perfect spot to get a full view of the fountain. I stood on the bench and allowed one leg to hang over the wall while the other leaned against the bench. He sat in front of me with both feet on the bench. I continued to enjoy what was left of my ice-cream.

"Are we really supposed to talk about our exes on a date?" he mused.

"So there is someone?" I probed.

He sighed. "I wouldn't even call it a relationship. It was a messy situation." Now I was curious. This is the first time I had heard anything about Giovanni being in anything remotely close to a relationship with someone. No one had mentioned it up until he did just now.

"I'm not going to judge you, Gio. I just would like to know," I said softly. I wanted him to open up to me. He finished the last of his ice cream and tossed the stick into the trash can by the bench. He ran his hands through his hair and looked over at me.

"Her name was Maya and we met when I was in my second year at business school. We started off as casual friends but the more time we spent together, the more I started to like her."

I couldn't help the annoying pinch of jealousy that lingered at the mention of him with someone else. It was dumb, I knew that but I didn't want to think of him with anyone other than me.

"So did you date?"

"It wasn't that simple."

"Why not?"

"She was already dating someone else."

My jaw dropped. "She was with someone else?"

He nodded. "I'm not proud of the decisions I made with Maya. No one even knew what happened between us and I regret a lot of it."

I was taken aback. I didn't expect him to share that his one and only relationship situation was with someone who was already taken.

"What exactly happened between the two of you?"

He leaned back against his arms. "First you have to understand that I was in a really bad space. I wasn't sure what I wanted out of my life but I knew I wanted someone. It was the first time I actually wished I had a girlfriend so a part of me was desperate for it."

My face remained unchanged as I allowed him to continue. He was opening up to me and I was in no position to judge his actions.

"Anyway, Maya and I started to see each other more and more. She started making flirty comments and passes at me. I didn't care that she was in a relationship at the time - I just wanted to be around her. We were friends at first but then she started to want to see me without anyone else around."

"Did you know the boyfriend?"

He nodded. "He was a dick, might I just add, and they fought all the time. It was one of those toxic relationships that migrated from high-school to university."

I finished the last bit of my ice-cream and tried to toss my stick into the nearest trash can. I missed horribly and Giovanni burst out laughing.

"You're terrible at that," he chuckled and got off the wall to pick it up for me. I smiled and he continued his story.

"I don't want you thinking differently of me because of this," he said sheepishly and came to stand in between my legs.

"I don't." I reached for his hand.

"Maya kept telling me that she was going to leave him because she loved me. I genuinely thought that I was in love with her too, at the time. We would sneak around and the deeper we got, the more it started to drive me crazy."

"How long did this go on for?"

"A few months. As I said, I'm not proud of it but she had me wrapped around her finger. I wanted her to leave him for me. I thought I loved her but I quickly realized that it was toxic and I knew what we were doing was wrong."

"Did the boyfriend ever find out?"

"I'm pretty sure he knew. Even when he was around, she didn't hide her interest in me. It was fucking messy but after her sister caught us together, it was like a lightbulb went off inside and I realized what I was doing."

"Did you really love her?" I wasn't sure if I wanted to know the answer to that question but I knew I had to ask him.

"I thought I did but thinking back now, there was no way that was love."

I remained silent, taking in everything he said.

"Since Maya, there's been no one else. I didn't trust anyone. I couldn't. There was no guarantee that someone wasn't going to do to me what she did to her boyfriend. I decided it was easier to just fuck around instead."

I understood his reasoning behind keeping things casual. It came down to him not wanting to get hurt. I was apprehensive now. He spent so much time being single and jumping from woman to woman, why would he suddenly want to be a one-woman kind of man with me? My insecurities started to creep in.

"So, you've never been in love at all then?" I asked as casually as I could. He thought for a moment before answering. "No. Wasn't even sure I believed in love."

That made me sad to hear. No matter what happened in my life, I had always believed in love. I was a hopeless romantic. Thinking back to my relationship with Nate, there was love there but not the all-consuming love that I believed you're supposed to experience. The kind of love that took your breath away and made you want to be better for that person in every way. I still believed in that. The idea that he wasn't sure if he believed in love brought on a rush of disappointment. *Would he ever be able to love me?*

"Please say something," he murmured. "I don't want you thinking differently of me, Isabella."

"I don't," I answered quickly. "I'm just trying to understand you."

"Understand me?"

I stared down at my hands. "Yeah, you've been hooking up with women for years now, Giovanni. It just makes me a bit scared. What if you want to do that again?"

He grabbed my hands and my eyes met his. "Trust me, *mi hermosa*, I don't want that anymore."

"How do you know that?"

"I know that because I've never met anyone like you before," he murmured. "I can't explain it but there is something about you that makes me want more. It's actually fucking terrifying."

I smiled. "Tell me about it."

"You're like sunshine to me." He leaned his forehead against mine.

My heart grew and a warm sensation washed over me. I leaned forward and wrapped my arms around his neck, pulling him closer to me. His lips reached mine and I felt him smile against me. I was consumed by him.

He pulled away and asked, "So you've never watched one of these shows?" I shook my head as he brought himself up onto the ledge next to me. He leaned back and I positioned myself between his legs, my head resting against his chest while we overlooked the fountain in the distance. I was soaking in every moment with him and I didn't want it to end. This date would be ingrained in my heart for the rest of my life - no matter what happened between him and me, I would always have this day.

We spent the next few hours exchanging random facts and interesting information about each other. I learned about his OCD tendencies while I shared my messy habits. Favourite colours, favourite shows, pet peeves, embarrassing moments - we exchanged it all. Every little bit of random information that we could and I was falling deeper into him. I watched him throw his head back in laughter and the way in which he ran his fingers through his hair as it kept falling forward. His dimple deepened with each smile and his eyes holding an intensity to them that wasn't there before. It made me nervous - it felt as if he was looking straight into my soul and I felt vulnerable.

"I got arrested once," he shared casually.

My jaw dropped. "You did not!"

He chuckled. "I did. For speeding of all things."

"Yeah, well given the car you drive, I don't exactly see you driving around like an old lady," I quipped. "So, what happened?"

"Well, I was going a hundred in a sixty mile an hour zone and I didn't see the cops as I came around the bend so I ended up getting locked up for the day."

I turned to him, shocked at how blasé he was about this story. "You're a criminal!"

He burst out laughing. "I am not a criminal, it was just really bad timing."

"That would have terrified me. Going to jail is not something that's on my bucket list."

"I should hope not," he joked. "So, what is on your bucket list?"

I pondered on it for a moment. "That's a really good question. I don't even think I have one."

"Everyone has to have a bucket list," he retorted. "We're going to have to think of some things to add to it."

"I'd like to get a tattoo."

He raised an eyebrow. "You would?"

I shrugged. "Could be fun."

I would never have thought of getting a tattoo or anything spontaneous before I met him but his nature was contagious. He made me want to take risks and try new things out. I craved the adventure that he brought into my life.

"We could make that happen. I think I know a guy," he joked.

I smiled. "What was the first tattoo you got?"

He pulled his right sleeve up to display an intricate rose tattoo he had on the inside of his arm. There was not a blank piece of skin available on his arm, it was filled with markings. The rose was big and went all the way up to his elbow. Tons of thorns were drawn around it, in between all the other tattoos he had.

"My mother's middle name is Rose and I wanted something to represent her so that was the first one I had done back when I was 18."

I ran my fingers slowly up and down it. "It's beautiful." He leaned down and kissed my hair.

"Are you and your mom close?" I asked.

"Very. We've always been that way."

"That's good. I'm sure she appreciated the meaning behind the tattoo."

"She wasn't a fan of me getting any at all," he chuckled. "But she quickly got over that."

I leaned back into him and soaked in the night sky. The sun had set already and we were waiting for the show to start. He wrapped his arms around me and I smiled to myself.

"I think my mom would love you," he murmured.

I leaned my head back to face him. "You'd want me to meet your mom?"

He kissed my forehead again. "Of course."

Oh, I was falling for him.

Harder and faster than I ever thought was possible and that terrified me. Once the show started we enjoyed it from our spot, wrapped up in each other's arms. I had never experienced bliss like this before but I wanted to hold onto this feeling for as long as possible.

CHAPTER 21:

Thursday morning I walked into the elevator at the bottom of Giovanni's apartment building, two cups of coffee in hand. After our romantic date over the weekend, he and I were swamped with work and today, I finally had the day off and I just wanted to see him. I wanted to spend every moment I could with him. He had access to the building straight from *Mala Mía* or through the additional entrance in the basement that I had to utilize when the club was closed. The elevator opened straight into his apartment and I casually strolled in, a murmur of voices spreading throughout.

"Giovanni?" I shouted out.

I placed the coffees and my handbag on his kitchen counter. A moment later a lady I had never met stepped into view with a huge smile on her face.

"You must be Isabella," she exclaimed, reaching her arms out to me and pulling me in for a hug.

I was taken aback but I embraced her. "Yes I am, nice to meet you."

"Ah dear, it's so lovely to meet you. Giovanni has told me so much about you," she said with a thick Spanish accent, "I'm Marcina, Giovanni's mother."

Looking at her now, I could see a hint of resemblance between them. Giovanni definitely carried more from his father but there was a certain familiarity in their facial structure that made him and his mother look related. She was a short, plump lady with the most wonderful smile. Her face had a youthful glow to it despite the crease lines by her eyes and forehead. Her rich chestnut brown hair was the same as Giovanni's and it hung just above her shoulders. She was smiling at me and I could see the happiness in her eyes. It made me happy to know that he's mentioned me to his mother. There was clearly something worth mentioning about our relationship.

"Mama." Giovanni strolled into the kitchen.

Every time I saw him, he managed to take my breath away. He was wearing a pair of grey sweatpants that hung nicely on his waist. He pulled a hoodie over his head as he walked in, hiding his naked torso.

"I see you've met Isabella," he said, stopping next to me.

"Bella, bella, bella..." she said, cupping my face in her hands.

I couldn't help but smile and mirror her happiness. She was so welcoming and had a beautiful energy to her. The complete opposite to his father and I found myself wondering how they could have ever been together.

"Okay, *Mama*," Giovanni chuckled. "I think you're scaring her."

"No, she's not," I answered quickly and turned to his mother. "You are so lovely."

"See *hijo*," she pulled me in for a hug. "She doesn't mind."

I giggled and embraced her. I was infected by her energy and already felt welcomed. Giovanni shared the same welcoming spirit and that was one of the many things I already loved about him. The buzzer to his apartment building went off and Marcina pulled away.

"That's *papá*," she said to Giovanni. "Let me get going." The question of whether his parents were still together lingered in mind and she now confirmed that they were still a couple. She pulled Giovanni in for a hug and kissed both of his cheeks. *"Te quiero, hijo,* take care of her."

He rolled his eyes and smiled. *"Sí, mama."*

She reached for me next and kissed both my cheeks. She couldn't stop smiling. "And you, I've heard so many wonderful things about you. You should join us for lunch sometime."

"That would be amazing." I smiled.

The buzzer went off again.

"Okay, I'm going," she said and walked to the elevator. The doors opened and with one last smile, she was gone.

Giovanni turned to me as we walked back over to his kitchen counter. "I'm sorry about her. She's just very excited."

"What have you told her about me?"

"Only good things of course," he said as he pulled me into his arms. This made me smile. He pointed to the coffee cups. "Which one is mine?"

"The left one," I said and reached for mine as well.

"I've missed you," he said as he leaned down and gave me a quick kiss. "You should come around more."

I took a sip of my coffee and placed it on the counter. "I missed you too."

I had my back against the counter and he placed his arms on either side of me, stepping closer to me. I breathed him in and flicked my eyes to meet his.

"This reminds me of something," he murmured and lifted me up onto the counter, my legs wrapping around his waist.

He was referring to the morning after our attempt at a one-night stand. I nipped at my bottom lip at the memory.

He leaned closer to my ear and whispered. "Do you remember, Isabella?"

I tightened my legs around him. "How could I forget?"

He brought his lips to meet mine. I flicked my tongue over his, the coffee taste still lingered. It had been a while since I had him the way I wanted him. I ran my fingers through his hair and down the back of his neck. He leaned closer to me and I could feel him come alive beneath me. It thrilled me to feel what I did to him. He ran his hands up and down my thighs, each touch igniting my body. Just as I started to reach out for him, his phone started ringing. He ignored it at first and kept his focus on me.

"Don't you have to get that?" I murmured.

"Probably but I'd much rather take you on this counter." My eyebrow raised as he piqued my interest. I brought my lips back down to his, intensifying the kiss but his damn phone wouldn't stop ringing.

He pulled away. *"Joder."*

"It's okay." I smiled. "Someone clearly needs to get a hold of you."

He kissed me quickly before reaching for his phone, finally stopping the insistent ringing. *"Si?"* he answered. *"Que?¿por esta noche?"*

He continued the conversation but I couldn't keep up. My Spanish was poor so I jumped off the counter and grabbed my coffee cup before making my way to my favourite spot on his couch. I dropped down and positioned myself comfortably as I waited for him to finish up. He closed off the conversation and hung up. He grabbed his coffee and came to join me. He sat down next to me, placing his hand on my thigh.

"So listen," he started to say. "There's an event tonight at *Mala Mía.* We've got a few new DJs coming in but I wanted to warn you that Casey is having her birthday there tonight." I stopped and flicked my eyes to him. Just the mention of her name made me involuntarily roll my eyes. She's never done anything to me directly but the idea of her with Giovanni drove me crazy. Not to mention the fact she was one of the most beautiful people I'd ever seen and that didn't help my own insecurities one bit.

"Yeah I thought you'd react like that," he mused. "I wanted to give you a heads up."

"I'm not even sure I want to tag along tonight," I admitted. As much as I wanted to spend time with Giovanni, the idea of being at *Mala Mía* without Reyna made me weary. She was my safety net and if I went tonight, it would be for the sole purpose of being with Giovanni the whole night. I was still toying around with the idea.

He reached for my hand. "Please come."

"Does Casey know that whatever was going on between the two of you is over now?"

"There's nothing going on between Casey and me."

"But does she know that?" I asked, lifting an eyebrow. "If you haven't made it clear then sometimes people have no idea."

He leaned down and kissed my forehead. "I'll make sure I make it clear to her then."

I was more apprehensive now. This conversation brought up a wave of unwelcomed concern. It was nagging at me and I had to talk to him about it.

"Is there anyone else that you need to make it clear to?"

He placed his empty cup down on the table in front of us and turned to face me. "Make what clear?"

"Make it clear that you're not seeing them anymore," I said, placing my cup down. "I don't want to be presumptuous about what is happening between you and I but you already know how I feel about all this."

I was referring to the fact that I refused to be one of his many women. We weren't dating but we were seeing each other and I wanted to be the only one he was seeing. Call it selfish but that was how I felt. I wanted him all to myself. He reached for me and pulled me into his arms.

"Isabella, I don't want to see anyone else," he breathed. "Just you." He leaned down and kissed me. I fell into the kiss and wrapped my arms around his neck. Each time he kissed me I could feel something deep inside of me - a constant growing feeling developing into something more. Something that both excited and terrified me. We broke the kiss and he leaned his forehead against mine. All these little things he was doing was making it difficult for me to protect my heart from him - he was slipping through those walls I built.

"Come on," he said, pulling away. "I've got a few things I need to do so let's get going." We got up off the couch and I slipped my bag over my shoulder. He grabbed his jacket on the rack by the elevator and pulled it on. He reached for my hand as we stepped in and he didn't let go.

***

After what felt like hours of hopping from one store to the next on the Giovanni shopping spree, we ended up at this quaint little restaurant just down the road from his apartment. It was small and had very few people in it so we found ourselves a little table inside right at the back. The lighting was dim and the overcast day outside really set a romantic mood we couldn't escape. I slid onto the chair, hanging my handbag on the back. Giovanni chose the seat next to me and ordered us a bottle of their house red wine. Our waitress was a young dark-haired woman who was completely taken with Giovanni - so taken that she hardly even noticed my existence. That was something I experienced for the first time today during our shopping trip. Everywhere he went, people took notice of him. He didn't look for attention but he couldn't escape it either and he received a lot of attention from other women. He held my hand while we walked and to the average passerby, we most likely looked like a normal couple but that didn't stop women from flirting with him. He was always very polite and I figured that a lot of his kindness was probably mistaken for flirting.

"Are you tired now?" he mused.

"You are worse than me when it comes to shopping," I commented. "My feet even hurt from all the up and down."

He chuckled. "Well, I promise I am done for the day. After lunch, we can head to my place and get ready for tonight."

A part of me was dreading tonight but I didn't share this with him. He asked me to be there with him and that was what I was going to do. I didn't want to pay attention to the fact that Casey was going to be there and I worked my hardest to push that out of my mind. I just needed to keep my distance from her.

"So, what's good here?" I asked, scanning the menu in front of me. "Do you eat seafood?"

I nodded.

"Then you should definitely try the *Paella de Marisco* - it's not as good as the original Paella you get in Valencia but it's a close second."

The waitress came around and took our order before disappearing to the back again. Giovanni poured us both a glass of red wine. I took my glass from him and he held his out, waiting to make a toast.

"To lunch together," he said, smiling. We brought our glasses together before bringing the glass to my lips. I took a small sip and was pleasantly surprised by the sweeter taste it seemed to have. I usually found the wine here in Barcelona to be more bitter so my immature palette was enjoying this new one.

"Look at this - our second date," I mused, lifting my eyebrow at him.

He smiled at me. "Is that what this is?"

"You tell me," I shrugged playfully. "This could be two friends having an innocent lunch together. No strings attached."

He cocked an eyebrow. "There's no way you and I could be just friends."

I flicked my eyes to his and noticed the simmer of desire behind them. The tension between us was always there - we couldn't deny it. We just picked our moments because we couldn't throw ourselves at each other every single time. Even if that was exactly what I wanted to do. Every time I saw him, I had to physically stop myself from giving in to my deepest desires.

"All or nothing then," I declared.

He was right. I could never be just friends with him - not now. After everything that's happened between us over the last few weeks, I could never go back to not knowing him. There was way too much between us and just being near him was enough to set me alight. If he wasn't in my life this way then he couldn't be at all because it would drive me crazy having him so close yet so far.

"All or nothing," he repeated. "That's quite the ultimatum."

"That's where we're at right now."

The waitress interrupted with our food. She placed it down in front of us and my stomach revealed just how hungry I was. It was a big bowl and I wasn't sure if I was going to be able to finish it but I couldn't wait to dig in. The smell of seafood surrounded us and I reached for my spoon.

"This looks so good," Giovanni said, rubbing his hands together.

We both tasted our food at the same time and I was sold. It was delicious - the seafood and rice were a combination I didn't think would work and yet it was amazing. It had a lingering spicy twang to it and I was really enjoying it.

"Can I ask you something?"

After he told me about Maya the other day, I had some lingering questions that I really wanted him to answer. The idea of him never being in a relationship reminded me that I could be right to have reservations about where this was headed.

Giovanni nodded while eating. "Of course."

"Why did you not want to get into a serious relationship? I know you told me about Maya but did you really not want to try at all after her? Was that intentional?"

He stopped for a moment and I could see him trying to put an answer together. I couldn't help it, I had to ask him. I know I said I wasn't interested in labels right now but I had to know that this was going somewhere. I couldn't let myself fall for someone who couldn't reciprocate what I was feeling. He took another bite of his food and then placed his fork down, reaching for his wine.

"Does the fact that I have never been in a serious relationship bother you?" he asked, deflecting from my question.

"It doesn't bother me," I explained in between bites. "I just don't want what is happening between us to be a lost cause. I'm sure you can understand that I don't want to get hurt again."

"I would never want to hurt you, Isabella," he murmured. "Like I've said before, I just had too much fun fucking around. I know that sounds like a terrible thing to say but that's the truth. I'd seen so many relationships around me fall apart and I didn't want that. Especially after Maya. I struggled to trust people. I didn't want to get hurt and I didn't want to be the one to hurt someone else so it was easier to avoid it all."

I was sure a part of that statement had to do with what happened between his parents as well. What happened with Maya happened way before his father's affair. I couldn't bring it up because he wasn't the one who told me but I was still waiting for that. I wanted him to open up to me but for now I was thankful that I understood him better.

"Just because you never got into a relationship with someone doesn't mean you didn't hurt them though."

"Yeah, I know that but I didn't have to take responsibility for that because I never made any promises to anyone."

It made me sad to hear him talk like that. I was pretty sure that there were a number of women out there who probably ended up hooked on Giovanni only to have him move onto the next one.

"I know it sounds so fucked up, Isabella," he said as he shrugged and I could see he felt bad about his past ways. "I'd never met anyone that I wanted to be with."

While I was happy to have him open up to me, I could sense a part of me waving the big red flag. Everything he was saying was reminding me that I could still potentially end up hurt by all of this and I didn't want that.

He reached for my hand and took it in his, caressing it with his thumb, "That was until I met you." My heart skipped a beat. I looked at him and there was a softness to the way he was looking at me. The same way he looked at me that day at the fountain. He was being genuine - I could tell that he meant what he just said. I never expected to find him and to feel this way. He continued to say everything I needed to hear. Just when I was about to let my doubts override my feelings, he swooped in and suddenly my feelings were sitting front row again.

"There is just something about you, Isabella. I just can't seem to get enough."

"I'd be lying to you if I said this didn't scare me, Giovanni," I admitted.

"What are you afraid of?"

"What's happening between us. The way I feel for you is scaring me already." I avoided looking at him. I didn't want to admit that to him but I couldn't stop myself. Losing Giovanni would be a different kind of heartbreak - it would be the worst and I could either take a chance with him and let myself fall or I could run for the hills. Both were terrifying options.

"Don't you think this is scaring me too?" he murmured softly. "This is all so new to me." His vulnerability was shining through and our concerns mirrored each other. Here we sat, two incredibly weary people in a tangle of feelings that we couldn't escape. All we could do now was take it one step at a time. I leaned across the table and kissed him. He still held my hand in his and brought it up to his lips. My heart yearned for him.

"As long as it's just you and me, Giovanni, I'm happy." I ran my fingers through his hair and rested my hand against his cheek.

"You and me, *mi hermosa*."

A huge smile spread across my face and the happiness consumed me. I didn't care about anything else but this moment here with him. He was perfect. Through every little imperfection, he was still perfect to me. He was so incredibly attractive and with an all-consuming confidence that you couldn't escape. His humour and vulnerability added another level of attractiveness that not a lot of people would get to see. The more time I spent with him, the more I started to realize that

I didn't want to spend time without him. He was exactly what I wanted.

"Let's finish up so we can get ready for tonight," I mused. He smiled and we ate the rest of our meal in comfortable silence.

CHAPTER 22:

Later that evening I was perched on a single barstool by the bar of Mala Mía. Giovanni had been running around for most of the evening trying to get a handle on the influx of people that filled the place. Thursday was the first night of the week that it opened and it was, surprisingly, their busiest evening. It was almost as if people didn't have jobs they had to wake up for the next day.

I was alone at the bar but I actually didn't mind, I was enjoying the chance to sit and watch people. It was one of my favourite activities - to see people in their element when they think they aren't being watched. Crowds of women trying to get the attention of the men and women alike, the men pretending they aren't noticing those exact women as they try their own ways to get their attention too. The dynamic of the crowd was fascinating to me.

A tall beautiful blonde entered the club, catching my eye and I immediately knew that it was Casey. It was impossible to deny her beauty - she had the perfect slender body and her long blonde hair cascaded down her shoulders. She was wearing a tight red dress that clung to her body perfectly. I couldn't help the wave of jealousy that came over me. I tried really hard not to compare but how could I not? She was a model - of course, she was a model. I rolled my eyes at that thought. She walked down the stairs with a group of friends around her. She was laughing at something that was said and her smile shone through the club. She walked straight over to Giovanni who was at the bottom of the stairs. As much as I needed to look away, I couldn't stop watching her. She threw her arms around him like an excited little girl. He hugged her back but it was a different energy with her than I had seen previously. He was really making an effort to show me that she wasn't a threat. She ran her hand through his hair and he moved away from her touch as politely as he could. I smiled to myself and looked away.

This was never going to work if I didn't trust him and I had made the decision to do just that. He expressed more of how he was feeling about me and I had to give him the benefit of the doubt here. My heart was so full and warm because of him and I was adamant to not let anything affect me. I ordered a gin and tonic from the bartender and went back to my previous crowd watching.

Moments later, I felt an arm snake around my waist. I turned and Giovanni had taken his place behind me, resting his head on my shoulder.

"There you are," he whispered in my ear over the blaring music.

"Here I am." I smiled and turned to face him.

"Have I told you yet how beautiful you look?" He nestled his head into my neck, kissing it.

I couldn't help but blush. I borrowed a tight black long sleeve bodysuit from Reyna that covered all the curves of my body. Paired with a pair of black pants and my high heel boots, I usually shied away from skin-tight clothing but something about this outfit was giving me the confidence I needed and Giovanni's affirmations just made it all better. I turned my body around so my back was leaning against the bar and he positioned himself in between my legs, wrapping his arms around my waist.

"You may have mentioned it once or twice," I teased.

He ran his hands down my waist and over my thighs. "Well, I will keep reminding you. I am loving this bodysuit by the way."

"I'm sure you'll love it even more when it's on the floor later."

He cocked an eyebrow and smirked. I have never been one to flirt like this but he brought out this sexy confidence in me that made me comfortable enough to share my deepest thoughts and desires.

He leaned into my ear and nipped at it. "Oh, hell yes!"

I had to bite my lip to remind myself to keep it together. We were in the middle of a crowded club and he was technically at work. I had to be patient and contain my desires until we were alone.

"Here's your drink," the bartender shouted, breaking us out of our trance.

I turned back to the bar and reached for my drink. "Thank you." He nodded and was off.

"Good choice," Giovanni commented. "That's usually really good."

I sipped on it and was surprised by the sweet taste. It definitely didn't taste like I was drinking alcohol. "It really is."

One of the bouncers from the door interrupted us. *"Patrón, ven conmigo por favor,"*

"Si, si."

Giovanni turned back to me. "I'll be right back. Be careful with those drinks, they're dangerous."

I chuckled and continued to sip on my drink. He left a small kiss on my forehead and he was off. I couldn't help the smile that spread across my face. *How in the world did I end up with Giovanni?* A man who had a reputation of running from relationships and yet, here he was making me feel like the only girl in the world. He made me feel wanted and I loved this feeling. As I leaned on the bar to enjoy the rest of my drink, I felt a tap on my shoulder. I turned my head and Casey stood next to me, a fake smile plastered on her face.

"I don't believe we've met," she said with a more nasal tone than I expected. "I'm Casey."

I knew exactly who she was but I must have been a big surprise to her. She was even more striking up close. Her eyes were a deep brown underneath her incredibly long fake eyelashes. Her skin was flawless against her sharp cheekbones but I also had to give credit to the amount of makeup she was wearing. I was thrown off by her sudden need to introduce herself but I forced myself to play nice.

"No, we haven't. I'm Isabella." We shook hands briefly and she leaned her back against the bar, flipping her hair back over her shoulder.

"So, how do you know Giovanni?" she asked casually.

I was unsure of how to explain what was happening between Giovanni and me. We weren't dating and yet, we had pretty much agreed to be exclusive - without using those actual words though. *Could I even say we were exclusive?* Ugh, all of this was too confusing.

"Uh well, I'm actually seeing him."

"Seeing him?" She couldn't hide the shock on her face. "How interesting."

I was incredibly uncomfortable. I didn't have to answer to her, but she was clearly doing an investigation of my relationship with Giovanni and I didn't like it one bit. Her fake happiness was replaced by her clear frustration from my answers.

"Why is that interesting?"

"And how long has this been going on for?" she asked, dismissing my question. She didn't even attempt to hide the bitchiness in her voice this time around.

I was awful at handling situations like this. I was really bad at conflict and as much as I wanted to tell her to mind her own business, I found myself intimidated by her and I hated myself for that.

"It's been a couple of months now."

Technically, we'd been sleeping with each other for a few months now. I couldn't even remember how long exactly. Saying it out loud reminded me of how intense our relationship was already. I felt like I have known him my whole life and the overwhelming feelings I was already having for him over such a short period of time were terrifying.

Casey scoffed.

"Is there a problem?" I asked, my patience slipping further away from me.

"I just find that interesting," she explained. "The timing is just off considering I've also been seeing him."

I was well aware of the fact that they had a history together. I was unaware of the details surrounding it but I knew enough to know that this was a clear display of jealousy from her side from seeing me with Giovanni. I reminded myself to keep my cool.

"Well, you're not seeing him anymore."

She lifted her eyebrows at me. "Can I give you some advice, Isabella?"

I remained silent.

"You may think you're seeing Giovanni, but just be warned that he and I always find our way back to each other. You're just a temporary stop and I'm okay with that. Gio and I have an understanding but I wouldn't want you getting the wrong idea about this."

I snapped. "With all due respect, you know nothing about my relationship with Giovanni. You may have been someone he casually hooked up with in the past but that's not happening anymore while he is seeing me and he will make that perfectly clear to you."

"Not sure how clear he was supposed to be considering the last time we slept together was a couple weeks ago, clearly overlapping the same time you two were seeing each other so maybe you're the one he needs to make that clear to."

Her words hit me like a slap across my face. I knew she was just trying to get a reaction out of me and unfortunately, it was working. The last thing I needed to be reminded of was that they had slept together during the same time he and I had been sleeping together. *What the actual fuck?* I could feel the heat on my cheeks and I was seething.

"Like I said, Giovanni and I always find our way back to each other so enjoy this while it lasts." And with one last smug smile, she turned on her heels and left.

I had a lump in my throat. I didn't know if I wanted to scream or burst into tears. I downed the rest of my drink and as I placed it back down on the bar, I made eye contact with Giovanni from across the club. He clearly witnessed my interaction with Casey. I was totally over this night now. I needed to get out of here and as much as I wanted to crawl up in my own bed, I was staying at Giovanni tonight and I did not want to walk to my place alone so late at night. I pulled my gaze away from his and walked towards the back - this environment suddenly suffocating me. I pushed through the crowds of people and made it to the back. I took in a deep breath and allowed the fresh air to fill my lungs. I walked past his office and went straight for the elevator. As I pressed the button, I heard my name being shouted.

"Isabella, wait!"

I turned and Giovanni made his way to the elevator. I couldn't bring myself to look at him - hearing that he was with Casey just a few weeks ago. It made me feel like an idiot all over again. *When was that?* I thought a few weeks back and it must have been around Reyna's birthday? What the fuck. I never would have continued to pursue him had I known about their on-going physical relationship. I felt like even more of an idiot because I actually had no right to feel this way. We were not dating but being with him like that meant something to me and now feelings were involved.

"What did Casey say to you?"

He reached for my hand but I pulled it away, crossing my arms. The elevator arrived and I stepped inside, he stopped the doors from closing with his hand.

"Isabella," he started... "What did she say?"

"Nothing worth mentioning," I murmured, looking down at the ground.

He let out an exasperated sigh. "Please just talk to me."

"When last did you sleep with her?" I asked, finally looking up at him.

"What?" He was taken aback by my question and I could see the confusion on his face.

"When last did you sleep with Casey?" I repeated slowly.

I could see him racking his brain for an answer. I stood my ground and waited for his answer. I was dreading hearing him confirm what I already knew but I needed to hear it from him. I was humiliated by that entire conversation with her.

"Isabella." He tried to reach for me again but I kept my arms tightly crossed against my chest. "Why would you ask me th-"

I interrupted him. "Giovanni, just answer the damn question."

He shook his head."Fuck, I don't know. A month ago? I don't track that shit. It was way before I realized how I was feeling about you."

"A month ago? That's not what Casey said."

"She's trying to get a reaction out of you."

I was screaming on the inside but my face remained unchanged. The last thing I needed was to cry in front of him. I had enough humiliation for one night. A part of me kept reminding myself that we weren't together at the time and I had no reason to even be upset but the other part of me, the part that was riddled with feelings for him, couldn't help the hurt I was feeling. Being with him was unlike anything I had ever experienced and while I was soaking him in as much as I could, his attention was divided.

"Please don't let her get in your head. She's part of my past. I didn't know what was going to happen between us, Isabella. I never expected any of this," he explained, the vulnerability in his eyes shining bright.

"You say months ago but I had seen you guys together so many times and then you still brought her to the bar that you knew I would be at a few weeks later?" I didn't even bother hiding my contempt.

"I already told you that was a mistake. I have a bad habit of fucking things up."

"I don't want to be a casualty of your fuck up, Giovanni."

"That's not going to happen again," he sighed. "Isabella, please don't let Casey interfere with what's happening between you and me. I don't want her. I want you."

I was torn. He was saying what I needed to hear right now but I couldn't ignore the part of me that was hurt by hearing that he slept with her again. He jumped between the two of us. It was wrong and yet this is exactly what happened with those fickle blurred lines that occur with relationships like this. I didn't want any more surprises like this. I didn't want to keep hearing about him with others.

"I want to go, Giovanni," I whispered.

We were interrupted by two people calling for Giovanni again. He ran his fingers through his hair in frustration and shouted back, *"Espere, por favor!"*

He turned back to me. "Isabella, please just wait for me upstairs. I need to just sort this shit out and then we can talk. Please. Promise you'll wait for me."

I kept my eyes firmly on the ground but the desperation in his voice made my heart call out for him.

"Okay," I murmured.

"Thank you."

And with that he was gone, the elevator doors shutting me off from this night.

***

The elevator doors opened to his warm apartment and I stepped inside. I always felt so welcomed here but now I was starting to doubt everything again. I was angry and upset. Who the hell did Casey think she was? Why did she have to remind me of their relationship? I was doing perfectly fine before she brought up every insecurity I had managed to lock away. Every piece of doubt I had towards Giovanni was now on the surface again and I was frustrated by all of this. I was angry at him for putting me in a position like that where I looked like such an idiot trying to defend our relationship when there were clear timing inconsistencies. I was angry that I didn't know he slept with her after sleeping with me.

Was I an idiot to have thought differently? I was angry that I felt so strongly for him that this was getting to me. Having these blurred lines in casual relationships was exactly where the fuck ups came in. You didn't know where you stood or what you could and couldn't get angry at because there was, *technically,* no real obligation. I couldn't be angry about him sleeping with her because at the time, I didn't even know if I was going to see him again and yet, here I was hurt by that new piece of information. The idea of him with someone else drove me crazy. I was being selfish now - I wanted him all to myself.

I wandered into his kitchen and went straight for the bottle of wine on the counter. I had been at his apartment so often lately that I knew exactly where everything was and I felt comfortable enough to make myself feel at home. From the first moment I met him, he made me feel comfortable. Never once did I feel like I didn't belong or I couldn't be myself. He felt like home to me. After finding the bottle opener and a wine glass, I was perched on the couch in his lounge.

Two glasses of wine later, Giovanni finally walked into his apartment. I looked over my shoulder at him and watched as he removed his jacket. I turned back to my glass of wine and took a sip. He walked into the lounge and sat on the coffee table directly in front of me. I kept my eyes firmly on the glass of wine in my hand. The alcohol mixed with my time to overthink was a terrible idea but there was no going back now.

"Thank you for waiting," he said softly.

"Didn't have much of a choice. Couldn't exactly walk to my apartment at this time of the night."

I was being unnecessarily sarcastic right now but that was the result of the wine.

"Come on, Isabella." He reached for my wine glass and took it out of my hand.

"I wasn't finished with that."

He held my hands in his and ignored my comment. He brought my hands to his lips and kissed each one of them.

"Can we please talk about this?" he murmured.

I remained silent. *What did he want me to say?* I was angry and hurt. I probably shouldn't have added alcohol into the mix but I just didn't know what to do. This was exactly the kind of thing I was afraid would happen. I was afraid that I would be left looking like an idiot for thinking I could have Giovanni all to myself. Every doubt I had managed to shut away was back and I hated that. I didn't want to second guess him - not after all the effort he's put in the last few weeks but I couldn't control it.

"Isabella," he repeated. "What exactly did Casey say to you?"

I shrugged. This was one of my terrible defense mechanisms - I shut off and then I became unable to speak. The words sat on the tip of my tongue but I couldn't get them to come out. I've never been able to express myself the way I would have wanted to and now that has molded me to keep quiet in situations - even ones where I should be expressing how I really feel.

Giovanni let out an exasperated sigh and ran his fingers through his hair. "This isn't going to work unless you speak to me. I'm not a mind reader, Isabella."

I rolled my eyes. "I am well aware of your lack of superpowers."

"Ah, she speaks," he murmured. "Now can you please tell me what she said to you?"

"She made it pretty clear that you and her always find your way back to each other and that I am wasting my time here."

"Do you believe that?"

I shrugged. "I don't know what to believe. I haven't been able to stop thinking about you since we first met and that hasn't been the same for you."

"Isabella-," he started to say but I held my hand up to stop him.

"You can't even lie about that, Giovanni," I said. "We slept together and then you slept with Casey and then back to me again. Is there anyone else that I should know about?"

He averted his eyes and my heart sank. Hearing he was with Casey was bad enough but now there was even more to the story.

"How many other women have you slept with since you've been seeing me?" My voice cracked from emotion and I took a deep breath in.

"That's not a fair question," he retorted. "We weren't together during that time."

I ignored that statement because I knew I had no leg to stand on, "Casey said you guys slept together a couple of weeks ago but you said it was a month ago? Why would she say that?"

"It's what she does. She's spiteful and she can see I'm happy now and wants to get in the way of that."

I ran my fingers through my hair, exasperated by this whole situation.

He continued, "When I came to you that night after I brought Casey to the bar and I apologized, you have been the only one I have been seeing. I didn't know what was going to happen between us, Isabella - I didn't know I was going to feel this way about you."

The suffocating feeling was back and I was suddenly overwhelmed by emotions. I stood up and moved away from him, pacing up and down.

"This is too much, Giovanni," I said as I threw my hands up. "I don't think I'm okay with being just an option."

"Isabella, you're not listening to me," he said as he stood up and walked over to me. "You're not just an option to me. Fuck, this is all so new to me. I don't know what I'm doing. No matter how hard I try, I keep fucking things up."

He looked defeated. All I wanted to do was reach out and comfort him but my pride was holding me back. No matter how much I really wanted to walk away from this situation, I was starting to realize that wasn't an option anymore. I wanted Giovanni. I wanted to be with him. But I was terrified.

"What are we doing here, Giovanni?"

"What's wrong with what we've been doing?" he sighed. "From the moment I met you, I knew there was something about you but I tried to push that out of my head. I didn't want anything with anyone. That's why I did the stupid things like sleep with Casey and bring her out because my defense is to sabotage these situations when anyone gets too close."

He grabbed my hand and pulled me closer to him. "I don't want to sabotage anything anymore, Isabella. I'm trying here."

"I know you are," I murmured softly. "I'm just so scared of getting hurt, Giovanni. I don't want to get hurt."

"I don't want to hurt you. I would never want that," he said as he placed his hand on the side of my face and ran his fingers softly through my hair. "I need you to trust me."

"I want to trust you. I do trust you," I sighed. "Everyone just keeps getting in my head and reminding me that you don't date. You are not a relationship guy and even though I'm not trying to force any labels, I'm getting in way too deep here with you and I can't bear the thought of losing this."

That was the truth. I knew my feelings for Giovanni were strong but after hearing Casey share what had happened between them, my deepest fear about being with him were realized. I couldn't hide it any longer that I was falling for Giovanni. He had been making so much effort with me lately, how could I not give him the benefit of the doubt? I needed to trust him completely if this was going to work.

"You're listening to everyone but me here, Isabella," he murmured. "They are right. I have had a reputation of running away from committing to one person but I never thought that I would find you. I never thought I would find someone who made me want more. And I do, *mi hermosa*, I want more with you."

I looked up at him and his eyes were begging me to believe him. I had seen so many different sides to Giovanni during our time together but this was the most vulnerable I had seen him. It made my heart ache. I reached out for him and wrapped my arms around his neck, resting my head against his chest. *How was I in so deep?* I couldn't believe how strong my feelings were for him at this point. I didn't want to accept that. It was too soon but the simple truth was that I wanted him in my life and I wanted to be with him.

"I just want you, Giovanni," I whispered.

"And you have me, baby. In every way, I am yours," he said as he kissed my hair. "Please don't let what everyone else is saying ruin what we have. I told you today already that it's just you and me and I meant that."

That was everything I needed to hear. I needed to be reminded of what he's been trying to show me all this time. He wanted me and he wanted to be with me. I knew about his reputation but he was trying hard to show me that he wasn't like that anymore. I couldn't believe any of this. I couldn't believe that my life brought me here to Barcelona but I felt inside that part of that plan was so I could meet him. The only man to set my heart, body and soul on fire. He was quickly becoming everything to me and I no longer wanted to fight it. I could spend the rest of my life terrified to take a chance because of my fear of getting hurt again but what good would that do? I would be alone and I definitely didn't want that.

I pulled myself closer to him, I needed him as close as possible. My heart was overcome with emotion right now and I needed to have him. I pulled away to look up at him. Our eyes met and in that moment, our hearts were calling out for each other. He pulled into me - it was soft at first but the minute his arms encircled my body, we had to have each other.

The urgency in our kisses increased with each touch. My heart was bursting. I was drowning in my feelings for him and the desire I had for him consumed my every thought. My body craved him and my heart ached for him.

My hands found his hair and I tugged at it as his lips moved from my lips and down my neck. I ran my fingers down his shirt and slipped them underneath, feeling the heat of his body. I pulled at his shirt urging him to take it off. He broke the kiss and pulled the shirt over his head, tossing it across the room. My lips found his again as he ran his hand down my back, pulling the zip along with it. He ran his hands down my body and with one swift motion he lifted me up, my legs instinctively wrapping around his body.

He carried me to his bedroom, never once breaking the kiss. He slowly placed me down on the bed and pulled away from me. He towered over me and ran his hands down my body. My breathing picked up - I couldn't control it. Every touch burned against my skin and I couldn't control how he was making me feel. He ran his hand further down my leg and lifted it. He slowly pulled my boots off and tossed them to the floor. He brought his hands back down to my body, running his finger along the lining of my pants. There was no urgency in his touch - it was more delicate this time which only increased the pressure between my legs. Feeling his touch against me and watching him as he took his time with each movement only made me want him even more. He pulled my pants off my legs and let them fall to the floor.

I helped myself out of the bodysuit and lay there in my underwear. He flicked his eyes up to me and his feelings mirrored my own. He brought his lips back down to mine and laid his body against me. We were skin to skin now and that set us both alight. I pulled him closer to me, feeling every inch of his body that I could. The image of him above me with both arms on either side and his muscles rippling throughout was so sexy. I needed to feel him - every part of him. I wanted to leave a trail of kisses down his body and over every inch of skin I could manage.

I was enthralled by him. A greater wave of desire rushed over me and I suddenly wanted to take control of the situation. I pushed him off me, making sure we changed positions. He laid against the bed and my legs straddled him. He looked surprised by my sudden need to take control but there was a definite desire burning in his eyes.

He was intrigued and I was adamant to be in charge. I wanted to make him feel what I was feeling. I wanted to take care of his body the same way he had always taken care of mine. I wanted to remind him that no one could make him feel the way I could. He had mastered my body and I wanted to do the same to his.

I ran my hands down his chest, feeling every inch of his body. They followed down further over his abs. I allowed my nails to gently scratch over them. His body reacted to my touch and I knew he was enjoying that. I carried on - slowly dragging my nails up and down his body. His breathing picked up and he already loved what I was doing to him.

I brought my lips down against his neck and started to kiss him. Stopping a few times to suck and nip at his neck. I reached his jawline and left a trail all the way to his lips. He kissed me back and I grazed his lips with my teeth.

"Fuck, Isabella," he breathed. "What are you doing to me?"

I smirked and pulled away. I moved my body further down until I was straddled over one of his legs. My hands reached for his pants and I pushed them down, dragging his underwear with it to reveal himself to me. He was ready for me and I wanted to make him feel good. I took him in my hands and he caught his breath. I flicked my eyes up to his as I slowly started to move my hands up and down. He threw his head back and the view of him basking in the pleasure I was providing him was driving my own body crazy. I wanted to take him in my mouth. I wouldn't call myself experienced in this department but he excited me and made me want to do all kinds of things. I wanted to learn new ways to make his body mine and I wanted to watch him get caught up in the ecstasy of it. He ran his fingers through his hair and I brought my mouth down over him, taking him in.

"Fuuuuuuuck," he breathed.

His hand instinctively went to my hair and he pulled at it. Hard. His newfound roughness awoke something deep inside of me and I moved my mouth up and down him, going deeper and faster. Small moans escaped his mouth - he was unable to control his body now and I knew I was in the driver's seat. I didn't stop - I just kept going. The faster I went, the harder he pulled.

"Isabella," he breathed my name and I lost it. Hearing my name in the midst of his pleasure was driving me insane and I had to have him.

I removed him from my mouth. "Giovanni. I need you."

The urgency in my voice was undeniable and he obliged. In one swift motion, he flipped me onto my back and he was back in control. I unclipped my bra and removed it as he slid my underwear down my legs. Our primal energies had taken over and I was dying to rip into him. He leaned over and reached for a condom from his bedside table. He ripped it open and rolled it over himself. I spread my legs for him and he positioned himself in between me. He entered me and I cried out of pleasure. My body was so ready for him and it welcomed him with ease. I wrapped my legs around his body and pulled him deeper into me. He was buried so deep inside of me and I could already feel my body pushing itself to the edge. He didn't hold back. Each movement with more urgency than before. He went faster and deeper and I clawed at his back, digging my nails deep into his skin.

"Yes, yes, yes," I screamed to the world, unable to hold back the vocalisation of what I was feeling.

He leaned his hand against the wall and thrust himself deeper into me. I had never experienced such intense passion before and I was losing myself in it. My body was reacting to what he was doing and I couldn't control my moans or the way my body was coming undone, over and over again. I threw my head back and cried out in pleasure. He gripped my hair and pulled it, arching my head back. I followed his rhythm and I knew my body wasn't going to be able to hold out any longer.

"Giovanni," I moaned. "Fuck, I'm close."

He pulled me closer to him and his lips reached my ear. He nipped at it and whispered my name into it as we both reached our climax. Drenched in sweat and caught in our synchronized heavy breathing, we both collapsed onto his bed. I lay on my stomach and watched as he tried to get control of his breathing. He turned to face me and smiled. I loved the way he was looking at me right now. It made me feel like I was the only woman in the world. There was no one else. Just the two of us at this moment, right now.

"Come here." He gestured for me to scoot closer and I obliged, resting my head on his chest and draping my arm over his body. My breathing matched his and my heart was bursting with emotion. I felt his lips against my hair and I tightened my arm around him. The sudden exhaustion swept over me and my eyes slowly began to close.

"Don't ever leave me," he murmured in the distance and before I could answer, I was welcomed by the sleepy darkness of my dreams.

CHAPTER 23:

The sound of the soft rain outside brought me out of the land of dreams. My eyes slowly fluttered open and I reached over to Giovanni's side of the bed to find it empty. I stretched my body across the bed and managed to open my eyes up completely. The sleepiness still lingered along with the pleasure from last night. I blushed immediately and a smile spread across my face. After my conversation with Casey, I didn't expect to still be in Giovanni's bed but I quickly realized that there was nowhere else I was meant to be. We were choosing each other now and there was no way that I could not have him in my life. I was so tangled in his web and there was no escaping this. As scared as I was to admit it, I was falling for him. I spent so much time pushing away my feelings for him but they were there the whole time. Being with him was idyllic and there was nothing else that could compare to it.

I wrapped the sheet around my naked body and went to find him. A distant voice hummed in the air and I followed it to the kitchen. Giovanni was leaning against the counter with his bare back to me and was on the phone. I leaned against the wall and waited for him to finish up. I didn't want to interrupt him and I enjoyed the opportunity to soak him in. I would never get tired of looking at him. The tattoos across his body allowed him to be a constant artwork that I had yet to fully appreciate. His back muscles were on full display. If there was one thing about Giovanni, he took care of his body and the sight in front of me right now was one I enjoyed. I loved running my hands over his body, feeling every inch of him. I noticed a few faint scratches on his back and realized that was from me.

Oops.

I couldn't help it. Last night was amazing and I didn't realize how deep I dug my nails into his skin until now. He said his last goodbyes on the phone and turned to face me.

"Good morning," he said as he smiled. "I didn't wake you, did I?"

I shook my head and walked over to him. He immediately took me into his arms and lifted me onto the counter in front of him. I wrapped my arms around him and he buried his head in my neck. I slowly started to softly scratch the back of his neck - an action I knew he loved.

"Mmm, that's nice," he murmured.

"Who was that on the phone?" I asked.

"Pedro. My one potential business partner from Valencia. I actually need to speak to you about something."

He pulled away to face me but still kept his arms wrapped around my body, "I have to head to Valencia early tomorrow. One of the buildings we wanted to look at for the next opening of Mala Mía just became available and this weekend is the only time we can both go and check it out."

A pang of disappointment flickered inside but only because I didn't want to be without him for the whole weekend.

"Well, that's great then," I said, kissing his cheek. "You definitely have to go."

"I know we had plans to spend the weekend together..." he started to say before I heard my phone ringing from his bedroom.

"Do you want to get that?" he asked.

I shook my head. "I'll just check it later."

"Okay well, I was actually going to ask you if you wanted to come with me?"

"To Valencia?"

He nodded. "Yes, why not?"

I smiled and just as I was about to answer him, his phone started to ring. He lifted it off the counter to check it. "It's Reyna."

Reyna? Now I was confused. He brought it to his ear, *"Hola? Si,* yes she's here with me. Okay, hold on, let me give her the phone."

I extended my hand out and he passed the phone over to me.

"Hi Rey - "

"Isabella, why haven't you been answering your phone?" There was a hint of franticness to her voice on the other side and I was confused by it.

"I'm sorry. I was in the kitchen and then I didn'-"

She interrupted me. "Okay it doesn't matter but you need to get a hold of your sister right now."

"Camila? Why? What's going on?" The concern in my voice was evident and Giovanni began to mirror my previous confusion.

She was silent for a moment and it was driving me crazy.

"Reyna, what is going on here? You are starting to freak me out."

"Nate's engaged" She blurted out.

I froze.

"Wait, what?" I managed to choke.

"I'm sorry, Izzy, but your family found out and they've been trying to get a hold of you but then you didn't answer so they called me and..." she rambled on but I didn't hear a word she said.

Nate's engaged? Nate? As in my former ex-boyfriend who broke up with me because he didn't want to settle down? The same man who didn't want to make a serious commitment like getting married was now engaged to someone else?

And my family knows. *Oh fuck.* My entire cover story was immediately tossed out the window and they knew it. They knew I had been lying to them. I felt sick to my stomach.

"Reyna, I need to go," I said, interrupting whatever she was saying at that moment.

"Okay," she murmured softly. "Please let me know what happens."

We said our goodbyes and I hung up. I was trying to wrap my head around what just happened but I didn't even know where to start. *How could Nate be engaged?* And to who?

"Isabella, what happened?" Giovanni asked, bringing me out of my own thoughts. I looked up at him and there was concern spread across his face.

"Nate's engaged."

"Nate?" He was confused. "Wait, as in your ex-boyfriend Nate?" I nodded.

"The one who broke up with you because he didn't want to settle down?"

"That's the one," I murmured, laughing at how ridiculous that statement was now. "The very same Nate who my family thinks I was still with this whole time."

"Oh fuck." Giovanni breathed.

"Yeah, oh fuck..." I repeated.

"Well, maybe it's a good thing," Giovanni suggested. "They were bound to find out sometime."

I didn't reply. He was right but it just fast-tracked a situation I didn't want to have to deal with. I jumped off the counter and went back to his bedroom to get my cell phone. As if right on cue, it started ringing again and my sister's name lit up the screen. I took a deep breath in and stared at her name. I did not feel like having to explain myself right now but I also couldn't avoid them forever. I gave in and answered.

"Isabella, thank goodness," my sister said. I could hear the irritation in her voice, "Why haven't you been answering your phone?"

"I know you don't care about that, Camila." I got straight to the point. "You're obviously calling because of Nate."

I knew my sister and she didn't have an empathetic bone in her body. She was doing the dirty work for my mother but I had no doubt I would hear it from her too soon enough. She would never miss an opportunity to remind me what a fuck up my life was in her eyes.

"Are you going to explain yourself?" The words dripped off her tongue. "Was Nate not your boyfriend? We didn't even know you weren't together. If I'm being honest, I had a feeling something wasn't right ever since mother told me you lost your job and you ran off to Barcelona. You were being too closed off abo-"

"Could you stop?" I interrupted her. "Yes, I lost my job. Yes, Nate was my boyfriend. He dumped me months ago but I couldn't exactly tell you guys that now could I? Mom already had a lot to say about me quitting my job, how could I possibly share that I was dumped too? The last thing I wanted to do was give you guys even more ammunition to use against me."

"Isabella..." Camila started again but I cut her off.

"Who is he engaged to?" I asked.

"Christina Michaels."

I recognized that name from the many society parties my family dragged me to. Her parents owned many properties in London and because she was an only child, she bathed in their lavish lifestyle. I never liked her - right off the bat you could tell how pretentious and spoiled she was. Clearly, Nate thought something different. I couldn't care less about who he was engaged to - it was the fact he was engaged at all that came as a shock to me.

"Hello? Isabella? I just don't understand you. How could you not tell us that you weren't together anymore?" Camila brought me out of my thoughts.

"Have you not been listening?" I sighed. "He dumped me, Camila. Nate told me things were getting too serious and he didn't even know if he wanted to get married at all. Kind of ironic now considering he's engaged - clearly, the commitment wasn't the problem."

I laughed. This was a joke.

"Well, mother is in a state again," Camila fumed. "It's enough now. You've had time over these last few months to do whatever the hell you've been doing but now you need to sort your life out and she wants you to come home."

She sounded exactly like my mother, it was eerie.

"I am home," I seethed.

"Come on, Isabella, be serious now," Camila dismissed me. "You can't be-"

"Camila, stop!" I snapped. "I am not coming home and you can tell Mom and Dad that I am sorry I lied to them but I can't deal with this right now. Don't call me again."

And with that, I hung up on my sister.

I dropped on the bed and let out the breath I didn't know I was holding. I was so confused and I didn't know where to begin to try and unpack my thoughts. Everything was unraveling now and what hurt me the most was that my family didn't care one bit about how I was actually doing - they were more concerned with how this was going to impact their image. I scoffed. This was typical Avery family behaviour. It was disgusting.

"Isabella," Giovanni murmured and peered into the room. "Are you okay?"

I nodded and he came to sit next to me. I unlocked my phone and went straight to my messages from Reyna. There was a screenshot of their engagement announcement on Facebook. There they stood, arm in arm with her left hand extended forward as the main focus of the image. The diamond on her finger was huge - very flashy and obnoxious. That was never Nate's style but then again, I clearly didn't know him as well as I thought I did.

"Does it bother you that he's engaged to someone else?" Giovanni murmured gently.

"I honestly don't care that he's engaged to someone else," I admitted. "I'm definitely confused though. Last I knew he wasn't ready for a commitment and didn't even know if he wanted to get married at all but now look. Oh, and my mother is in a state apparently."

"But, it's not about her."

"Oh, but it is," I scoffed. "She and my sister couldn't care one bit about how I must be feeling. She's probably more concerned about the mess she has to clean up in their own little society. They have always cared far too much about what other people think."

This was the first I had even heard of Nate even being in a relationship. I tried to check up on him a few times through social media over the last few months and on his family but there was never anything about him and Christina. How long had they been seeing each other? Half a year and they're engaged? Or was something happening before? I could feel my head about to explode.

"Come to Valencia with me," Giovanni urged gently. "I don't want you to be alone right now."

Without hesitation, I answered, "What time do we leave?"

***

Over 24 hours later we were in Valencia and it was beautiful. It wasn't difficult for Giovanni to get me a first-class ticket next to his and I was thankful to be able to tag along. It took us an hour to get to Valencia and we spent the morning wandering around the old-fashioned city before Giovanni left for his meeting. That worked out perfectly for me because in between the fast-paced tour of the city and the news of Nate the day before, I was exhausted. Mentally and physically. Hours later I woke from my nap feeling refreshed and focused, ready to put all that bullshit out of my brain. There was no point in dwelling on the Nate situation - no matter how many unanswered questions I still had for him. He clearly lied about having commitment issues and I was the issue. Or maybe he did have those issues but meeting Christina changed that? He didn't want to commit to me but who cares? Here I was with a man that actually cared about me and even though the irony lay in his own notorious commitment issues, he told me he wanted me and that was all I needed to hear.

I took a quick shower and strolled over to my overnight bag on the floor by the bed. We were in a five-star hotel in the middle of the city center. Valencia was different to Barcelona - both were just as beautiful but Valencia held that more home-like feeling due to the significantly lower number of tourists. Barcelona was always busy and you could easily get caught up in the energy of the city. Valencia was calmer and I needed that right now. Giovanni had promised to take me to one of the best restaurants in town and I wanted to look good for our date. I pulled on a pair of leather pants and paired it with another black long-sleeve bodysuit of Reyna's that I knew he loved. Thankfully she left it behind - it hugged my body, accentuating my fuller breasts in just the right way. I strolled into the bathroom as I pulled my hair into a high ponytail and added a pair of hoop earrings to complete the look. I was putting on the last of my mascara as Giovanni strolled into our suite.

"Look at you," he said as he stopped by the door frame of the bathroom and gawked at me. "Fuck you're beautiful."

I looked at him through the big mirror and blushed. "Welcome back." He walked over to me and wrapped his arms around me, looking at the two of us in the mirror, "I'm not sure I wanna show you off to the world. I might want to keep you in my bed all night."

I chuckled. "Oh no. You promised me a great dinner at this great restaurant you speak so highly of..."

He playfully rolled his eyes. "You're right. It would be wrong of me to deny you such great food."

I turned to face him and reached up to kiss him. He was intoxicating to me. I wanted more of him every single time. I ran my hand through his hair, tugging at it as his tongue flicked over mine. My teeth grazed his lip and I pulled at it.

He groaned. "You're making it difficult for me to not rip your clothes off right now." I leaned into him and felt him against me. I broke the kiss and flicked my eyes up to meet his. The tension between us was well on its way to derailing the evening we had planned and I was about to let it happen until his phone started to ring.

"I don't have to check that," he murmured.

"You probably should," I sighed. "And I didn't spend all this time getting dressed up to go nowhere."

He chuckled and pulled his phone from his pocket. *"Hola, Pedro, Si si, yo necesito..."*

He strolled out of the bathroom to continue his conversation and I turned back to the mirror. My cheeks were flushed now and I could feel my body was still on edge but I decided to lock the tension away until tonight. Then I would have my way with him.

***

Later that evening I was perched on a barstool leaning against the counter waiting for the drinks we ordered. After we finished our dinner - which really was a meal to write home about - we decided to grab a couple of drinks before heading back to our hotel. The bar was packed with people but we managed to find a place right against the bar.

"You were right about the food," I admitted. "That was probably one of the best meals I've had in a long time."

He took me to a small restaurant called *Racó del Túria* to have a traditional *paella* meal. He explained that no one did a traditional *paella* better than Valencia and I now agreed with him on that. It was so tasty and the home-cooked atmosphere of the restaurant made the experience even better. I was enjoying how comfortable I was feeling here in Valencia with Giovanni. We moved in perfect synchronization together. He felt like home to me and it was nice to take a break from all of the drama - no Nate, no Casey, no unwanted family members. Just the two of us in our bubble - a bubble I didn't want anyone or anything to pop.

"I love the food here," he commented as the bartender placed our drinks in front of us. "I've been here a few times and I have never had a bad meal."

We reached for our drinks and clinked them together before sipping on them. The Gin was strong but I didn't mind. My palette seemed to be adjusting to the alcoholic drinks I was enjoying lately.

"You know you can talk to me about this Nate situation." Giovanni leaned against the bar, moving closer to me. "You don't have to pretend it isn't bothering you."

I sighed and took another sip of my drink. "Of course it's bothering me but not in the way you might think. I really don't care about Nate being with someone else - I was just blindsided by this whole thing."

"I get that. He lied to you."

"Yeah, he did and I'm just putting off the inevitable by not answering my parent's calls but I just don't want to deal with it." I pulled him closer to me and wrapped my arms around his neck, "Tonight, I only care about being here with you."

He smiled and ran his hands up my thighs, "I can't stop thinking about how much I'm going to make you scream later."

I raised an eyebrow and my legs tightened. The pressure between my thighs intensified and I had to remind myself we were in a bar full of people. Looking at him now, I wanted to rip his clothes off him and have him take me right here on the bar.

He leaned closer to my ear. "What are you thinking about, Isabella?"

His breath on my neck made me shudder. I had no control of my body around him - he had mastered it and it bowed down to him.

Before I could even answer him he whispered to me, "I'm thinking about how I'd like to perch you up on this bar right now and have my way with you. I don't even care who sees."

"Giovanni," I breathed his name and pulled him closer to me. "We can't do this here."

He chuckled and looked down at me. "But it would be fun."

"To have sex in front of all these people?" I cocked an eyebrow at him.

He shrugged. "They'd just be wishing they were us."

I smiled and reached for my drink. I glanced back at him and suddenly his whole mood had shifted. He was staring dead straight ahead of him, his mouth had settled into a hard line. The sudden anger burning in his eyes was undeniable. I turned to follow his gaze and there was his father locked in a passionate embrace.

But with a woman who was not Giovanni's mother.

In one swift movement, Giovanni was walking towards his father and I knew this wasn't going to end well. He pushed his way through the crowd, not caring who he bumped into on the way.

"Giovanni, wait," I said as I tried to pull at him to get him to stop for a moment but he kept going. He reached his father and pulled him apart from the woman.

"*¿Qué carajo?*" Giovanni bellowed.

Everyone around us turned to see the commotion. I tried to reach for Giovanni again but he stepped towards his father till they were face to face.

"Giovanni, *¿Qué haces aquí?*" His father couldn't hide his surprise.

"What the fuck do you think you're doing?" Giovanni raised his voice even louder.

"Don't you dare speak to me like that," his dad scolded and pushed him away. "*Joder!* Who the fuck do you think you are?"

"Who the fuck do you think you are?!" Giovanni repeated and pointed to the woman his father was kissing. "*¿Quién coño es este?* How can you do this to *Mama* again?"

"Giovanni, you stop-"

He interrupted his father. "Do you have no respect for her? You come to a public place and think people aren't going to find out!"

People were staring now and I didn't know how to stop this. Giovanni was seething. He stepped closer to his father and they were face to face again.

"You fucking disgust me!" he shouted. "*¿Qué carajo?*"

He shoved his father backward and the anger in Cecilio's eyes flared. These two were going to fuck each other up and they weren't listening to anyone trying to stop them.

"Giovanni, please!" I shouted and reached for him, terrified of what was going to happen next.

"Giovanni, you better mind your own fucking business," Cecilio seethed.

"Mind my own business?" And with that Giovanni swung at his father, his fist connecting with his jaw.

The crowds dispersed and I couldn't get a handle on what was being said over the shouting from everyone trying to break up the fight. Two men in close proximity managed to pull Giovanni and his father apart but not before Cecilio managed to swing back at Giovanni and connected his fist right underneath Giovanni's eye.

"Giovanni!" I screamed and reached for him. "Please, stop."

A stranger helped me pull Giovanni further away from his father before this became a blood bath. I stopped in front of him and he was bleeding now.

I cupped his cheek. "Giovanni, please let's get out of here." He said nothing but the rage was burning in his eyes. Security came just in time to tell us we were no longer welcomed here. Giovanni remained silent, turned on his heels and headed towards the exit. I followed closely behind him. We made it outside and I was so thankful for the fresh air that hit us. Our hotel was a couple blocks away and Giovanni took off walking down the street.

"Giovanni, wait." I picked up my pace to catch up to him. I grabbed his arm and forced him to stop. "Hey, stop. Giovanni, look at me."

He kept his eyes on the floor as I reached for his face. I slowly pushed his chin up to reveal the swelling already happening under his right eye. There was blood on his cheek. I wiped it away and made him look at me.

"Giovanni," I breathed. "Are you okay?"

He finally made eye contact with me and I could see the sadness in his eyes. He shook his head, "He's done this before."

He started to open up to me. "He pulled this shit on my mom years ago. She had to find out about his cheating ass in the press - it was a fucking mess and here he is doing this again."

"I'm sorry." I murmured.

"Forget it." He dismissed the conversation and reached for my hand, "Let's go." He kept me close to him as we took off down the street back to our hotel in silence.

***

We made it back to our hotel room and Giovanni went straight to the bathroom. I sat down on the bed and removed my shoes. My feet were now aching from that walk back. These high-heeled boots were not designed for walking uphill. I heard the water from the shower as I took a moment to replay what had happened tonight. It all happened so quickly. One minute we were flirting and enjoying ourselves and the next Giovanni was in this fit of rage. I couldn't blame him. It was upsetting what his father was doing - especially since this wasn't the first time. I felt so bad for Marcia. She deserved so much better than this and so did Giovanni. His relationship with his father was already hanging by a thread but there was no doubt that it was non-existent now.

I needed to be there for him now. He was starting to open up to me and that was exactly what I wanted. I wanted him to confide in me. I wanted to be part of his life in every way - the good and the bad. I slipped out of my pants and pulled my shirt over my head, dropping it on the floor. I pushed the bathroom door open and the steam from the hot shower escaped. I closed the door behind me. Giovanni stood in the shower staring at the floor, the water running off of him. I pulled my bra off and stepped out of my underwear. I opened the shower door and joined him. He didn't move - he stayed underneath the water, lost in thought. I wrapped my arms around his body and leaned my head against his back.

"I'm here," I whispered. "Let me be here for you."

He turned to face me. "I don't want to think right now."

The previous anger and sadness in his eyes were no longer present. He slowly ran his hands up and down my arms. The heat from the shower overcame me but that wasn't the heat I was feeling. Seeing his wet, naked body in front of me was causing a wave of desire across and through me. He slid a finger across my collar bone and down between my breasts. I held my breath as he traveled down my belly button and further. He stopped before I wanted him to and flicked his eyes to meet mine. Everything else slipped away and I knew he wanted me. In one swift motion he lifted me up and my legs wrapped around his waist. Our wet bodies colliding in an all-consuming passion. The hot water beating down against us as his lips found mine in an urgency I hadn't experienced before. His arms encircled me, pulling me closer to him as he pressed me up against the wall. The cold of the wall made me gasp but so did the kisses he was leaving along my jaw and down my neck. My body was aching for him right now.

"Giovanni," I breathed.

"Tell me you're mine." He purred in my ear.

"I'm yours, Giovanni," I gasped. "All yours."

My arousal was spiraling out of control. I pulled myself closer to him as my lips found his. I pulled at his hair, needing him closer than ever. His tongue flicked over mine with urgency. He needed me and I needed him. He lifted me up and positioned himself between me and just like that, he was inside of me where he belonged. I cried out in pleasure as I felt all of him. He ran his hands over my breasts, squeezing and pinching me feeding my arousal. We moved together in an animalistic fashion - never being able to get enough of each other. His lips found my neck where he sucked on my skin as he thrust deeper inside of me. We were the closest we had ever been and it was

invigorating. I was high on the ecstasy of him right now. The way he
filled me up made me pull on his hair with such an intensity that I was
sure I was hurting him. My lips found his again and I tugged at his
bottom lip making him groan.

I threw my head back crying out in pleasure. The combination of
the hot water, the steam and Giovanni deep inside me was pushing me
off the edge. It was vivifying to feel all of him like this. Not just
physically but emotionally. There was so much more to this. The
pleasure overwhelmed me and I moaned his name. I couldn't care less
who could hear me right now. The only thing that mattered was
Giovanni and the ability he had over my body. He thrust deeper inside
of me and we both quickened the pace.

"I'm so close," I moaned, the pressure between my legs mounting
to its climax.

I pulled myself harder against him and came undone to the sound
of his name. I was the one moaning it and yet the euphoria of my climax
disconnected me from my own reality. He pushed deep inside me one
last time before pulling out to reach his own. My legs were still
wrapped around his body but he leaned me against the wall - both of us
trying to catch our breath. He eventually placed me down and I had to
place my hand on the wall to keep my legs from buckling underneath
me. I was overwhelmed - I felt like I could hardly breathe. I was
completely consumed by Giovanni in every way. The pleasure lingered
in every part of my body but it was the suffocating feeling in my chest
that flummoxed me. I was so enthralled by him and those feelings I was
denying for so long drowned me. I couldn't control it any longer.

CHAPTER 24:

"**Y**ou can see now that my relationship with my dad is pretty fucked up," he explained.

After finally dragging ourselves out of the shower, we were lying in bed together - my head against his chest as he played with my hair. I didn't say anything more to him about what happened with his father but he was at the point now where he wanted to let me in so I listened intently as he explained what happened to his family.

"A few years back my dad's company was working on the *La Sagrada Familia.* He had made quite a name for himself in society and that meant the press was always interested in our lives. We had to attend various society parties and make appearances at public events - at the time I was enjoying being in the public eye but that was until a story broke in the press that had pictures of my dad with another woman."

I lifted my head from his chest and propped myself up on my elbow to look at him while he spoke. I kept my face as neutral as possible and allowed him to explain more of his story.

"It was a pretty fucked up situation and I was there when my mother found out. The news broke and she found out along with the rest of the public. It was brutal to watch."

He was staring off in the distance and I could see the pain in his eyes. The pain he was still carrying from this. It was such a terrible situation to be in - mostly for his mother but it affected the entire family and to have it in the press like that just made it so much worse. When you're on the media's radar, you couldn't control what information they were going to share and they didn't care how painful it could be to those on the receiving end. They just wanted a story.

"She broke down and I was the only one there to pick up the pieces. I've never seen her like that - it killed me to see the pain he caused." His eyes were empty and he was too far into this memory for me to try and break him out of it. "I was so fucking angry. I tried to keep it together but the minute he walked through the door, I hit him."

I gasped. "You hit him?"

"Yeah, tonight wasn't the first time I've punched him," he said. "I didn't give a shit. I had to stand up for my mom - what he did was fucked up."

Everything he was sharing made sense to me. The anger and hostility he had towards his father were completely justified. His dad not only broke his mother's trust but the trust of the entire family. When you have children, they're immediately involved in whatever happens in the relationship - whether it's intentional or not and with a situation like theirs, they could not escape it. It was out there for the world to see and for all of them to deal with.

"My dad hit me back. Like he did tonight. That time he managed to dislocate my jaw though and that just upset my mom even more. Hitting him wasn't my finest moment but I was just so angry at him."

"I can understand." I reassured him that his feelings were justified.

"It was all downhill from there. It became more about me getting involved in a situation that, according to my dad, had nothing to do with me," he scoffed.

He was carrying so much pent-up anger and resentment towards his father with no healthy outlet. I could tell this conversation was forcing him back into a dark place where he had to recall the past and I didn't want to push him deeper into his looming darkness. I reached out and slowly ran my nails against his body, drawing circles on his chest. I wanted to be close to him and I wanted him to know I was here for him.

"Long story short, my mom took him back," he muttered. "I moved out and got my own place. Took years before we started to even speak again but we both knew that things would never be the same again. We tolerate each other for the sake of my mom. He also likes to remind me that the only reason we have a successful business is that he gave us the opportunity."

"You worked hard for what you have, otherwise it wouldn't be successful. Just because you were given the start-up doesn't mean that he deserves all the credit."

He scoffed, "Don't tell him that. We pay him rent for the building anyway so even though he gave it to us, it wasn't a free gift."

It made me so sad to hear about his family dynamic. When I see families like Reyna's, it made me wonder why people like him and I got stuck with the families we had. I've always wanted things to be different with my own family but they were never going to be like me and I had to accept that. Watching the way Giovanni and his dad went at each other really showed me just how far gone their relationship was. Giovanni was still struggling with this. I couldn't blame him - I felt for him and all I wanted to do was take away his pain.

"Are you going to tell your mother?" I asked softly.

He ran his fingers through his hair, like he had thoughts racing through his mind.

"I'm going to have to," he said as he sighed. "I don't want to see her hurt again. It was fucked up to witness but I can't lie to her."

"It's the right thing to do," I assured him. "Do you think she'll forgive him again?"

"Who knows," he said. "But I won't. He can't continue to hurt everyone around him and not have any consequences."

He pulled me closer to him and I draped my leg across his body. I left kisses along his chest, constantly wanting to reassure him that I was here for him no matter what.

"Thank you for telling me." I had both hands on his cheeks now, cupping his face. "You're such a good man."

And I meant that. He only wanted to stand up for his mother when she was so publicly disrespected like that. I didn't know how anyone would have been able to handle a situation like that. Looking at Giovanni in this vulnerable state really made my heart go out to him - he was sharing this with me because he trusted me enough with it and I loved that. I wanted him to trust me and lean on me. I wanted to be there for him.

He leaned into my touch and whispered to me. "You're so beautiful."

I blushed and brought my lips to his. He was such a good man and I was sinking deeper into him. His arms tightened around me and I knew there was nowhere else I was meant to be but in his arms. Forgetting all the bullshit we both had to deal with from our families, we had each other and he was starting to feel like home to me.

Giovanni tightened his arms around me. "Can I ask you something?"

"Of course."

"If Nate had asked you to marry him, would you have gone through with it?"

I thought about this for a moment before answering. "Truthfully, if he had asked I would have said yes. It was what was expected of me and I had accepted that a long time ago."

He was quiet and stared straight ahead, lost in thought. I probably would have married Nate - I wasn't in love with him but I never thought that was supposed to be a big part of marriage. My parents had painted a great picture for me of what a successful life was and the marriage part was more of a decision that suited the plan. I never questioned it - I had thoughts about their way of living but it was all I knew. It wasn't until I was honest with myself that I realized how miserable I would have been if I had gone ahead with that.

I reached up and rested my hand on his cheek. "What's on your mind, Giovanni?"

"I don't know if I wanna get married," he confessed.

Why was he telling me this? Hearing that didn't really surprise me. How could it? I've been made so aware of his commitment issues, the last thing I'd think he'd want to do would be to get married.

"I'm just trying to figure out where you're at," he explained. "A few months ago you were ready to get married and now here we are. I just want to know if that's still something you want."

I was taken aback by his words but I tried to think about things from his perspective. I've never pushed for any kind of commitment with him other than respecting me enough to only sleep with me. He was free to change his mind at any point which made me incredibly vulnerable in this situation. Why would we even need to talk about marriage at all right now?

"I'm not ready for marriage, Giovanni. My life is a mess right now, I'm not even thinking about that if that's what you're worried about."

"Your life isn't a mess."

"Well, it's not what I thought it would be. There's still so much I need to figure out so trust me when I say I'm not expecting to get married any time soon." I pulled away and looked up at him,

"I'm not putting any pressure on what this is," I indicated to him and me. "All I know is I wanna be with you."

That was all I wanted. I wanted to be with him. I wanted to wake up with him and be the reason for his smile. I wanted to be who he turned to. I was enthralled by him in every way and I wanted him to be mine but I would never put pressure on what was happening between us to get that.

"I've never felt this way about anyone," he whispered to me so softly I wasn't sure if he wanted me to hear. I brought my lips to meet his and I sunk into him.

CHAPTER 25:

"**W**ill you call me after?" I put my bag down on the counter and turned to Giovanni, "I'll be here for you for whatever you need okay?"

He pulled me into his arms. We spent the rest of our time in Valencia tangled in each other's arms. We were both seeking comfort in any way we could get it and I didn't want the weekend to end. I wanted to live in my bubble with him and ignore all the other shit we had to deal with. Unfortunately, we weren't able to do that and he had to drop me back at my apartment. He wanted to walk me up before heading out to meet his mom. He was about to have a terribly uncomfortable conversation with her and it wasn't my place to tag along. He needed to do this alone.

"I know, *mi hermosa*," he kissed my hair. "Thank you."

I pulled away and smiled up at him. "Thank you for letting me come with you. I needed to get away."

"I'm glad you came with me," he said as he pulled away but still held my hand. "Okay, I need to go and get this over with."

I could see the pain and frustration in his eyes. He kissed me one last time before leaving my apartment, closing the door behind him. I sighed and pulled my phone from my pocket and dialed Reyna.

"Izzy," she answered excitedly. "Where are you? Do you want to have lunch?"

I laughed. "Honestly Reyna, it's like we're the same person. I was just about to ask you the same thing. I just got back and thought I'd pop by your office."

"Yes, please. These people are pissing me off today so I need to get out of here."

I chuckled. "Okay, I'll see you in a bit then."

"See you soon." We ended the call and I went to get ready.

Thirty minutes later I was on a train to the city center. It was more packed than usual so I chose a seat in the far corner. I placed my earphones in. Reyna's office was a fifteen minute train ride away and I needed my music. I leaned against the window and swiped down to see my recent notifications. I still had missed calls from my mom and plenty of messages from her and Camila. I sighed and opened them.

"Isabella Avery, you better give me a call. I can't believe that you lied to us about Nate. We are incredibly disappointed and embarrassed we had to find out like this!"

I rolled my eyes. Being told they were disappointed didn't sting as much as the last time she said it. I guess I was used to it by now.

I opened another one.

"Isabella. Call me NOW!"

I swiped through it and opened one from my sister.

"Bella, please phone mom back. She's in a state about all this - everyone is asking questions and she doesn't know what to say. That's not fair on her."

I rolled my eyes and shut my phone. They aggravated me so much. Not one of their messages asked me how I was doing with all of this. I know it was wrong of me to have lied to them in the first place but couldn't they see why I did? I wanted to avoid feeling like this. My phone buzzed again and I glanced down to see a message from Giovanni.

"Just got to my mom. I'll call you later. Thinking of you."

I smiled and replied, *"Good luck. I miss you already."*

I meant that. My heart was his and I missed him when he wasn't around. I had already become so accustomed to having him in my life.

Fifteen minutes later I stepped off the train at the stop closest to her office. I made my way through the crowds of people trying to get on and was greeted by the bright sun as I stepped out of the station. I breathed in the cold air and smiled. I would never be able to get enough of this place.

I turned down the street towards Reyna's office. She worked for a high-end media company in the city. She had started there as an intern after she graduated and was now one of the creative directors. It was a big company and she played an important role in the marketing campaigns they ran. I was a few minutes away so I removed my earphones and placed them in my bag.

Suddenly, I heard my name in the distance. I looked around to see who it was and I was surprised to see Lorenzo waving at me excitedly from down the street.

"Isabella!" he shouted again.

I waved back at him and walked to meet him. He was wearing a well-fitted navy suit and I was definitely attracted to this new look of his. He was smiling and I only noticed now how great his smile was.

"Lorenzo, hi," I said and reached for a hug.

"Didn't expect to see you here," he embraced me. "Do you work in the area?"

I shook my head and pulled away slowly, "My friend, Reyna, she works down the street."

I pointed in the direction of Reyna's office and he nodded. "Well, I'm really glad I bumped into you. I tried calling a few weeks ago but I never heard back."

He was referring to the time Giovanni answered my phone, he just avoided mentioning him. I averted my eyes and tugged at my lip like I always do when I'm nervous. *Why was I being so awkward?* Memories of the last time I saw Lorenzo came back to me and I couldn't help the warmth spreading across my cheeks. I didn't even know him but I still felt bad for how I used him that night.

"Well, you look great," he continued. "I really enjoyed that night at the bar."

I blushed, "Sorry about that. I felt really bad about just leaving like that."

And for kissing you to make Giovanni jealous. I ran my fingers through my hair, the awkwardness I was feeling around him continued. Definitely a full 180 from the last time I was with him. Alcohol really gave me the confidence I needed.

He reached out and placed his hand on my arm, "Don't worry about it. I just haven't stopped thinking about you since."

We locked eyes and there was this sudden lingering tension that wasn't there before. I pushed it out my head - *What the fuck, Isabella?* I couldn't deny he was attractive but surely there was nothing more.

"Listen, Lorenzo, I'm sorry if I led you on but I'm actually seeing somebody."

"Giovanni Velázquez?"

I nodded.

"Wasn't he dating that model?" He didn't bother hiding his very obvious contempt for Giovanni. They both had the same reaction to each other. I knew it had something to do with Lorenzo's sister but I really didn't want to know more about Giovanni's past. I'd heard enough about that.

"That's over now," I answered quickly.

It seemed like everyone was aware of Giovanni and Casey's on-again-off-again relationship. I pushed my jealousy aside and reminded myself to control that. I couldn't get upset every time someone mentioned the two of them. That was in the past now.

Lorenzo looked apprehensive but he shrugged. "Well, I certainly hope so. He better treat you right."

I smiled. "He will, he does."

He reached out and tucked a piece of hair behind my ear. I held my breath at his unexpected touch. There was something different about

D o m i n i q u e   W o l f

Lorenzo this time round. My obvious emotional state last time around clouded the very obvious tension between him and me. It was unexpected and I didn't like it. I was focused on Giovanni and me right now.

"Listen, I have to go now," he started. "But I really hope to see you again. Take care of yourself, beautiful."

"Bye, Lorenzo."

With one last look, he turned and took off down the street. I let out a breath and recalled that incredibly strange interaction. I was definitely attracted to Lorenzo but not in the way I was attracted to Giovanni. That was all-consuming. Lorenzo didn't even bother hiding his interest and while I was flattered, I didn't reciprocate that. Hearing about Casey again left a bad taste in my mouth but I pushed all of that out of my mind and continued heading to Reyna.

I dialed her number as I started to approach her office.

"Are you here?" she answered.

"Yeah, I'll wait downstairs for you."

"See you now."

We ended the call and I slipped my phone into my handbag. Her office building looked just like every other building in Barcelona. Skyscrapers and modern architecture were scarce in the city - it didn't need it. Reyna strolled out of the building, handbag and cellphone in hand. She was wearing a smart long-sleeve pencil dress and her thick hair was pulled into a neat bun. She had a way of carrying herself that showed she meant business. She smiled when she saw me and pulled me in for a hug.

"I feel like I haven't seen you in forever!" she shrieked.

I chuckled. "I know. I've missed you."

She pulled away. "Where do you want to eat?"

"This is your area. What do you recommend?"

"Follow me. There's a great Italian restaurant down there."

We turned in the direction of the restaurant and fell into a comfortable rhythm side by side. Winter was starting to creep in but it was great to have the sun shining on us bringing some warmth to the day.

"So?" I asked. "How was Madrid? How are your parents?"

"It was great, Izzy. You know how much I love going back home. I don't think I mentioned to you that Katrina is still there."

"No, you didn't. How long is she there for?"

"No idea, but I know she really wanted to introduce Sergio to our parents so he's flying up to meet her this weekend."

"Meeting the family?" I was surprised but happy for her. "That's serious."

"Oh yes. They're definitely in love. My parents are going to come down for a weekend next month and I really want them to meet Diego."

"That's so great!" I exclaimed.

We got to the small little Italian restaurant Reyna was referring to. We chose a table inside, away in the back corner. They were pretty busy so we wanted to keep our distance from the other tables. It was a sweet little family-owned restaurant. This was evident by the artwork and storytelling quotes they had on the walls of the place. I breathed in the aroma of basil and garlic and my stomach reacted. I was hungrier than I realized. We slipped into our seats as a cute waiter came to take our order

"*Hola, hermosas.*" He smiled.

He must have been just shy of eighteen years but you could see the confidence he exuded. He was definitely attractive but in a youthful way. Reyna ordered us a round of cocktails to start off with and he nodded.

"Coming right up."

Reyna turned to me. "So back to Diego. I really want to introduce him to my parents. I feel like this could be something great."

Her eyes twinkled as she spoke about him. She was completely smitten and this was the first time I had ever seen her like this. I reached out for her hand and squeezed it.

"Diego is great. They're going to love him."

"I think so, too. You know me, I don't introduce anyone to my parents but I've also never felt like this before."

The waiter was back with our drinks and placed them in front of us. I didn't know what it was but I trusted Reyna's judgment on this.

"Can I get you ladies anything to eat?" he asked.

We scanned through the menus quickly and both settled on a simple margarita pizza to share. He took the menus from us and was off again.

"Don't think you're going to get out of explaining to me what went down with your family, Izzy." She raised her eyebrow at me.

I rolled my eyes. "There isn't much to tell. Cats out the bag - they know for sure now that I was lying and I've been avoiding them since I last spoke to Camila."

"How do you feel about Nate being engaged?"

"Well, I was fucking surprised by it. I didn't even know he was seeing anyone and you know why he broke up with me so it just doesn't make sense to me now that he's doing exactly what he told me he didn't want to do."

"Yeah, it was surprising for me to hear too. I didn't expect that from him. Do you think there was something going on with that woman while you were still together?"

"The thought definitely crossed my mind but I have no idea and I'm not going to ask him. I know that he was feeling the pressure from my family about the whole getting married thing - I was feeling it too, but we just weren't right for each other."

I sipped on my drink and was pleasantly surprised by the tangy grapefruit flavour that came through. Nate and I weren't right for each other and I was okay with that now. Hearing that he was engaged definitely came as a shock but it also brought me the closure I didn't realize I was seeking.

"I was worried about you," Reyna admitted. "This has been a difficult year for you and I know how crazy your family can be."

"Yeah, they definitely didn't care at all about how I was actually doing. They're just so angry that I lied and put them in such a difficult situation because everyone is asking questions and blah blah blah."

Reyna scoffed, "That's the Avery's for you."

She was right. My family has always been like that and Reyna has been around enough times to see them live in action.

"How was your weekend in Valencia?" She changed the subject and I was thankful for that. I didn't have much else to say about Nate and my parents.

"Oh, there was some drama," I said as I brought my drink to my lips and continued to sip in between explaining. "Giovanni and his dad got into a fight."

She choked on her drink, "I'm sorry, what?"

I chuckled, "Yeah it was madness."

"Spill the beans."

I knew Reyna wouldn't share this with anyone else - that was part of the best friend's code of conduct.

"We went out for dinner and decided to go for a couple drinks at this bar before heading back to our hotel. Turns out Giovanni's dad was at this same bar but with a woman that wasn't his wife."

Her jaw dropped. "No! Fucking! Way!"

The waiter arrived with our pizza and placed it down in front of us. It was a large one but it was perfect for the two of us to share. It smelled amazing and I couldn't wait to dig in.

The waiter lingered and smiled at Reyna with his boyish grinning. "Can I get you anything else?"

"We're good, thank you." She smiled and he left us to enjoy our meal.

I reached for a slice and brought it to my mouth. The tangy tomato and basil taste was the perfect combination with the copious amounts of cheese they had spread throughout.

"The nerve of his father to do that again," Reyna commented, shaking her head. "What a pig."

"Yeah, Giovanni didn't take it well. He ended up punching his father but he also got hit in the process. I met his mother, Marcia, the other day and she was just the most wonderful lady."

"It's always the good ones that end up with shit like that," she shook her head. "So how's Giovanni handling all this?"

"Not well," I admitted. "He's actually at his moms right now telling her what happened. I can't imagine that's an easy conversation for him to be having."

"God no, that must be awful."

"He still harbours a lot of anger from the last time that happened. He was telling me how he was the one who found his mother after the news broke the first time and it was devastating for him to witness."

"I can't believe his father would put their family through that again."

"I told Giovanni to call me once he's spoken to his mother. It didn't feel right for me to tag along."

Reyna brought her drink to her lips and sipped slowly. "How's it going with the two of you?"

My mind lingered back to this past weekend with him and the heat spread across my cheeks.

"Oh my God, you're blushing already." She laughed.

"I can't help it," I admitted. "I think I could really fall for him."

Reyna rolled her eyes and smiled, "I think you can admit to me that you've already fallen for him, Izzy."

I didn't want to say that out loud but she was right. Saying I could fall for him gave me the sense of security that I could stop that at any point. I could stop before I hit the bottom but the truth was I was no longer in control of my feelings.

"He consumes me," I explained. "I have never had passion like this with anyone before. He excites me and for the first time ever I feel comfortable to be who I am. There are no hidden agendas. He was never part of the plan and that's what I love. He completely took me by surprise."

I downed more of my drink and continued, "And it's not just that he's incredibly hot, he's got a soft side to him too. He's opened up to me and I feel like we truly get each other. He really makes me feel like I belong."

I looked up at Reyna who was smiling at me across the table.

"What?" I asked.

"You're in love with him," she said as a matter-of-fact. "I can see it in the way you talk about him. Your eyes light up with this *thing* I've never seen before."

"I'm not in love with him."

She scoffed, "Izzy, you don't have to lie to me. It's okay to admit it."

I shook my head, "I can't. The minute I admit that I lose all control over this and I can't afford to do that."

"Control over what? Your relationship with him?" She asked. "Does he feel the same about you?"

"I think so," I murmured. "I know he cares about me but I also know that he's never been in love."

"He's also never made the kind of effort that he's made with you."

I smiled. Everyone was so quick to make me aware of Giovanni's lack of commitment but he wasn't like that anymore. I refused to believe he wasn't committed to me. Our relationship became a lot more serious very quickly. I was there for him with what happened now with his dad and he wanted to lean on me. He opened up to me and I believed him when he told me that he cared about me. I could see it in the way he looked at me. It took my breath away at times.

"It's okay to love him, Izzy." Reyna reached out and squeezed my hand.

We continued our lunch and her words repeated over and over in my mind. *Was I in love with him?* Already? How could I tell? I used to think I was in love with Nate but the feelings I had for him were nowhere close to what I was feeling for Giovanni. It didn't even crack the surface. It terrified me to feel this way about him. I pushed that from my mind.

"I couldn't love him already - there's no way."

"Who are you trying to convince here?" Reyna asked. "Me or you?"

CHAPTER 26:

*Y*ou're in love with him.

That phrase lingered in my mind the whole way back. Just thinking about him made my heart skip a beat. I was definitely completely infatuated with him, but in love? I was trying to convince myself that it was too early to feel that way about him. There was still so much we needed to learn about each other. Wasn't there? I glanced at my phone expecting a message from him but there was still nothing. It had been hours since I last heard from him. My lunch with Reyna went on much longer than I expected but I was happy to have that time to catch up with her. She was headed to Diego's place tonight so I wanted to find out if Giovanni could come over. I got off the stop closest to my place and contemplated my next move. I dialed Giovanni's number but it went straight to voicemail. I wasn't sure if I should go back home or if I should head to his place? What if he wasn't there?

I tugged at my lip nervously. I was dying to know what happened with his mother. I wanted to be there for him after such a horrible conversation. There was no way it was going to go down well. Hearing that your husband cheated on you again couldn't be easy at all. The fact that you would put your trust in someone again and they had no problem breaking it made me sick. It wasn't even a situation that involved me directly and yet, I felt so strongly about it. I could only imagine how this must be affecting Giovanni.

Without thinking, I turned down the street in the direction of his apartment. If he wasn't home then I'd just walk back but if he was then I could at least be there for him. The sun was starting to set and I was thankful that I decided to bring my coat with me. The minute the sun started to disappear, the lingering cold air started to settle and remind us that we were in for a cold winter this year. I pulled my coat closer to my body and crossed my arms as I eventually reached his apartment building. I went through the basement entrance and waited for the elevator. I tried to dial him again but his phone was still off. He could still be at his parent's place. The elevator approached his apartment and I could hear music blaring from inside. The doors opened and I stepped inside.

"Hello?" I shouted. "Giovanni?"

I looked around the living room and I couldn't find him. Music was playing at full volume on his surround sound and I went to turn it down. He's got to be here somewhere.

"Who the fuc-" he shouted at the top of the stairs before realizing it was me.

"Oh! Isabella," he slurred. "When did you get here?"

He had been drinking. He came downstairs, stumbling over his own feet as he walked into his kitchen. I'm guessing the conversation didn't go very well. I placed my handbag down on his couch and walked over to him.

"Giovanni," I said softly, placing myself in front of him as he leaned against the counter. He reeked of alcohol.

"Hello, baby," he mumbled, pulling me into his arms. "I tried- I tried to call but I lost my phone and then -"

He mumbled the end of his sentence and I couldn't make out what he was saying. Sadness lingered in his dark brown eyes and my heart reached out to him. I cupped his face and turned him to face me.

"You look hot," he breathed and pulled me in for a kiss. "So hot."

His lips met mine and his arms wrapped around me. His tongue flicked over mine and my arousal came to life. I wanted him but I also wanted to know that he was okay. I pulled away from him but kept my arms around his neck.

"Giovanni, what happened?"

He looked away. "I told her and she broke down as I knew she would. This is the second time now I've seen my mom become a broken woman."

Poor Marcina. I went to pour him a glass of water. He downed the whole thing as I grabbed his other arm and pulled him to the couch. He didn't fight me - he followed me and dropped down. He was defeated. I sat next to him and ran my fingers through his hair.

"Talk to me," I whispered.

"I hate my father," he said as the sadness in his eyes turned to anger. "He broke my mother and he broke our family."

"You don't hate-" I started to say but he interrupted me.

"Yes, I do. I hate him. He's not a man," he spat. "You don't do that to your wife. And this is the second time. *Joder.*"

I took the glass from his hand and placed it on the table.

"What's your mom going to do?"

"No idea. She said she needed to be alone to think about all this. I left her and I knew she was broken," he clenched his fists. "I fucking hate him for what he's done to her."

I grabbed his hands and squeezed them. "Hey, you did the right thing by telling her. She deserved to know."

He said nothing and stared straight ahead. His eyes were filled with anger and sadness and I wanted nothing more than to take his pain away. I hated seeing him like this. I hated that his father did this to him. I slowly rubbed my thumb against the bruise by his eye.

He turned to me and his eyes softened. "How did you know I was here?"

"I didn't," I admitted. "I tried to call but you didn't answer so I thought I'd see if you were home."

He leaned his head against my shoulder and I was glad I decided to come and find him. I didn't want him to be alone after today. No one should have to break that kind of news to their mother.

"I'm glad you're here."

He pulled me to him and my lips met his. The strong taste of whiskey still lingered as I flicked my tongue across his. The urgency of his kiss increased as he pulled me onto his lap. I couldn't hold back the constant lingering tension between my legs anymore. Whenever he touched me or kissed me, my body came to life. I was always ready for him. I ran my fingers through his hair and rocked against his body. He groaned against my lips and my arousal increased. How did he always have this effect on me? It didn't matter the situation, my body was always ready for him. I pulled away from him.

"Giovanni, I want to be there for you," I said softly. "Whatever you need."

"I just need you," he said as his eyes burned with desire. "I don't want to think about anything else right now. I just want to hear you screaming my name."

I was flushed. He was never afraid of expressing what he wanted and we both knew he had the ability to push me off the edge every time.

"Don't you want me, Isabella?" He whispered into my ear, his breath against me sending my body into a frenzy.

"Of course," I breathed.

"I need to know that you're mine." He looked up at me, the desire still burning in his eyes but there was something more now - a sense of longing I hadn't seen before.

"I'm yours, Giovanni."

"Only mine?"

He needed reassurance right now. His lingering but inevitable trust issues were being brought to light by the situation with his parents. I looked down at him. *Oh, what a beautiful man he was.*

"I don't want you to be with anyone else, Isabella," he murmured.

My heart swelled at his words and I could no longer hold back my feelings for him. I needed him to know how I felt.

"You have my heart, Giovanni," I whispered softly.

Looking down at the beautiful and vulnerable man in front of me, I wanted to admit how I truly felt but I was terrified. I was terrified that he didn't love me back.

"And I want to be there for you, whatever you need," I continued. "But how about we get some food into your system first?"

His face fell for a moment before he sighed, "Order in."

***

I woke to the sound of thunder booming across the night sky. My eyes flung open and I sat right up, taking in my surroundings. It gave me such a fright and it took me a few seconds to find my bearings. I ran my fingers through my hair. The curtains in Giovanni's room were still open and the only light was from the street lights beaming through the pouring rain. I glanced down at a sleeping Giovanni next to me, his chest softly rising and falling as he lay peacefully. We spent the last few hours wrapped in each other's arms. The alarm clock on the side of his bed told me it was just after midnight and I was surprised at how many hours we had already slept. I was wide awake now and my stomach growled. We devoured our pizzas earlier but my appetite was asking for a midnight snack. I wrapped my body in one of the blankets on his bed and slowly tip-toed to close the curtains and then out the room, careful not to wake him. He had such a trying day dealing with his family - he deserved to rest.

I strolled downstairs into the kitchen in search of a midnight snack. I'd been here enough times to know that Giovanni always made sure to keep his pantry and fridge fully stocked so there was bound to be something. I opened his pantry cupboard and a box of Pringles immediately caught my eye.

"Yes please," I said to myself and reached for them.

I made myself comfortable on his couch, pulling the blanket closer to me to block off the light cold breeze that hovered in the air. I stared out at the beautiful city through the window. The storm was coming down hard and it brought over a wave of calmness that made me feel right at home. There was nowhere else I was meant to be right now. I dug into the chips as I enjoyed the nighttime view. I replayed Reyna's words over and over in my head.

You're in love with him...

I could try and convince myself all I wanted but I knew she was right. I was completely taken by Giovanni, since the first moment I saw him at Mala Mía. It's crazy to think that the first time we met was only a few months ago - a part of me felt like I had known him my whole life. He was exactly what I needed. He was strong, compassionate and confident. The kind of confidence that made you stop and stare whenever he walked into a room. He didn't seek the attention, it just happened to find him. Besides the fact he was incredibly attractive, there was a softer side to him that slowly crept into my heart. The walls I spent months building around my heart was a complete waste of time because Giovanni Velázquez managed to squeeze his way through. With all his dirty jokes and goofy nature. He was everything I didn't know I needed. I wanted to tell him how I felt - hell, I wanted to scream it from the top of this building but I was terrified that he didn't feel the same. I knew we had a connection, that much was obvious but as far as being in love goes, how would I know?

I was suddenly starting to feel overwhelmed by the fear of the unknown so I pushed that out of my mind and placed the empty box of chips on his table. *Stop overthinking this*. There was no reason for me to say anything to him now about how I felt. I just needed to wait it out a bit and see where this was going to take us. He was dealing with his family falling apart again and I was completely avoiding mine. We weren't really devoid of things to deal with right now so I forced myself to focus on just being there for him in any way I could be. I made my way back to his room and dropped the blanket to the floor. He was tucked underneath his duvet and I slipped myself in. He was facing my side of the bed with his one arm tucked underneath his pillow. I shifted closer to him and his other arm instinctively lifted, allowing me to position myself right up against his body.

"Where'd you go?" he whispered.

I didn't even realize he was awake.

"I was hungry," I said sheepishly.

"Again?" He chuckled. "Did you find anything to eat?"

"Pringles."

"Good choice."

"How are you feeling?" I asked softly, turning to face him.

"Better now that you're here with me."

He wrapped his arm around me and I felt the heat from his body against mine. He kissed my hair and I slipped my hand through his. This was so much more than the one-night stand I intended it to be. This was everything to me right now.

"Isabella?" He whispered into the darkness.

"Yes?"

"I'm glad you're here."

I smiled to myself. "There's nowhere else I'd rather be."

There was enough light still peering through his curtains that I could see his face in the darkness. He had sleepy eyes but he was smiling down at me.

"I owe Reyna for bringing you to Mala Mía that first night." He kissed my forehead.

"I never would have thought that it would have been such a good idea," I admitted.

"This is a one-time thing." He mimicked me.

I giggled. "Well, I didn't know how great you were in bed. How could I ever just have you once?"

His eyes were closed but he remained smiling.

"You caught me by surprise," he admitted. "You're changing me, *mi hermosa.*"

My heart skipped a beat. I rested one hand underneath my head and used my other one to slowly stroke my fingers through his hair. Here we were sharing late-night confessions with each other and I was dying to know what else he was going to share. It was crazy for me to think that this was the same textbook bad-boy with commitment issues that everyone warned me of. They just didn't know him the way I did.

"I hope that's a good thing," I murmured.

He slowly opened his eyes to meet mine, "The best thing. I never knew I needed anyone until you."

Oh, I loved him. Staring into his deep brown eyes while he bared himself to me confirmed everything I already knew. I reached up and his lips met mine. This kiss was different - it had so much more behind it. I wanted to tell him that I wasn't going anywhere because I loved him. I wasn't ready to form the words but he would know one day.

Suddenly, he pulled me closer to him and his lips met mine with a hunger that I now mirrored. I was slammed with the love and desire I had for him. Every overwhelming feeling I had was sitting front row and I needed him to know I was his. His hands traveled up and down my body as I pulled at his hair. He loved that and it told him what he needed to know. I had to have him - now. His lips traveled down my neck at a hungry pace as he gripped the shirt I was wearing. In one swift movement, he pulled me on top of him and I was now straddling him, never once breaking the kiss. He broke away from me and pulled his shirt over his head, throwing it across the room. I followed his lead and removed the shirt of his I had helped myself to earlier. His strong arms wrapped around me and he turned me over, my back now against the bed. He slowly brought his lips down on my body, leaving kisses across my collar bone and down my chest. My breathing picked up as his lips burned my body. He ran his hands down my body.

"Giovanni." I breathed.

The anticipation of what was coming next was suffocating me. He made eye contact with me as he moved across my body and his intense gaze sent my body into a frenzy. He knew exactly what he had to do to drive me over the edge. He pushed his pants down, exposing how ready he was for more.

He brought his body over mine, his arms on each side of me. He slowly brought his lips to my neck again and up to my ear.

"I need you," he whispered.

A small gasp escaped my lips. The combination of his body over me and his breath against my skin was pushing my arousal further and further.

"Giovanni," I breathed.

I spread my legs for him, inviting him where he needed to be. The light peeping from between the curtains was enough for me to notice his smirk as he positioned himself between me. Without breaking eye contact, he pushed deep inside of me. I gasped as he filled me up, perfectly, like he always does. Having him inside of me was euphoric - there was nothing more that I needed. I needed him, always. We belonged together, as one... and I was becoming more and more sure of that. Our bodies moved slowly at first and then we were overcome by this animalistic desire. He lifted both my arms and pinned them above my head, holding them down as he moved deeper. I lifted my legs, welcoming him further and further inside of me. I couldn't get enough. I threw my head back against the pillows moaning his name into the night.

CHAPTER 27:

"**A**re you sure you want me to come with?" I asked.

This morning Giovanni got a phone call from his brother Alvaro inviting him over for lunch. Giovanni had been avoiding his father's calls for days and after Alvaro spoke to their mother he picked up that something was going on. It wasn't exactly the kind of situation you should explain over the phone so Giovanni was going to visit his brother today and tell him what happened with their parents. He asked me to go with him but I was starting to wonder if it was my place to tag along for something like this.

"I need you to come with me, Isabella, I don't want to do this alone."

He grabbed his wallet and car keys from his kitchen counter and turned to me. I sat on the staircase, tying the laces of my boots. He was wearing a pair of black pants and paired it with a pair of dark brown combat boots. The weather was more unforgiving today and we both had our coats on to keep the cold weather at bay. I stood up and closed my coat as Giovanni walked over to me. I was on a higher step that allowed us to be the same height for the first time ever. He slipped his hands around my waist and mine found their place around his neck.

"I need you to be there with me," he murmured. "You're in my life now and I also want to introduce you to Alvaro and Penelope. I wish these were better circumstances but it is what it is."

He's mentioned Alvaro's wife, Penelope to me before. She was quite far along in her pregnancy now and they had just purchased a house outside of the city which was where we were headed today.

"Okay," I reached out and kissed him. "You know I'll always be here for you."

He smiled, "Shall we?"

***

Half an hour later we pulled into the driveway leading up to a very modern-looking house. It was the most modern architecture I had seen in Barcelona so far. It was a square white double-story house with a balcony on the top overlooking the spacious garden in front. Giovanni turned the car off and turned to me.

"You ready?"

I nodded. He reached out and squeezed my hand before getting out of the car. I followed behind him as his brother came to greet us.

"Hola, hermano." Alvaro greeted and pulled Giovanni in for a hug.

There were plenty of similarities between Alvaro and Giovanni but they were also so different. Alvaro had long curly brown hair but they both had the same dark brown eyes. Alvaro was cleanly shaved and his style was more reserved and laid-back than Giovanni's. They were the same height but Giovanni was a lot broader. There were enough similarities between them to never have you question whether they were related or not.

Giovanni stepped back from the hug and pulled me closer to him. "Alvaro, I'd like you to meet my girlfriend, Isabella."

Girlfriend? *Oh my God* - he said it. I tried to keep my composure as I stepped forward to greet Alvaro in the typical Spanish fashion - a kiss on each cheek.

"Pleasure to meet you."

"Lovely to meet you, Isabella," Alvaro smiled. "Never thought I'd see the day when this guy over here got a girlfriend."

I blushed. Hearing that word again made me smile. I didn't expect Giovanni to introduce me that way but I was so happy that he did. We were in a relationship and he was no longer shying away from that. A petite blond stepped through the front door and came to greet us, her very pregnant belly leading the way.

"*Hola*, Giovanni," Penelope greeted Giovanni and then turned to me. "You must be Isabella. We've heard so much about you."

"All good things I hope."

"Of course." Alvaro chuckled.

"Welcome to our home," Penelope smiled. "Please come inside."

Alvaro and Penelope walked in front of us through the front door. I reached for Giovanni before he went inside.

"Girlfriend?" I mused. "Where did that come from?"

"I don't want to be with anyone else, Isabella," he slipped his hand in mine. "So it's what you are now - if that's what you want of course."

I giggled. "Of course that's what I want."

He smiled and kissed my forehead. I followed him through the large wooden front door and was welcomed by their home. The ceilings were high and there was a staircase to the right of the house as you entered. We strolled through the open plan kitchen and I placed my handbag down on the counter. The kitchen opened out onto their wooden patio, overlooking their back garden and the clear water of the pool. They had a lovely home. It was much colder today but the sun shining down on us was definitely helping.

"Isabella, can I get you anything to drink?" Alvaro asked.

He stood behind the bar they had at the end of the patio. Penelope had taken a seat at the table and gestured for us to do the same.

"Yes, please."

Giovanni went to join Alvaro behind the bar, "What do you feel like, baby? They've got wine, gin, water..."

Baby? I couldn't believe the sudden change in Giovanni. Don't get me wrong, this was everything I had wanted but I still didn't expect it.

We were here to have an uncomfortable conversation with Giovanni's brother but I was smiling from ear to ear.

"I'll have a glass of wine, thank you."

Alvaro and Giovanni carried on with the drinks as I took a seat across the table from Penelope. She was very pretty. She has straight blonde hair that sat just above her shoulders. She had light brown eyes and light freckles across her cheeks and nose. Her face was plump but pregnancy would do that to you.

"We're glad to meet you, Isabella," Penelope chimed. "For a while, I thought Giovanni would end up as a terminal bachelor."

I chuckled. "From what I've heard, that's what everyone thought."

Giovanni strolled to the table and sat down next to me, placing my wine glass in front of me. Both he and Alvaro settled for a glass of whiskey. Giovanni kept one hand on my thigh and the other on his glass.

"Now as happy as we are to have you guys here, I know you have something to tell me, Giovanni," Alvaro continued. "I called *Ma* yesterday and something was off."

"Yeah it's not the kind of conversation either of us wanted to have over the phone," Giovanni sipped on his drink. "I caught dad with another woman last weekend in Valencia."

Both Alvaro and Penelope couldn't hide the shock at the information Giovanni was sharing. They didn't expect that and I could see Alvaro trying to process this.

"Was it the same woman?" Alvaro asked.

Unlike Giovanni, he remained calm about the situation. I could see the anger and frustration on his face but the delivery of his words remained unchanged.

"I have no idea," Giovanni said. "But I punched him and yesterday I went to tell Ma what happened. I couldn't lie to her."

"No, of course not. You did the right thing."

Penelope remained silent and reached for Alvaro's hand. He was processing the information and I felt bad for him. I felt bad for all of them.

"And how did *Ma* take it?"

"How do you think?" Giovanni scoffed and took another sip of his drink. "She was a fucking mess again. How could she not be? You were there when he said he wouldn't do this again and now look."

"Well, she needs to leave him," Alvaro stated. "How many times is she going to get hurt by him?"

A flicker of emotion flared in his voice. I agreed with him - it wasn't my place to say it but their mother deserved better than this.

"She told me she needed time to think about all of this. I didn't want to leave her yesterday but you know how she can be. I don't think she knows what to do right now."

"Well, of course not," Penelope joined the conversation. "She's been with your father for how many years?"

"You can't just stay with someone because of your history." Giovanni scowled.

"I'm not saying that, Giovanni," Penelope replied gently. "We should ask her if she'd like to come here for a few days. It will give her time to process everything away from your father."

I glanced up at Giovanni. The lingering anger from this situation shone in his eyes and I squeezed his hand, reassuring him I was here for him.

"Have you seen dad since?" Alvaro asked.

Giovanni shook his head, "He's tried to call a few times but I ignored him. He wasn't there when I went yesterday and I'm glad. I'll fuck him up."

"You can't do that," he scoffed.

"I can and I will," Giovanni retorted. "He deserves it."

"We have to see what *Ma* is going to do first before we retaliate."

"Well, I don't want anything to do with him anymore," Giovanni downed the rest of his drink. "And you can't expect me to."

Alvaro shrugged, "I wasn't going to. I understand how strained your relationship has always been."

Alvaro didn't seem to have the same distaste for his father that Giovanni had. They seemed to be the ones to constantly bump heads.

Alvaro turned to me and smiled. "I'm sure this isn't the most pleasant conversation to have for the first time meeting us."

We all chuckled at his attempt to lighten the mood.

"Not exactly, but I wanted to be here for Giovanni."

Giovanni turned to me and smiled. The anger slowly started to leave his eyes as the affection he held for me made its way through. The way he looked at me sometimes took my breath away - he made me feel loved.

"So apart from all this other bullshit," Alvaro continued. "What did Pedro say about Valencia?"

They delved straight into business so I focused on getting to know Penelope a little better.

"So, how long have you two been together?"

"About three years now. I knew him back in school but we never dated or anything and then one day we bumped into each other and now here we are." She smiled and rubbed her belly.

"It's so nice to see things work out." I smiled at her. "Congratulations on your baby. How far along are you?"

"Got about five weeks to go," she said as she glanced down at her belly with so much love in her eyes. "He's already such a big boy though, I look huge."

I giggled. "You look amazing - you've got that pregnancy glow everyone talks about."

"It's called sweat," she mused. "It definitely takes a toll on you but it's such a blessing."

I smiled. It was so lovely to see a couple like Alvaro and Penelope. They seemed to be genuinely happy with each other and they had built up a great life together.

"Well, I hope you're getting plenty of foot rubs from your husband," I joked.

"Of course she does," Alvaro jumped in. "I wasn't very good in the beginning but I got there eventually."

Penelope rubbed her thumb against his cheek and smiled. They were completely smitten with each other, you could see it through the way they looked at each other. Giovanni placed his hand on my thigh and squeezed gently trying to get my attention. I turned to him.

"Thank you for being here with me," he said softly enough to just keep the conversation between the two of us.

I slipped my hand into his. "Well, you are my boyfriend now."

He chuckled. "I like the sound of that."

He leaned over and kissed my cheek. I was so happy with where we were right now. We were officially together and I couldn't believe that I could call this beautiful man mine.

"So, what shall we do for lunch?" Alvaro asked. "I was thinking we could order something." As they continued talking, I heard my phone start to ring from inside. I excused myself as they went through the options. I reached my handbag and dug out my phone, not recognizing the number on the screen.

"Hello?" I answered.

"Isabella," my sister's voice came through the other side. "Bella, you need to come home."

My stomach dropped at the unexpected emotion in my sister's voice. Her voice was breaking and she sounded as if she was crying.

"Camila, what's going on?" I couldn't hide the panic in my voice.

"Dad had a heart attack."

Oh no

"They're struggling to get his heart to stabilize. Bella, you need to come home now, they don't know if he's going to make it."

I was overcome by a wave of emotions at her words and the tears started streaming down my face as I struggled to process what she was saying to me.

Dad had a heart attack.

The words played over and over in my head.

"I'll get on the next flight."

We disconnected and I couldn't hold myself together any longer. Everything I had held in over the last few months came flooding in as I tried to grapple with the news she just told me. Giovanni rushed inside to me as I started to cry.

"Baby, what happened?" Giovanni was frantic. "Isabella, speak to me."

He held me close to him as I cried against his chest.

"My dad had a heart attack."

"Oh, baby no." He pulled me closer to him.

"They don't know if he's going to make it," my voice cracked.

I couldn't get a handle on my bearings right now. I was in a state. Penelope and Alvaro hovered around us speaking to Giovanni but I couldn't focus on what they were saying. My father had a heart attack and I wasn't there. I hadn't spoken to him in so long and now I had to go back home because they didn't know if he was going to make it.

Oh my God...

The more I thought about it, the harder I cried. Giovanni tightened his arms around me.

"Isabella," his voice sounded so distant. "Izzy, we need to go to London now."

He held onto me as we walked towards the entrance. I was so disconnected from reality - I felt as if I was watching myself from above. All I was thinking about was getting home. *What if he died and I didn't get to say goodbye?* I felt sick to my stomach. We said our goodbyes - both Alvaro and Penelope giving me big hugs and wishing me luck and before I knew it we were back in Giovanni's car, speeding down the road as he comforted me as best as he could.

"Isabella, I need you to listen to me baby," he said softly. "We are going to your apartment and I need you to pack what you need okay? I'll organize our tickets on the next flight out."

I remained silent but I held onto his hand tightly.

"I'm here for you. Everything's going to be fine," he murmured.

He didn't know that. No one did.

CHAPTER 28:

By the time I got back to my apartment, I was numb. Giovanni walked me upstairs, his hand in mine the whole way. He unlocked the door and we stepped inside, greeted by the emptiness.

"We need to pack a bag and grab your passport," Giovanni explained softly, "Do you want me to do that for you?"

I shook my head. "I'll do it. Could you call Reyna and let her know?"

"Of course." He kissed my forehead.

I walked down the hall to my room and grabbed a bag from the floor. I threw it on my bed and started shoving whatever I could find in it. *My father had a heart attack.* I couldn't fight the sick feeling of guilt that sat deep inside of me. I couldn't even remember the last time I had a full conversation with him. We spoke briefly a couple of months ago. He always reminded me that no matter what, he loved me. Unlike my mother, he tried to be more caring and understanding. He didn't ask too many questions - he just wanted to know I was okay. *Why didn't I make more of an effort with him? I* was so angry at myself. I didn't even realize that tears had started to form again until they spilled over, running down my cheeks. I dropped on my bed next to my bag and hung my head in my hands. What if he didn't make it? What would have been the last thing I said to him? I never thanked him for being a good father and he was, no matter the difficulties I faced with my mother and sister, it had nothing to do with him. He just got caught in the middle of my mother and me - the constant bickering and disagreements. Her constant disapproval of my choices and the pressure I had always felt from her. All of that seemed so irrelevant at that moment.

"Isabella?" I looked up at Giovanni standing in the doorway. "Baby are you ready to go? Our flight leaves in an hour."

I wiped my cheeks as he walked over to me and wrapped his arms around me.

"It's going to be okay," he murmured into my hair.

"You don't know that." I sniffed.

"We'll be in London soon and then you'll be able to see him. I'm sure your family has the best doctors working on him."

That was probably true. My mother was pedantic about so many things in life - she would definitely ensure my father was being taken care of. I gathered myself together and took a deep breath in. Giovanni grabbed my bag.

"Do you have everything?"

I quickly grabbed my passport from my bedside table, "Yes, let's go."

***

It was already nightfall by the time we pulled up in front of St. Jude's hospital. I didn't know how Giovanni organized everything so quickly but we were in London and I was about to see my family for the first time in months. We stopped at the hotel room he booked and dropped our bags off first before heading to the hospital. The sick feeling in my stomach got worse at the thought of going inside - the guilt and the anxiety were now doubling over. I had no idea what to expect when I stepped through those doors. I didn't want to have to talk about anything from the last few months - I just wanted to focus on my dad. That's why I was here.

Giovanni grabbed my hand, pulling me out of my own overthinking. "Are you ready?"

I shook my head. "I don't think I am. This is the first time I'm going to see my family."

"You're here for your father, *mi hermosa*," he said as he kissed my forehead. "That's all you need to focus on."

I shrugged and took a deep breath in. All I wanted to know was that my father was okay. We walked through the lobby and I went over to the older lady sitting behind the desk at reception.

"Hi, I'm looking for my father. Oscar Avery."

"Yes dear, let me have a look for you." She fixed her glasses and turned to her computer screen.

I tapped my nails nervously on the counter.

"Isabella?" A deep voice said from behind me.

I turned to see Smith walking through the hospital lobby. He had put on a bit more weight since the last time I saw him. His soft, kind face was rounded out and I was surprised by the full chrome beard he was now sporting. Camila was never someone who liked facial hair so I was surprised her husband had such a thick beard. The bags under his blue-grey eyes gave away his clear lack of sleep but they were full of concern.

"Smith, hi," I reached out and he pulled me in for a brief hug. "I got here as soon as I could. Is there any news?"

"They managed to stop the pain but he's not out of the woods yet. We're still waiting to hear from his doctor."

Giovanni stepped beside me and extended his hand to Smith. "Hi, I'm Giovanni. Nice to meet you."

Smith was taken back by Giovanni and looked over to me.

"Oh sorry, Smith, this is my boyfriend, Giovanni."

He tried to hide his surprise and shook his hand. "Nice to meet you, Giovanni. I'm Smith - Isabella's sister's husband."

Smith was kinder than my sister and mother combined so I wasn't sure how they were going to react to Giovanni. My mother was so convinced I was going to marry Nate and with the latest relationship updates from the last few weeks, I didn't think she was going to be prepared for me to have a new boyfriend. Especially one the complete opposite of what she would approve of. I didn't want to have to deal with that now though - I was here for my father and nothing more.

"I'll take you to his room," Smith said and led us down the corridor.

Every hospital was the same. The piercing bright white lights shining down on you and the smell of disinfectant all around. I hated hospitals. They were too often filled with families riddled with uncertainty as they waited for news on their loved ones or families overcome by sadness over the loss of someone. It made my heart sore.

I stepped closer to Giovanni. "I don't know what's going to happen when you meet my mother and sister."

He shrugged casually. "I'm here for you, Isabella, so whatever happens, I'll take it."

I tightened my hand around his as Smith turned us down the aisle marked "Cardiac ICU" and my family came into view. My mother and Camila were sitting side by side on the chairs against the wall across from the ICU doors.

"Isabella," Camila gasped and got to her feet.

I let go of Giovanni's hand and went to greet my sister. Her brown eyes are all puffy from crying. She threw her arms around me and a lump started to form in my throat, suddenly overcome by the emotions again. I had never seen my sister like this.

"It's good to see you, Bella," she whispered in my ear.

"You too, Camila."

My mother stood up and turned to face me. Gloria Avery had never looked older. My mother had always held a youthfulness to her face but the latest creases in her eyes and forehead started to give away her age. Her dark brown hair was cut short just below her chin. Her face remained unchanged - not a flicker of emotion in her light brown eyes.

"I'm surprised you're here," she sneered, clipping her words in her formal delivery.

Seriously? Her husband was in ICU fighting for his life and she still decided to address me in her usual, unemotive ways. I wiped my eyes and crossed my arms, my sadness now replaced with frustration.

"Of course I'm here," I retorted. "Dad is fighting for his life right now."

She snorted and Camila turned to her. "Mother, please don't do this now."

I was thankful for my sister's interruption. I was not in the right headspace to get into anything with my mother right now. She flicked her eyes past me landing on Giovanni.

"And who is this?" She snapped.

I turned to Giovanni and reached for his hand.

"This is my boyfriend, Giovanni." I announced.

I watched my mother clench her jaw as she looked Giovanni up and down. She was not happy at all.

"Boyfriend?" she repeated, not bothering to hide her distaste.

Giovanni stepped forward and very politely extended his hand to Camila, "Hi, Camila, I'm Giovanni."

Camila shook his hand and politely greeted him but I could see the surprise on her face. None of them were very good at hiding their feelings. Giovanni extended his hand to my mother next.

"Nice to meet you, Mrs. Avery."

My mother looked down at his hand and crossed her arms. "Wish I could say the same."

"Mother!" I snapped. "There is no reason you have to be so rude."

Giovanni dropped his arm and stepped back beside me. He kept his face very neutral and I was thankful for his level-headedness right now as one of us had to be that way.

"Isabella Avery, you do not want to get into this with me right now," she warned. "You think you can just waltz back in here after all your months of lying, deceit and blatant disrespect? I don't even recognize the daughter standing in front of me right now."

Shots fired. She didn't hold back. A part of me thought she would have at least contained herself until we were alone but I was foolish to have thought that. My mother had never had a maternal bone in her body. I clenched my fists, the anger inside of me boiling up.

"Mother, please!" Camila hissed. "Now is not the time or place."

Thankfully, the doctor pushed through the ICU doors just in time before I opened my mouth. I wasn't sure I would have been able to hold back everything I wanted to say. I was overwhelmed with emotions right now and my mother was pushing me over the edge.

"Mrs. Avery?" The doctor stepped towards us. "I'm Doctor Greenwood."

He must have been in his late 40's. He pulled the material cap off his hair exposing his dirty blond hair. His jawline was very defined and his blue eyes reminded me of a human-looking Ken doll. He pulled his gloves off and shoved them into his dark blue scrubs.

"We've managed to stabilize him but we still need to assess the damage done. He is still in pain but we are unable to give him any morphine at this stage as that would drop his heart rate way down and with the instability of the beating right now, it could stop his heart."

Giovanni stood close to me, reaching for my hand again as I listened intently to what the doctor explained.

"These next 24 hours are crucial. His heart needs to start beating at a regular pace again by itself and right now that's not happening. We need to wait for it to stabilize before we can think of the next step."

"And what if it doesn't?" my mother asked.

"I'm sorry but you and your family need to be prepared for the worst. All we can do at this stage is continue to monitor him and hope that his heart begins to stabilize again. This was a very severe heart attack and I think it might be best for you all to go in and see him and say your goodbyes just in case."

The lump in my throat worsened as I tried to hold back my tears. My father could die in the next 24 hours and we had to be prepared for that.

How the fuck do you even begin to prepare for something like that?

My mother followed Dr. Greenwood into the ICU room. I turned to face Giovanni, concern spread across his face. He cupped my face in his hands.

"He's going to be okay, baby. You need to believe that he's going to be fine," he consoled. "I'm going to be right out here waiting for you."

I leaned my head against his chest and his arms tightened around me. *Was I supposed to say goodbye to my dad?* Would this be the last time I ever saw him? How could I possibly begin to be okay with that? The nauseating feeling that washed over me got worse with each thought.

"Isabella, you can go next," Camila said as my mother came outside again.

I avoided her eyes and walked straight into the ICU. The constant beeping sound surrounded me as I laid eyes on my dad in the hospital bed. My eyes filled with tears at the sight of him. His eyes were closed with his hand resting on his stomach. He was hooked up to so many machines it made my heart ache. His hair had started to grey out but he still had so many years left inside of him. I approached his bed and slowly reached for his hand. His eyes fluttered open.

"Isabella?" He breathed. "Is it really you?"

The tears slid down my cheek. "It's me, dad. I'm here."

I could see the tears starting to form in his eyes and I had to tell myself not to break down at the sight of that.

"You're here," he kept repeating as he tightened his hand around mine.

"I'm here and I'm so sorry, dad," I whimpered.

He slowly moved his other hand over mine. The movements highlighted how weak he truly was in that moment.

"I'm sorry about everything and I'm sorry I haven't been here. I love you so much, dad. You have to be okay." I couldn't hold back the tears as they streamed down.

"Shhhh, Isabella," he murmured. "I'm going to be fine."

"I'm so sorry." I kept repeating, overcome with emotions at the sight of my frail father.

"I want you to be happy, Izzy. Tell me that you're happy."

I looked up at him and his light eyes filled with emotion. He always had kind eyes. That was one thing about my father - he could comfort you with just one look. After everything that has happened, all he wanted to know was that I was happy. His forgiving nature made me even more emotional.

"I'm happy but I need you to be okay," I sniffed. "That will make me truly happy."

"I love you, Izzy."

"I love you too, dad."

I held onto him until a friendly nurse came to tell me that my sister wanted to come inside but it was only one visitor at a time. My dad's eyes were closed again but his chest was slowly moving up and down. I kissed his forehead one last time before leaving the room. I entered the corridor and Giovanni sat alone on the couch in front of the doors. My mother was nowhere in sight.

"Where did she go?" I asked him.

He shrugged his shoulders. "She wouldn't say a word to me. She just came out and took off in that direction."

He pointed down the hall but she wasn't there. Smith stood awkwardly at the doors to the ICU, waiting for Camila. I wiped my cheeks and took in a deep breath.

"Smith, we're going to head out," I announced. "You can tell Camila I'll be back here tomorrow morning for visiting hours."

He nodded and gave me a weak smile. Smith never had a very strong nature to him but he always tried to be kind, especially to me. I grabbed Giovanni's hand and we made our way to the exit of the hospital.

"The taxi will be here in two minutes," he said.

We pushed through the doors and in true London fashion, we were greeted by the rain. We stood close together underneath the roof while we waited for our transport back to the hotel. It was freezing and I couldn't wait to get out of here.

"So, you're just going to leave again without saying goodbye?" I heard my mother say.

I turned to the side and my mother climbed the few stairs to the top where we were standing. She had her coat on and held an umbrella above her head.

"I came here to see dad and I will be back tomorrow for visiting hours," I said coldly.

"You have a lot of explaining to do, Isabella," she snapped. "Don't think you can just show up here as if nothing has happened."

I rolled my eyes. "Yes, heaven forbid you'd be able to contain yourself. Even in situations like this, you have to act so heartless and make this about you."

My mother was seething now but I didn't care. She had a terrible way of getting under my skin and I couldn't stop myself from snapping at her.

"You're the one who has been heartless," she spat. "You disappear for months after blatantly disrespecting me and running away to God knows where. Your career and relationship were in absolute shambles and you lied to us about it!"

"You don't know what you're talking about!" I objected. "How could I possibly turn to you? You've never cared about how I felt. You've only ever cared about yourself and your status."

I wanted to scream. My blood was boiling over and I knew that if I didn't leave right now, I would say something I would regret. Thankfully our taxi pulled up in front of the hospital just in time. Giovanni started to walk towards the taxi and I followed behind him.

"How dare you?" my mother exclaimed, "I'm the parent here - I've always done what's best for you."

I stopped and turned to her. "No you've always done what's best for you."

Giovanni opened the door for me and I stepped inside, not even bothering to hear what else my mother had to say to me. I stared outside the window and the pouring rain as we sped off into the night. I was exhausted - mentally and emotionally.

"Are you okay?" Giovanni whispered to me.

"Not at all."

He put his arm around me and pulled me closer to him. I closed my eyes and rested my head against his chest. Everything that happened was spinning around in my head and I couldn't stop it. I really thought my mother would have contained herself for the sake of my dad and what was happening but I was wrong to have expectations. All I needed was a hug from her to tell me everything was going to be fine. Isn't that what parents were supposed to do? They're supposed to comfort you and make everything better but instead, my mother dismissed how I must be feeling and went all in. I knew she had so much more to say but I couldn't give her the time of day - I was too overwhelmed.

"I'm sorry my mother was so rude to you."

"That's not your fault."

"I know, but still. She can be a real bitch sometimes."

Giovanni chuckled. "I can handle your mother. She's not the one I'm here for."

I reached up and planted a soft kiss on his lips. He was my only comfort right now and I wanted to hold onto him for as long as I could.

CHAPTER 29:

We made it back to our hotel and Giovanni led the way up to the top floor. He unlocked the door and opened it, gesturing for me to step inside. I strolled into the room, shrugging my jacket off and placing it on the coat rack by the door. It was a spacious room with a double bed in the middle. There were large windows ahead of us with the curtains still open, giving us the perfect view of rainy London. We had a single chair in the corner of the room and a flat-screen TV on the wall across from the bed. Below it was a mini-bar and table filled with all you need to brew a hot cup of coffee.

"I want to go take a shower quickly. Do you want to order room service?"

I shook my head and Giovanni walked over to me. He reached out and placed his hands on my shoulders.

"You need to eat something baby. You haven't eaten all day," he said softly.

"I know. I just can't think of food right now."

He leaned down and placed a kiss on my forehead. "I understand. Let me order something small just in case you get hungry later."

He grabbed the menu off the table and started looking through it. I strolled over to the windows, taking in the storm. The rain had picked up and the thunder boomed across the sky. The city was dark but there were moments where the lightning illuminated it enough to reveal the beautiful view we had of Big Ben. I could see most of the city from our room and I had forgotten how beautiful it was. I had always loved living in London but I loved Barcelona more. The vibrancy of the city consumed me and there was something more freeing about Barcelona. It made me feel like I could be whoever I wanted to be. London was tainted by my family's ever-controlling ways and as much as I loved it here, I didn't think I could ever live there again.

"I've ordered something small. It should be up soon so I'm going to hop into the shower quickly."

I nodded and smiled at him before he disappeared into the bathroom. I turned back to the view of the city and took a deep breath in. *What a day.* I thought my biggest problem today was going to be whether or not Giovanni's brother liked me or not. I certainly didn't think I was going to end up back in London with my father fighting for his life. The deep pain in my chest resurfaced and I had to stop myself from crying. *He's going to be okay.* I kept repeating that to myself - it was the only thing keeping me from breaking. It was surreal to see my family after so long. I wish they had been under better circumstances but thinking back, I doubt I would have returned to London at all. I didn't want to face the music with them. I was ashamed of how my life went and I knew I was a disappointment to them. Now, I was here and none of that mattered to me. I didn't want to marry Nate and I was thankful we never went through with that. Everything that happened brought me to Giovanni and he was all that was important to me.

A few minutes later, a soft tap at the door brought me out of my own thoughts. I wiped my eyes and went to open the door. An older gentleman stood outside with a trolley of food that was ordered.

"Evening, Miss," he greeted politely. "Here is your order."

"Thank you so much."

I grabbed the trolley and brought it inside. With a sweet smile, he turned and I closed the door behind me. I left the trolley by the table. I had no idea what he ordered but it smelled great. I lifted the lid and two grilled cheese sandwiches sat on the plate. My stomach awoke at the sight of it and revealed just how hungry I actually was. I grabbed one half of the sandwich and bit into it. *Holy hell that tasted good.* The melted cheese mixed with an array of spices made it taste like I was eating a pizza.

Giovanni stepped outside of the bathroom with just a towel around his waist.

"That was quick," he said, glancing at the room service tray. "See, I knew you were hungry."

I smiled. "This is the best sandwich I've ever had."

He chuckled and ran his fingers through his wet hair. He strolled over and grabbed one half for himself.

"Okay, you were right. This is pretty good."

I smiled at him and finished off my half. My stomach now pleased with me that I actually decided to stop depriving it.

"Do you want a drink?" Giovanni asked.

"Definitely. I could use one."

I didn't want to think right now. I needed a distraction from everything going on. He opened the mini-bar and observed it's contents.

"Okay, we've got some red wine, white wine, whiskey, vodka..."

"None of that is strong enough so I guess I'll settle for the white wine."

I sat down on the bed as he handed me my wine glass and proceeded to pour himself a whiskey - neat. We sat in silence for a moment, both of us lost in thought. I had so much going on with my family but so did Giovanni.

"So, is your mom going to stay with Alvaro?" I asked.

Giovanni sipped on his drink. "They're going to go visit her tomorrow and suggest that. I don't know what's going to happen to be honest."

He leaned against the wall next to the mini-bar. Every time I looked at him I felt a rush inside. He was so fucking sexy. The way he brought his glass to his lips and tilted his head back was surprisingly arousing to me. He ran his fingers through his dark hair again and stared into the night - his deep brown eyes full of worry. I just wanted to take it all away. Here I was dealing with my own shit but I just wanted to be there for him - the same way he had been there for me.

I downed my wine and held my empty glass out for him.

"You know you're supposed to sip that?" he mused.

"Not tonight. If there was tequila, I would have opted for that instead but this will have to do."

He said nothing and topped me up. I worked my way through that glass quite quickly and eventually went over to grab the bottle to top myself up. I didn't know if it was still the lack of food in my system or the pure exhaustion I was feeling but I was already tipsy. One half of a grilled sandwich was definitely not enough to soak up the amount of alcohol I was now putting into my system.

"Slow down there, baby," he murmured.

"I don't want to think right now."

I felt the alcohol spread through my body and my concerns began to fade into the back. I stopped myself from thinking of what happened today - I didn't want to think of anything and it was easy for it to become white noise with alcohol in your system. I watched Giovanni down his drink and for some reason I couldn't keep my eyes off him. His strongly defined chest and abs are all covered in his tattoos that I found so attractive. Each time he lifted the glass to his lips, his arms flexed and I couldn't help but bite my lip. Of all his tattoos, the ones on his arms were my favourite.

"What?" he asked as he caught me staring at him.

"Nothing." I shrugged. "I'm just looking at you."

He placed his empty glass down and walked over to the bed. He leaned on the edge of it and flicked his eyes up to mine.

God, he looked so fucking hot.

"You're just looking at me?" He murmured. I tugged at my bottom lip and nodded.

He moved closer to me, "And do you like what you see?"

"I love what I see."

I tilted my head back and emptied my glass once more as he smirked at me. He grabbed my empty glass and leaned forward to place it on the bedside table. He was so close to me now so I breathed him in. *Fuck, he always smelled so good.* How in the world was this man all mine? He leaned closer to me, our faces inches away from each other. The palpable tension rising with each longing look and slow movement, inching closer to each other. I couldn't hold back any longer and I wrapped my arms around his neck.

"What do you want, Isabella?" he breathed.

"You, Giovanni. I've always wanted you."

He leaned down and his lips met mine. The taste of whiskey lingering as he flicked his tongue over mine. He was intoxicating. All the alcohol in the world couldn't measure up to the inebriated state he put me in whenever he was around. It consumed me - every touch, every kiss set my body on fire and I couldn't help it. And the fact he was all mine now? How was that even possible?

I broke the kiss and asked. "Did you mean it earlier when you called me your girlfriend?"

He was inches from me and I could see the lingering desire in his eyes, "Of course I did. I realized I could have found a better way to ask you but there was no other way I wanted to introduce you to my family."

I smiled. "So, you really want me to be your girlfriend?"

"Yes. I fought my feelings for you for so long but I don't want to do that anymore, Isabella," he murmured. "I want to be with you."

I was happy to hear what he was saying. I've wanted this for so long but I also wanted him to be sure. I wanted nothing more than to be with him.

"And you're sure that you're ready for a relationship?"

"*Si, mi hermosa*," he said as he sat down next to me and gently reached out to tuck a strand of hair behind my ear. "I know we're both dealing with stuff right now but that's what made it all clear to me."

I reached for his hand and squeezed it tight. He stared down at them and I could see the vulnerability in his face. He was being vulnerable with me and I loved that - I wanted to do the same with him. I wasn't afraid of getting hurt anymore because the stakes were high for both of us. I wasn't feeling this alone and I didn't know if he loved me like I loved him but I knew he cared about me and that was enough for now. With everything going on right now, I was thankful I had him to distract me. I needed him to.

"It fucking terrified me to say any of this out loud," he murmured. "I've never felt like this about anyone before so I know I don't want to lose that. I don't want to lose you - I need you in my life."

"I don't want to lose you either, Giovanni."

He looked up at me and smiled. *Oh, how I loved that smile.* I reached out and rested my hand against his cheek, his facial hair brushing against me.

"I love this," I said and ran my fingers against his beard. "And this..."

I moved my hands to his chest and across his tattoos, "I love all your tattoos."

I could sense the alcohol assisting me with the constant use of the word 'love'. I wasn't intentionally hinting at anything - I just knew I wanted him to know how I felt.

"What else do you love, baby?"

I flicked my eyes up to his and the previous lingering desire made its way through again. He loved it when I touched him and I was running my hands up and down his body. I wanted to feel him all - I needed to. I shifted closer to him, our faces just inches from each other.

"I love the way you kiss me," I whispered.

He brought his hand up to my hair and pulled me closer to him, our lips meeting.

"Like this?" He asked in between our kisses.

"Mmm-hmm."

He pulled away, a level of concern had reached his eyes. "I want to be there for you, Isabella, whatever you need."

"I just need you, Giovanni," I murmured. "I don't want to think. I just need you to take it all away, even if just for a moment."

He leaned his forehead against mine. "Are you sure, baby?"

I nodded and he slowly leaned into me. There was only one towel separating me from having all of him. I increased the urgency in our kiss - I wanted him and my own animalistic desires took charge. His insistent lips parted mine and his desire mirrored my own. My body was awoken to the sensation of his kiss - he wanted me and to feel like a wanted woman, and that was the most beguiling feeling in the world. I pulled my shirt over my head and tossed it across the room, returning my lips to his. He made me forget everything I didn't want to remember. Everything disappeared and it was just him and I. My hands found their way through his hair and I tugged at it as his lips reached my neck. After all this time, he was still tantalizing to me. He laid me against the bed and towered over me. His lips found my neck again and moved across my collarbone and down to my chest. I threw my head back and closed my eyes. I couldn't help the quickening of my breath - every kiss making my body shudder with desire. Every movement of his had a purpose. He was careful and calculated and yet, he didn't hold back. He pulled at my hair and nipped at my neck. His lips reached mine and I couldn't help but tug at his bottom lip.

"Isabella," he groaned. "You're killing me baby."

"Now, Giovanni," I breathed.

Without hesitation he reached for the button of my jeans and undid it, sliding my zip down along with it. I pushed my pants off and my underwear was next. I leaned up and he unclipped my bra, that too joining the pile of clothes on the floor. He stood up and removed his towel, exposing himself to me. *Fuck he was so ready for me.*

CHAPTER 30:

"**C**an I get two cups of coffee, please? One black please?" I asked the friendly grey-haired lady behind the counter at the cafeteria at the hospital.

Giovanni and I spent the rest of the night in each other's arms and only managed to get a couple of hours of shut-eye before we had to be up for early morning visiting hours. He was the perfect distraction from the mounting sadness I had inside of me. I ordered our coffees while he finished off his phone call with his business partner, Pedro. They were close to closing a deal for the building in Valencia and it was a time-sensitive agreement. I took a seat at one of the tables while they made our coffee. The hospital was quiet this morning. Visiting hours were spread out to three different times a day but I was too anxious to wait till later. We still had half an hour until we were allowed to go in. We hadn't heard anything during the night and I was thankful for that - if they were going to call, it would have been with bad news so I was feeling optimistic today.

"Here you go my dear," the lady behind the counter said as she set our coffee cups down on the table in front of me. "Is there anything else I could get you?"

"No, this is perfect, thank you so much."

I handed her the cash for the coffee and with one last smile, she returned back to behind the counter. I reached for my cup and took a small sip. It was still very hot but the warmth spread through me and I could already feel myself starting to wake up a bit. I was pretty sure the idea of having caffeine in the morning was a placebo but I'd take any help I could get at this point. If I turned to face the entrance behind me, I could see Giovanni from where I was sitting. He was still on the phone outside pacing up and down. I tapped my fingernails anxiously on the table as I sipped my coffee.

"Isabella?"

I heard my name and I turned back to see Camila walking towards me. She looked just as drained as I did. The bags under her eyes gave it away. I couldn't blame her as I didn't think any of us got any sleep last night. Her wavy short hair was pulled into a low ponytail, hidden briefly by the big scarf she was wearing. She paired that with a big navy coat and jeans with her rain boots reaching just below her knee. It was definitely cold but she was dressed for a storm.

"Hi, Camila." I stood up and gave her a quick hug before returning to my seat. "Are you here alone?"

She nodded and took a seat across from me. "Smith and Mother had to head to the office today. There are a couple of things they needed to sort out."

"In other words, our mother is avoiding me," I said bluntly.

Camila shrugged. "She's not avoiding you, Izzy."

"Yes, she is," I scoffed. "Don't worry - that's fine with me. I'm only here for dad."

"You can't blame her, Izzy," Camila said softly. "You just disappeared."

"I don't have enough coffee in my system to even attempt this conversation right now."

"Well, it's time you stopped avoiding it."

I rolled my eyes at my sister. She was definitely less emotional than yesterday and I knew she was going to have plenty of questions about the last few months. As much as I wanted to avoid it, I also wanted to get everything out in the open. I was tired of this back and forth - I didn't want any of it anymore.

"Where's your boyfriend today?" she asked, a flicker of contempt lingered in her voice.

I pointed behind me to Giovanni outside and Camila followed my gaze.

"How can you have a new boyfriend, Izzy?"

I took a deep breath and reminded myself to remain calm. "Nate dumped me months ago, Camila. He didn't want to get married and he dumped me."

"Why didn't you tell us any of this?" She asked. "You guys broke up, you lost your job and then you disappeared. Why did you run away?"

"You don't know what it's like, Camila," I snapped. "You were the golden child. You always got everything right and I had to grow up in your shadow. I tried to be just like you but I always fell short - whether it was with my grades, my job, my relationship."

"You didn't have to be like me."

"Oh but I did," I sniggered. "You knew what mom was like. She had a plan for us and we had to follow it and whenever I didn't, I felt like such a disappointment and I was tired of feeling like that."

I could feel a lump forming in my throat. The last thing I wanted to do right now was cry but this all brought up so much I hadn't dealt with yet.

"You could have told us," Camila murmured. "But instead you ran off to Barcelona and we didn't know why. You may have fooled mom and dad in the beginning with the story about meeting Nate there but something just felt off."

"Yeah, I'll admit it wasn't a solid story but it was easier to avoid all of you than to have to be confronted by the facts."

"So what are the facts now, Isabella? I don't know anything about your life," she said and I noticed there was a hint of sadness in her voice and it actually surprised me to hear it.

"The facts are that I have a life in Barcelona now and it's one that makes me happy."

"And your job? What happened at Oak Tree?"

"I didn't get the promotion. He gave it to someone else and with the whole getting dumped thing, I needed to leave London."

"But you were supposed to come and work for the newspaper. We were all supposed to work together."

"I didn't want that, Camila," I admitted. "Honestly, I had no idea what I wanted. Our lives were painted out so perfectly for us and I realized that it wasn't the life I wanted."

Camila looked confused and I didn't blame her. She was programmed her whole life to follow what my parents said and she had done that perfectly. My blatant act of rebellion was foreign to her and she would never be able to understand it.

"They just wanted us to be successful, Isabella. You can't hate them for that."

"I don't hate them for that. I hate that I always felt like an outsider in my own family."

I took another sip of my coffee to keep from crying. I could feel my voice wanting to crack and I refused to give in to my emotions right now.

"I didn't know you felt like that," she murmured.

"I know you didn't and mom didn't either. She was always adamant that we stuck to her plan and I know she's disappointed in me and the life I have chosen but this is the first time in my life I have ever been truly happy, Camila."

"Well, I suppose that's what matters then."

I was surprised by her response. I could see her fighting all her natural urges - the urge to tell me that I made a mistake and that I had no plan. She was too similar to my mother and the idea of not following a life plan was something she couldn't relate to. I appreciated what she was doing because I knew how hard it was for her.

"And Giovanni?" She asked. "Are you happy with him?"

I blushed at the thought of our relationship. "I've never felt this way about anyone before."

"Not even Nate?" She was confused. "I thought you loved him."

"I definitely had love for Nate but thinking back it was very platonic. I convinced myself back then that I was in love with him but I never was."

"But you guys were together for so long."

Her back and forth defense of my old life was starting to get on my nerves. She had moments where she wasn't being judgemental but she couldn't hide her true feelings for too long. I wanted her to listen to what I was telling her. For the first time in my life I was opening up to my sister and I wanted her to understand me.

"That doesn't mean anything, Camila," I snapped. "I'm in love with Giovanni."

Her eyes widened at my confession. I didn't expect to say it but it was the truth and she needed to know this was serious.

"Hi, Camila," Giovanni said from behind me and I froze.

Oh my God. Did he just hear what I said? Camila got up and greeted Giovanni and I kept my eyes firmly on my cup of coffee.

"Is this mine, baby?" Giovanni asked, pointing to the second cup on the table.

"Yes, I hope it's still warm enough," I said as calmly as I could manage.

I was freaking out inside. There was no way he heard me right? He would have given me some kind of indication but he was perfectly normal. He grabbed a chair from an open table and sat down next to me, placing his hand on my knee. Camila observed us and thankfully said nothing more about what I said.

"Is everything alright with Pedro?" I asked.

"There's a couple things I need to deal with but I'll do that when we get back to the hotel."

I nodded and sipped on what was left of my coffee. We sat in awkward silence and I wanted to scream. *What the fuck, Isabella?* There was no way he didn't hear what I said.

"So, what is it that you do, Giovanni?" Camila asked politely.

"I'm a business owner. My brother and I run a club in Barcelona called *Mala Mía*," he explained.

"A club?" She couldn't hold back on her very clear judgment. "That's, uh, very nice."

I rolled my eyes. "You could have tried a little harder to hide your judgment, Camila."

"It's okay, Isabella," Giovanni assured me. "I'm sure that could seem like an unconventional choice but it's a business nonetheless and it's only successful if you work to make it that way and we have."

"Well, I don't know much about that kind of scene. I was never fascinated by the clubbing culture."

Her condescending tone was infuriating to me. She was just like my mother - once they made up their mind about something, you couldn't sway them and she had clearly already decided she was not going to accept Giovanni.

"Well, that's where I met your sister." Giovanni kept his tone very polite and I was thankful for his ability to remain calm.

"You guys met at a club?" She blurted, not bothering to hide her judgment this time round.

"Yes, Camila, we met at a club," I snapped. "You're starting to piss me off with your judgment. This is the exact reason why I never wanted to share anything with you guys. You're all the same."

"I'm sorry, Isabella, but I just feel like I don't have any idea who you are anymore," she chastised. "You ran away to another country and now suddenly I'm supposed to be happy for you that you're with some random club owner who, no offense, looks like bad news."

I felt like I had been slapped. I was horrified and embarrassed by her judgemental tendencies. It was completely out of line and the similarities between her and my mother were shocking.

"With all due respect, Camila, you don't even know me," Giovanni remarked. "You don't know anything about me or how I feel about your sister. I am here for her and I'm not going anywhere."

I stood up. "I am here to make sure dad is okay. You and mom are exactly the same and if you guys are going to continue to be like this then I don't want you in my life."

"Don't be ridiculous, Isabella." Camila clicked her tongue. "We're your family."

"Giovanni is my family now." I extended my hand to him as he stood up. "Now, I'm going to go and see dad. I suggest you and mom stay clear of me."

I didn't wait to hear what else she had to say. I turned on my heels and made my way through the hospital with Giovanni. Just when I thought I was making progress with my family, they went and proved to me that once again they would never change. I was angry at my sister for being so disrespectful to Giovanni and to our relationship. Just like my mother, she couldn't be happy for me.

"So, your family is really... something."

I burst out laughing at his diplomatic response to what just happened. First my mother and now my sister - I felt so bad he had to deal with them.

"You're way too polite for your own good." I chuckled.

We turned down the hallway to the Cardiac ICU. We still had to wait another ten minutes but I couldn't sit there with Camila any longer.

"Giovanni, I can't apologize enough for my family. I'm sorry about my mother yesterday and now my sister. She had no right to say any of the shit she said and I'm so angry at her."

"Isabella, listen to me." He stopped and pulled me closer to him, cupping my face. "No offense but I don't give a shit about them. I care about being here for you and if that means I have to take a couple cheap shots from your family then bring it on 'cause I'm not going anywhere."

I was about to reply but he interrupted me with a kiss. I sunk into him and immediately felt myself start to calm down. He pulled away but leaned his forehead against mine.

"I mean it, Isabella, I'm not going anywhere," he murmured. "Because I'm in love with you."

My jaw dropped. *Oh my God.* He said it.

"You're in love with me?" I beamed.

"I heard what you told your sister..." he started.

"Oh my God - you did hear that." I covered my face in embarrassment.

"Hey, don't cover your face," he said as he slowly removed my hands and cupped my face in his. "I have never been so happy to hear what you said, *mi hermosa,* and I wanted you to know I feel the same."

I smiled and felt the tears fill my eyes. All the emotions I had been feeling came bubbling over and resulted in this unexpected happiness I never thought I would have. I wanted to jump up and down like a little school girl. I couldn't believe it - Giovanni loved me.

"I can't believe you feel the same." I was in shock.

"Of course, I feel the same, I love you, Isabella."

I threw myself at him, my lips crashing down on his. I had never felt such a rush - it was euphoric.

"I love you, Giovanni."

He smiled down at me and I could see the love in his eyes. It mirrored my own and I felt like the luckiest girl in the world.

"I wish I had told you in a more romantic place but I needed you to know," he murmured and kissed my forehead.

I wrapped my arms around him and pulled myself closer to him. I couldn't believe this. This was all I ever wanted to hear and I was happier in that moment than I had ever been. Whatever happened from here on out, that moment would be ingrained in my mind forever.

"It's time for you to go see your dad," Giovanni said, pulling away from me. "I'll be right out here waiting for you."

I nodded. "Thank you. If my sister comes here, please ignore her."

He chuckled. "I can handle myself, baby."

I smiled and pushed through the ICU doors. I stopped to sanitize my hands and walked over to my dad's bed. He was fast asleep, his chest rising and falling softly while the machine beeped with each breath. He looked so peaceful and I didn't want to wake him. I stopped by the nurse's table in the middle and an older woman sat behind the counter.

"Hi my love," she greeted politely. "How can I help you?"

"My father - Oscar Avery - was admitted yesterday after a heart attack. I wanted to find out if there have been any updates on him?"

"Doctor Greenwood hasn't been around this morning but we watched over your father last night and it seems like his heart has started to stabilize. I shouldn't speak out of turn as Doctor Greenwood will know more about where your father is at but he managed to finally get some rest early this morning."

I sighed a breath of relief. "Okay, that's great news. Do you have any idea when the doctor will be in?"

"He usually does his rounds just before lunchtime so I'm sure we'll have more information for you after that."

"Could I please leave my number with you? I want to know what the doctor says but I don't know if I'll be here to get them. Would you mind letting me know?"

I didn't want to take this poor stranger through my family drama but I definitely didn't want to have to ask my mother or sister for any updates. They have both proven that they cannot separate their feelings so I'd have to find out myself.

"Yes, of course, dear." She handed me a piece of paper and a pen.

"Thank you so much," I said and wrote my number down. "I'm just going to say hi to him and then I'll be out."

"No problem. I'll let you know what Doctor Greenwood says later."

I smiled at her and strolled over to my dad's bed. I didn't want to wake him but I wanted to take a couple of minutes to sit with him. I pulled the chair next to his bed closer and I leaned my arm on his bed, taking his hand in mine. He didn't wake and I heard his soft snores. He needed the rest.

"Hi, dad," I murmured. "I don't know if you can hear me but I just wanted to let you know that I'm glad you are resting now. I didn't want to wake you up."

I was happy that he was headed in the right direction but I was still anxious to hear what the doctor had to say.

"I'm sorry I ran away to Barcelona. There's so much to that story and I'm not going to get into it now. All I want you to know is that I am happy and I am in love and I hope that when you're all better I can bring Giovanni around to meet you."

I leaned down and kissed my dad's hand. The skin was soft and his veins were protruding out like they always had.

"I never wanted to hurt you by running away. I just needed to find myself and I think I have now so it's all about you getting better now."

I doubted he could hear me but I felt like I had to say what I said. Out of everyone, my father was still the kindest to me and I never wanted to disappoint him.

"I'm going to go now but I promise I'll be back later to see you."

I stood up and slowly pushed his hair back. I leaned down and left a soft kiss on his forehead. "I love you, dad."

He continued his deep sleep and I was just thankful to see him in a peaceful state. I thanked the nurse one last time before I stepped through the doors of the ICU. Giovanni sat alone in the chair waiting for me. He looked up from his phone.

"Are you done already?"

"Yeah, he's asleep and I didn't want to wake him," I explained. "I left my number with the nurse to update me once the doctor has done his rounds."

He nodded and reached for my hand, intertwining it with his. "Let's get out of here."

"Yes please."

***

Later that day the nurse stayed true to her word and updated me after Dr. Greenwood had been to see my father. His heart had finally started to stabilize by itself through the night. After running tests, they found that he had massive blood clots in the left anterior descending artery which was what ended up causing the heart attack. The next step was to place stents in those arteries in order to open them up and avoid something like that from happening again. I was incredibly relieved by the news - it was a step in the right direction.

"Thank you so much for letting me know," I said to the nurse on the other line.

I ended the call and let out the breath I was holding. *Thank goodness.* I sat against the bed and felt the anxiety I was holding onto slowly start to slip away. Now I just felt relieved. I just wanted to make sure he was going to be okay and now that they knew what was wrong, they were able to rectify the problem.

Giovanni walked back into our hotel room carrying two brown paper bags. "Honey, I'm home."

I smiled at his playful nature and went to greet him. He placed the bags down on the table and left a kiss on my forehead.

"And?" he asked. "Did she call?"

"Yes, he's going to be fine. He had a blood clot in his artery so they need to put some stents in but the doctor is very confident that he's going to be fine."

The relief set in across his face. "That's great news, baby!"

He wrapped his arms around me and I leaned my head against his chest. He was scheduled for his operation in the next couple of days. I was thankful that this nightmare was slowly starting to come to an end.

"So, hopefully by the end of this week, he'll be home and in recovery."

"You must be so relieved."

"I am." I sighed. "These last couple of days have been a nightmare."

"It wasn't all bad," he murmured. "I learned a beautiful young lady loved me so there's that."

I pulled away enough to look up at him and he was smiling down at me. His happiness was contagious and I couldn't help but mirror it. I still couldn't believe he told me he loved me - it was a moment I kept playing over and over in my head.

"Well, she does love you," I said playfully. "But only if you brought back doughnuts like you said you would."

He chuckled and let go of me. He reached into one of the bags and pulled out a small box of mini doughnuts dusted with sugar and cinnamon on them, just like I wanted.

"Yes!" I exclaimed. "See, this is one of the many reasons why I love you."

He smirked and emptied the contents of the brown bag. Microwave popcorn, chocolates, sweets - he had it all for our little movie night we had planned. We were in London but we weren't exactly here under the best of circumstances and I couldn't bring myself to be in the 'touristy' mood and show him around. Giovanni suggested we gather all the snacks we needed, get into bed and binge-watch a movie or two. Who could resist that?

"Did you ever hear back from your brother?" I opened the box in my hand and grabbed one, the doughnut melting in my mouth.

"My mother is there now. Apparently, she had locked herself in the guest room - she didn't want to face my father so thank fuck they went to get her."

"And was your father there?"

He shook his head.

"You know you can talk to me about that," I murmured softly. "I know all this shit was happening with my dad but you're also dealing with what happened."

He sat down on the bed and I walked over to him, positioning myself in between his legs.

"There's not much to say. My dad is a dick and I don't want anything to do with him," he said flatly. "And I want my mother out of that house. She deserves better than this."

"Do you think she'll leave him?"

He shrugged. "No idea to be honest."

"If she doesn't, what are you going to do about your dad?"

"Nothing. If she stays with him, she'll have to respect that I don't want to see him again."

I understood his frustration. He just wanted to protect his mother and he had every right to.

"I'll deal with this when we get back to Barcelona," he said.

I slowly ran my fingers through his thick hair, "Speaking of, you need to let me know how much all this cost you. The flights, the hotel - I need to pay you back."

He scoffed.

"What?" I asked.

"I don't want your money, baby." He rubbed his hand up and down my arm.

"But this was all unexpected," I objected.

"Isabella, I mean this with no arrogance but money is not an issue for me."

I was definitely aware that he was well-off. If his car and apartment were anything to go on, he lived more than comfortably.

"Plus, what's mine is yours now," he said as he pulled me closer to him. "We are in a relationship are we not?"

He was being playful now and I couldn't help but smile. I loved hearing him reference our relationship. This was all I had ever wanted. I wanted Giovanni all to myself and now I had him.

"I do believe we are."

I leaned down and my lips met his. I could never get enough of kissing him. He pulled away from me.

"Listen, we better get this movie marathon going because I'm dying to have those Oreos I bought."

I chuckled. "Fine, you pick a movie and I'll make the popcorn."

CHAPTER 31:

Two days later my dad was scheduled to go in for his surgery that afternoon. The sun had decided to make an appearance today and a sense of hopefulness surrounded me. He needed to get through this surgery and he would be okay to go home. I just wanted him to be home. After chatting to the lovely nurse again, she assured me that this is a very low-risk surgery and he should be out just after an hour. I had planned to go to the hospital and wait until he was out. I hadn't seen my family since my last encounter with Camila but I was going to swallow my pride and be there for my dad. I pulled my hair into a high ponytail and applied mascara to my otherwise, natural look. Giovanni's phone rang from outside the bathroom door. I heard him answer it and I went back to finish off my look. I placed my mascara back into my makeup bag and left the bathroom. Giovanni had his back towards me as he spoke.

"Alvaro, she's going to be alright. You need to stay calm."

Alvaro? What was going on? I could feel a sense of worry start to build inside as I walked over to him. He couldn't hide the concern that spread across his face.

"Let me just talk to Isabella and I'll be on the first flight out." He ran his fingers through his hair. "Let me know when you are at the hospital. *Adiós hermano.*"

He disconnected the call and turned to me. "Penelope went into labour."

"Already?" I was shocked. "But she still has a month to go."

"That's why they're worried about the baby. They are on the way to the hospital now and Alvaro is freaking out."

I felt so bad for them. They were such a lovely couple and I knew how excited they were for this baby.

"You need to go," I said.

"But what about your father?"

"He'll be fine." I reached out and cupped his cheek with my hand. "The worst is over now and once he gets this surgery then he'll be back home, but your brother needs you right now."

"Isabella, if you want me to stay just say the word."

"You need to be there for your brother. Once I know my dad is okay, I'll be on the first flight back to Barcelona."

He pulled me closer to him and wrapped his arms around me. I rested my head against his chest that was rising at a faster pace than usual. I could sense the underlying fear in his body. He was worried about Penelope.

"You sure?" He needed reassurance.

I pulled away with enough space to look up at him. "I promise you, I'll be alright."

He leaned down and kissed my forehead. "Please keep me updated and if you need me back here, I'll come right back."

"And I love you for that," I murmured. "But you need to be there for your family right now and I need to be here for mine."

***

A couple of hours later, Giovanni and I went our separate ways. He managed to get the next flight out to Barcelona and I headed to the hospital. He told me I could extend my stay at the hotel for as long as I wanted. The last thing I wanted to do was have to ask my mother or sister if I could stay with them. I would much rather stay in my own space. I arrived at the hospital with my heart in my throat. I didn't want to face my family without Giovanni and his absence brought on a sudden emptiness inside. I was completely besotted with him and he made these last few days bearable - he was my comfort throughout and as much as I knew it was the right thing for him to go be there for his brother, it didn't make me miss him any less.

I pulled my phone out and sent him a quick text.

Just arrived at the hospital. Let me know when you land. I love you.

He was already in the air so I knew he would only read that once he landed back in Barcelona. I dropped my phone in my handbag and walked into the hospital. I would never get used to the blinding fluorescent lights as I made my way down the corridor. He had been moved to his own private room while awaiting the surgery. Visiting hours weren't for another 30-minutes so I took a seat outside. I leaned my head against the wall and attempted to compartmentalize the activities of the last few days. It had been such a rush of emotions that I hadn't quite dealt with yet. My phone started to ring, forcing me to press pause on my thoughts. I grabbed my phone and Reyna's name lit up the screen.

"Hi, Reyna."

"There you are!" She exclaimed on the other side of the line. "How's your dad doing? Has he gone in yet?"

I kept her updated throughout the week with what was going on with my dad but she made a point of checking in every day to make sure I was okay.

"Not yet. He is scheduled to go in at about three so I'll have updates for you after that."

"Okay, that's good. He just needs to get through this and before you know it, he'll be back home."

I smiled. "Yes, that's all I want."

"And Giovanni? Is he with you?"

"He's actually on his way back to Barcelona."

"What?" She gasped. "Why in the wor-"

I interrupted her before she got any bad ideas about why he wasn't here. "Alvaro's wife went into labour early. Like a month early."

"Oh no!"

"They're worried about the baby, so of course I told him he had to go be there for his brother."

"Of course," she agreed. "I'm just sorry that you're there alone. Do you want me to come? I can fly out."

I chuckled. "Reyna, you'd never make it in time. Don't worry about it, I promise I'm okay."

"You sure?"

"Positive. I'm going to make sure all goes well with the surgery and then I'll be back home in a day or two."

"Okay, well if you need anything, you let me know."

"I will and I'll call you with an update later after the surgery."

"Please do, love you, Izzy."

"Love you, too."

We disconnected the call just as my sister strolled down the corridor, my mother following closely behind her. I mentally prepared myself for the interactions I was about to have with them.

"And, where's your boyfriend?" My mother asked, the contempt dripping off her words.

"He had a family emergency," I said as I kept my tone as monotone as I could manage. "His brother's wife went into labour early."

I was expecting either one of them to have some snarky come back but instead, they kept quiet and took a seat next to me. The tension in the air was suffocating and I tapped my fingernails nervously against my armrest.

"Isabella, please," Camila said, stopping my hand.

I took a deep breath in. Memories of being back in high-school came flooding in and how my nervous twitch would cause me to constantly tap my nails against any surface I was leaning on. My mother was usually the one to tell me to stop as she found it annoying.

Camila must have got that from her too. She really was the spitting image of my mother in every way.

We sat in uncomfortable silence and I was happy that neither of them had any more questions for me. Dr. Greenwood came down the corridor in his scrubs and greeted us politely before disappearing into my dad's room.

"Will we get to see him before they take him in?" I asked.

"Yes, Dr. Greenwood said we can have about five minutes to see him before they'll take him back," my mother explained.

We said nothing more to each other. Just like clockwork, five minutes later we were ushered into my dad's room. I allowed my mother and sister to go ahead of me, both of them hovering over him. He was already looking much better than when I last saw him. He had colour back in his face but he was sporting a new grey beard that was slowly spreading along his jaw. My dad was always one to remain clean-shaven but given the circumstances, he wasn't able to get rid of it.

"We're going to be right outside here," my mother explained softly. "And then once you're all done, you'll be home in no time."

She ran her hands slowly over the top of his hair. It was the most affectionate I had ever seen her be. It was unusual.

"Isabella, you're here!" I could hear the surprise in his voice. "It's good to see you."

I stood awkwardly at the foot of his bed. "It's nice to see you too, dad. I wanted to make sure you were okay."

"I thought I was dreaming the other day when you were here. I wasn't sure what was real."

My chest tightened. "Of course I'd be here. I had to see you."

He smiled up at me just as his doctor came to announce that it was time. I stepped closer to him and extended my hand. He took it in his and squeezed it.

"Love you, dad," I whispered.

"Love you, Bella."

He said his goodbyes to everyone else before the nurses wheeled him out of his room. The unsettling feeling inside of me continued to rise. I just needed him to be okay. We resumed our places outside on the chairs and we began the waiting game. I was happy to sit in silence but Camila had other ideas.

"So, how long are you staying in London for?" Camila asked.

"As soon as I know dad's alright, I'm going to go back home."

My mother scoffed, "London is your home."

"London was my home," I objected. "I have a new life in Barcelona."

"Are you ever going to explain yourself?" she asked.

She wasn't going to let this go.

I sighed. "What do you want me to say, mother? Nate dumped me and I had enough of having to follow the plan you laid out for me. It wasn't the life I wanted."

"So, your idea of a good life is running away to Barcelona and doing God knows what with God knows who. What do you even do there? Do you even have a job?"

A flicker of anger started to reveal itself and I had to physically stop myself from reacting with emotion. If I did, it wasn't going to go down well. I took a deep breath in before responding.

"Mother, why can't you just accept that I am happy with my life the way it is?" I asked. "It's not what you wanted for me but it's my life, not yours."

"We had a plan, Isabella," she retorted.

"You had a plan. A plan that I was so sick of. I didn't even want to marry Nate but for six years I stayed with him knowing that it was what you wanted and I was actually so relieved when he dumped me."

"You didn't even tell anyone. You just ran away."

"How could I tell you? You have never been afraid to make it known that you're disappointed in me and the last thing I needed was to constantly feel that way."

She remained silent.

"I need you to accept that I am never coming back to London. I am happy with my life in Barcelona and I am happy with Giovanni."

"The club owner," she stated, not bothering to hide the same condescension that Camila had when she found out.

I rolled my eyes. "Yes, the club owner. He works incredibly hard to have a successful business so I'd appreciate it if you'd dial down on the judgment."

"Don't think I haven't done my research on that boy," she clicked her tongue. "I know all about his lady-man reputation and that father of his."

It was no secret that if you researched their family their skeletons were tossed out of the closest and straight onto the web. It angered me that she felt the need to research him and make assumptions about him and his family based on what was in the press. She of all people should know that there is always more to a story. Instead of trying to get to know him, she went with the garbage she found on the internet.

"You don't know anything about the kind of man Giovanni is. You didn't even bother having a conversation with him - you flat out dismissed him because he wasn't Nate and then you have the audacity to claim you know all about him. You know nothing," I snapped.

"Isabella, we just want what's best for you," Camila murmured.

Oh for fuck sakes. I felt like I could pull my hair out at any moment throughout this conversation.

"No, you don't, Camila. You want what you think is best for me but I know what I want and I don't want to be controlled anymore. You may be happy with having them dictate your whole life to you, but I'm not."

The emotions were rising inside of me and I needed to get out of here.

"I need some air." I turned down the corridor and didn't look back.

CHAPTER 32:

My dad's surgery went on longer than we expected, but he was finally back in the recovery room with two stents successfully placed in his arteries. His doctor was happy with how everything went and told us that he could head home as early as tomorrow. Relief rushed over me - the worst was over now. My mother and sister followed the doctor into the recovery room but I stayed outside, needing a moment to take this all in. It had been such a rollercoaster of emotions these last few days, I was thankful to have the moment to soak in that everything would be okay now. I knew it meant it was time to head back home and I needed to say goodbye to him. I pushed through the door and walked over to his bed. My mother and sister were in conversation with his doctor so it was the perfect opportunity for me to have a moment with him. I grabbed his hand softly and wrapped it around my own. His eyes opened slowly and he smiled at me.

"Hi, dad," I whispered. "Everything is going to be alright now."

"Are you leaving again?" he murmured, a flicker of sadness in his voice.

I held back the tears that started to form in my eyes and nodded. "I don't belong in London."

He squeezed my hand. "I understand."

Those two words were all the comfort I needed to hear from him. He wasn't like my mother, he was always the softer of the two of them. *How was he so understanding?*

"Just promise me that you'll be happy," he whispered. "And that you'll call more."

I nodded and a tear escaped my eye. "I promise dad, I'm so sorry."

He pulled me in for a hug and I could no longer hold back the tears. They ran down my cheeks as I buried my head in his shoulder.

"Don't cry, Bella. It's okay now."

I pulled away. "I know and I'm glad you're okay."

He smiled and squeezed my hand again just as my mother and sister came to join us. I wiped my tears and stepped away from the bed, allowing them to have their time with him. I smiled at him one last time before turning to leave the room. I came to make sure that he was okay and now that he was, there was nothing left for me here. I reached for my phone and dialed Giovanni's number. Last I heard from him he had arrived in Barcelona and was headed to the hospital.

On the second ring, he answered. "Hello, baby."

"Hi!" I smiled at the sound of his voice. "Are you at the hospital?"

"Getting out of the car now. How's your dad?"

"He's out of surgery. Everything went well and they said he can go home tomorrow."

"That's amazing news!" he exclaimed. "So, does that mean you'll be coming home soon?"

"I'm going to head to the hotel now to book my flight."

"Good, cause I miss you."

"I miss you too. Please give Alvaro my love and let me know how Penelope and the baby are."

"I will." He stopped to ask for directions before returning to our conversation. "Sorry about that. Can I call you later?"

"Yes of course," I said. "I love you."

"I love you."

We disconnected the call and I was smiling from ear to ear. I would never get tired of hearing him say those words. It filled my heart with a warmth I had never experienced before.

"So, you're leaving?" Camila said from behind me.

I turned to face her. "Yes, that was the plan."

She was silent but I could see she was itching to say something.

"I know you want to say something."

She crossed her arms defensively. "I just can't relate to your life decision, Isabella so it's difficult for me to understand why you would keep running back to Barcelona."

"I'm not running back to Barcelona. That's where my life is now and I wish you would try to understand it, or at the very least, respect it."

"You don't have to leave. You can stay in London. Mother had spoken to Nigel about getting your job back and he-..."

I held a finger up to stop her from finishing that sentence. Of course, my mother would go behind my back and do that. It angered me that my decisions couldn't be respected.

"Listen to what I'm saying here, Camila." I turned to my sister. "I'm not coming back to London ever again."

Gloria Avery stepped out into the corridor where we were and I wondered if this would be the last time I saw my mother. I had every right to turn around right now without another word to the two of them but a part of me didn't want that. Even after all this, I didn't want to have such a strained relationship with them - I wished things were different.

"Mother, I'm letting you know that I am leaving London and even though you and Camila disapprove of my decisions, at this point I really couldn't care less."

I fully intended to remain polite but that didn't go according to plan. "And I hope that while I'm gone, you'll think about things from my perspective and try to understand the choices I have made."

My mother remained silent and her face unchanged. I sighed. I tried but if they weren't going to meet me halfway, there was nothing I could do about it.

"Right," I murmured and rolled my eyes. "Well, there's nothing else for me to say so I'm going to go now."

I turned and made my way down the corridor. A part of me had hoped that either of them would have said something or at least tried to make amends but they were too proud. My mother had a stubbornness to her but I didn't expect it to be something she would cling to in a moment like this. A sadness spread through me and I knew I would always long for things to be different.

CHAPTER 33:

The earliest flight I could get was tomorrow morning so I was stuck in London by myself until then. I lay in the bed in my hotel room, staring up at the blank ceiling. The last few days had been a rush of emotions and I was starting to physically feel how drained I truly was. Everything with Giovanni's parents happened, I met his brother, my dad had a heart attack, rushed over here to London then he had to rush back because of Penelope's early labour - it was a lot to take in and I was trying to wrap my brain around it all. The anxiety I was holding onto because of my father started to subside, he was going to be fine now and that was what was most important. A part of me was surprised at his understanding of my choice to leave but when it came to the three of them, he had always been the more open-minded one. Unlike my mother who was stubbornly set in her ways. A lingering sadness always hovered around me whenever I thought of my mother. When I first met Reyna's family, that was when I started to question the dynamic of my own. I watched how warm and loving they were to one another and it really highlighted the fact that I would never have that. I couldn't connect with my mother on an emotional level and now there were wounds that we wouldn't be able to heal.

I pushed that out of my mind and rolled over, reaching for my cellphone on the bedside table. I unlocked it and dialed Giovanni's number. It had been a few hours since I heard from him and I was worried about Penelope. The phone rang and rang but no answer. He must have been preoccupied with things at the hospital but I was so nervous to know more that I dialed his number again. On the third ring, he picked up.

"Hello?" His voice carried a hint of annoyance in it.

I was surprised by the tone of his greeting, "Giovanni?"

"Isabella, sorry about that," he murmured. "I didn't realize it was you."

What, no caller ID?

"That's okay. I just wanted to see if you had any updates."

I could hear a muffled voice on the other end. Definitely a female voice but I couldn't work out who it was.

"*Espere, por favor,*" he snapped at the person before returning to the call. "Sorry, no - no updates yet."

The voice murmured something in Spanish again. She was too distant for me to pick up on anything that was being said.

"Who's that with you?" I asked, an uneasy feeling settling over me.

"What?" He asked but then continued, "No one - don't worry. Listen, can I call you back later?"

"Giovanni, what's going on?"

"Nothing, Izzy, please, I'm just worried about the baby okay?" His tone softened, "I have to go now."

"Okay, I lo-," I started to say but before I could get the words out, he disconnected the call.

What the fuck?

I tossed my phone to the other side of the bed in frustration. *What the hell was all that about?* I understand that emotions can be high in a situation like that but he didn't have to respond like that. And who was he with? Why couldn't he tell me? I knew it was a female - that much was clear but who? His mom? Penelope's family? A nurse for crying out loud? Why say it's no one?

Isabella, stop!

The hovering insecurities that remained in the back of my mind started to push their way through. I knew I had to trust him - I did trust him but right now, I had an uneasy feeling about what just happened. It was obviously someone he didn't want to tell me about.

Or it really was no one of importance?

But then he could have just said that right? And he snapped at them in a way that made it seem like they were familiar with each other. He doesn't just snap at anyone. So who was it? I ran my fingers through my hair in frustration. I didn't want to second guess him, I knew I had to trust him.

"Fuck it." I said, exasperated as I pushed myself out of bed.

This overthinking wasn't going to help. I needed a distraction because I couldn't stay trapped in my head for the next 12 hours. I grabbed the remaining snacks that we had and reached for the remote. I settled back into bed and turned the TV on. I wasn't going to dwell on that interaction. He was clearly just in a highly-emotional situation and I had to be more understanding of that.

You tell yourself that.

The voice at the back of my head was becoming a real bitch so I muted her as best as I could and found a mind-numbing movie to distract me. I just needed to get through these next few hours and I'd be back in Barcelona in no time.

Everything would be okay.

CHAPTER 34:

"**P**enelope and the baby are fine," Giovanni explained. "They are going to keep the little one in the NICU just to be safe but the doctors are confident he'll be just fine."

I let out a sigh of relief. "Thank goodness. I am so glad they're both okay."

I strolled through the airport towards my gate. I was thankful that it didn't take long for sleep to find me last night but when I woke this morning, I was reminded of all the reasons I had to be anxious. Thankfully, Penelope and the baby were not one of them anymore. I was so relieved to hear that they were fine.

"Me too. Alvaro was beside himself when he met his little boy." There was an unusual distance in his voice.

"And you? Are you sure you're okay?"

His distanceness and the strange interaction from last night didn't help the uneasy feeling nagging in my stomach. It made me more anxious to get back to Barcelona and see him. I'd feel better when I was with him again.

"Yes," he answered quickly. "Are you at the airport yet?"

"I am. I've just checked in so I should see you soon. I'll probably take a cab back t-..."

"I'll fetch you," he interrupted.

I appreciated the gesture but I couldn't ignore the feeling that there was something else going on. "That would be great, thank you."

"Have a safe flight and I'll see you in a couple hours."

"See you soon."

We ended the call and I went to my gate. That entire interaction left me feeling worse than before. Something was different in Giovanni's voice - I could hear it. I knew him well enough to recognize when there was something missing. Was there something else going on? Or was it just the whole situation with his nephew that had him on edge? I couldn't quite place it but I reminded myself that overthinking the situation wasn't going to help it at all. I couldn't wait to get back home. I left Reyna a message letting her know I was on my way back. They eventually started allowing passengers to board. I handed them my passport and made my way down the corridor onto the plane. After finding my seat and placing my earphones in, I got comfortable and allowed sleep to overcome me as we ascended into the air.

***

Two hours and ten minutes later, I was back on Spanish soil and all the animosity and anxiety I was feeling started to leave my body as soon as I stepped off the plane. Giovanni was on his way to fetch me and I couldn't be more excited to see him. I pushed all unnecessary thoughts out of my mind. I was back home now and everything was fine again, in both our lives. I was ready to get back to my new routine with him. I made my way through passport control with my bag in hand. Thankfully, I didn't need to check in any luggage and I could head straight to the parking lot to meet him. I strolled past one of the convenience stores they had in the airport with a huge Oreo display. I decided to grab a couple boxes for Giovanni knowing how much he loved them. There was a line in front of the counter so I stood patiently waiting my turn. Out of the corner of my eye, a familiar face caught my eye. I turned to the display of newspapers and my stomach dropped. Spread across the front page of one of the tabloids was a picture of Casey and Giovanni leaving a hospital. They were standing close together and looked deep in conversation. I grabbed the paper to get a closer look at the headline.

"*La modelo, Casey Fonseca sale con su papá, Giovanni Velázquez, por primera vez desde que anunció su embarazo.*"

Of course, it was in Spanish and I didn't understand a word that they were saying. I quickly grabbed my phone and translated the headline.

"*Model, Casey Fonseca steps out with baby-daddy, Giovanni Velázquez, for the first time since announcing her pregnancy.*"

I was going to be sick. Casey was pregnant and Giovanni was the father.

What! The! Fuck!

My heart shattered. My breathing became ragged and unnerved. A wave of dizziness overcame me and I couldn't help the overwhelming amount of emotions that hit me like a slap in the face. I stared at the headline as the words repeated over and over again in my mind. I didn't even hear the lady calling me until someone tapped my shoulder as it was my turn to check out my items. I couldn't do that. I turned abruptly and shoved the newspaper back on the rack and dumped the boxes next to it. I couldn't care less about what I was doing, I just needed to get out of there. I pushed through the crowds of people and made it out of the store. I leaned against the wall, trying to get control of my breathing.

Casey was pregnant with Giovanni's baby.

"No, no, no," I kept repeating. "This can't be happening."

Pools of tears started to form in my eyes. He didn't tell me anything. He called me and didn't even bother mentioning it. Was that who he was with yesterday? I asked and he said it was no one but clearly I had every reason to doubt him. I was fuming. *What the fuck?* How dare he keep this from me? She was there at the hospital with him while Penelope was giving birth and he hid that from me. He lied to me. A single tear finally escaped my eye and I knew I had to get out of here before I completely broke down. I reached for my phone from my handbag and turned down the corridor towards the exit. I was just about to leave when I heard a familiar raspy voice from behind me call my name.

No. Way.

It can't be.

"Isabella!" The voice repeated and I slowly turned around to face the familiar blue eyes I hadn't seen in months.

"Nate." I breathed.

THE END

Printed in Great Britain
by Amazon

67750084R00187